A VILLAIN PARANORM
COMPLETE

WRATH & REIGN

NIKKI ST. CROWE

BH

BLACKWELL HOUSE

Published by Blackwell House LLC
ISBN 13: 979-8-9854212-7-9

Cover Design by Joy Author Design Studio
Proofreading by Elemental Editing & Proofreading
and Jane Beyer

BEFORE YOU READ

Some of the content in this book may be triggering for some readers. If you'd like to learn more about CWs in Nikki's work, please visit her website at:

https://www.nikkistcrowe.com/content-warnings

AUTHOR NOTE

Wrath & Reign is a collection of books 1 - 3 of the complete trilogy.

This omnibus collection includes the following full-length novels:

- Ruthless Demon King: Book One
- Sinful Demon King: Book Two
- Vengeful Demon King: Book Three

You can expect lots of tension, action, twists, hate kissing, and a villain you love to love. I hope you enjoy the read!

-nikki

RUTHLESS DEMON KING

PROLOGUE

Everyone has a story about where they were when the Demon King arrived.

I was alone in my condo trying to swat a fly.

Looking back, it really was ultra-thematic, considering.

Fly swatter in hand, I stood in the middle of my living room trying to track the buzzing beast when my phone rang and my mom's freckled face popped up on the screen.

I answered and put the phone on speaker. "Hello?"

"Baby, it's Mama."

She said that every time I answered the phone, as if I didn't have her name programmed in.

"I know, Mom. What's up?"

The fly buzzed past. It was one of those fat flies, the kind that defies gravity and logic.

It zoomed past me, and I swung the fly swatter, missing.

"Goddammit," I muttered.

"Baby, what are you doing? Have you watched the news?"

"What? No. Why would I watch the news?"

I had a strict no-news policy because the news was depressing. The world was burning. A mass shooting every other day. Political discord. Governmental nutjobs. I was already not excelling at life. I didn't want to add to the shit with more shit.

"Turn on the news," Mom said.

I only had streaming services. I didn't even know how to *turn on the news.*

With a grumble, I took the phone in hand and logged into Twitter.

And that's when I first came across his name.

The Demon King.

I'm not sure who named him, if it was a media thing, like the Zodiac Killer, or if *Demon King* was the name he arrived with and some brave soul dared to ask him for it.

After scrolling my feed for a bit, I stumbled on the first image of him—a grainy picture snapped in the dark by some amateur photographer who used an on-camera flash.

But while the image was low quality, it did its job.

The Demon King was otherworldly gorgeous.

Judging by the tweets, everyone else was having a similar reaction.

We were all captivated by him, starved for beauty, greedy for drama, attracted to power like a moth to the flame.

We were all hungry to burn.

And this man, this gorgeous man, had walked into the White House, demanded to see our leader, then disappeared when he was taken into custody.

Not disappeared as in *someone lost track of him.*

Disappeared as in *twelve witnesses watched him* literally *disappear.*

He found our president a few hours later and demanded her supplication. He was shot. The bullets bounced off of him.

Not long after, the U.S. government declared war against him.

But everyone who tried to take him out failed.
Miserably.
Spectacularly.
Like me with that damn fly.
We never stood a fucking chance.

1

SIX MONTHS LATER

I'M A PHOTOGRAPHER, AND I HATE TAKING PICTURES OF PEOPLE.

"Josiah," I say to the little demon running from me and my camera, "make a funny face!"

He turns around long enough to flip me the bird and then darts behind a tree, laughing.

"Josiah!" his mother shouts. "Get back here right now!" She gives him chase in her pretty boho dress as Dad stands by, hands in the pockets of his khakis looking bored and annoyed all at the same time.

Dads are sometimes harder to come around than the kids.

I got into photography because of my mother, and I *do* love the art form, but everything leading up to that final image is a nightmare.

Somedays I think if I have to take one more sun-drenched photo of a perfect (dysfunctional) family on the beach or in a field, I might scream.

But here I am, taking more photos, chasing after more monsters, wondering where the hell I went wrong with my life.

Well, that's not entirely true. I know where I went wrong. It's my temper. It always gets the best of me. I've been fired from more than one minimum wage job because I yelled at a customer or told a manager to fuck off.

I'd like to blame it on my mother, but that's just a lazy excuse. I was raised by her, though *raised* is a stretch. She's a product of a hippie commune, a vegan, new age woman who always smells of lavender and patchouli. She's a world-renowned photographer whose images hang in the lobbies of billion-dollar corporations. Sunshine Low, or Sunny Low as everyone calls her.

It's no surprise that my hippie, vegan, new age mother named me Rain.

Growing up, I traveled with her when she chased one idea or another, but she had always been hands-off with her parenting, leaning into that whole freewill, feral-child parenting style. It made me extremely independent, but also stubborn and wild, if I'm honest.

I learned how to use a DSLR camera on manual when I was eight. I know all about shutter speeds and aperture and chasing the perfect light. I learned how to take photos from one of the best photographers in the world, but what my mom photographs isn't what I want to photograph. Mountains don't move me. An artful curl of an ocean wave doesn't spark passion. Not that family photography is where my heart is either. It's like I'm searching for something through my lens that I just haven't found yet.

For now, family photography pays the bills, and I'm my own boss, but it's starting to feel like every session I do chisels a little more off my soul.

My cracks are widening, and I don't know how to fix it.

If I'm not successful at the one skill I have, then what more can I possibly do with my life? I have my mother's wandering spirit, I think, but while Mom is perfectly happy with the wandering, I'm in a hurry to reach the destination.

I just don't know where that is or what I have to do to find it.

Josiah finally warms up to me, but Dad doesn't, and by the end of the session, once the sun has descended below the horizon, I have about seven hundred images of Dad scowling.

I wrap up, promise to have the images processed within two weeks, and then say goodbye.

Leaving Riverside Park where I held the session, I head on foot to the heart of downtown Norton Harbor. It's a picturesque tourist town on the shore of Lake Norton, about thirty minutes from Saint Sabine.

In the summertime, every day feels like a vacation. Colorful beach towels hang out to dry on picket fences, while locals and tourists alike travel the cobblestone streets in golf carts. Live music can be heard around every street corner.

Though I'm a homebody, there's something about Norton Harbor's energy that I just can't get enough of. It's one of the reasons I decided to call it home after traveling like a nomad with my mother most of my life.

I love the sea of pedestrians and the buzz of conversation and the glow of string lights.

Everything about it is perfect.

Except for the Demon King.

It's been months since the last confrontation with him. I'm not sure if the country just gave up trying or if some kind of peace was agreed upon. The government isn't making those details known.

Three months ago, the Demon King started appearing regularly in Norton Harbor, so now the picturesque lakeside town is a haven for Demon Devotees.

If my photo session didn't make me crabby enough, the horde of fangirls and boys outside Par House have me toeing the line of damn near volcanic.

The Demon King loves Par House.

That's a sentence I never thought I'd utter.

Hands balling into fists, I approach the crowd that is growing by the second. A woman has her phone up and trained on the front door, filming, waiting for a glimpse. Sometimes I think he does it on purpose, this building of tension and apprehension.

When will he come out?

Who knows, and I don't fucking care.

"One of the waitresses who works here said he was in last week and he ordered a sushi platter!" a redhead says.

Her friend hangs on this fact like it's made of gold and tied in ribbon.

It makes me sick. It makes me hate him more.

This reminds me of what used to garner our attention—the pages in glossy Hollywood magazines. *Stars, they're just like us! They tie their shoes and buy batteries!*

So the Demon King eats sushi. Big friggin' deal.

I skirt past a newspaper box and see the Demon King's face on the front page. The headline reads, "*Can We Have Peace with Wrath?*"

That's his other name. Maybe his official one? I don't know.

Wrath the Demon King.

A scrawny guy fluffs his hair and says, "I nearly brushed up against him in the town square a month ago, and I think I levitated."

His friends laugh.

Since his appearance, and the U.S. government's failure to kill him or send him back to whence he came, the Demon King has been making a name for himself.

There are thousands of fan accounts dedicated to him on all of the social media platforms. Countless internet memes and websites and devoted clubs.

He's everywhere. All of the time.

We fear him and bow to him—sometimes literally.

But no one seems to know what the hell he wants or even how

he got here. Was he always here and we didn't notice until he wanted us to? Was he summoned? Was he lying dormant in some dank hole and finally crawled out?

Or my favorite theory—he comes from another universe. This is the one that has string theorists and multiverse nerds losing their goddamn minds. If there are other worlds, then how do we access them?

Humans love to discover new land then destroy it.

But that sounds like kicking a hornet's nest to me. The Demon King cannot be killed. Do we really want to explore where he came from?

No thank you.

I think the biggest question I have is why now? Rumor is he's looking for something, but what, no one knows.

The crowd's twittering grows louder, and I look back over my shoulder to see a bald man step out of the restaurant.

The crowd lets out a collective and disappointed *oooooh.*

I text my best friend Gus. *Fangirls be fanning at Par House.*

Come to the T shop, is his reply.

I am. Almost there.

Collie's Tea Shop is owned by Gus's aunt, and he helps her run it. It's at the end of the short block just behind Par House. It used to be a millinery back when Norton Harbor was first founded, and the shop still has a lot of the late 19th century charm.

The door to Collie's is heavy and massive, and it always takes me two hands to pull it open. It slams shut behind me when I step into the cool, air-conditioned interior, and though I've been here a million times, it still makes me flinch.

Soft coffee house music plays through the sound system while the three matching ceiling fans that hang from the tin ceiling lazily churn the already chilly air. Just below them, zigzagging across the shop, Edison bulb lights glow brightly.

Collie's might be my favorite place on the planet.

None of the furniture matches, and at least half of it is losing its paint. In some spots, the old plaster has been allowed to crumble away from the lath, giving it this rustic look that I absolutely love.

Nothing is perfect in this world, and allowing something to show its cracks should be beautiful. Not in our glossy, social media obsession though. Every photo should be perfect. Every angle well-lit. The mess hidden. The lipstick flawless.

I hate that on my own social account, the photos that get the most attention are the ones that are staged. Then again, I've never been brave enough to post the flawed images.

For a Thursday night, Collie's is packed. There's a game of backgammon going on in the far corner, a group of friends at the benches to the left, and a trio of older women taking up the toile settee by the piano.

As I make my way to the counter, I'm immediately hit with the smell of fine Earl Grey tea and fresh scones. Gus smiles at me as I slide onto one of the vintage soda shop stools. "Hey, babe," he says. "Is it a dirty tea night or an herbal blend night?"

"Give it to me dirty," I say.

He immediately hands me a cup of iced tea and grins. "Figured."

I take a sip through the straw. He's made me a half-and-half spiked with rum. Black tea, lemonade, and all the booze a girl could get.

"I love you," I say.

He winks. "I love *you*."

Gus was one of the first friends I made when I moved to Norton Harbor. At the time, my mom was living here too, and she had joined a group of new ageists and became fast friends with a woman named Gloria. Mom had a best friend before I was born, Tatiana was her name, but they drifted apart after a while, and I got the distinct sense Mom had always been looking for a new kindred soul.

The new ageist group was hosting a get-together with a

psychic. Mom wanted me to meet Gloria and then maybe snap some pictures for their blog.

Turned out Gloria was Gus's mom. Gus came along for the food. When we left that night, we were practically best friends, and when Gloria died a few years back from breast cancer, it really cemented our friendship. It somehow made us closer, losing someone we loved.

Losing Gloria drove my mom back onto the road though. She's been traveling pretty much ever since.

Gus puts his elbows on the worn counter and curves his hand along his jaw. "Tell me the worst thing about this session."

I take another sip of the drink and then tell him about Josiah flipping me off. Gus hangs his head back and laughs at the ceiling, his bleached blond hair flopping over his head. When he sobers again, his single cross earring swings back and forth from his ear.

"That's a good one," he says, "but that still doesn't come close to the kid that farted on you."

I curl my upper lip. "Bosley. That kid was a menace."

"Such a menace."

The rum is already hitting me, sending warmth through my limbs and a bit of euphoria to my brain. The stress of the night starts to dissipate.

The backgammon crowd roars with laughter.

"What are your plans for the rest of the weekend?" Gus asks. "Adam is taking me to Saint Sabine to see a show. Want to come?"

Adam is Gus's sorta boyfriend. They aren't exclusive yet, despite Adam's eagerness for it. Gus has always been independent, and a little flighty, if I'm honest. He's a Gemini and he loves to flirt. I think he's worried that by being in a serious relationship, he'll have to tone down his personality.

He's not entirely wrong. Adam is former military and still acts like a rigid soldier. I can never seem to get anything out of him. He's stoic, distant, and has no compromising bone in his body.

But I don't tell Gus that. Obviously. While I like to be straightforward in just about everything, my best friend's love life isn't something I meddle with.

"While that sounds like fun—"

Gus gives me a look like he knows I'm lying.

"—I have a ton of pictures to sort and process. Maybe next time?"

"Liar," he says. "You don't like Adam."

I take a long sip of my drink, then, "I don't *not* like him."

"Isn't that the same thing?"

"Is it?"

The heavy door slams shut with a new customer, and when Gus looks up, he makes a face. "Incoming," he mutters.

"Rain! Hey!"

I swivel on my stool to see Harper Caldwell coming at me, arms open for a hug. I shrink back as if I can avoid the physical contact, but Harper is relentless. She wraps me in her arms, overwhelming my nose with the smell of her expensive perfume. It's sharp and irritating in the back of my throat and immediately makes me think *prostitute in Paris*.

Two years ago, she slept with a guy I was dating at the time. She said she didn't realize we were exclusive, which is a total lie because I'd literally told her we were just the week before.

But Harper is the type of rich, spoiled brat who thinks whatever she wants can be taken without consequence.

I've hated her ever since, and while I've made my distaste for her quite clear, she seems completely oblivious to it.

"How are you?" she asks.

"I'm fine." I twirl my straw in my drink, then take another sip. "How are you?"

She widens her eyes, and her fake lashes swallow up her eyebrows. "It's been a *day*. I was just at Par House for drinks with Daddy, but he stood me up because of some dumpster fire in DC. Anyway, Wrath was there holding court as he does, you know?"

Gus and I nod even though we don't. Not really. I mean, you

hear the stories about Wrath, about the powerful people who gravitate to him and orbit him like he's a planet, but we've never literally witnessed it. I've avoided Par House or really any place Wrath is. I don't want to fawn. I don't want to beg for his attention.

I think a little part of me is afraid that I'm not as immune to him as I want to believe.

I just want him to go away.

"Anyway," Harper says, "the service was horrendous tonight because when the Demon King walks in the door, everyone else turns into a toad, apparently. I just wanted a lavender margarita. It took over a half hour to get it and then it was light on Patrón!" She makes a growly noise in the back of her throat as she slides onto the stool next to me. "Can I have a dirty tea, Gus?"

"Sure. Coming right up." He hurries away to make the drink, abandoning me with Harper.

"To make matters worse, I was practically steamrolled when I came out of Par House," Harper goes on. "I don't know why the devotees huddle around the front door like that. It's like, duh, the Demon King can literally poof out of the restaurant and poof to wherever he lives in his dark castle or whatever."

"Totally," I answer as I slide off my stool. The world sways a bit.

Might have drunk too much too soon. I duck down and grab my camera bag, looping it over my body.

"I should probably go," I say. "Lots of work to do."

Harper pouts. "You never hang with me."

The pout manages to squeeze a drop of guilt out of me. Harper really knows how to manipulate people. "Maybe next weekend?"

"Fab." She claps her hands together.

Gus eyes me over his shoulder. He knows the chances of me cancelling are at about 99%.

"Have fun in the city," I tell him. "Let me know how the show is."

"If you change your mind," he says, leaving it open, knowing I won't.

Drink in hand, I head out and take a shortcut through one of the cobblestone alleyways where more string lights glitter in the growing dusk. Norton Harbor loves its string lights. I will admit, they do add some coziness to a photograph.

I check my social accounts to take care of some media work while I walk.

A bride-to-be has commented on one of my new mom sessions to ask if I do weddings.

If family sessions are a nightmare, weddings would be absolute torture. I try to respond as best as I can, but it's hard typing with only one hand.

Autocorrect changes, "Congrats on getting married!" to "Congrats on getting murdered!"

"Well, that might be fitting—"

I cut off when I slam into something.

My plastic cup is crushed between me and the thing I ran into, and spiked half-and-half spills down the front of me.

"Fucking motherfucker!" I quickly pull my camera bag off and away from my body. I haven't backed up any photos! Losing an entire session of Josiah and his disgruntled dad would just be my luck. I do not want to have to repeat that session—for free.

When I'm sure the camera is safe, I look up to see what the hell got in my way.

There's rage in my veins and I'm about to burn this place to the ground.

But it's not some drunk tourist.

It's the Demon King.

2

When my mother photographed the Grand Canyon, she said it made her feel small and insignificant.

I didn't understand what she meant at the time.

But now I think I do.

Looking at the Demon King is like peering into the heart of an underwater cave and knowing that the darkness is looking back.

Goosebumps lift on my arms despite the summer heat.

The hair rises at the nape of my neck.

Maybe I am levitating.

I swallow hard and feel my eyes well with tears.

I don't know what the fuck is happening, but I can't breathe and I can't think and my mouth is dry and—

Fuck he is...

Hot.

Like so hot it hurts to look at him.

Like so hot I'm already tingling between my legs.

What. Is. Happening?

Straight nose. Sharp cheekbones. A mouth that bows with a sensual curve. Dark hair that swoops back from his forehead.

And his eyes. Not gray, not blue, not green. Something in between. All of the colors and none of the colors.

A gaze that penetrates and cuts and observes and *knows.*

He's wearing all black. A long coat with a high collar that stands sharply against his pale face. He's flawless. Not shining exactly, but radiant. Ethereal.

I get now why our social media world is obsessed with him.

Everything about him is overwhelming.

"The English language has its beauty," the Demon King says in a voice so rich, it's practically sinful, "but it has its filth too."

"Huh?" I say.

I realize I've never heard him speak until now. I'm sure there are videos online, but I've never sought them out. I never had a reason to.

But if I had, maybe I'd be prepared to hear the deep tenor of his voice, the way it rakes over my skin like sharp fingernails.

I shiver. I can't help it. I can't help anything about this entire encounter.

"You cussed," the Demon King says. "Rather spectacularly."

I finally take a full breath. "You ran into me."

He narrows his eyes. "Did I?"

The spiked half-and-half is seeping into my bra and starting to grow sticky on my boobs. I look down quickly to see how bad it is. My black lace bra is starting to show through my wet t-shirt.

When I glance up again, I catch the Demon King eyeing my chest.

I curl my lip at him. "My eyes are up here."

"I'm glad you're aware. Perhaps use them next time."

"I... *What?*"

I'm breathless again, and a lump grows in my throat.

I don't feel so good. I have to get out of here.

"There he is!" someone shouts behind me.

The Demon King looks over my shoulder and the scowl deepens on his elegant face. Footsteps pound down the alleyway.

I almost don't hear him over the screeching. *Almost.*

"Bow," he says, with an edge of disdain.

"Excuse me?

"Bow to me," he says, raising his voice.

The crowd reaches us, and like good little idolaters, they fall to their knees.

But I keep standing.

I can't tell if it's a good idea though. Am I the lighthouse standing against the raging storm? Or the single dandelion trying to face a tornado?

The Demon King turns those fathomless eyes on me. I think I know which I am.

My mom said that after she photographed the Grand Canyon, she sank to her knees and wept.

Tears spring up again, and I can feel my chin wobbling as I grit my teeth. I don't know why I'm close to sobbing, but I am, and it doesn't make any fucking sense.

The Demon King takes a step toward me, and I inhale sharply.

The air turns frigid. The crowd goes silent.

"Bow," he says again, voice sharp.

My head goes a little swimmy. I sway on my feet.

Maybe I should do as he commands.

How hard is it to sink to my knees?

I might not read the blogs dedicated to him or the news articles about his exploits, but it's impossible not to hear about the bad stuff. The Demon King has killed countless men and women in the initial fight between him and the country.

I know he can easily kill me.

But thinking about surrendering to this man makes my chest tight and my blood boil.

Whenever I'd throw a mini tantrum when I was a kid, my mom would turn to the witnesses in the grocery store or the library and just shake her head and say, "She's an Aries," as if they should know that meant I'm stubborn and I have a temper and I hate being told what to do.

And I do.

I really, really hate being told what to do.

I level my shoulders, bunch my hands into fists, and stare into those bright, bottomless eyes of the Demon King and say, "No."

3

The Demon King cants his head. "No?"

There's the telltale sound of feet shuffling over cobblestones and footsteps fading away as the crowd thins and people run.

There is a single moment where I think, *What have I done?*

The string lights flicker and go out.

The crowd starts shrieking, but it's a sound controlled behind gnashed teeth and hands clasped over mouths.

Too much noise might draw the king's attention, after all.

It's at this moment that I realize just how much shit I'm in.

My distaste for the Demon King means that I've somewhat kept myself in the dark about him. It got to the point that if I saw an image of him, I scrolled quickly past, as if my indifference would somehow keep him out of my life.

I hate men who think they're powerful. Who think they can tell people what to do.

If I learned anything from my mother, it's how to stand on my own two feet, dependent on no one.

But by not bothering to learn about the Demon King, I've put myself at an extreme disadvantage. Because now I'm standing in front of him, and the lights have gone out, and the people have run away, and I don't entirely know what he's capable of.

My heart is beating so hard in my chest, I think it might leap out of my skin.

Shit. Shit.

I can just hear my mom in the back of my head. *See what that temper has gotten you into? Rainy baby, you have to stop and breathe and think these things through.*

Well, Mom, now what?

The shadows take shape around me. I frown and step back. The Demon King hasn't moved. He's looking at me like I'm a bug that dared to sully his picnic.

Like he's ready to squash me.

And then, right before my eyes, the shadows become shadow men. Six of them in total, three on either side of the Demon King. Dark mist rises from them. Their features are indistinct from one another, smudged along the edges.

They step toward me.

"You should have bowed," the Demon King says.

Oh fuck.

The shadows lunge for me. Adrenaline shoots through my veins. Everything gets fuzzy and faraway.

I'm dead. I'm so dead.

I can feel their bruising hands on my skin trying to tear me apart. I squeeze my eyes shut. Maybe if I don't look at them, maybe if I retreat as far into my head as I possibly can, maybe it won't hurt as much. Maybe it'll be over quickly.

I should have bowed. I should have surrendered.

I should have... Wait. *No.*

Fuck no. I'm Rain Low. Wild child. Aries woman.

I surrender to no one.

Who the fuck does this guy think he is? Barreling into our world, into *my* town. Who the fuck does he think he is, demanding *I* bow to *him*?

Heat scorches through me. Bright red light flashes in my field of vision.

I can't tell if it's the surrounding light or pure rage.

The light burns like fire, flickering, warming my skin. As the light spreads out, the shadow soldiers rear back, lifting their arms like shields.

They burn up like kindling, there one minute, gone the next.

The only thing that remains is a curl of bright red smoke.

I look over at the Demon King. There's a deep frown on his face, his dark brows sunk in a V. His hands are tightened into fists, and there's something glowing beneath the collar of his shirt.

It's too much to absorb. Too much has happened. Too much doesn't make sense.

I do the only thing I can do—I turn around and run.

4

As soon as I'm out of the alley, the city comes alive again. The string lights are lit. The crowds are gathered. There's the clinking of glasses and the din of conversation.

But I'm running.

I'm running for my fucking life.

I just stood against the Demon King and...I won?

I don't know how the hell that happened. I don't know *what* happened. I don't want to look at it too closely because there are more questions than answers and I hate when I don't have answers.

I run down Stearns Boulevard, then cut left, away from the heart of downtown. My lungs tighten up. My shirt is plastered to my skin, sticky and wet. My legs ache. But I can't slow down. Not yet.

What the hell am I going to do?

When my building comes into view at the end of Platte Avenue, relief flares in the center of my chest. And when I punch in the code on the main entrance and the lock clanks open, I lunge inside and yank the door closed behind me.

I scan the street through the thick glass, heart pounding in my ears. Everything looks normal. I don't see the Demon King in any of the shadows.

At the elevator bank, I punch the arrow and pace in front of it as I wait. Once inside the car, I collapse against the back and suck in a deep breath.

I'm okay. Everything is going to be okay.

I hurry down my hall and then into my condo.

Am I safe?

I'm not sure anywhere is safe at this point. When the military sent a small squadron of men and women to fight the Demon King, he destroyed the troops. Killed them all.

Now I know how. He's got his own soldiers, monsters that can appear at will and tear a person apart. Except...how did they disappear? Did someone light a fire? I mean, if it just took fire to defeat the Demon King, I'm sure the army would have figured that out by now.

I make sure my deadbolt is locked behind me and then stumble into my living room, kick off my shoes, and drop onto my couch. I don't turn on any lights. My condo is on the waterfront and lampposts line the marina walk down below. There's always been plenty of light in my house.

I can hear the water of Norton Lake lapping against the concrete barrier down below. I left one of my balcony doors open when I left for my photo session and—

Oh fuck. My camera bag!

I dropped it when I spilled my drink, and I never bothered to pick it back up.

Laying my head back, I groan at the ceiling. How fucking ironic that right in this moment, I'm dreading another Josiah photo session when I literally just flipped the Demon King the bird?

Maybe he'll just forget about it?

Ha. He's probably plotting my demise right this second. Not

that I think I'm special enough to take up any space in the Demon King's head.

I need a drink.

Something to calm my nerves.

I get up and flick on the under-cabinet lighting in the kitchen. It sends a soft glow around the room.

Ducking into the fridge, I find lots of takeout and several bottles of white and red wine. Wine helps me relax, helps me think.

Pulling out the corkscrew, I tear off the wrap on a bottle of white and pop out the cork. The glug-glug of the wine as I fill my glass is a familiar sound and it makes the night feel normal. Except when the fridge kicks on, I yelp and nearly leap out of my skin.

"Calm down. You're home now. Everything is fine and normal, and you'll probably never see the Demon King again."

Wine glass in one hand, and the bottle in the other, I head out to my balcony and lie on one of my chaise lounges. The first sip of wine, the sweetness of it on my tongue, helps soothe some of my nerves.

Across the lake, million-dollar homes glow in the night. Yachts and sailboats bob in the water in the marina. I can hear people chatting and laughing on the boardwalk down below.

I take another long pull from my wine glass.

It's a little sad how easily we accepted the Demon King into our lives, taking over our towns and our minds.

The first month he was here, I seriously thought we were headed for the apocalypse. I mean, Demon King? What else comes to mind other than brimstone and hellfire and destruction?

There were a few weeks there where everyone was urged to stay home and stay off the streets after dark. But several days into it, when nothing happened, when no hellfire filled our streets, we grew bored and antsy.

There were only two major confrontations with the Demon

King—the fight that broke out when he first arrived and tried to dominate our president, and the second in a field in Indiana.

After the first confrontation where the government learned bullets did little damage to him, they tracked him down to a field in Indiana. Troops showed up. Men and women dressed in tactical gear, carrying assault rifles.

I guess they thought that if handguns didn't work, an onslaught of bullets might do the trick.

That was the first and only time I watched video of the Demon King.

Somehow body cam footage was leaked to the internet, and the jerky footage showed the team opening fire on the Demon King and blasting him with hundreds of rounds of ammunition. Nothing landed. He slaughtered half the troops there, forcing the army to retreat.

After that, there were rumors that he offered the government a treaty—let him do what he came here to do, and he wouldn't harm anyone so long as they didn't get in his way.

Since then, over the last several months, the Demon King has popped up all over the country, doing whatever he came here to do, but leaving most people to their business.

Of course, there are a few rebel groups that have been promising to kill him. Religious fanatics and militia men.

But for the last several months, the Demon King has only been spotted in Norton Harbor. Which is wild, considering the only thing to be found here is fro-yo, tie-dye tourist t-shirts, and lots of boats.

What could he possibly be looking for?

And also, did I just break the one rule of the treaty? Did I get in his way?

Technically he was in *my* way, since I was just minding my business heading home.

I drain the rest of my glass and then pour a second. Maybe I should leave Norton. My mom has been traveling the world again and right now...well, I can't remember where she is right now, but I bet it's somewhere far away from the Demon King.

The second glass of wine goes straight to my head, and soon the twilight sky is just a blur of light.

I think I'm drunk.

Officially.

Oh, my cup is empty.

I bend over the side of the lounge chair to grab my bottle but overreach and end up rolling off the chair and to the concrete patio.

"Fuck fuckity," I say to the sky. "Also ouch." I fumble around for the bottle but spot it on its side far out of reach. Apparently I drank it all.

"I should just rest here a second," I tell the sky. "I bet in the morning all of this will feel silly. I bet in the morning the Demon King will have forgotten about the girl in the alley with the wet t-shirt."

I close my eyes against the heaviness. The world spins in the darkness.

But when I wake in the morning, it's not just a headache I'm fighting off.

The Demon King hasn't forgotten about me.

In fact, now he's hellbent on finding me.

5

I wake to the sun burning brightly overhead. Everything hurts and my skin is so tight, it feels like it might break open at the slightest prick. I probably look like an ill-prepared tourist with skin the color of a tomato.

I get onto all fours and immediately regret it.

The dull pounding in my head rushes to my eyes, thumping through my eye sockets and into my sinuses.

"Oh god. *Regrets*."

My phone is ringing incessantly somewhere inside the condo. I stumble through the balcony doors and the ringing stops.

Once out of the sun, there's a slight respite on my skin and the burning subsides a little bit. I need aloe, stat.

The phone rings again, and a sharp flare of annoyance lights in my chest. Fucking phone and its stupid ringing!

I finally locate it on the kitchen counter. My mom's face beams up at me from her contact photo.

"Hi, Mom," I say, putting it on speaker as I rummage inside the fridge for the bottle of green aloe goo. I wish I could say this is the first time I've ever fallen asleep in the sun, but living in a tourist town on the water, you get used to summer burns. You always gotta be prepared. Cold aloe goo is a godsend.

"Baby, where are you?"

"Where are *you*?" It sounds like she's standing in a tornado, the wind whipping past the phone.

"I'm in the Scottish Highlands. Never mind where I am!"

Spotting the aloe in the door behind my massive collection of ranch bottles, I pull it out and squirt a puddle into the palm of my hand. The second I rub it on my burnt arm, it's like fucking nirvana.

"Oh god, that's better," I say.

"Rain!" Mom shouts.

"What?"

"You're on the news!"

"I—*what?*"

"Turn on the news."

Turn on the news. I can't turn on the news!

I pick up the phone with my aloe-free hand and go to Twitter.

The burning returns to my skin immediately and now throbs as the blood rushes to my face.

What the fuck?

I have thousands of messages.

Holy shit.

What the hell is happening?

"Are you watching the news?" Mom asks.

I scroll through my messages.

Are you alive?

How did you stand against the Demon King? Tell us your secrets!

How the hell did you not cream your panties? someone says with several squirting emojis.

And then I come across a video clip.

Hand trembling, I hit play.

The footage is grainy and shaky, but I can make out myself on the left and the Demon King on the right. Whoever is shooting the footage is hiding behind a dumpster, I think, because half the frame is dark, and their vantage point looks like it's right behind Chef John's across the alley from where I ran into the Demon King.

It's hard to make out our words.

"Rain," Mom says.

"Shhh."

My heart is beating loudly in my head and in my chest, and I'm hot all over.

It's almost like I'm watching someone else stand against the Demon King, and I'm afraid for the girl, even though I know how this ends.

The Demon King's shadow soldiers rush at me and then—

A flash of red light so bright, the person filming yanks back. There's some clunking in the sound, a gasp, then the camera goes back up, and I'm gone.

It's just the Demon King standing in the alley staring after me.

That's where the footage ends.

Goosebumps roll up my arms.

Was that really me? Was that really how it happened? And what was with that light?

"Rain," Mom says, panic lacing her voice. "Did you see the Demon King?"

"It's complicated, Mom. I ran into him, or rather he was in my way and—"

"Not last night," she cuts in. "This morning. He was on the news."

"Oh? Oh." I click through to my main feed, and he is *everywhere*.

I quickly find a clip of him. His ethereal face nearly glows in the camera's frame. I can just make out bookshelves behind him, like an entire wall of them. His house, maybe? No one seems to know where he lives, but for some reason, I never pictured him having a library.

I thought he lived in a cave. Or in hell.

Taking in a breath, I hit play.

His smooth voice glides over my fevered skin.

"Many of you have watched the footage from last night," he says, "and I'm concerned for the safety and well-being of the young woman in the footage. I've been able to identify her."

His gaze narrows, and it feels like he's peering straight through the camera, right into my soul.

"Rain Low," he says.

A shiver rolls down my spine, making my body quake.

My hearing diminishes as blood rushes to my head.

"If you have any information on this woman," the Demon King says, "I'm offering a reward. Price is negotiable depending on the validity and value of the information."

The video ends, frozen on the Demon King's pale, gorgeous face.

I hate everything about this man, and yet...

I'm clenched up tight, trembling and excited and fucking terrified all at the same time.

"Rain," Mom says, reminding me that she's there. "Baby, what happened? Is that really you in that footage?"

"I...Well..."

"*What happened*?" she asks again.

I answer with the only thing I can. "I don't know."

There's a buzz at my door. I hurry over to the control panel to check the camera only to find a small crowd at my building's front door.

That can't be good.

"Mom," I say, "I have to go."

"Where, though, honey? Where are you going to go?"

"I don't know, but...I'll keep you up to date, okay?"

I hang up, because if I know my mom, she's got a dozen suggestions and not all of them are good. Sometimes, when I didn't feel like traveling, I'd stay home while Mom went on assignment.

I'm no stranger to figuring things out. I've practically been taking care of myself since I was twelve years old.

As soon as I end the call, a new call comes through from a number I don't recognize. The door buzzer sounds again.

"Fuck!" I put my hands on the counter and suck in two quick breaths. The rage is burning through me now. I just want to be left alone!

Who does the Demon King think he is?

I look up, aloe goo drying on my hand, and try to make sense of everything that has suddenly gone wrong.

My skin is still throbbing in time with my headache, and I could really use a shower and my condo is still a mess and I still have photos to process for work and—

Okay, work can wait. Shower can wait. I need to leave until I figure out what to do.

My phone rings again from an unknown contact. I silence it and hurry to my bedroom and toss a few things into a bag. Next, I yank off my clothes from the night before, the material stiff from the spiked half-and-half. I pull on a fresh white t-shirt and a pair of cut-off shorts.

Maybe I need a disguise?

I tie up my dark hair with a rubber band, then thread the ponytail through the back of a Par House baseball cap.

On my way out the door, I put on sunglasses.

Since there's a crowd growing at the building's front door, I decide to go out through the parking garage. I don't have a car. I've never needed one in Norton Harbor where everything is within walking distance. But I'm guessing I might be able to slip out that way without being spotted.

Except when I get down to the garage, I can hear the voices of people gathered at the entrance.

Son of a bitch.

I press myself against the wall just outside the elevator and suck in a deep breath. I've dealt with high-stress situations before. There was that one time in Greece—I was barely thirteen—when my mom was run over by a motorbike and knocked unconscious. I punched the asshole in the nose and then got to work finding Mom some help.

And when Gus and I got trapped in an elevator for over an hour when we had a blackout in a snowstorm? Gus freaked out. I did not.

I've always been able to pause my anxiety and focus on the crisis at hand, but somehow this is different.

This isn't a crisis. It's a manhunt and I'm the man.

I scan the garage and spot Mrs. Mulhang at her Audi, her cute little Bottega Veneta bag hanging from her forearm. I stay to the perimeter of the garage and then weave through several vehicles until I reach the Audi.

"Mrs. Mulhang!" I whisper-shout.

Hand at her chest, she shrieks and whirls around.

"Oh, Rain, you scared me half to death! I thought you were a thief!"

"Sorry. Are you leaving? I need a ride out of here."

Her gaze cuts to the garage entrance. "I heard you had a run-in with the devil."

I wince. "Yeah, you could say that."

"Well, get in." Her bag bangs against her hip as she gestures for me to go around to the passenger side.

"Thank you, Mrs. M."

As soon as I'm inside the dark, lush interior of the Audi, I feel better. This is a solution, one that will get me to the next step of my nonexistent plan.

Mrs. M sets her bag in the backseat and presses the ignition button. The car purrs to life. She's approaching seventy and drives like it, so the slow backup and the crawl out of the parking garage feels like an eternity.

When we approach the entrance, I duck down in my seat,

grateful for the dark tinted windows. I hold my breath as Mrs. M presses the button for the guardrail and it slides open.

Within seconds, we're out of the garage in the late morning light, breezing past the gathering crowd. I exhale, close my eyes, and say a silent prayer to all the gods even though I'm not the least bit religious.

"Where do you want to go?" Mrs. M asks.

That's a really good question. I can't go to my mom's condo. Even if someone is unfamiliar with me, they'll easily see the connection with a simple internet search. Sunny and Rain.

I could go to Gus's...

Wait, he's probably already in the city with Adam.

I need to go somewhere no one would think to look.

And then it comes to me—Harper's house. Ugh. It's a good idea. Harper isn't a best friend and we're rarely tagged in each other's photos online. She's a close enough acquaintance that I could ask for help, but not so close that people would think to look at her house.

As Mrs. M heads down Platte Avenue, I pull out my phone and text Harper.

I need a place to lay low. Would you be willing to let me crash at your house?

Harper replies quickly. *OMG Rain. I can't even believe this is happening. Come over. You can stay here. And you have to tell me everything.*

I never thought I'd be so relieved to have Harper.

I give Mrs. M directions, and within ten minutes, I'm climbing out of the cool, dark privacy of her Audi. "Good luck," she says, moving her Bottega bag to the front seat. That thing probably cost more than my camera. Which I now realize I've lost to the Demon King. Fucking hell.

Mrs. M drives off, and I hurry up the paved path to Harper's front door. She lives on the south end of town in one of the quieter neighborhoods with its own private marina. I'm pretty sure her dad bought her the house with cash. He's a U.S. senator worth millions. I'm not sure what her mom does. Harper doesn't talk about her much.

Despite the wealth of Harper's family, her house is a quaint little cottage with gray cedar shake shingle and a black tin roof. There are several varieties of flowers growing in the manicured flower beds—that I'm absolutely certain Harper has never touched—and a little white picket fence around the yard.

In the cool shade of the front porch, I pull down the bill of my hat and knock on the screen door. "Come in!" Harper calls, and I quickly duck inside.

The screen door bangs shut behind me. She can afford a nice, quiet screen door, but here in the south end of Norton Harbor, it's all about the *authenticity*.

I find Harper in the all-white kitchen slicing an avocado. It smells like there might be bread in the toaster. There's definitely fresh coffee.

"May I?" I ask and nod at the coffeemaker that might as well be a spaceship. The authenticity can only go so far.

"Oh for sure. Help yourself."

I've been to Harper's a few times when she hosted a get-together, so I know where to find the cups. I pull down a white mug, find the oatmilk creamer in the fridge, and add it to a cup of coffee.

The toaster pops up, revealing bread so seedy, it might as well be a bird treat.

"So," Harper says, "you saw the Demon King last night." The smile that comes across her face can almost be described as *maniacal*.

I lean against the marble counter and fold an arm over my middle, coffee cup in the other hand. "I did."

"So like, *how* did that even happen?"

I take a sip of the coffee and damn near moan with delight.

Harper only drinks the good stuff, and the coffee is rich and nutty. It's a small comfort that makes me a little emotional.

"It's a long story," I answer when really, it's not. I just don't feel like talking about it.

She spreads mashed avocado on her toasted bread. "What was he like?"

My headache has lessened a bit, but being suddenly dislodged from my home with a hangover is making my soul hurt more than my brain. "Smug," I answer.

Harper picks up her plate and her own cup of coffee and tips her chin for me to follow her. We go out the back door to a giant deck that overlooks one of Norton Harbor's many parks.

More potted flowers flutter in the breeze and the air smells crisp and sweet.

I've never had to struggle with poverty, but we haven't always had the best in life. There was that time we stayed in a seedy motel outside of the Mojave Desert where their idea of a continental breakfast was fruit loop cereal in an unmarked plastic container and a pitcher of room temperature orange juice.

And I can't forget the budget apartment in Florida when Mom went through her wildlife photography phase, and was hellbent on photographing alligators. Half of the windows in that apartment were painted shut and there was no AC. The heat and humidity were so bad, I spent most of our time there feeling like I was swimming in our own apartment.

Harper's life is just a reminder that some people have it so easy, and really have no idea how easy they have it.

We sit at one of two patio tables. There's a large umbrella open above us, driving away the summer sun.

"Demon King was smug," Harper says as she takes a slice of toast in hand. "Tell me something I don't know."

Shrugging, I kick off my shoes so the breeze can hit my bare feet. "I don't know what else there is to say."

Harper sucks avocado off her thumb. "Really? You faced off

against Wrath and lived to tell the tale. How about that? Like how did you manage to get away?" Her eyes light up whenever she says the Demon King's name.

"I don't know. There was light and chaos and...I just ran."

She narrows her eyes at me. "You just...*ran*?"

"Pretty much."

She blinks several times, the fan of her long, fake lashes fluttering against her cheeks. "That is...crazy."

"Yeah."

She shakes her head and then takes a bite of her toast. The bread crunches between her white teeth.

After she swallows the bite, she takes her coffee cup in hand. "Daddy said they're working on a way to deal with Wrath. He won't tell me what, exactly." She pouts and then takes a sip of the coffee. "Daddy never tells me the important things. He says I can't keep a secret, which is so not true."

Uh, yeah it is, because she was literally the one who told me she slept with my sorta-boyfriend.

"I don't know what they can possibly do to combat him." The clouds thin, sending sharp sunlight down around us. I pull the sunglasses from the top of my head and slide them over my eyes.

Harper eyes me across the table, then leans in and lowers her voice. "Well, I did overhear Daddy saying something about someone working for them who knows a thing or two about Wrath. Like from his world."

"Really?"

She nods and then takes another bite of toast.

Maybe that someone really can help us defeat the Demon King, and then I can forget any of this ever happened and I can go back to my normal life.

Even if I do sorta hate where my life is headed.

With a sigh, I hang my head back and watch a sailboat glide past in the harbor.

Right now, here on Harper's deck, things *feel* normal, but I know outside of this little bubble, I have a lot of trouble waiting for me.

If someone had told me a year ago that today I'd be sitting at Harper's house trying to hide from a demon, I would have literally run away from that person because I would have seriously thought they were crazy.

It's a little unsettling how easily we accepted him into our world, how our world immediately absorbed him, and turned him into a commodity.

Does he hate that? Does he think we're all mindless and vapid? Sometimes I think so. Sometimes I hate this world we live in.

"Well," Harper says, "you're welcome to stay here as long as you'd like. But like, what's your plan?"

I slouch down and rest the coffee cup on the arm of the chair. Good question. Thankfully I'm saved from answering her by the ringing of my phone. I had put it on Do Not Disturb except for my favorites, which means it's either Gus or my mom calling.

When I dig my phone out of my pocket, it's Gus's name flashing across my screen. Though I've fended for myself most of my life, there's a sliver of relief when I answer the phone and hear his scratchy voice.

"I leave town for one day and you go and make friends with the Demon King?" he says, bypassing a hello entirely.

I set my coffee on the table and walk down the deck steps to the grass. The grass is soft between my toes. "I most definitely did not make friends with Wrath," I answer, and as soon as I think about him, about our face-off, I'm clenched up tight, my belly soaring.

I'm sure it's just his effect on people, but fucking hell does it rattle me.

It makes me feel out of control. A mindless slave.

Like the Demon King is a drug my body can't get enough of.

Maybe he is a drug, like pheromones or something. Like whatever his power is, it slithers into our brains and makes us crazy.

I feel crazy.

Because there's this little voice in the back of my head that says I want to see him again just to feel that weightless delirium at the center of my chest.

"Should I come home?" Gus asks.

"What? No way. It's really not that big of a deal."

I can literally hear Gus frowning at me through the phone. "Mm-hmm," he says.

"I'm serious. Enjoy your show. I'm fine. I came to Harper's house for now."

Gus guffaws. "Harper's? Seriously. You must really be desperate."

I glance at her over my shoulder. She smiles at me over the rim of her coffee cup and waggles her fingers.

"I was," I reply.

"Listen," Gus says, "there's something about Adam I've never really gotten into with you, because I know you hate the whole Demon King thing and, well, I didn't think it mattered to you one way or another. But now that you're Demon King Enemy Number One—"

"He's the villain here," I argue. "I am most definitely not an enemy."

"—there's something you should know about Adam."

"Okay, what is it?"

Gus takes in a breath and lowers his voice. Does Adam know he's telling me whatever this secret is?

"Adam is part of a group that is working to get rid of the Demon King."

"Oh. *Oh*."

"Yeah."

"And by group, do you mean...the militia men?"

"Not MAW," Gus says.

MAW or Men Against Wrath. They're a group of armed and tatted white men promising to blow the Demon King to smithereens. The only problem is, the one time they came face-to-face with him, seven people died and six of their members disappeared.

They aren't exactly adept at fighting villains.

Adam is black, so MAW is a stretch anyway, but there are lots of rebel groups working against the Demon King with varying degrees of capability, insanity, and fervor.

Take back our country from the vile heathen! is one group's slogan.

Another group, the Citizens Against Darkness, likes to hold rallies carrying handwritten signs that say things like, *Don't become a slave to evil!* They're the religious fanatics. And another group, Order of Alius, is promising End Times, that the Demon King's arrival is some kind of prophecy coming true.

But for every group against him, there are easily two *for* him. It's not hard to imagine Wrath being the winning side of whatever our future might bring. I haven't given our future much thought, to be honest. I'm pretty adaptable, though if the apocalypse came, I would seriously miss showers and Wi-Fi.

"Adam can help," Gus says. "There are safe houses, places you can go—"

Hiding out in a stranger's hut sounds worse than hiding in Harper's beach cottage.

"Thanks, Gus, but I think I'm good here for now until I can figure this whole thing out."

Not that I know how to go about that, but...

"No," he says. "Adam is exactly the guy you want on your side after a run-in with the Demon King."

I believe him. Adam can be scary when he wants to be, which is all of the time. He's six-four and pure muscle. I think he's like a black belt in some kind of martial art too, and he spent several years in the Army. The guy knows his stuff.

But what can he really do to fight the Demon King? Guns don't kill him, knives are as effective against him as a pipe cleaner, and he's apparently got some shadow demons at his beck and call.

"I don't want you to end your weekend early because of me," I say.

"How about this," he says. "We'll watch the show tonight and come home after. It might be late, but at least I'll be back in town. You're more important than a weekend in the city."

I sigh. As much as I like to pretend I can handle everything on my own, I would absolutely love having my best friend by my side. "Okay. Yeah. If you're sure it's not too much trouble."

"Of course not. Lay low at Harper's for now, okay? Promise me."

"I promise."

I really do have the bestest friend in the world.

We say goodbye and I return to the deck. Harper is scrolling through her phone. "You should see what people are saying about you."

I wrinkle my nose. "No thanks."

"You're like famous now or something."

"People will forget about me by tomorrow."

"I don't know," she says, her attention still on her screen. "The Demon King has been trending number one on Twitter since he arrived, and he's the most searched hashtag on Insta. He's never been interested in one of us like this. I doubt you're just going to fade into the shadows. Besides," she adds, "now that we know you can stand against the Demon King, it won't be just Wrath that wants you."

I had no idea at the time just how right she was.

Harper leaves for half the day to attend a yoga class, a Pilates class, and then a nail appointment. She invites me to all of it, but I'm officially on the lam and don't want to be spotted in town.

I nurse my sunburned skin with aloe I find in Harper's fridge, then try to formulate a plan while hydrating on Harper's deck. The sunburn starts to feel better by late afternoon, and the hangover is gone by then too. Harper texts me that she's going to the city with a friend a little after five, but tells me to stay at the house and make myself at home.

She's being so nice, it's making me feel like an asshole.

Harper's cottage has two guest bedrooms, so I take my pick after I order takeout. I go with the little room in the back of the house because it has its own bathroom. The stand-up shower is tiled in marble, and there's a dual showerhead that surrounds me in hot water when I decide a shower is exactly what I need before bed. It feels absolutely glorious.

Exhausted with the day, I go to bed early and slip into my favorite oversized tie-dye Bob Marley t-shirt I snagged at a yard sale last summer.

Cocooned in Harper's high thread count white sheets, I fall asleep fast thinking I'm safe.

That turns out not to be true.

Because several hours later, I'm jolted awake and yanked from my bed by the Demon King himself.

6

MOONLIGHT SHINES ON HALF THE DEMON KING'S FACE AS HE THROWS ME against the wall.

This might be the rudest awakening I've ever had.

Oxygen bursts out of me in a useless gasp as my eyes bug out of their sockets. He lifts me off my feet.

Black mist trails off the Demon King's shoulders, blotting out the silver moonlight behind him.

"What are you?" he says.

My feet pedal in the air.

With his other hand, he yanks down the collar of my shirt, but only far enough to eye my clavicle before he lets the shirt go.

What did he think he'd find there?

I scrabble at his grip, but his fingers are like a vise.

He gets in closer. The smell of him fills my nose. It's a heady, rich, deep smell that acts like a light switch. I'm suddenly buzzing and hot. My clit throbs.

This is some perverse fucked up shit!

"Fuck you," I manage to choke out.

He grits his teeth. His irises bleed to red and glow in the dark as black mist swims around us. His face sharpens, morphing into a monster right before my eyes.

This is the true demon. The monster hiding beneath.

"What. Are. You?" he asks again, his voice rumbling in the quiet.

I can't breathe. I wrap my hand around his wrist and push.

And somehow, the mighty Demon King is thrown back against the wall.

He catches himself easily enough, but the look on his face registers everything.

Shock.

I've surprised him.

He gets his bearings again and the monster returns as he lunges at me. I duck and he misses only to come back around and catch me by the hair.

He's faster than I am, and he's clearly done this before.

I let out a yelp as he throws me on the bed. A lamp is knocked over and shatters on the floor.

The Demon King puts a knee between my legs and bears down on me. "Who are you?" he says, trying a new line.

I might not be a black belt in karate, but my mom did get me into self-defense classes for a summer.

I bring my leg up and around and kick the Demon King in the sternum. He falls back on the floor. I leap off the bed and straddle his waist.

The Demon King is lying on an expensive rug in a beach cottage in Norton Harbor, and he's lying there because of me.

Except he doesn't look as defeated as he should. And that's when I realize I'm straddling him in nothing but an oversized Bob Marley t-shirt. Not exactly the attire of a warrior.

"You've got me on my back," he says. "Now what?"

"Now? Now...you leave me alone."

His face has returned to its ethereal beauty, the monster gone. His hands come to my bare thighs, and a shiver races through me.

"I can't do that," he says.

"Why not?"

The air grows charged. His hands come to my waist, and in one quick, smooth motion, I'm suddenly the one on my back, the Demon King on top of me.

A startled breath stutters up my throat. My heart thrums in my chest as his eyes glow again. The Demon King puts a knee between my legs, pressing at my center, and a needy thrill buzzes at my clit.

Maybe I do understand the obsession with this man, but only on a primal level.

I fucking hate him, and I think we're trying to murder each other right now, but I'm also dangerously close to wanting to rip his clothes off and fuck him until I can't stand upright.

What the fuck is wrong with me?

He leans over and more of his weight comes down, and I can feel his hardness through his pants.

Knowing that he's as turned on as I am makes me feel fucking powerful.

It makes me feel greedy for more of him, even though it's really the last thing I should be thinking about.

His voice caresses the curve of my neck as he says, "You are somehow immune to me, and I cannot abide that."

Shadows fill the room and coalesce into his shadow soldiers.

Panic grips me by the throat.

The Demon King lifts off of me and jerks me upright with a handful of my shirt.

The shadow soldiers lunge for me as Wrath steps back, letting them do the dirty work.

I can feel the cold, damp hands of the shadows against my skin, their fingers digging into my flesh. Tears burn in my eyes as I try to scream, but no sound comes out.

They're smothering me, overwhelming me. My chest burns, and it's like they're stealing all of the oxygen out of the room.

Pinpoints of light blink behind my closed lids. There's a disconnect between my brain and the rest of my body, like I'm being dragged to the cold, dark ocean floor. Everything is weightless, and all the light is sucked out of the world.

And as I sink lower and lower into it, instinctively, I reach up, up, desperately scrabbling for something even though I can't see, even though I can't tell where my hands are.

There's a moment where I think this is the end. Where I think, hey, your stubborn temper really got you into some shit this time, didn't it? You should have just fucking bowed.

And then—

The shadow soldiers shriek and pull back. I'm able to open my eyes and see and—*holy shit.*

Light blazes in the room almost like it's on fire. Wrath has a hand at his chest, teeth gnashed, face contorted...*like he's in pain.*

The shadows burn away.

The Demon King scowls and stumbles back, sucking in air.

A door bangs open in the front of the house.

The Demon King steps into me and I dance back, bumping into the bedside table. "This has only just begun," he says, and then he's gone. There one minute, gone the next, and I blink at the spot he just inhabited until Adam bursts into the room, a large gun in hand, two more strapped to his waist.

I yelp until I realize who he is.

"The Demon King?" he says.

"I...He..."

"Gone?" Adam says, a little breathless from the adrenaline.

I can only nod.

"Rain is clear," Adam says, and it takes me a second to realize he's talking to someone through an earpiece.

"Come on." He gestures me forward. "Grab your things. We're taking you somewhere safe."

Numbly, I toss my few belongings into my bag.
I'm not so sure a safe place exists.
I'm now the enemy of our enemy.
And apparently the only one he sees as a threat.

7

I BARELY NOTICE CLIMBING IN A DARK SUV. I BARELY NOTICE THE DRIVE somewhere, or when I'm helped out of the SUV and guided into a building that I've never seen.

Adam's by my side, but he's barely said two words to me. His finger is still dangerously close to the trigger of his giant gun.

There are more people, men and women dressed in tactical gear, that follow us down a dimly lit hallway.

When we emerge into a central room, Gus is suddenly there, wrapping his arms around me, and I sob into him.

I don't know where I am, and I don't know what is happening and I'm fucking scared.

"It's all right, babe," Gus says by my ear. "You're safe now."

I close my eyes and drink in the smell of him, like sugar cookies and Earl Grey tea and lavender. Gus is as close to home as I've ever gotten. He might not be blood family, but he's my safe space, one of two people I trust in this world.

I like to pretend I don't need anyone, until I do.

I can't do this alone.

I needed Gus, but I was too proud to take the help he was offering.

When the tears finally dry up, I pull back and realize there are at least a dozen people—strangers—standing awkwardly around me, and I'm still standing in my oversized Bob Marley t-shirt.

Christ, could this day get any worse? Or...wait, I think it's after midnight so it's a new day. Already off to a brilliant start.

Adam appears on my left, a tissue in hand.

"Thank you." I dry my face and wipe my nose.

"We should talk," Adam says.

"Give her a minute," Gus says.

I crumple the tissue in my hand. "It's okay. I'm okay."

Gus frowns at me and tucks a hair behind my ear. "No you're not."

He's not wrong, but what am I going to do? Curl into a ball in the corner and cry myself to sleep? That's not my style. Power through, right?

I look around the room. We seem to be in some kind of warehouse or gutted factory. There are large windows around the entire room, but all of them have been covered in newspaper. Several desks and worktables fill up the large space and—damn, lots and lots of guns. There are guns on tables, guns in racks on the walls, guns strapped to hips.

This must be one of the militia, Adam's team, and apparently their headquarters.

"Is there coffee somewhere?" I ask.

Adam cuts his dark gaze to a short guy across the room. The guy darts away without so much as an order.

"Anything else?" he asks me in a deep, gravelly voice. Gus once told me that voice alone could make him come, and I have to admit, it does hold some weight.

I look down at my bare legs. "Pants?"

"I have some extra fatigues here," a girl says. "I'll go grab a pair."

"Thanks, Sanjay," Adam says, and the girl hurries away.

Adam takes off his giant gun and hands it to someone. "Come on," he says to me. "Let's sit down for a chat."

"I feel like I'm being led to the principal's office," I mutter.

Gus puts an arm around my shoulders. "You should see what happens when Adam hands out a detention." He winks.

"Gross," I say with a laugh.

Adam sends a disgruntled look over his shoulder, and Gus bites his lip, trying not to grin.

These two are honestly the oddest pair.

Adam leads us through the central room to a set of iron stairs that wind back and forth up two flights before spilling us into what must have been a control room. All of the machinery has been stripped, but the counters remain. There's a utilitarian table in the middle with green metal chairs sitting around it.

Up on the wall, three giant TV screens are currently on mute but playing through news feeds. On the opposite wall, four smaller screens show surveillance footage, maybe from the outside of the factory?

Before I sit, Sanjay shows up with a pair of army green pants. They're a little short, since I'm a bit taller than she is, but they button up just fine, so I don't complain. And right after that, the short guy arrives with a steaming cup of coffee.

"Wasn't sure how you'd take it," he says in a Southern drawl, "so I brought you some sugar and cream."

"Thank you..."

"Eric," he answers.

"Eric. You're a lifesaver."

He smiles and his pale skin flushes.

I doctor up my cup of coffee and take a tentative sip. It doesn't even come close to Harper's expensive brand, but I'll take whatever I can get.

Exhaustion and stress are making me a little ill.

Sanjay sits at the table on my right side. She's petite, but I definitely spy some toned biceps peeking out of the sleeve of her white t-shirt. Her long, black hair is braided tightly into a French braid, and it hangs over her shoulder. She's wearing no jewelry, but I can just make out an empty hole for a piercing on her left nostril.

I suppose when you're fighting bad guys, jewelry is a hazard.

Gus pulls out the chair on my left, and Eric sits on the other side of him. Two other burly men who introduce themselves as Pitch and Tommy fill up the rest of the table.

Adam stays standing, muscular arms crossed over his chest.

He really does cut quite the figure.

His dark hair is cropped close. There are a few black tattoos winding over his arms, but in the sharp fluorescent light, I can't make out what they are.

"Rain," Adam says, "this is my crew. We don't have a name. We're not out for fame and chaos like MAW or religious zeal like the Citizens Against Darkness. We're here to do a job."

I nod when he stares at me because it's hard not to fall in line like a dutiful soldier when Adam is looking at you. "And what's the job?"

The others glance at each other like they're trying to decide if the secret should be spilled even though I think I already know what it is.

"Neutralize the Demon King," Adam answers.

"And by neutralize, you mean..."

"Kill him," Pitch says.

I let out a puff of air. It sounds like *pah.*

No one says a word.

"He's unkillable," I say. "The entire United States government has tried to take him out. And you think you're somehow going to do a job they couldn't?"

Adam's nostrils flare. I make out the bulge of a vein in his forehead. Clearly he's trying really hard not to put me in my place.

"Every man has a weakness," he answers.

"He's not a man." I set the cup of coffee down. It rings out on the metal table. "You plan to what, use some flood lights against him? Burn him to a crisp?" I get a flash of memory, of Wrath's face contorted in pain, and the surprise that registered in the glint of his colorless eyes. "I mean...the fire or whatever it was seemed to do some damage, but—"

The others shift in their seats and look at one another.

"What?" I say.

"That wasn't us," Sanjay answers.

I frown. "It wasn't?"

She shakes her head.

I rake my teeth over my bottom lip, trying to recall exactly what happened and *how* it happened. It was all a blur, fear and adrenaline putting me in a reactionary mode instead of allowing me to take in the details.

"If it wasn't you guys, then who was it?"

Adam uncrosses his big arms and puts his palms on the edge of the table. When he hunches forward, shoulders rising in his army green t-shirt, it makes him seem bigger, like a bull getting ready to charge.

"Every man has a weakness," Adam repeats. "And the Demon King? You're his."

8

Oh crap.

They can't really believe that, can they? This ragtag group of highly trained and motivated men and women armed to the teeth.

They can't really think I can somehow help them take out the Demon King.

Can they?

I stand up, the chair groaning across the concrete floor as I push it back. "No," I say and shake my head for emphasis in case they didn't hear my very loud objection. "*No.*"

"Rain," Gus says, reaching for me.

I yank my arm away.

Adam straightens. "Sit down, Rain."

The room goes quiet when Adam speaks. He and I have a showdown of intense stares.

Maybe my reluctance to get to know Adam has to do with our stubbornness. The clashing of horns. Though I think he's a Virgo, which is the virgin, so maybe that metaphor is wrong. Maybe Adam's stubbornness comes from his deep well, his patience to wait out my Aries ram.

With a huff, I sit and fold my arms over my chest. I suddenly feel silly in my thrift store Bob Marley t-shirt.

"No one has stood against Wrath," Adam says. "That is a fact."

So okay, maybe that's true.

"Which means you are the closest we've come to a defense."

"But...I'm no one special."

"You're something," Sanjay says quietly, reassuringly.

Tommy and Pitch nod at me. "Sorry, darling," Pitch says, "but it is what it is."

"So, what, I'm like Wrath's kryptonite or something?"

"That's not a perfect example," Eric says, "because Superman is repelled by Kryptonite, and the Demon King seems to be both drawn to you and affected by you and—" He clamps his mouth shut.

I'm gathering Eric can't function once he realizes everyone is looking at him.

Adam finishes for him. "You're immune to Wrath, but I don't think he's immune to you. He's drawn to you."

"That's not true," I argue.

"Oh?" Adam raises a brow and comes around the table so he's directly across from me. "He came straight to you tonight, and he could have possessed you. Instead, he toyed with you because we think he's struggling to take you down."

"Wait...*Possess* me?"

Tommy mutters something in a language I don't know. I think it might be Russian.

"What'd he say?"

Adam translates for me. "Have you been living under a rock?"

"Rain has been trying hard not to learn anything about the Demon King," Gus explains. "She's almost made it a professional sport."

"I have my own shit to deal with," I answer.

"Well, if you'd been paying attention," Adam says, "you'd know that one of the Demon King's powers is to possess humans.

That's what his soldiers are. They were originally members of MAW."

My mouth drops open. "Are you serious?"

I do remember hearing about several MAW members disappearing after a confrontation with the Demon King, but I had no idea he literally stole them and made them into some kind of enslaved dark soldiers.

Of course, it makes sense now, considering he's *literally* called the Demon King. And what do demons do in our very own lore and mythology? They possess us, steal our bodies and our minds.

It opens up a whole other can of worms—what else from our mythological history might actually be real? And was our mythology based on the Demon King and whatever world he came from? It can't just be a fluke, can it?

"How...How does the Demon King possess humans?"

"His dark magic," Gus answers.

"The shadows," Adam adds.

Was he trying to possess me? Sic his soldiers on me to try to turn me into one of his monsters? All because I withstood him in the alley and made him look weak.

I take in several deep breaths.

The Demon King is going to come for me. He's going to keep trying to kill me or enslave me and—

Oh god.

And here I thought the worst thing on my plate was dealing with Josiah at my last family session.

How good I had it!

And then something occurs to me.

"If he found me at Harper's, can't he find me here too? Aren't you guys worried about your safety?"

Adam goes back to the head of the table and juts his chin at the surveillance monitors. "We have this place heavily guarded, but..." He trails off. Adam is not a trail-off kind of guy.

"What?"

"I know this has been a lot to take in for one night," Gus says.

"What? Just tell me."

"I'm a witch," Eric answers. "And I put up a protective barrier around the building."

"Oh. Ha. Ha *ha*."

No one else is laughing. Even Adam. Stoic, no-nonsense Adam is standing there like Eric didn't just literally call himself a witch.

"What?" I say.

Gus rubs my back again, trying to calm me.

"What?" I shout.

Tommy says something in Russian, and Adam nods at him.

"What is happening?" I say.

Adam snaps his fingers at Pitch, and the burly man goes to a cabinet along the far wall.

"I can't," I say, and Gus nods and coos at me.

"I know, babe," he says.

"Witches? Demons? *Possession*?" I can feel my blood pressure rising, my face flushing.

By sticking my head in the sand, I've put myself at an extreme disadvantage. I suppose it shouldn't be much of a shock, the fact that witches are a thing when a demon literally orders sushi at Par House.

But if witches are real, then probably other things that go bump in the night are real too.

And I don't currently have the mental capacity to reckon with that.

I don't fucking want any of it. I want to go home, and I want everything to be normal, and hell, I'll even do family photo sessions for the rest of my life until the cows come home. I'll take all the demon children over the very real, *very* gorgeous, *very* infuriating Demon King and—

Pitch uncaps a bottle of whisky and gives my coffee a generous pour.

"Drink," Adam orders.

I lurch to my feet. "I'm not drinking! Drinking got me into this mess! I was drinking a spiked half-and-half when I was on my way home and I ran into the Demon King and that's what started this whole thing and—"

Adam comes up beside me. He easily towers over me by a foot. "The spiked half-and-half started this?" One of his dark brows rises in an arch. "It was the booze that gave you the ability to stand up against that devil? So if I get drunk, I can slap him around a bit? No worries at all?"

I sputter to a stop.

He picks up my coffee and hands it to me. "I need you." He gestures to the room with a wave of his arm. "*We* need you. So take a drink. Take a beat. Take a breath. And then help us *stop him*."

There are tears burning in my eyes. I lick my lips.

They need me. *They need me?*

"You can't ignore this anymore," Adam says.

I sniff and nod. It's easy to ignore the threat the Demon King poses on our future when our social media obsessed world has turned him into a celebrity, into a commodity.

The thing is, I'm no one special. I'm not a decorated soldier like Adam, or a badass like Sanjay. And I don't possess Gus's optimism and positivity.

I certainly can't manhandle a gun like Russian Tommy and burly Pitch. And I'm no witch like adorable little Eric.

They think I'm the only one that can help them.

But what do I think?

I think I'm in over my head.

I take the cup of coffee from Adam and drink. The coffee has already started to cool, but the booze makes it burn down my throat.

Once the alcohol hits my stomach and floods my veins with warmth, I do feel a little more settled. And as long as I don't take too much, the booze will help with the anxiety more than popping a pill.

I need to make sure I have my shit together from here on out. I can't be lagging when the Demon King wants to hunt me down and possess me.

"Good?" Adam says.

I nod. "Yeah. I'm good."

"Gus," he says, "get her something to eat."

Gus stands up and hooks an arm around my waist. "Come on. This way. There's always good takeout leftovers here."

"I ate the tacos," Pitch says.

"There's leftover Chinese food," Sanjay says.

I let Gus guide me back down the stairs and down a hallway and to a giant kitchen that looks more like a cafeteria. He deposits me at one of many metal tables while he goes behind the counter to the industrial refrigerator.

"Ahh," he says to the interior, and then pulls out two cartons of Chinese food and two cans of sparkling water. He returns to me and sets the food down. There are Mason jars on each table filled with silverware but no chopsticks. Gus grabs two forks instead.

I take another long drink of the spiked coffee, then push the mug aside.

Even though I'm in an unfamiliar place, forced from my home, eating leftovers with Gus is the most familiar thing I can think of and it makes me feel settled and safe.

Knowing me well, Gus hands me the container with the chicken fried rice.

I unfold the top and the smell of rice, veggies, eggs, and salty, tangy soy sauce fills my nose. I can tell by the box that it's from Little Sheep Gardens, my favorite.

The first spoonful serves as a weight, pulling me back down to earth, to reality.

"I didn't realize how much I needed this," I say around a mouthful.

Gus is eating rice and sesame chicken. "Chinese food always makes everything better."

"Mmm," I say and stuff more food in my mouth.

"So," Gus says as he pops the top on one of the cans of sparkling ice water. "You want to talk about it?" He slides the can across the table to me, then opens his and takes a drink.

Using the tines of the fork, I push around a few carrots, looking for bits of chicken, avoiding eye contact with Gus. I'm afraid that if I look at him while I talk, I might just start sobbing again.

"None of this makes sense," I say.

"Upheaval rarely does."

"You've got a point. But seriously, Gus." I drop my fork in the takeout container. "Does this track for you? Why the hell is this happening to me? I don't get it."

The lump of his Adam's apple sinks in his throat as he swallows, looking at me like I'm a delicate flower that needs soft words and gentle watering or else I might wilt. I'm not used to feeling fragile or vulnerable, and the way Gus looks at me makes me think he isn't sure what to do either.

"You're Rain Low," he says. "Stubborn Aries, fiery queen. Of course you stood up against a villain. Remember when you socked Ben Hightower when he called me a fairy?"

I snort a laugh.

Gus grins. "I'll never forget that look on his face as blood ran from his nose, like he was confused as to how he got there."

"He never saw it coming," I answer. "Bully for him, underestimating a girl, picking on my best friend. Bastard deserved it."

"See? You've never backed down. And yeah, maybe it's a mystery why you're immune to the Demon King, but the fact that you have the balls to do it? That's not surprising at all."

I'm already feeling better.

"Thanks, Gus."

He reaches across the table and squeezes my hand, his cross earring swinging from his ear. "You don't have to thank me. I've got your back, and so does Adam. He might be all stoic soldier dude on the outside, but the guy has a heart of gold, I'm telling you. It takes a lot of work to get through his defenses, but once you do, watch out, he'll move heaven and earth to protect those he cares about."

"It's not like he cares about me, though."

"But he cares about *me,*" Gus says. "Which by extension means you too."

"Yeah, so let's talk about that for a minute, shall we?"

Gus screws up his mouth. "Um, no."

"When are you making it exclusive?"

The can of sparkling water glints in the fluorescent light when Gus upends it, swallowing down the rest of it.

"Gus."

The can clangs loudly when he sets it down. "You know me, I like my freedom." He pretends to whip back his hair, even though his has always been short and coiffed to perfection. Lately, he's been combing over his bleached blond hair and taming it with so much product, the shine on it could be seen from space.

"I know you like your freedom," I say, "but if Adam is as golden as you make him out to be, he's only going to stick around for so long. I'd hate to see you miss out on something special out of fear."

"I'm not afraid."

I give him a look. "Oh really?"

"Well, maybe a little."

Gus had his heart broken a few years back by a guy that I disliked from the very beginning. I mean, I *am* extremely protective of Gus, and no man is ever good enough for him. And maybe that's also why I've kept Adam at arm's length—deep down, I know he *is* good for Gus, maybe even too good. And I'm afraid of losing my best friend to love.

Fear keeps us all in our boxes, locked away safe and sound. I think in a lot of ways, doing family photography is my safe little box. I whine and bitch about it, but have I done anything to change it? No. Because it's safe. Because doing it means I don't have to take any big risks, it means I don't have to face failure, or discomfort.

I eat the last spoonful of fried rice and then shove the carton aside. "Well, this got deep real quick, didn't it?"

Gus sighs. "This is your usual MO though, babe."

"What are you talking about?"

"When faced with your own obstacle, it's much easier for you to focus on other people's problems."

I frown. "That maybe sounds familiar."

He hangs his head back and laughs at the ceiling. The sound echoes through the large cafeteria. Gus has the best big laugh. It warms my gut.

When he straightens again, he quickly sobers. "Just like you've always helped me through my shit, I'm going to help you through this one. Got it?"

I put my chin in the palm of my hand. "What if I don't want to do this?"

"Babe," he says and ducks his head so he can look me right in the eyes. There's concern pinched between his brows and a frown on his lips. "I don't think you have a choice."

Fuck. My stomach flips.

He's right.

He's so fucking right.

The Demon King is coming for me whether I like it or not.

9

IT'S SANJAY WHO SHOWS ME TO A ROOM I CAN CRASH IN. HER LONG, BLACK braid swishes behind her as she walks down a wide hall. The girl can move quickly despite her small frame, and I find I have to power walk to keep up with her.

"So how long have you been working with Adam?" I ask.

She glances at me over her shoulder. "We served together, so I've known him about seven years, but after I got out of the Army, I went back home to Detroit and tried to pretend I was cut out for a domestic life. Or an academic one." She looks at me again with a grin on her face. "Spoiler, I wasn't. Much to the chagrin of my parents. They wanted me to either go through with an arranged marriage or go into medicine, but I wanted to fight for something."

She turns a corner, and I scurry after her.

"I've always been that way," she carries on. "Medicine is great for saving people, but so is fighting."

"God, I love you," I say.

She smiles again. She has a dazzling smile that reminds me of a daisy opening up. When she turns that smile on you, you just want to bask in it.

"Anyway," she says when she stops at an unmarked door, "when Adam told me he was putting together a team to try to stop the Demon King, I was all in."

Sanjay opens the door to my new room and flicks on a light switch. I poke my head inside.

Like everything else about this place, it's unadorned and practical. There's an iron-framed bed against the wall with a lumpy mattress on it. Sheets and a green blanket are folded precisely at the foot of the bed. There's a metal cabinet next to the bed with a curved-arm lamp on top.

There aren't any windows.

I suppose that's for the best. No one can crawl in while I sleep.

I go in and turn a circle. "Have you guys figured out what the Demon King is looking for?"

Sanjay crosses her arms over her chest and leans into the doorframe. "Not yet. But we suspect whatever it is, we don't want him to have it."

I nod. That makes sense. "So the plan is to stop him from finding it."

"Pretty much."

"And you guys really think I can help with that?"

"You're closer than we've ever gotten."

I drop to the bed and the frame squeaks loudly. "I wish I had your confidence, Sanjay."

"I wish I had whatever your power is to withstand the Demon King."

An unladylike snort comes out of me. "It's not a power. Probably a fluke."

"If you say so."

I glance at her, checking for sarcasm. What I find instead is more frightening—hope.

She, like everyone else, is hopeful that I can stop Wrath. But that voice in the back of my mind keeps saying it's all some kind of mistake and that they'll realize their optimism was misplaced in me.

Or worse—someone will end up as one of Wrath's enslaved monsters.

I don't want to be the reason Adam loses his team because I couldn't do what he needed me to do.

The trouble with always fending for myself means I've never had to shoulder the responsibility of anyone else, and I'm finding I don't like it. The feeling chafes.

"I'll let you get some rest," Sanjay says. "Bathroom is at the end of the hall. If you need anything, my room is just two doors down."

"Thanks, Sanjay. I mean it. I really appreciate your kindness."

She smiles again. "No need to thank me for that."

We say goodbye, and she pulls the door shut behind her. I click on the desk lamp and flick off the harsh overhead lights.

I've never been the type of person to get whiny about my surroundings, but this...this is hard to adjust to. Having no windows is great for safety, but I'm feeling closed off, hedged in, isolated. I don't like it.

I already miss my condo, my bed, and my bathroom.

Trying to distract myself, I make the tiny twin-sized bed with the sheets that have been left out. The material is scratchy, but the white cotton is clean and I can smell the bleach that was used to wash it.

Clean is good. I can handle this.

Once the bed is made, the pillow fluffed, I lie down and flick off the light.

For a massive space like a repurposed factory, you'd think there'd be all sorts of sounds. Clanking and rustling and groaning. But this place must have been built to withstand a bomb because it's silent. Absolutely fucking silent.

I turn onto my back and blink up at the ceiling even though in my windowless room, there's nothing but darkness.

What if this is my destiny? For the rest of my life? To hide away in a barren, windowless room while the ruthless Demon King hunts me down simply because I'm immune to him?

The tears that spring to my eyes catch me off guard.

This isn't something to cry about!

I'm safe. I have a roof over my head. Not everyone can say that. And I'm surrounded by friends and I have a mother that cares about me and—

My face wrinkles up in the dark as the tears come.

I hate that I hate this.

I hate that I can't just be happy with what I have.

But isn't that how I've always lived my life? Nothing is ever good enough. Perpetually dissatisfied. My mom always said as much.

"Like you're always chasing a drug," she would say, "but you don't know what the drug is."

She's not wrong. I feel like I've been searching for *something* my entire life, but I don't know what that is, and now not only do I not have something better, I have something worse—a windowless room in a gutted factory and a very shaky future.

Because Wrath isn't going to let this go. He may have signed a treaty with the government, but when it comes down to it, what do they think they'll do if he breaks it? Nothing. There's nothing anyone can do.

Tears trail down my temples, soaking my hair. I brush them away, but more just replace them. I can't stop. I'm overwhelmed and fucking mad and frustrated and scared and—

"Tears are for the weak."

The voice slithers out of the darkness, caressing my skin.

The tears immediately stop as my heart kicks up in my chest.

Did I just hear that?

I hold my breath as blood pumps hard through my body, goosebumps sending a shiver across my shoulders.

He takes a breath. I can hear it in the dark. I can feel it like a fingertip dragging across my skin.

"You're not here," I say.

"Am I not?" he answers.

Fuck.

Fuck.

I can't see anything but...are the shadows coalescing? He's going to possess me. Fuck.

The Demon King is here somehow, someway. He's here and he's going to take me and then I'll just be a mindless slave made of darkness.

On three, I'm turning on the lamp.

Anticipation coils in my bones.

One.

My heart races beneath my ribs.

Two.

I slowly reach my hand to the lamp's hanging chain.

Three.

I yank it down and soft golden light fills the room.

And the Demon King is standing not three feet away.

All of the air dries up in my throat and I think my heart stops beating.

"I'm coming for you," he says, and then his face contorts into that sharp monster as he charges me, teeth bared.

10

I SCREAM AND SQUEEZE MY EYES SHUT, PULLING THE BLANKET UP LIKE I'M A child again hiding from the monsters under my bed.

I scream and scream.

The door bursts open.

Boots pound into the room.

When I open my eyes, I find Adam with a gun up, the stock tight against his shoulder as he scans the room through the sight. Sanjay and Eric flank him.

"Clear," Adam says.

Sanjay and Eric pull back. Sanjay says, "Rain is clear."

"What happened?" Adam asks.

"I—"

I look around the tiny room. The Demon King is gone. There's nowhere to hide here except—

I leap off the bed and then slowly, tentatively, check under the bed only to find it empty. How the hell am I supposed to explain this one?

"Rain?" Adam says.

"I thought..." I fold my arms over my middle. "I thought I saw something." I look up at him, my face still wet with tears. I must look like a lunatic.

He's probably starting to get the drift—I'm a liability.

I might be the only person immune to the Demon King, but I'm also losing it.

Gus hurries into the room half dressed. He spots me, then looks to Adam. Adam gives him a quick nod before Gus rushes over, his hands on either side of my face.

The tears come again and this time, blood pools in my cheeks from the embarrassment. I'm not a damsel in distress, but I feel like one and I can't stop crying.

"You all right?" Gus asks. His hair is askew and there are bags beneath his eyes. He looks tired and worried and stressed and it's all because of me. He's supposed to be enjoying a weekend in the city with his sorta-boyfriend. Not taking care of me in a depressing factory.

"I'm okay," I say, feeling stupid. Maybe I was dreaming and didn't realize it? I could have sworn Wrath was here. I *felt* him. But I can't tell them that or they'll really think I'm losing it. Maybe I am.

"I think I'm just really tired," I answer.

"Was he here?" Adam asks, his expression blank.

My heart kicks up again and butterflies fill my belly.

Was he here?

Wrath. The Demon King.

Did he come right to me?

Why does it feel like my body is hoping he was? It's turning into a damn traitor.

"I...I *thought* I saw him," I admit. "But that's not possible, right? Because of the barrier thing?" I wave my hand vaguely through the air as if I even understand what a witch barrier is.

Adam casts a glance over his shoulder. Eric nods and hurries off.

"Anything is possible with Wrath. Let's not forget that," Adam says. "We'll search the grounds."

Gus tucks me protectively into his side. He's warm and familiar, and being near him unwinds some of the knots in my chest. I'm so grateful to have him that the tears burn in my sinuses again before I sniff them back.

"She can't stay in here alone," Gus says.

"Agreed." Adam drops his rifle. It's strapped to his body by a black nylon strap, and when he cinches it up, the gun tightens to his chest, the barrel pointed at the floor. "We'll move her to the living room and keep eyes on her at all times."

"Can she go there now?" Gus asks.

"Wait until we clear the building," Adam answers. "Tommy and Pitch," he shouts as he leaves the room. "Guard Rain."

"Aye, boss," Pitch says.

Tommy says something that sounds like *pon-you*.

Gus guides me back down to the bed, but doesn't leave my side. It isn't until he drapes the army green blanket over my shoulders that I realize I'm shivering.

I don't like feeling like I can't take care of myself, like I'm weak.

The Demon King is making me feel like a grade A loser.

"If he's here, Adam will find him," Gus says as he rubs warmth into my arms.

"And if he does? Find him, I mean?"

Gus frowns, but he doesn't answer.

We both know what happens.

It doesn't take Adam's team long to clear the building, and they find nothing. Not even a window screen out of place. While I'm glad they didn't run into the Demon King, I'm a little defeated by it because it makes me think maybe I did imagine him.

Still, as Gus takes me to the living room, I can't shake the feeling that Wrath is still with me, watching, waiting, and that eventually, he will come to me and there will be nothing anyone can do to stop him.

The living room is much smaller in size than the central room, and it feels cozy despite the sterile gray paint on the concrete walls. Like Collie's Tea Shop, the furniture here is mismatched and has clearly been thrifted or commandeered from other places.

I sit on the end of a gray tweed sofa that smells faintly of a grandma.

An 80s movie plays on the flat screen TV hanging on the far wall. The characters are wearing button-up shirts with wild patterns, hair slicked back.

"Wish I would have found the bastard," a scrawny guy says in the corner. He's sitting at a round table with another guy. There's an unfinished game of chess between them. "I would have put a bullet straight through his brain."

Sanjay is sitting on the arm of a side chair, her rifle close at hand. I've never been around guns much and it's a little unsettling how comfortable everyone is with them. I'm used to being surrounded by coffee table art books and camera equipment.

"You could have tried to put a bullet through his brain," Sanjay says, "and then you would have had your heart ripped out by the Demon King when you failed."

One of the other guys laughs.

The scrawny guy turns red. "Why we keeping this girl around anyway?" He tips his chin at me. "Maybe we should use her as bait."

Sanjay's eyes go round like she's silently telling the guy to shut it.

And that's when Adam steps up.

He crosses his arms over his chest and his muscles strain against his sleeves.

The room goes silent.

I'm learning that when Adam levels his shoulders and crosses his arms, it's akin to a cobra opening its hood.

Somebody is about to get bit.

"Rain is one of our own," Adam says as he looks over the room. Most of those assembled avoid eye contact with him. "Do we sacrifice our own?"

The scrawny guy opens his mouth like he's about to argue, but Adam silences him with a glare. "Do we sacrifice our own?" he repeats. "Darren?"

The scrawny guy, Darren, apparently, shakes his head. "Sorry, boss."

I look across the tweed sofa and see Gus practically drooling as he watches his man bring the room to heel.

I can't say I blame him.

"Rain," Adam says when he turns back to me. "Sanjay and Pitch will be your personal guards. They'll follow you everywhere. Do not stray from them. Understood?"

Even though I'm not one of Adam's soldiers, I still find myself dutifully nodding my head. "Understood."

"Tommy and Eric," Adam says. "With me."

When they leave the room, conversation filters back in.

Gus leans into me and whispers, "I can't wait to fuck that man tonight. Or is it day?"

"How can you even think about sex right now?" I scrunch into the couch's corner, tucking my knees up into my chest, pulling my Bob Marley shirt over my legs. I'm so frickin tired, and yet I can't seem to commit to sleep. What if I did dream about the Demon King? And what if he comes back?

"Sex helps me relax," Gus answers, shifting himself sideways on the sofa so he can spread out his long legs. His feet are bare and he arches his toes my way. "It's a natural anti-anxiety med."

I close my eyes. I might not be ready to sleep, but my eyes are burning so badly, I just need a few minutes of respite. "Maybe I should proposition Eric then. I could use all the anti-anxiety I can get."

"You could try," Sanjay says, "but he's asexual."

"Tommy then," I say and look over at the burly man watching the doorway.

When Gus laughs, a lock of blond hair flops over his forehead. More proof that my freak-out roused him from bed. He's disheveled, not coiffed like usual.

"What's so funny about that?" I ask.

"Oh nothing, other than Tommy is old enough to be your dad."

"Maybe I have a daddy fetish. How will I know until I try it?" Except when I think about having sex, the first image that pops into my brain is the Demon King.

It immediately makes me clench up, and I untuck my legs, disliking the rush of blood to my clit at just the mere thought of the Demon King between my thighs.

Guilt wends into my gut. These people are risking their lives to protect me from Wrath, and here I am fantasizing about screwing him?

It's just...every breath he exhales around me feels like a storm rolling in, like I'm the ocean, and he's the thundercloud churning my insides.

I can't fight it any more than the ocean can fight the storm.

This isn't good. Not good at all.

It must be a facet of his power. It would explain why we're all gaga for him.

Summoning all of the mental energy I have left, I shove down those thoughts and turn my focus to the TV and the 80s movie nearing its montage. But as I sit here, I can feel Darren and his friend watching me warily.

Adam might have made it clear that I was off limits, but how loyal are these people? My gut instinct says I can trust Sanjay and Eric and Tommy and Pitch, but there's something about Darren that makes my skin crawl.

I inhale to settle my nerves. I have a lot of good people on my side. I just have to trust in them.

But for how long?

How long do I have to surrender to this hide-and-seek life?

I doze on the couch for a while, but keep my legs tangled with Gus's just to ensure my subconscious that a friend is nearby.

My sleep this time is blissfully uneventful, but when Gus shakes me awake sometime later, instinct has me lurching upright like I'm under attack.

"It's just me," he says, holding up his hands.

"Sorry." I scrub my eyes. "What's going on?"

"You gotta see this." He shows me his phone, and I wince at the light, my eyes still burning with sleep.

"Oh, hold on." He turns the phone back around to slide down the brightness. "Here."

I sit up and run my hands through my hair. I can already feel it getting greasy and knotted. I take a shower every day without fail, and I'm now overdue. It's like my hair has an expiration date and as soon as it hits, it's full-on dirty. It's just one more reminder that I'm not at home and nothing is normal.

I haven't checked out the bathroom situation here yet—do they even have showers?

Phone in hand, sleepiness fading, I finally focus on the screen.

Gus is logged into Instagram, and he's landed on a photo-shopped picture that makes me go cold.

It's me and the Demon King.

My photo is from two years back when I was experimenting with fine art self-portraits. My hair was shorter, and I'd gotten a blowout specifically for the photo, then promptly mussed it as soon as I got home to give it an artfully messy vibe.

Bright sunlight filtered in through a window behind me,

turning everything hazy and warm. I was wearing a men's oxford shirt fully unbuttoned baring a sliver of flesh and some serious cleavage.

I thought I was being risqué, but in today's Instagram world, the photo was practically biblical.

Now someone had taken the photo and composited it with an image of Wrath and his pale, gorgeous face.

The artist added shadows around Wrath, and mood and texture to the final image. Dark mist wreathed the edges, and pale filigree stamped the corners.

There was a quote written in small, slanted cursive just below Wrath.

A light here required a shadow there – Virginia Woolf

Looking at the image, I feel a chill slither down my spine.

My mom taught me that no art can be dismissed. Anything that's made with creativity is art. Even this photoshopped image on Instagram.

I've lived and breathed all kinds of art my entire life. I once lived in the back of a gallery with my mom when I was a kid when she took part in a live exhibit.

I *know* art. I know that not all of it makes sense, but that good art makes you feel something.

And right now...I feel like that ocean again, weightless, boundless, *restless.*

There's an excited flutter in my chest, one that I try hard to ignore.

I open up the comments to read what others think about it.

I ship it.

I hate this girl and I want to be her all at the same time.

I volunteer!

Couple goals.

If she's not currently jumping his bones, I will gladly take her place.

I scroll back up to the image.

It's like Wrath is looking at me through the phone's screen. Everything about this man makes me...

No. No. Everything about him makes me irate.

If he shows up again, I'm going to stab him.

"You think that's bad?" Sanjay says as she points the remote at the TV and turns up the volume.

There are news teams and amateur YouTubers racing after a dark figure on the street.

It doesn't take much to recognize the broad shoulders of Wrath. Or maybe it's the confident, determined gait, as if he's headed for a battle he knows he's already won.

"Wrath!" someone shouts.

"Your Highness!" another man yells.

Oh, we're giving him titles now, are we?

"Mr. Wrath," a woman yells. "Can you tell us more about Rain Low and why she's so special?"

Wrath abruptly stops, and everyone chasing him bounces off of each other as they come to a halt.

Lights flash, cameras click. There's a crowd gathering on the street curb.

My heart is beating like a drum in my chest.

Why am I so special? What is he going to say?

I desperately want to know.

The sharp cut of Wrath's jawline comes into stark relief as he turns just enough to speak to the cameras. He doesn't look at the viewer, but it's clear he's speaking to us.

Or maybe he's just talking to one person in particular.

Me.

"I wish only to speak to Rain," he says, and then adds, "Alone."

I lick my lips. All of the exhaustion is gone from my bones and I feel charged up, electric.

I sit upright and lean toward the TV.

The most wanted/most popular man in the country is currently talking about me on national TV and all over the internet. It's easy to pretend this is just my problem in my little bubble, but this, the Instagram post, it all proves just how big this has gotten in a very short amount of time.

It's no longer a fluke.

It's no longer something I can bury my head in the sand over and wait it out.

This is very, very real and it's snowballing.

"In fact," Wrath says, "I'm upping the reward."

The crowd murmurs around him. More cameras click.

"If you have Rain's current location," he says, the deep timbre of his voice filling the speakers, wending through the room, slithering over to me on the couch and lifting the hair at the nape of my neck. "I'm offering one million dollars to anyone who can tell me where to find her."

"Holy shit," Gus says.

"Holy shit is right," Sanjay says.

Pitch pipes up behind me. "That's not good. Tell the boss."

Sanjay pulls out her cell phone and taps in a message. Their panic has me panicking, and it's suddenly hard to breathe.

I stand up, thinking that walking around might help, but my head swims and I have to catch myself on the arm of one of the side chairs.

"Rain?" Gus says.

My stomach rolls.

This isn't good, Pitch said. Not good. Fuck. If he's worried...

"I think I'm going to be sick." I clamp my hand over my mouth.

The room erupts in a flurry of movement and then someone shoves an empty bucket beneath me at the exact moment I start retching. What little I ate immediately comes up, burning through my sinuses, lighting my throat on fire.

My stomach is in knots and my chest hurts and it's all too much.

Someone holds my hair back. I think it might be Gus, but I can't be sure. I keep retching, unable to stop it, my body violently opposing this shit show. And I've gotta say, I'm right there with it.

When it finally stops, I collapse against the wall. Putting my hands on my knees, bending over, I suck in several deep breaths. Someone hands me a wet rag and I paw at my face, flushed and probably covered in red splotches. I always break out in hives when I vomit.

As I stand there, half hunched over, pristine black boots appear in my line of sight. I can feel Adam's energy before I look up at him. He's like the lion sauntering into the circle. I don't want to face him. He and I might not be the best of friends, but being around him just serves as a reminder that I don't have my shit as together as I thought I did.

I'm supposed to be okay fending for myself, but Adam keeps having to rush in to save me.

I wish I could summon just an ounce of his unshakeable demeanor because I really am losing my shit right now.

"Rain," he says.

I wince and straighten. "Yeah?"

"You all right?"

Gus is standing just behind him, a pinch of concern between his blond brows.

"I'm fine," I answer.

Adam frowns but says nothing.

"I'm fine," I repeat like I'm trying to convince him as much as myself.

"Come with me."

"What? Where?"

"Come on." He's already moving toward the door.

I shoot Gus a panicked look. "I'll come with you," Gus says, hooking his arm through mine.

We follow Adam from the living room and down the hallway. We pass a few people dressed in varying shades of army green and camouflage. They nod at Adam and shoot looks of curiosity and wariness my way.

Do they know the bounty has been raised on my head? A million dollars is a lot of money. How the hell is Adam ignoring it anyway? He could outfit his entire team with all the bells and whistles and then really have a fighting chance against Wrath. Maybe. Probably not. But they'd look damn good doing it.

Adam finally comes up to a set of double doors. They're the kind with a metal bar for a handle and the bar clanks loudly as Adam pushes through. The fluorescent lights buzz high above us. Several caged ceiling fans churn out tepid air.

Half the room is covered in a blue floor mat, the other a thinner black mat. One side seems to be for sparring, while the other, with several barbells and weights, seems to be for lifting.

I look around. "What is this?"

"You're going to make her workout?" Gus says.

Adam goes to the blue mat and loosens up his stance. "You feel out of control."

It's a statement, not a question, and I can't help but give a quick nod.

"Why?"

I'm still clinging to Gus when I answer, "I'm afraid."

That's the honest to god truth, and I hate that it makes me feel weak. I mean, this entire time, I knew that Wrath was dangerous. I knew that he posed a real threat to our way of life, but it isn't like he went looking for a fight anywhere. It isn't like he blew up buildings or planted bombs or started opening fire on innocent bystanders.

Our world is already dangerous, but it's a danger I'm familiar with.

Wrath is a new monster, but he's one I was naive enough to believe wasn't *my* problem. I thought I could ignore him.

But now that I'm the center of his mission? Now that his eyes are on me?

I'm fucking terrified.

Why can I withstand him? And does he really just want to talk? Or is that a ploy to get me alone so he can turn me into one of his obedient soldiers?

I've always fended for myself, but I enjoyed that freedom. I was always grateful to have it. And now? Wrath and his very existence threaten to take that away, and I don't know what to do about it or how to fight it.

I don't know how to take his eyes off me.

And there's some depraved part of me that doesn't want to.

And what the hell does that say about me?

He's enemy number one, and I'm practically buzzing just thinking about being alone with him.

Maybe in the long run, that's what scares me most, how badly I want his attention. Because that makes me no better than the rest of them, so hungry for the spectacle, the power.

Wrath is living, breathing art.

And a little twisted part of me wants to be overwhelmed by him like my mom at the Grand Canyon, staring into the chasm.

Adam slides on a pair of boxing pads. "Punch."

"Why?"

"Because hitting something will make you feel better, will make you feel in control."

"I'm not going to box with you," I say.

"Why not?"

"Because!"

"Because why?"

I turn to Gus. He holds up his hands, excusing himself from the entire scenario. "I like the guy," he says, "but sometimes his methods are weird."

Adam snorts. "You once tried to give me advice through a deck of cards."

"Hey, hey now. Do not disrespect the Rider-Waite."

With a sigh, I walk onto the cushy blue mat. Adam waits for

me. When I get within swinging distance of him, he asks, "Do you know how to make a fist?"

I roll my eyes. "Of course I do."

"Good." Adam brings up the mitts. "Take a swing then."

I bring my fist up and Adam shakes his head.

"What?"

Dropping the mitts, he comes over and grabs my hand. "Like this." He tucks my fingers into my palm, curling my thumb over my index and middle finger. "Keep your knuckles level, and make sure your fist is in a straight line with your forearm to prevent your wrist from buckling."

So maybe I didn't pay that great of attention during the self-defense class.

Once my fist is to Adam's liking, he steps away again and slides the pads back onto his hands. "Now go."

I feel a little out of sorts, but I've never been one to back down from a challenge.

I step toward him and throw a punch. It lands uselessly on the pad.

"Again," he says.

I throw another punch.

"Again. Harder this time."

I punch and keep punching, and the more I punch, the more frustrated I become as Adam keeps yelling at me to keep going. I grit my teeth as sweat beads on my forehead.

My breathing quickens as my heart rate spikes.

"How are you feeling?" Adam asks.

"Angry." I throw a punch at his right.

"Why?"

I inhale, fill my lungs, and throw another punch. "Because...I want...my own bed."

My knuckles are starting to ache, but I keep going. There's a pressure in my chest like I'm either about to scream or sob or maybe both.

I want to go home. I want my life back. I don't want to be stuck in a factory guarded by others like I'm some weakling.

I punch again, then alternate and punch with my left. Adam remains stoic, his boxing mitts taking the beating. Soon the knots in my stomach loosen, and some of the stress melts away and a smile comes across my face.

Maybe Adam does know what he's doing.

And then someone calls out his name and he pulls the mitts away.

I step back, hands on my hips, chest heaving. Sweat trickles down the side of my face and down my spine. I've never been the gym type, but I'm starting to rethink my resistance to exercise. I feel fucking great.

"There's something you need to have a look at," Tommy says from the doorway.

Adam returns the mitts to a rack along the wall. He stops by my side before he leaves. "I'll get you home again. You just gotta trust me."

I give him a quick nod, and then he's gone.

"What he didn't say," Gus says, "is that the tarot deck gave him some excellent advice."

I laugh and push sweaty hair off my forehead. "The Rider-Waite never lies."

"He doesn't like anything he can't verify with his eyes."

"I bet Wrath's arrival here threw him for a loop."

We walk toward the double doors. Pitch is there, having taken over guard duty for Sanjay. He holds the door open for us.

"I think it threw most of us for a loop," Gus admits. "I mean, maybe not so much for people like you and me. Our mothers believe in fairies and sprites."

"Yeah, maybe Eric being a witch shouldn't have surprised me as much as it did. My mom once spent a month with a shaman. Remember that?"

"How could I forget? When she came home, she made us drink her special tea every day for a month to cleanse our souls."

"It was awful tea."

"The worst."

We spill out into the hallway. It's ridiculously quiet, and I realize I have no idea what time it is. Not sleeping straight through the night, and the lack of windows here, makes it feel like a black hole of time.

"Are there showers?" I ask.

Pitch falls into step beside me. "Yes. I can show you if you'd like. And I can ask Sanjay to take over for me so—"

"That's not necessary. She was up all night. I trust you, Pitch."

He gives me a serious look. "I'm duty bound to protect you. I'll even clear out the bathroom for you."

"Thanks."

"I think I'm going to crash for a while too," Gus says. "I'm beat."

Gus is the type of person who can operate just fine on three hours of sleep, but glancing over at him, I note the heaviness beneath his eyes. "Of course," I say and give him a hug. "Thank you for sitting with me earlier. The only reason I was able to sleep was because you were there."

He squeezes me back. "Don't thank me. I love you. That's what friends do."

We part ways and I return to my room for my bag. It feels like a boon, the fact that I had the foresight to pack clean underwear and a clean sports bra.

"Bathroom is this way," Pitch says and takes me to the door at the very end of my hall. "Wait here." He deposits me at the door and then goes inside, checking the stalls, then the shower. "All clear, Ms. Low. You'll have the bathroom to yourself."

I pat the big guy on the shoulder as I pass. "You're a godsend, Pitch."

He beams at me. "My mama used to say the same thing."

"And did you believe her?"

He chuckles, his barrel chest heaving up and down. "I once told my teacher I didn't have to do my math homework. 'And why's that?' my teacher asked. And I said, 'Because I'm a godsend. And god doesn't want me to do math homework.'"

I laugh with him as I hang up my bag on one of the metal hooks. "Your teacher let you get away with that?"

"Not a chance." He goes to the door and pulls it closed, but not all the way. "I'll be right here if you need me, Ms. Low."

"Rain, please."

"Rain then." He doffs his baseball cap at me and takes position just outside the door.

There's a rack of clean white towels along the tiled wall. I unfold one and hang it on the hook next to my bag.

There are three shower stalls in the communal bathroom, each separated by a green tiled wall. A plastic shower curtain hangs from rings on the doorway. I pull mine closed, the rings clanging against the rod.

When I turn on the showerhead, cold water blasts me in the face, and I clamp my hand over my mouth, trying not to scream. Don't want the entire factory running to me in the shower.

It takes the water a while to heat up, but once it does, and the steam starts to fill the alcove, I breathe out a sigh of relief.

A hot shower can seriously repair any bad day. I stand beneath the spray for several minutes just drinking in the heat and the steam. I find shampoo and conditioner in a dispenser on the wall.

It's probably cheap surplus soap, but right now, I don't care. I pump out several globs and scrub it into my scalp. It smells like strawberries and reminds me of when my mom and I stayed at a rural cabin just on the edge of a strawberry farm. She had dreams of writing a book about creativity, and the cabin was supposed to be her writing oasis.

We ended up spending most days picking strawberries by the carton and getting paid in pints.

We ate a lot of strawberry shortcake and fruit smoothies that summer.

And thinking of that reminds me I haven't called Mom back. She's probably stressing.

In fact, I haven't checked my phone in a while.

I rinse out the shampoo, then rake some conditioner into my ends. I'm just rinsing it out when I hear shouting outside the bathroom.

I step out of the spray to listen and then—

Pop-pop.

Were those gunshots?

Pop-pop-pop.

Holy shit.

I shut the shower off and quickly wrap myself in a towel. "Pitch?" I call, as water drips from my soaking wet hair.

There's no answer. More shouting. A grunt. Another *pop-pop-pop.*

I tie the towel around my body.

Something heavy hits the wall and the door rattles on its hinges. I slink back with a yelp, then clamp my hand over my mouth again.

Fear needles along my spine as I tiptoe to the doorway.

I poke my head out to see Pitch fighting a man dressed entirely in black, face covered with a tactical mask. Pitch grunts. He's the one who got slammed against the wall, and he's fighting the other guy, who has a dagger pointed at Pitch's neck.

"Oh my god!" I yell because I'm an idiot.

Pitch flinches.

I suck in a breath, terrified tears already burning in my eyes as the assailant drives the knife into Pitch's throat.

Blood spurts from the wound. Pitch chokes on it as he slumps down the wall.

I just stand there frozen, eyes wide, mouth hanging open. The only thing I can think about is how Pitch just told me a silly story about math class and his mom and now he's bleeding out right before my eyes.

Holy fucking shit.

This is real.

This is very real.

The guy turns to me, the bloody dagger clutched in his hand.

I do the only thing I can do—I turn around and run.

11

My wet feet slap against the concrete floor as I charge down the hallway having no idea which way I'm going. Is this the way to the sparring room or the central room? Where's Adam? Where's Gus?

Oh shit, Gus.

Please let him be okay!

Footsteps pound behind me as the guy gives chase. I can feel him getting closer and closer. It's like a spider crawling up my back.

Any second he'll be on me.

I jam through an unmarked door and charge into the darkness. It takes me a few seconds to realize my feet are no longer on concrete, but dirt, and I'm no longer inside the factory—I'm in some kind of courtyard.

I spin around as my eyes adjust to the darkness. There's a dead tree to my left and a bunch of scrub bushes to my right. The entire courtyard is surrounded by a brick wall easily seven feet tall.

There's no way I can climb that.

The door bursts open behind me and the assailant comes to a stop.

I stand on an old pathway, clutching the towel to my body, wet hair plastered to the side of my face. The guy brings his hand up. He's no longer holding a dagger. Now he has a handgun and the barrel is pointed right at me.

A useless scream gets lodged in my throat, and even if I could get it out, there's no one here to help me.

I'm going to die in a barren courtyard at some nameless factory all because I got drunk and ran into the Demon King.

The assailant, his face still hidden behind a mask, aims the gun at me and pulls the trigger.

I brace, body clenched up tight.

This is how it ends.

I'm dead. I'm dead.

The air snaps, and suddenly Wrath is in front of me, black mist trailing off of him like the tentacles of a dark, terrifying monster.

The bullets hit him and plink uselessly to the stone path.

"Shit," the assailant murmurs and then backs into the door.

With water still dripping from my body, I step to the side so I can see over the broad line of Wrath's shoulders.

The assailant yanks at the door handle, but it doesn't budge.

Wrath advances.

"Help!" the guy screams. "Fucking open the door!" He pulls harder, boots dug into the ground, knees bent. "Fuck. Help!"

Wrath disappears.

The air goes still. A bead of water wends down my spine.

There's a feeling in the air, like we've stumbled into a dark jungle, a predator watching us from the shadows. I pull the towel closer, hands shaking.

"Help!" the guy screams again.

Wrath reappears right next to him and grabs him by the throat. The guy tries to yell again, but it just comes out as a wet, garbled mess. His feet leave the ground and pedal in the air. Wrath's pale hand stands out in the darkness, fingers tightening as the swaths of mist emanating from him sharpen to spears.

The guy kicks and scrabbles as the telltale sound of bones cracking rents through the night.

"Please," the guy gasps out as blood trickles from the corner of his mouth.

The shadow spears pull back and then charge through the air, impaling the man against the door.

One final gasp bursts from his throat and then his head lolls to the side, blood spurting from the wounds.

I step back, heart ramming in my chest and in my throat and—

Wrath turns to me. The shadows trailing off of him pull back, and the impaled man thuds to the ground.

Oh fuck.

I clutch tighter at the towel as I scan the surrounding courtyard for a weapon. But what's the point? If I was defenseless against a human with a gun, I'm hopeless against Wrath, the Demon King, invincible, untouchable.

"*Dieva*," he says, his voice like liquid metal rolling down my spine.

"No." I backpedal, get tangled in a fallen tree limb, and then lose my balance. I tip sideways, my arm out to catch me.

But I don't land. Instead, I hang in midair, my wet hair dripping to the stone.

When I look up, I find Wrath's deft fingers wrapped around my wrist, his eyes glowing red in the weak light.

He yanks me upright, and I twist my arm, trying to pull out of his grasp. It only manages to bring me closer to him when he tightens his hold.

My head sways as my nose fills with the rich, sweet scent of him. I'm shivering again, but for a different reason.

"Let me go," I say, tapping a fresh vein of courage.

His jaw flexes when he grits his teeth. "I save you and this is how you repay me?"

"I didn't need saving."

"Oh?" The way he says the one word makes his eyes narrow

and his brows sink, like I'm an annoying toddler who's just said something profoundly stupid.

"Yes." I test his grip again with another yank, but his fingers don't budge.

"There's another on his way here," Wrath says , and his eyes glint in the dark. "Shall I lead the way to him? I'm sure he'll be delighted to put a bullet in your brain."

I look past Wrath to the lump of a man lying at the door. I can't hear anything beyond the blood rushing through my ears, but I'm sure there are more men and women in black tactical gear with plenty of knives and bullets for me.

But I'm not sure which is the lesser foe—them or Wrath.

No, scratch that, I do know.

No one can kill Wrath. Therefore he's the greater adversary.

But I can't ignore the fact that he *did* just save me, and while his grip is tight, it isn't painful. I haven't seen one of his possessed soldiers either, so that's a good sign.

"What do you want from me?" I ask.

He cants his head, a sliver of moonlight finding his face. There is something dangerously beautiful about him, like a blade made of glass. "I'm not sure yet."

Something slams into the courtyard door, making me jump. Wrath's attention slides away from me briefly, and the absence of his attention is like losing the sunlight on a cold winter day.

I shiver. Wrath turns his gaze back to me. "If I gave you a choice as to whether you came with me or stayed here to face the cretins of the Citizens Against Darkness, which would you choose?"

"The Citizens?" I say, my arm still clutched in his hand, his body still impossibly close. "How do you know that? The soldier was wearing all black."

The door pushes open again, but there's currently a dead body blocking it. Is it Adam trying to get through? Gus? Or just another soldier?

"They're wearing patches," Wrath says like it should be obvious, like I should have noticed this small detail while being chased by a knife-wielding murderer. "Answer the question."

"Why?"

"Because your answer matters."

My heart kicks up again. From the little I know about Wrath, nothing any human has ever done or said mattered to him.

"Why?" I ask again.

The courtyard door opens another few inches, and the sharp fluorescent light of the hallway spills out into the darkness.

"Ticktock," he says.

You'd think he would have learned by now that I don't like being told what to do.

"I'd choose the Citizens," I say, more out of spite than anything else.

"Wrong answer." Wrath twists me around and wraps his arm across my torso. Butterflies take flight in my stomach as his next exhale pours down the curve of my throat.

The dead soldier finally rolls away and the door swings open.

It's not Gus or Adam. It's Darren at the head of three other Citizen soldiers.

That little piece of shit!

Darren pulls his gun from the holster at his hip and slides his finger onto the trigger.

"He's going to shoot," I shriek and push against Wrath, trying to get out of the way.

Swaths of his dark mist bleed into the air around us like ink dropped into water. The darkness cages us in as a gun goes off. Wrath growls at my ear and the darkness pulls in on itself, perfuming the air with a scent that's deep and dark and reminds me of starlight and burning wood.

The bullet hits the Demon King's dark magic and falls to the stone pathway.

"Hold on," Wrath says.

"Hold on? For what?"

Suddenly, the ground disappears and I'm yanked backwards, my hair flying in front of my face, blocking out the courtyard and the factory beyond.

I squeeze my eyes shut as the world tilts and my center of gravity goes with it. It's not unlike being on a carnival ride, the gravitational force flattening me against Wrath's body.

I clutch at his arm, and he tightens his hold on me.

When I can sense solid ground beneath me again, I open my eyes and look around.

We're no longer outside. In fact, I don't recognize *where* we are.

The floor is rough stone and it's cold on my bare feet, but the fire crackling in the fireplace to my right helps drive away some of the chill.

That, and Wrath is still wrapped around me, his chest to my back. He's warmer than I would have thought. Everything about him makes me think of a dark winter night, but the comforting heat of him is driving away the chill of my damp hair still dripping on my shoulders.

And realizing that I'm currently pressed against him has a depraved thrill racing from my belly down between my legs.

I'm still naked in nothing but a towel, and Wrath, the Demon King, the *villain*, is so close his breath tickles at my neck and spills beneath the hem of the towel, down the valley between my breasts.

I lurch away and stumble toward the fireplace. No, no, no. I am not going to be one of those crazed fangirls that turns to a blubbering mess when Wrath comes within a square mile of them.

"Where are we? How did we even get here?"

Wrath stands beside an overstuffed leather side chair, his hands hanging by his side. His eyes are no longer glowing, and all of that black magic that trails off him is gone, but even so, even when he's standing by as casual as can be, there's something menacing about him that disturbs the air like he's a volcano that could blow at any moment.

It makes my heart thump in the hollow spaces of my body, this constant closeness to something that could destroy me with such little effort.

"I've brought you to safety," he answers, and I snort.

"I doubt that."

I gaze around the room. The ceiling height is easily twenty feet, if not more, with heavy wood beams running from one end of the room to the other. The leather furniture is arranged in a half circle around the fireplace, but there are two more seating areas—two large sofas by the floor to ceiling windows and another overstuffed chair in the far corner, an iron floor lamp beside it.

Persian rugs, several of them bigger than my entire living room, are spread over the hardwood floor. The room is dark and cozy.

"Is this your house?"

Wrath just looks at me and says nothing, which I think says enough.

It's not what I expected, but now that I'm in the space, drinking in his rich, spicy, wintertime scent, it's exactly what it should be.

"How did we get here?" I ask again.

"I brought you."

"Obviously. But *how*?"

He disappears, dark mist pluming in his wake.

I sense him behind me and whirl around.

"Like that," he answers. "I believe your scientists will someday describe it as traveling through the sub-dimension."

"Will? Can you predict the future too?"

There's a hint of a smile at the corner of his mouth. "No. They just need time to catch up."

This entire conversation is making my head spin. "So what's a sub-dimension?"

He thinks for a second, his gaze going far away. I like watching him consider for me, as if my question has merit.

It makes a faint flicker of warmth light in my sternum.

"Think of an old house with plaster and lath walls," he says. "The space between those walls is the space between dimensions. The walls keep the dimensions from spilling into one another. I can travel through that space—the sub-dimension."

"So that's how you disappeared from custody the first time you were taken in," I say.

He gives me no indication that I'm wrong.

The scientists who've been enamored with Wrath's very existence would likely nerd out over this detail. But is it magic or science?

"Can anybody travel through the sub-dimension?"

His face is still blank when he answers, "Absolutely not."

I turn away, back to the fire. I'm starting to shiver. I'm still in nothing but a towel, and I'm dripping all over Wrath's pretty Persian rugs.

The heat of the fire is enticing, and I gravitate toward it like a cat to a patch of sunlight.

But as I turn, the air grows charged again, and Wrath is suddenly behind me, his hand fisted in my hair.

"Ouch!"

I fight to get away, but he yanks me back, his other hand on my bare shoulder, holding me in place.

That flame ignites in the center of me as adrenaline pumps through my veins, that prey flight instinct screaming *go, go*.

"What the hell?" I shout.

"Where did you get this?"

"What? Get what?"

"This mark," he says. His thumb trails down from the ridge of my shoulder blade, just barely grazing the space where I know my birthmark sits at the base of my neck.

I ball my hands into fists, fighting the urge to lean into him even though he's got my hair in his grip and his hand on my naked shoulder, forcing me still.

Shame wedges into my chest. I shouldn't be feeling this way

with the enemy. Adam would give me the world's biggest scowl if he saw me now, practically mewling at Wrath's touch.

But fuck if it doesn't ignite something in my core.

I don't like it. And also, I like it very, very much.

And both of those emotions have me reaching for what I'm most comfortable with—anger.

I grab his left wrist and try to disengage from him, but he just pulls my hair harder.

His mouth is suddenly at the soft shell of my ear, his voice like silk on my skin. "If I brought you here with barely any effort at all, imagine where I could deposit you now, *dieva*, naked and trembling."

Fuck.

"I'm not trembling," I argue, even though my voice breaks on the words.

"Oh?" His other hand, the one on my shoulder, trails down my arm, teasing goosebumps on my skin. I'm suddenly wet again, and not just from the shower.

He's toying with me, and goddammit, my body is here for it.

I close my eyes, a breath stuttering up my throat. I don't want this to end. I want him to keep touching me even though everything inside of me is screaming to snap out of it.

His hand moves from my arm to the curve of my waist.

My waist and my hips have always been the place that gets me going, that makes me ravenous for more.

My chest rises and falls with quicker breaths. It would be so easy to let the towel go, let it fall to the floor, to feel Wrath's hands on my—

"Where did you get the mark?"

I swallow hard. "It's a birthmark. The answer is in the name."

"You're lying."

I snap my eyes open. "Why would I lie about that?"

Black mist kicks up around me. Not even twenty minutes ago,

that mist was protecting me, but now I get the distinct impression it's meant to do the opposite.

The darkness blots out the firelight.

My desire is dripping down my thighs, and now I'm on the edge of being murdered by the Demon King. It's perverse and wrong and I hate what he does to me.

The darkness solidifies.

Fuck, fuck.

Think, Rain.

Adam kept saying I was the only one who could stand against Wrath.

I just...I need to focus. I bet Wrath has some kind of power that turns people into mewling sycophants and I'm just falling prey to it.

I rack my brain for the self-defense tactics I learned. It was so long ago...

Kicking was always a tactic the instructor recommended using when you had your back to your attacker.

I lift my leg and jam it back, kicking Wrath in the knee.

He grunts and drops my hair. I whirl around only to find him gone, the son of a bitch.

I spot the door on the other side of the room. There are windows beside me, but fighting to get them open is only going to waste time, and I have no idea what floor we're on or how far of a jump it'd be.

I run to the door.

Wrath reappears ten feet away. I swivel—window it is—when he's suddenly on me. He grabs me by the wrist, swings me around, and throws me against the nearest wall, my back to his chest again as his body cages me in place.

I'm not getting out of here, not alive anyway.

Wrath is indomitable, untouchable.

Nothing I have in my very limited toolbox comes even close to matching his power. It's no wonder our army is useless against him.

"I'm going to ask you again," he says. "Where did you get that mark? Was it a witch? A traveler?" He presses even closer as I wiggle beneath him, the heat of his body, the heady scent of him overwhelming me.

My breath fans out loudly against the wall. "It's a fucking birthmark," I say.

"Lies," he says in the most menacing voice I've ever heard.

My heart drops to my gut as his anger becomes its own monster. I can literally feel it seething behind me.

Hand at my throat, fingers tightening, he says, "Tell me, *dieva*, or I will break this pretty little neck."

I hate being called a liar. I rarely lie. It was a characteristic my mother loved to brag about to her friends. My mom always knew she could trust me.

"I don't know what else you want me to say!"

The darkness kicks up again, almost sentient.

He's going to snap at any second, but I don't have the answers he's looking for. I don't know what he wants from me.

"It's the truth!" I shout again.

Out of the corner of my eye, I see the shadows sharpen. Will it hurt to be gutted by his black magic?

I brace for it and wait for my life to literally flash before my eyes when the door to the room bursts open and a girl spills in. She comes to an abrupt stop when her eyes land on me.

"Oh," the girl says. "I didn't realize you were bringing *her* here."

I don't miss the way she refers to me like I'm a toad covered in warts even though I'm literally pressed against the wall by a monster, his dark magic billowing around me.

"As if I need your permission," Wrath says to her.

"She's a liability."

I breathe out with a little hiccup of relief.

Who is this girl? She looks close to my age, early twenties. She reminds me of some of the rich girls I went to school with—long blond hair, perfect features aligned in perfect symmetry, and lips too big for her face.

"What do you want, Lauren?" Wrath asks, still holding me against the wall.

"Arthur needs you."

"For what?"

"Rhys Roman."

Wrath lets me go and steps away, but I stay there pressed against the wall, unsure of where I go from here.

He just threatened to kill me. He didn't, obviously, but would he have?

I hear Adam's words echoing in my head—*you're immune to Wrath, but I don't think he's immune to you.*

Before now, no one was safe when it came to the Demon King. I almost think the fact that I *am* somehow puts me in *more* danger. Or maybe the line between *immune* and *dead* is an extremely thin one.

Maybe he doesn't know what to do with me either.

Wrath stalks for the door and breezes past Lauren. "Show her to a room," he says, "and get her some clothes."

Lauren scrunches up her face, looking me up and down. "What am I, her personal stylist now?"

Wrath stops at the door. The black mist lifts from his shoulders. When he turns just enough to look at her over his shoulder, his eyes are glowing red.

The monster is threatening to snap.

Lauren licks her lips. "Fine, I'll see what I can find," she says, but the bite to her words has been filed down to a dull edge.

Wrath says nothing more and disappears, *literally*.

I put my back to the wall and clutch at the loosening knot of the towel. It's a damn miracle the thing hasn't fallen off yet.

When Lauren turns her gaze on me again, her eyes narrowed, scrutinizing, I straighten my spine and lift my chin. I'm older than she is—I think—and I don't suffer no bullshit.

Even when I'm at her mercy.

"Come on," she says. "Follow me."

Lauren leads me out of the room, and I look for the nearest exit only to find closed doors.

"Where are we?" I ask again.

"Upstate New York."

Well at least I'm still in the same state.

"Do you have a phone I can use? My friends back at the factory—"

"Your friends are probably fine," Lauren answers.

"Probably? We were under attack when Wrath showed up. I need to know if they're all right."

Lauren sighs and pulls a cell phone from the back pocket of her jeans. "Make it quick."

I punch in Gus's number and clutch the phone to my ear. Please, please answer.

It rings four times before he picks up. "Hello?"

"Gus?"

"Rain! Where are you? Are you okay?"

"I'm fine-ish. Is Adam good? What about Pitch?"

"Pitch is..." He sighs. "Pitch is dead. Adam is fine. Where are you?" he asks again.

"You're never going to believe me," I start, and then Lauren yanks the phone out of my grip and ends the call.

"Hey!"

"Your friend is okay. That's what you wanted. I don't have time for a long-winded conversation." She swivels around and keeps walking.

With a groan, I follow after her.

We go down a wide hallway where oil paintings hang in gilded frames. There are a few of familiar landscapes—the Cliffs of

Moher, Tuscany, a Greek island where white stucco buildings crowd the shoreline—and dotted throughout are portraits of old white men looking down on me with judging eyes. There's a military commander in full decorated uniform and another man in a heavy velvet jerkin. A man with an aggressive moustache stands beside a throne wearing a puffy white collar.

"Wrath has some unique taste in art," I mutter.

"It's not his."

"Oh. Someone else lives here?"

We come out to a central corridor, and Lauren's voice echoes down the hall when she speaks. "The castle was given to Wrath."

Castle? Holy shit.

"Given or taken?" I ask.

"Sometimes they're the same thing, aren't they?"

"Umm...no."

Lauren snorts and keeps walking.

"Are you a friend of Wrath's? I didn't think he had friends here."

"*Friend* is a mortal word and one Wrath detests."

"I'm assuming since you're here, you're an ally then at the very least."

"You would assume right."

"So...what are you?"

"What are *you*?" She sends a scathing look back at me.

"A photographer."

"You and everyone else these days."

She's not entirely wrong about that. I used to complain to my mom about all the rookies claiming to be professional photographers online. People who made obvious mistakes in their photography, like using the on-camera flash for portrait sessions. Just thinking about it makes me grimace.

My mom liked to point out that everyone had to start somewhere. "No one is born an expert," she said.

But I know that's not what Lauren is asking me. She wants to know why I can withstand Wrath, not what I do for a living. I would give her the truth if I had it.

Lauren slows her pace and yanks down the collar of her shirt. There's an intricate tattoo on her skin—delicate filigrees and a small medallion just above her ample cleavage. "I'm a demon." She lets her shirt fall back into place.

"Whoa. Seriously? Like Wrath?"

"Comparing me to Wrath is like comparing a rock to an asteroid. But yes, if you want to label us as something, we're both demons."

"And the mark has something to do with that?"

"All demons have a mark."

My first encounter with Wrath comes back to me. My shirt had been soaked with spiked half-and-half, and he'd checked out my chest. At the time, I thought he was ogling me, but this makes more sense. He was looking for a mark.

"What's the mark mean?" I ask.

"It shows their rank."

"There are different types of demons?"

She nods. "Like humans, we're all different. But there's a hierarchy too, a royal line—the king and five princes. The royal line can bestow rank to lords. Everyone under a lord is just a demon."

"Which are you?"

She doesn't answer, so I'm guessing that means she's just a low-level demon. She strikes me as the type of person who would brag about royal blood or a title if she had it.

And the fact that I'm even thinking about *royal demons* blows my mind. How is this my life?

"And here I thought 'Demon King' was something the media came up with," I say.

We eventually come to a massive staircase that goes up to a landing where gorgeous, arched, stained glass windows glow beneath the golden orbs of wall sconces. On the landing, we turn left and go up another set of stairs to the second floor.

Another long, wide hallway runs for what seems like miles. Like literally, I think it would take me a good ten minutes just to reach the end where a half-moon window is lighting up with early morning light.

I stop to gaze around the space, and Lauren quickly pulls ahead, so I have to jog to catch up with her. “How long have you known Wrath?”

She side-eyes me. “For some of us, we’ve always known him, even when he was in Alius.”

Why does that name sound familiar?

Right. “Isn’t there a fanatic group called Order of Alius?”

“There is.”

“What does that mean? Alius?”

“It’s where all supernaturals come from,” she says with an air of superiority. “Demons. Witches. Vampires. Fae. Shifters.”

I come to a halt. Did she just say what I thought she said?

“There are more than demons and witches?”

She sniffs. “Of course there are.”

I shouldn’t be surprised by this, but...

This is a lot of information to take in while wearing only a towel after traveling through some portal through time and space.

Lauren cuts left down another hallway without warning, and I backpedal to switch directions. We stop at the third door on our right, and Lauren uses a skeleton key to unlock it, pushing the door in. I peer around her, aware that at least here, I’m always on the cusp of getting my head lobbed off.

“It’s not booby trapped,” she says as she goes inside and flicks on a few lamps.

I step into a bedroom with a giant four-poster bed to my right, flanked on either side by heavy wooden tables with vintage lamps. There’s another massive rug beneath the bed, this one in shades of emerald and red and cream.

There’s a barren fireplace across from the bed and two wing-back chairs in front of it.

"There's a bathroom through that door." Lauren tips her chin at a closed door beside the fireplace. "I'll see what clothes I can find for you on such short notice. You clearly won't fit into mine."

"I'm sorry...have I done something to offend you?"

She looks me up and down again. I tighten the towel around my body.

"A few days ago, no one knew your name." Lauren crosses her thin arms over her chest. "Now everyone is salivating over you, including Wrath. I don't like it. It makes him look weak."

"I don't think he's salivating over me."

She rolls her eyes. "Who even are you?"

"What do you mean?" Does she want my name? My blood type?

She steps into my personal bubble, but for some reason, I just get angry with her. I'm not afraid of her, even though I think maybe I should be.

I've seen some of Wrath's powers. As a demon, what can Lauren do? Can she possess others too?

"Are you a spy?" she asks.

"For who?"

"What's your game?"

I wrinkle my nose. "I don't have a game."

Her eyes sweep over me again. I really wish I'd thought to grab my bag from the hook because this towel is starting to seriously irk me. It puts me at a disadvantage and worse, makes me uncomfortable.

"If you're not a spy..." Lauren scowls at my chest, then her eyes flick up to meet mine. "If you're just some rando, then I have news for you—you don't understand what you've stepped into."

"I totally agree," I say, because that's the honest truth.

"So leave."

"I've tried," I say, "but Wrath doesn't seem to want to let me."

That pisses her off. Fine lines appear around her eyes as the air takes on the scent of something sickly sweet, like cheap floral perfume.

"I hope he destroys you," she says.

"Well, I'd say the odds are good considering that's what he seems hellbent on doing to our world."

"Is that what you think?"

Now it's my turn to snort my derision.

"You don't even know what you stand to lose or how hard Wrath is working to save your ass and this entire world and you—"

She clamps her mouth shut, lip curling at the corner.

"What?" I coax. I think Lauren's spilled some tea I'd very much like to taste.

I mean, I buried my head in the sand about Wrath for too long, and now that I'm in the middle of it, with no prospect of getting out of it, I need to arm myself with information. No one really knows why he's here. This is the most I've heard of the details since he popped up months ago.

But Lauren shakes her head again and turns for the door. "I'll be back with clothes. If you want the blood to stay in your body, I suggest you stay here."

With that, she slams the door closed, leaving me alone.

I wait a good twenty minutes and then check the bedroom door and find it unlocked.

Okay, so not entirely a prisoner here. I poke my head out and find an empty hallway. I want to try for an escape, but clothes would make it a hell of a lot easier.

As I wait, I check the windows. Both bottom panes open without complaint, but I'm on the second floor and the bushes below look prickly and sparse, not enough to soften my fall.

A yawn escapes me as I pace the room, trying to think of an escape plan. The plush bed practically calls out my name every time I pass it.

"I'll just test it out," I mutter like I'm Goldilocks or something.

But as soon as I lie back on the bed, exhaustion washes over me. Before I know it, I'm fast asleep in the Demon King's castle.

12

I WAKE TO THE DOOR OPENING AND LURCH UPRIGHT, BLEARY-EYED AND disoriented and apparently naked in the sheets.

I don't remember dumping the towel, but damn if these sheets aren't the softest white cotton I've ever slept on.

Lauren comes in, her arms full of clothing. Outside the windows, the sky is gray and overcast.

"What time is it?" I ask.

"A little after four. Here." She tosses me the clothes.

I blink through the sleepiness and smooth over my hair as if I can somehow match her prettiness. I probably look like hell.

On the top of the clothing pile, I find a pair of jeans. I'd prefer leggings but I'm not going to complain in a time like this. Except when I hold up the jeans, I can't help but scowl at them.

"What the hell are these?" There are so many holes and tears in the jeans I'm not sure they could even be called pants.

"It's trendy," Lauren says.

The t-shirt advertises something called Deer Camp Fun Run from 1997. The material is like tissue paper between my fingers, and when I put my hand inside, I can clearly see my fingers.

"No bra or panties?" I ask.

"It's the best I could do on short notice." She tosses me a pair of cheap flip-flops and a comb. "You're welcome." She swivels for the door and leaves me again.

It takes me another hour just to get through my tangled, knotted hair. Apparently traveling through a sub-dimension is not good for a girl's hair. I curse more than once when I have to rip out a knot.

When I finish up, I check my reflection in the giant, gilded mirror hanging on the wall in my temporary bedroom.

I look like a fucking wreck. My hair is at least tamed, but letting it air dry without brushing it has left a weird swoop in my bangs.

My nipples are pebbled in the shirt and sticking out so badly, I think I could write my name in the sand. And with the tears in my jeans, my bare lady bits are practically flapping in the breeze.

With a sigh, I turn away and go to the door. I pull it open and peek out into the corridor. The place is vast and silent.

What is Wrath really going to do to me if I explore?

Kill you.

That voice in the back of my head is thinking rationally, but my gut instinct tells me something else. That maybe he plans to keep me around for now because he has yet to figure me out.

And what was with his fascination with my birthmark? Because it's between my shoulder blades, I tend to forget it's there. My mom used to call it my off button because it's shaped like a ring.

Whenever I'd descend into a tantrum, she'd press that spot between my shoulders and say, "Rainy baby, it's time to power down."

Sometimes it'd get a laugh out of me. Sometimes it'd just rile me up even more.

I leave my room behind, my heart rate kicking up in my chest. It's almost like I'm daring Wrath to appear to chastise me. The thought sends butterflies skittering across my belly.

I make a left turn at the next intersection of hallways and quickly get lost in the labyrinth of the castle. Most doors I test are locked, so once I manage to find my way back to the stairs, I go down.

On the ground floor, I pause for a beat to listen. For being a giant castle, the place is oddly quiet. I follow the hallway to the left and stop at one of the arched windows in the stone wall.

The window has a lead muntin with stained glass in the three top panes. I check out the location and the grounds.

There's only greenery as far as the eye can see.

There's a road leading from the castle, but it disappears in the trees so I can't tell where it leads. Down below is a stone roundabout with a fountain in the center. The faint sound of trickling water can be heard through the bubbled glass.

I can't help but feel like I'm in an entirely different world.

What does Alius look like anyway? And was Wrath trying to *escape* it? Lauren hinted at something greater than Wrath, though whether that was another demon or a greater power or some kind of social experiment, I don't know.

Maybe he's trying to bring us the dark holy spirit. The way our society is fawning over him, he's quickly becoming a cult leader.

Farther down the hall, I finally come to a door, and when I pull it open, a footpath leads away from the castle and into the woods.

I look over my shoulder and scan the hallway. I'm alone, and as far as I've been able to tell, there are no cameras here.

I could walk right out this door and run.

But something keeps me frozen in place, my bare feet just on the other side of the threshold.

What would running accomplish? Wrath can find me just about anywhere, I suspect. Unless Eric creates another one of those witch barriers, and even then, I'm not so sure that's a viable option.

Am I really going to hide for the rest of my life? The stubbornness in me wants to see this through and find a solution. Not a temporary fix.

I shut the door and keep walking, finding numerous sitting rooms, then a large dining hall with heavy dark wood tables. In another room, I find three billiards tables and a bar stocked with every kind of liquor imaginable. If I wasn't literally in the den of a monster, I might pour myself a drink. I could certainly use one right about now.

Down another hallway, a rich aroma makes my stomach growl, and I quickly follow the trail of it into a kitchen three times the size of my condo. Steam rises from a pot on the industrial stove top and red sauce bubbles in a pot next to it.

There's a man at the stove stirring something in a pan.

When he spots me, he looks up and frowns. "The mighty Rain, I presume?" There's a hoarseness to his voice that reminds me of my grandmother who smoked two packs of cigarettes a day. She died from lung cancer when I was nine—surprise, surprise.

"Hi," I say as I come around the long kitchen island. "Who are you?"

"The name is Arthur."

I recall Lauren mentioning an Arthur. I'm surprised Wrath has people. I guess I always pictured him as a solitary creature.

Arthur is much older than Wrath or Lauren with a salt and pepper beard trimmed neatly on his tanned face. His hair matches the beard and is closely cropped along the sides, longer on top.

Heavy wrinkles surround his brown eyes. The man is all muscle and sinew without an ounce of fat on him, and he's not much taller than I am.

"What are you making?"

"Spaghetti." He gives the meat another stir. "Are you hungry?"

My stomach growls loudly. "I'm starving, actually."

"Sit." He nods at one of the metal stools by the island. "This is just about done."

I watch Arthur drain the pasta, then put a generous helping on a plate. Next, he drowns it in sauce and meat and finishes it off with a fresh slice of garlic bread that he pulled from the oven.

"Eat it while it's hot," he says, and I dive right in. I don't even care about the risk of poisoning. Seems like an awful lot of trouble to go to just to poison me when Wrath could literally impale me with his dark magic.

My first bite is heavenly. I had leftover Chinese food and then promptly barfed it up. I can't even remember the last meal I had before the leftovers.

"This is really good," I say around a mouthful.

Arthur makes himself a bowl that he eats standing up. "I'm glad to share it. Wrath doesn't eat much, and Lauren avoids carbs."

I finish off the food in record time, barely coming up for air or conversation. When my plate is empty, I drop my fork and it rings out.

"That was exactly what I needed." I fold my arms on the marble countertop. "I didn't realize how hungry I was."

"Food is good in a crisis." Arthur spins his fork in the last of his spaghetti.

"I've had the pleasure of getting to know Lauren," I start, when Arthur smirks and says, "Pleasure, was it?"

"Exaggeration, maybe. Anyway, she said she's a demon. Are you one too?"

Arthur takes our dishes to the sink. "I'm human."

"Really?" I slid off the stool and lean against the counter. "How the hell did you get hooked up with the Demon King then?"

I know there's no shortage of sympathizers and fangirls and people clamoring for Wrath's power, but I have to assume very few are worth Wrath's attention. And probably not deemed trustworthy enough to be in his house.

"I was the first human that Wrath encountered when he came to our world."

"Came to our world," I echo. "That still blows my mind. So what happened when you met him?" I ask.

"Well, I'm an alcoholic and I was extremely intoxicated at the time." Arthur rinses our dishes and laughs. "And you know what alcohol does to you."

"Makes you bold."

"Precisely. I was stumbling around downtown Saint Sabine, and I asked him for money. He told me he'd give me something better if I helped him. I couldn't imagine anything better than booze or the money to buy it, so I tried to rob him."

"You *what*?"

Arthur laughs. "I know. It's a miracle I'm still alive."

"What happened?"

"He gave me the equivalent of a slap to the face, let's just put it that way. He said he could help me. I said no one could help me. I'd been broken for a long time. Didn't think it was possible to heal."

"What do you mean?"

"Bad car accident." He turns and lifts the back of his shirt to reveal a very distinct box-like shape beneath his skin.

"What is that?"

"It's a spinal cord stimulator for chronic back pain. I damaged my spine in the accident." His gaze goes far away. "Amongst other things."

"Ahhhhggg. That sounds like it hurts."

"Oh, it does."

"So what did Wrath do?"

Arthur deposits the dishes in a stainless steel dishwasher, and it occurs to me that the Demon King has a dishwasher. But does he know how to use it? Probably not.

"Wrath's power can give me temporary relief from the pain. Better than any pill, better than the stimulator. It allowed me enough of a reprieve to get clean."

I can see where this is going. "He dangles the power over you like a carrot, doesn't he? Just giving you enough to keep you coming back for more."

"No." Arthur pops a soap pack into the dishwasher and presses a button. The appliance churns to life. "There's a limit to what he can do."

For one blinding second, my opinion of Wrath changes. Arthur doesn't look like a broken man, an addict. He looks healthy and strong and happy. And Wrath helped him do that? All I know of Wrath is the scary monster, the man who kills and destroys all for some unknown mission.

But then I have to remind myself that he *is* the destroyer, the man who threatened our president, who decimated an entire troop of soldiers. The same man currently holding me hostage in his pretty castle.

"Where is he now?" I ask. "Wrath?"

Arthur's gaze jets to a space just beyond me and I whirl around, yelping when I see Wrath standing behind me, arms clasped behind his back.

"Holy shit. You did that on purpose. You were probably listening the entire time."

He scowls and steps forward. "Contrary to what you may think, *dieva*, I do not spend all of my waking hours fretting about what you say or do."

"Could have fooled me."

His scowl deepens.

"What's *dieva* mean anyway?"

He comes up beside me, towering over me. The kitchen is massive, but with Wrath in it, it shrinks in size, not just because of his toned biceps or his broad shoulders, or all his inches over six feet, but because he exudes power.

Because when he steps into a room, it's clear he'll always be the one in charge.

His scent overrides the tang of spaghetti sauce, and my breath unconsciously quickens just so I can drink in more of him.

I hate him.

I really hate him.

"It means," he says and peers down his pale, perfect nose at me, "*little girl.*"

My mouth drops open. "That's demeaning."

"Is it?"

"Why do you always do that?"

"Do what?"

"Challenge me with a question. It's so...so...pretentious and arrogant."

"Is it?" he says again.

"See?" I look at Arthur as if he's really going to commiserate with me. Arthur just gives me a shrug.

"Can I go home now?" I ask.

"No," the Demon King says, and then he looks up at Arthur. "Rhys Roman will be here soon. I need you by my side."

"Of course."

"Who is this Rhys Roman anyway?"

"A vampire." Wrath turns away.

"Seriously?" I look to Arthur again. There's something about him I know I can trust. Arthur raises the line of his brow like, *Surprise*!

Because I have nothing better to do and I'm a brave soul, I follow Wrath out of the kitchen. "What do you need with a vampire?"

"It's not the vampire I want, but his witch."

"Does he own her?"

"She's loyal to him, so in a sense, yes."

Wrath is wearing a different outfit than before. Gone is the long black coat. Now he's wearing black jeans and a black t-shirt. It's so very human that it almost makes me forget who and what he is.

"What do you need a witch for?"

"You."

"*Me*?"

Arthur comes up alongside me. I notice there's a slight stoop to his posture, but his gait is strong, and I don't detect any pain on his face. Gus's mom, toward the end of her life, was in constant pain, and she was so doped up, sometimes it was hard to have a coherent conversation with her. I don't know how anyone lives day to day with chronic pain. It's either the pain or the drugs and no happy medium. I felt so bad for Gloria. It was an impossible situation to be in.

"You won't tell me what you are," Wrath says over his shoulder, "so the witch will tell me instead."

We go down a hallway I haven't explored yet and enter another one of the countless sitting rooms. This one has the distinct feeling of being used though. There are books stacked on side tables and disheveled newspapers on one of the buffets.

"I've already told you," I say, "I'm human. I'm not trying to keep anything from you."

Maybe I can save my life and get the hell out of here if I can convince him of that truth.

Wrath goes to a mini bar and pours himself a drink of some expensive bourbon. He slings the tumbler back.

The Demon King drinks. I'd think silly mortal stuff would be beneath him.

I glance at Arthur out of the corner of my eye. There's no indication of craving the booze.

"Pour me one." I come up alongside the mini bar and look up expectantly. Wrath's gaze goes to my chest, but this time, I know he's not looking for a demon mark. Instead, his eyes go straight to my hard nipples.

When his eyes lift to mine, his irises are glowing red.

I'm not sure if I should fold my arms over my chest to hide my boobs or arch my back to tempt him. A little thrill pulses in my clit.

Wrath's nostrils flare, the tumbler clutched tightly in his grip.

I put my hands in the back pockets of my borrowed jeans, pushing out my chest even more, and the Demon King takes a step toward me.

Arthur clears his throat.

The glow disappears when Wrath blinks. He turns to pour one shot into a second tumbler that he hands over to me. “Here, *dieva*.” His voice purrs when he speaks. “Drink your fill.”

Is that a challenge?

I take the glass and drink the liquor in one gulp. It burns all the way down my throat and warms my belly. Holy shit. This stuff is no joke.

“Man, that stuff is weak,” I say, my voice reedy, just on the edge of a cough. The alcohol quickly hits my veins.

The Demon King just looks at me silently, calling out my lies.

I set the glass down. “So what are you going to do when Mr. Roman tells you I’m a nobody?”

“If he tells me you’re only human, it’ll be a lie,” Wrath says, “so I will kill him.”

My mouth drops open just as the doorbell rings.

13

Rhys Roman is gorgeous. Like 90s Brad Pitt meets Greek god gorgeous.

His dirty blond hair is raked back over his forehead, and his piercing blue eyes search everything as he steps into the room.

Beside him is a girl that looks like a doll compared to his long, lethal body. Her hair is dark and wavy around her face. She looks sweet, but there's an authority to her that I like.

On Rhys's right side is a man with dark hair and amber eyes and a smoothness about him that feels like mischief.

On the other end is a tall, statuesque woman with plump ruby red lips and a body to die for. She's wearing an emerald green dress that plunges low on big boobs and nips in tightly at her tiny waist.

When her eyes land on me, I can tell she's the one who's come here for a job. She must be the witch.

The newcomers cross the room and stop in front of Wrath.

Wrath is a foot in front of me, almost like a shield. His hands are clasped behind his back, and though a vampire has just walked into the room, it's not the vampire that holds my attention, but the pale hands of a demon king, the strong, deft fingers.

Those fingers were wrapped around my throat not that long ago, and thinking about that makes my insides quake and a thrill sink to my clit.

With the alcohol still humming along through my bloodstream, and my head a little fuzzy, desire rears its ugly head.

The vampires look at me. Wrath turns his strong, pale jaw toward me.

"Did we interrupt something kinky?" the dark-haired man asks.

Rhys sends a scathing look his way, but the man barely flinches.

The air crackles. Wrath disappears. Rhys Roman shifts his body in front of the small girl, his eyes glowing neon blue.

Wrath reappears in front of the dark-haired man, and his slick, sharp magic forms a blade that pierces the man's chest.

I yelp, startled.

The girls step back as blood spurts from the wound.

"Holy shit," I breathe out.

Wrath is eerily still. I can't see his face, but I imagine his eyes are glowing too, but in a more sinister way, all fire and rage. "Be respectful," he says evenly, as the spear retracts. "Now get on your knees."

Rhys growls. The dark-haired man clutches at the wound in his chest, blood gurgling through his fingers. His teeth are set in pain, and as the blood leaves his body, his face grows pale.

The small woman goes to her knees.

Rhys scowls down at her. "What are you doing?"

"I don't know," she squeaks as she bows her head.

"She's a demon. She cannot refuse me," Wrath explains.

The dark-haired man sways on his feet.

"Is someone going to help him?" I ask. "Arthur?"

"He's a vampire," the witch says. "He'll survive."

"He'll survive if he gets on his knees," Wrath says, his gaze still pinned on the man.

With a groan, the man shakily sinks to the floor.

The witch sighs. "I didn't come dressed for supplication."

Wrath looks over at her. "Then next time, come prepared."

There's cat-eye eyeliner on her wide eyes that grows sharper as she arches a brow.

"Rhys?" the witch says.

Wrath's dark magic billows up like a cloud of locusts, and the darkness quickly takes shape. Within seconds, he's surrounded by his possessed men.

Rhys Roman scans the shadows. "Impressive. What do you call them?"

"The *norrow*," Wrath answers. "It means *the enslaved*."

"How quaint," Rhys says.

Wrath stands still, waiting.

Frustration pinches at the corner of Rhys's mouth, but he finally gives in and gets to his knees. "Bow, Kat," he says, and the witch—Kat—hikes up her dress to mid-thigh so she can get to the floor. I don't miss the murder eyes she gives Wrath.

If the Army had a witch or two, could they finally match Wrath's power? The Citizens and Wrath got through Eric's barrier, so I don't know how useful a witch can be. Or maybe the barrier only works on supernatural beings who aren't Wrath. Nothing seems capable of stopping him.

"Are you happy now?" Rhys asks.

Wrath walks away. "This wasn't for my benefit."

"What the fuck is that supposed to mean?" the dark-haired vampire says.

"Dane," Rhys warns.

"If a ruler demands supplication only to stroke his ego, then he's doing it wrong." Wrath comes up beside me and turns to face his guests currently on their knees.

"Does everyone bow to you?" I mutter beneath my breath.

He gives me a pointed look. "Not everyone." He turns back to the group. "Get up," he says warily.

Rhys is on his feet in a blink, and he gives the shorter girl his hand, which she happily takes. Dane is a blur as he goes to help Kat. I try not to show my shock or amazement. I guess vampire speed is a thing pop culture got right.

The girl smooths over the front of her silk blouse, and the collar pulls down an inch, revealing a thread of what looks like a demon mark. Wrath *did* say she's a demon.

So two vampires, a demon, and a witch.

I bet outside of Wrath, this group is a power to be reckoned with. And it must be extremely irritating to have to bow to him.

"Can we get on with this then?" Kat says, her gaze darting to me.

Wrath holds out his hand to me. I look from it to his face. I don't want to cooperate with him. Like Kat, I didn't come for supplication, but Wrath just stabbed a man for...well, I'm not exactly sure why he stabbed Dane. Some minor slight, clearly. If I disobey him now, what'll he do to me in front of all these people?

I can just hear Adam in the back of my head—*unnecessary risk.*

I need to play along for now.

I lick my lips and take his hand. My body hums to life at his cool touch. He walks me across the room to Kat. Up close, she's even more striking. Not a hair is out of place and her skin is flawless.

"Rain Low," she says. "It's nice to meet you. I'm Kat." She gestures to the shorter girl. "This is Emery, Rhys, and Dane. We're from House Roman in Saint Sabine."

"Nice to meet you all." I take a settling breath, trying not to freak out about meeting two vampires, a witch, and a demon.

Have these people always been living amongst us and we just never paid attention? I suppose if they didn't want to be found, they had ways to keep their secrets.

"I'm a witch from the Redheart line," Kat explains. "We are known for our ability to read the body. It won't hurt and it shouldn't be uncomfortable in any way. All right?"

For some reason, I look to Wrath, almost for reassurance. I hate that I do. And I hate that he knows exactly what that means. Instinctively, I want his approval.

Thankfully, he gives me only a blank stare. There's no nod, no gesture to speak of permission or reassurance, but his presence at my side feels like it just the same.

"I'm ready when you are," I tell Kat.

"Just stand still. I don't have to touch you, just so you know what to expect."

"Okay."

She takes a step toward me. Out of the corner of my eye, I see Wrath's darkness kick up.

"Calm down, Demon King," Kat says. "I said I wouldn't hurt her."

Butterflies fill my stomach.

Kat stands by my shoulder and puts one hand over my chest, the other at my back between my shoulder blades. She sucks in a deep breath and closes her eyes.

There's no indication that she's using magic, but something coppery and sweet coats my tongue and the hair at the nape of my neck rises.

No one speaks as Kat works, and I try not to freak out about what she might tell us.

There's no way I'm anything other than human. I would know. If I had magic, I would have used it by now.

Magic.

The thought is ridiculous. Me, have magic? I'm a photographer who hates her job, who has no idea what she actually wants to do with her life.

"Well?" Wrath says.

Kat sighs and drops her hands. "You're not going to like the answer."

"Let me be the judge of that."

What is that supposed to mean? Sweat beads on my lower back.

I'm human, goddammit!

"When I read someone," Kat says, "it's like opening the pages of their book. I read the text and I know the answer."

Wrath clasps his hands behind his back, causing his biceps to swell against the sleeves of his black t-shirt. "Go on."

"Rain's book is blank."

"What?" I say.

"What does that mean?" Wrath asks.

Hands on her hips, Kat answers, "Any number of things. A binding. A shield. Some other kind of magic. Or..." She trails off, her gaze going distant.

"Or what?" Wrath prompts. I can hear the faintest tremor in his voice. But is it excitement? Fear?

Kat frowns. "Or I don't know the language?"

"No. No, no." I shake my head. "I know what you're all insinuating. I'm not from your magic fairy land. I don't have magic. I'm human!" The panic forms a lump in my throat. "I'm no one."

Kat tilts her head, brows sinking in concern. "They're just theories, Rain."

"No," I say with more venom than I mean. "I'm not like you."

Emery steps forward, her hands up. "It's okay to freak out."

"I'm not freaking out," I argue through gritted teeth, while I most definitely freak out.

"Can I talk to her alone for a second?" She looks to Wrath for permission, but it's Rhys that steps forward.

"Absolutely not."

She scowls at him over her shoulder. "I don't need your permission."

"But you need his?" Rhys says, fangs sharpening in his mouth.

If I didn't believe he was a vampire before, I definitely do now.

Emery frowns at Rhys, then turns to Wrath. "May I?"

Wrath gives one dip of his chin, and Emery hooks her arm through mine and guides me out the door.

As far as I know, Emery has never been to the Demon King's castle, but she leads me down the hallway with a determination and surety I admire. We duck into another damn sitting room, and she sits me down on a cushioned window seat that overlooks a pond surrounded by cattails and dotted with lily pads.

If I had come here under any other circumstances, I'd be completely enamored with this place and out exploring the grounds. It would make a fantastic location for photo shoots.

But this isn't some other circumstance, and photography is so far away right now, it almost feels like another life.

"Okay," Emery says, "take a deep breath."

I inhale, filling my lungs, shoulders rising.

"Good. Now. I know this is a lot to take in—"

"How would you? You're a demon. I'm just...I'm..."

Emery smiles at me and takes my hand in hers. In the cool light of early evening, she looks like a woodland sprite with freckles dusting the tip of her nose and the apples of her cheeks.

"In this world, nothing is as it seems," she says. "In fact, a year ago, I didn't know vampires were real, and I had no idea I was a demon."

"Really?"

She nods. "Rhys was cursed," she says and shakes her head, making a face like it was a whole thing that she doesn't feel like getting into. "It was chance that we ran into each other, or at least I thought it was at the time. Turns out it was my destiny all along."

"And now?" I ask because I'll take any distraction.

"And now?" She looks at the door, but I can tell she's really looking in Rhys's direction. I can see love and admiration on her face. A demon and a vampire. How about that?

"Now," she says with a small smile, "now I have mind-blowing sex with that gorgeous man practically every day."

I burst out laughing, and Emery laughs with me.

"That's not what I expected you to say."

"I aim to surprise," she says.

"Does he...like..." I make fangs with my first two fingers and she blushes.

"Yes. It's actually...*sensual.* If you can believe it."

I think of Wrath, the way he terrifies and excites me all at the same time.

A few days ago, I wouldn't believe Emery. Today I do.

"I know it's overwhelming right now, but thankfully you had a bit of a head start with Wrath. You've known about him for a while."

"Yes, but I never thought I'd get pulled into his world, into the spectacle and the drama."

"I think we were all pulled into his world when he arrived."

"I suppose that's true. I just tried really hard to resist it."

"If you find out you're something else, you will get through it, and I'm here if you need me. Any time of day or night."

I roll my eyes. "Thanks, but I'm not something else. I'm really not and—" I cut off when Emery tilts her head, eyes pinched at the corners. "What?"

"I can't read your mind."

"Umm." I pull back. "Is that a thing that you normally do?"

"Demons can read minds," she says matter-of-factly.

I level my gaze at her. "Demons can read minds. Like *read...minds.*"

She nods. "I'm not sure if all of them can, but *I* can and I'm guessing Wrath definitely can. But it's harder for me to read supernatural beings. They usually know how to shield their minds. Are you shielding me now?"

I laugh nervously. "Am I shielding you from reading my mind?"

Tears well in my eyes, I'm laughing so hard. I think I'm a little delirious.

Emery squeezes my hand again.

"No, I'm not shielding you from reading my mind!"

"Okay," she says. "So..."

"So?"

"So?" She shrugs. "I'm not sure what that says other than you probably aren't entirely human." Her voice rises in an upward inflection, the way someone might deliver news no one wants to hear.

Like me. I'm that person.

"No," I try again, because maybe if I tell these people no enough times, they'll stop thinking crazy things.

"Rain," she starts, but I stand and pace in front of the window, trying to make sense of all of this.

"Wrath can read minds?"

"I'm guessing so, if he's king. He's way more powerful than I am." Her body does a little shiver, but from her, I read it like a spider crawling along her skin. There's no enjoyment on her face.

"Have you ever been unable to read a human?" I ask.

"Not that I'm aware of. Before Rhys, I hadn't really met anyone I couldn't read."

"Maybe your power is broken. Maybe Wrath is doing something to it."

She bites her lower lip, then says, "Maybe? What do you know about your origins?"

I stop pacing. "What do you mean?"

"Your birth?"

"Uneventful," I answer. "My mom had me at Osco General in New Hampshire on March 30th."

"And your dad?"

My mom has always been open and honest with me about my biological father. They met on a group camping trip and had a wild two weeks together. They parted ways, thinking nothing of it.

Except a month later, Mom realized she was pregnant and had no way of getting hold of him. She, like me, had always embraced independence, and she decided she was all right with raising me alone.

"I never knew my dad," I say, feeling a slight wedge of panic jamming between my ribs.

"Okay. Well. This gives you somewhere to start, right? See if your mom has any information on him. Then go from there."

I breathe in deep and then exhale.

Could it be that my birth father was something other than human? Did my mom know? And how the hell can I find out now? Even Kat the witch couldn't find anything definitive about me.

I grimace and run my hand through my hair.

Emery stands and cuts off my path. She's a few inches shorter than I am, but something tells me she could stop me if she wanted to. She's a demon, after all.

"It's going to be all right," she says. "You just have to take it one step at a time."

I close my eyes and sigh. She's right. I can handle this. I'm no stranger to powering through.

When I look over at her again, I smile. "You're really good at this, you know."

"Well, my own freak-out was not so tidy, but I used to be an executive assistant. You have to prioritize and keep a level head when dealing with an inept CEO."

"I'm a family photographer. You think there are similarities between an inept CEO and bratty kids?"

"Oh, I'd imagine that's a yes."

We laugh together.

"Thank you, Emery. Really." I breathe out in a rush. "I didn't realize until now just how alone I was feeling. It's like there's Wrath and all of this in one hand, and my life, my friends, and normalcy in the other. I needed something in between."

"It's my pleasure."

"Maybe we should get back? Your vampire boyfriend and my..." I trail off. Was I about to refer to Wrath as mine? He's not *my* anything.

My enemy.

The bad guy.

The villain.

Emery finishes the sentence for me. "The thorn in your side?"

"Yes, exactly."

She nods and heads for the door. "Something tells me leaving those two alone for long could be a very bad thing."

"Like two lions in a den?"

"Precisely."

14

THANKFULLY WE FIND EVERYONE IN ONE PIECE WHEN WE RETURN, THOUGH there's considerable tension between Rhys and Wrath.

"If I should need you again," Wrath says, and lets the sentence hang in the air.

Rhys's jaw flexes. "You can call on me," he finally answers.

Wrath nods, and Rhys weaves his arm around Emery and leads them out.

"Well, that was insightful," I say.

Wrath scowls. "Are you being sarcastic? Arthur, is she being sarcastic?" The tone of his voice says he already knows the answer, but Arthur answers anyway.

"I believe she is."

Wrath pours himself another shot and drinks it, his back to us.

"Can you read my mind?"

Arthur shoots a look between me and Wrath.

Wrath does that thing again where he turns his head just enough, chin meeting the line of his broad shoulder. "No," he answers.

I cross the room. "Can you read others?"

"Ms. Low," Arthur starts, but Wrath cuts him off.

"The *dieva* already knows the answer, Arthur. I see no reason to keep it from her."

Arthur frowns. I get what he's trying to do. He's protecting Wrath. Wrath saved him, and for that, Arthur will always be loyal to the Demon King. But if he's going to hold me prisoner here, I need answers.

"Yes," Wrath says. "I can read minds." He turns to us, a refilled crystal tumbler in the grip of his pale fingers. "No mortal can shield themselves from me. Very few supernatural beings can either. In Alius, I am king. No one outranks me."

He levels me with a stare, and a breath stutters up my throat. It's so easy to forget about the royal title. I mean, even here, royalty is losing its power, it's stature. Yeah, we go a little gaga over the English royalty, but do they really hold power over us? If they asked us to bow to them, we'd laugh. Or do it just for the novelty.

When Wrath asks us to bow, we get to our knees.

Well, *most* people do.

Wrath drinks back the bourbon and winces when he exhales.

"What about Rhys? Can you read him?"

"Not entirely. With him, it's more of an impression rather than a clear thought."

"Emery?"

He puts the glass down and sweeps across the room. "Emery is a demon. There is nothing she can hide from me."

Interesting.

"And me?"

He stops. Tension pulls into the space between his shoulder blades. I'm not sure if he's on the verge of gutting me with a spear or laughing at me.

I think I already know the answer, but I want to hear it from him.

"No," he says, his voice low and threaded with wariness.

The earlier panic flickers like a flame in the dark. “What does that mean?”

He looks at me over his shoulder, a curtain of dark mist hiding the flare in his eyes. “If I knew, Ms. Low, I wouldn’t have brought the witch here, now would I?”

Then he exits through the door.

When Arthur comes up beside me, his stoop is more pronounced, but he still shows no discomfort on his face. “Careful, Ms. Low. Just...be careful, okay?”

“How am I supposed to do that when he’s holding me captive? When he’s insinuating I’m not human? I feel like I’m losing my damn mind, Arthur. I want to go home.”

“He has his reasons.”

Lauren said something similar, didn’t she? Something about Wrath’s plan, and how he was trying to save our world and we didn’t even realize we needed saving.

But isn’t that the opinion of all dictators and ruthless kings? They think their way is the only way.

“What are his reasons?” I try.

Arthur shakes his head. “Just be careful.”

“Of what?”

His gaze darts from me to the door. “Sometimes the king’s methods are ruthless,” Arthur says, “and I don’t want to see you get hurt. Don’t test him, all right? If I give you any piece of advice, it’s that.”

I frown but nod, and Arthur leaves me.

His warning is a sound one. I know what Wrath can do. But there’s another nagging thought in the back of my mind.

The fact that Arthur had to warn me not to test Wrath at all leads me to believe...

I might be the only one who can.

I watch dusk turn to night through one of the large arched windows in the sitting room. The castle has gone silent again. Am I supposed to just sit here waiting like Sleeping Beauty until Wrath decides he needs me?

Fuck that.

I can't get Emery's words out of my head.

What do you know about your origins?

I sometimes wondered about my birth father, but in an abstract way. It's hard to think anything concrete when you have nothing to go on.

My mom was always upfront about him and his absence. She wanted me to know how lucky she felt to have me in her life and that my father's absence was just bad luck.

I think I need to talk to her. Maybe there's some detail she remembers that could help shed some light on this whole thing, and I haven't spoken to her since I left my condo. She's definitely going to yell at me for not checking in.

I leave the sitting room and search the castle for Lauren, but I find every room empty, and I get to a point where I'm unsure of whether or not I'm checking the same rooms over and over.

This place is a labyrinth.

When I come to a side door that clearly leads outside, I decide what the hell, might as well take a look. If I'm not supposed to be outside, I'm sure Wrath will go all misty and pop up to stop me, and then I'll really know I'm a prisoner.

The door creaks on old iron hinges when I pull it back. I pause to wait and listen, but no possessed soldiers—the *norrow*—show up, so I trudge on. Pea gravel crunches beneath my flip-flops. Victorian lampposts shed golden light on the footpath that leads around the side of the castle and through a garden archway where little purple flowers bloom from waxy vines.

I eventually come to a garage, though *garage* might be an understatement. It's a two-story structure with five dormers and three large bay doors. There's a newer model Ford Mustang parked in the driveway. It's done entirely in black.

I try the door handle and find it unlocked. The interior is dark and empty, so I slide into the driver's seat. The leather is buttery soft. Though there's nothing personal about the car's interior, it smells distinctly like Wrath. Like a cool, dark night.

The car has a push-button ignition, but I don't see a fob anywhere.

"Worth a shot," I mutter and press the brake pedal, then the button.

The car purrs to life.

"Holy shit." I look around the driveway and the grounds feeling like a kid that just stuck his hand into the cookie jar. No one comes running.

That rebellious fire that my mom always loathed and loved burns brightly in my chest. I need answers, and I'm not going to get them locked away in Wrath's castle.

I pull the door closed and put the car into drive.

I guess I'll just have to find the answers myself.

Holy shit, I just stole the Demon King's car.

I'm a little punch-drunk with the thrill as I drive the car down the long, winding driveway, the headlights sweeping through the surrounding woods. He's going to kill me. I can't wait to see the look on his face when he tries.

The driveway eventually spills onto a main road that is vaguely familiar. Lauren said we were outside Norton Harbor, though I don't know which direction. The road follows the rise and fall of gently rolling hills as I pass red barns and wheat fields and cute little farmhouses.

I think Wrath's castle might be northwest of Norton Harbor farther inland.

It takes me about twenty minutes to finally come into the city limits, and I breathe a sigh of relief. It feels good to recognize my surroundings again, and I decide what I really need is to go home.

My hands are shaking on the leather steering wheel, and the butterflies in my stomach have turned into a storm. It's almost like I'm daring Wrath to try to stop me. Can he? Would he?

When I spot my building at the end of Platte Avenue, I nearly weep. I punch in the code to the parking garage and the gate swings open. Even though I don't have a car, I do have a parking space. Time to put it to good use.

I finally locate the key fob in the center console and grab it, locking up behind me.

Stealing the Demon King's car is one thing, letting it get stolen by someone else is quite another.

Stepping back, I can't help but admire the car. It's so very Wrath. Dark and sleek and striking.

I take the elevator up to the third floor and follow the hallway down to my condo. Everything is normal, the same, everything except for me.

At my door, I tap in the code and the deadbolt thuds open. I push inside. I can smell my coconut plug-in air freshener and the faintest hint of the chicken I cooked the other day. The balcony door is still open. Apparently I forgot to shut it.

I drop the key fob on the island and go in search of my tablet. I might have lost my phone, but all of my devices are connected to messenger. I can call my mom that way.

In the living room, I flick on a lamp and pull my tablet from the bottom shelf of the end table. I fold the case open and prop it so it stands up on the coffee table.

The screen lights up when I activate it, and I find a kajillion missed messages, calls, and alerts.

I swipe out of them and go straight to messenger, then tap on my mom's name. She's been trying to reach me since yesterday.

Guilt turns to stone in my gut.

I tap on the phone icon and the tablet starts ringing. Mom picks up on the second ring.

"Where have you been?" she shouts at me.

Her wavy, auburn hair is twisted up in a messy bun and several frizzy strands flutter in a breeze around her face. The bags beneath her eyes are so big, it's almost like they're holding up the thick, black-frame glasses on her face.

She's tanner than when I saw her last, so her freckles have almost disappeared on her face.

"I'm sorry, Mom," I say with a wince. "It's been a journey."

"Baby, I've been worried sick. You couldn't pick up the phone?" Her eyes are big and wide.

"I lost my phone," I explain. "But the good news is I'm okay."

No matter what, I've never burdened my mother with the exact details of how bad something is. My mother will bend over backwards for me, but I don't like bugging her with stress she doesn't need.

Mom huffs out a sigh and repositions her phone. I can just make out a small living room behind her and a large picture window that's dark with the night. "Should I come home?" she asks.

"No. I'm okay. Really."

Some of the tension leaves her face. "So what happened? What is going on?"

"It's a long story. Basically Wrath—"

"Wrath?" Mom echoes like she's surprised to hear me speak his actual name and not his title.

"The Demon King," I correct. "He thinks I'm someone important when obviously I'm not."

"Is he there now?" She tries to peer around me, but the rest of my condo is dark.

"No. I'm home alone."

"You should stay away from him."

"I'll try." If only it was that easy. He's not like an ex-boyfriend who I can just block on my cell and social media.

Mom picks up the phone and the picture shakes as she walks, setting me down on what I assume is a kitchen counter. She starts filling a teapot with water. "I just don't like it."

"I know. Listen, Mom, there's something I've been wondering about."

"What's that, baby?" She shuts off the tap and puts the teapot on the stove top.

"What can you tell me about my birth father?"

She smiles at the mere mention of him. It's always been this way. Though they were only together those two weeks during summer, I think she really did fall head over heels for him. Her gaze goes far away, and I lose her to the memories for a second before she blinks back. "I've told you most of what I know." The stove's burner clicks as she lights it beneath the teapot. "His name was Jeffrey. He might have told me his last name, but I don't remember it. He loved to collect fossils and rocks. He could cook the most amazing chicken over an open fire." She smiles again. "Why do you ask?"

"Did you ever try to find him?"

A cupboard door opens, blocking my view of her face as she reaches inside. "I asked a few people from our camping group if they knew him, but he was a friend of a friend of a friend. That kind of thing. And if I'm honest" —the cupboard door shuts, and she tears off the top of a tea pouch— "I was conflicted about telling him. I got the impression he didn't want kids." She frowns at the phone, at me. "I'm sorry, baby. I don't want you to think... well...he never—"

"No, I know. I get it."

I don't care if this man wants a Father's Day card or not. I just need to know if he's human.

A chilly dread crystalizes in my chest.

I might not be human.

I might not be human.

That can't be true.

Please let it not be true.

Mom puts her hand on her hip and angles toward the phone. "Why do you ask?" She's wearing one of her favorite outfits—a white t-shirt beneath a silk kimono in shades of brown, black, blue, and burnt orange. My mother loves her kimonos and earth tones.

"I'm just curious," I say, trying not to get too specific. "It's just...maybe if I had the details and I could prove to Wrath that I'm just a normal person, he'd leave me alone."

Mom laughs. "A normal person? Rainy baby, none of us are normal."

"You know what I mean."

"But why this sudden fascination with you? What does he think you can do? I saw the video, of course. I saw the light. But you and I both know light artifacts and light pollution are to be expected in photography, especially with an amateur."

"I know. And especially in Norton Harbor where there's a string of lights around every corner."

"Exactly."

I breathe out. Talking to my mom is making me feel so much better. She's absolutely right. There's probably a very good reason for the light in the video.

"Anyway, I just need to do some legwork to prove to him that I'm nobody. Can you tell me how I might get a hold of someone from the camping trip? Someone who might know the friend of a friend of a friend?"

"Oh geez, it's been so long," she says out of frame and then comes back into view of the camera, a teacup in hand. "I just don't want to see you disappointed is all."

I frown even though she's not looking at me and instead busies herself with the tea bag. "I promise I won't be disappointed. Can you give me a name? Any name?"

"Let me see..." She looks at the ceiling, sorting through the memories. "There was...Susanna and Tatiana—"

"Tatiana was on the camping trip?"

"Oh sure. That's how I met her."

"I didn't know that."

"She hated camping." She laughs as steam starts to churn from the teapot. "In fact, we ran into her on the trail and found her with no bag, no provisions. She was the worst camper."

Mom talks about Tatiana in the same way she talks about Jeffrey—wistfully and reverently. Sometimes I wish I could have gotten to know her. She had to move not long after I was born.

"Do you know how to get in touch with Tatiana?"

"No. She hated phones."

"What about this Susanna?"

"Oh sure. Yeah. She's on my social. Susanna Narvaez. She's a ceramicist now. Makes millions making coffee cups. The world is a glorious place these days."

I snort. I don't know if I'd go that far. The world is a dumpster fire on most days.

"Thanks, Mom. I'll look up Susanna."

She sinks the tea bag into her cup and nods. "Sure, baby. I'm planning on coming home in another week, but if you need me before then, you'll let me know?"

"Of course."

She air kisses by the phone when she picks it up again. "Be careful, please."

"I will."

"I always feel like that's a lie when you say it, knowing you."

I roll my eyes at her, but she's not wrong. Besides, how can I promise to be careful when a demon is after me?

We say goodbye and I close out of the app, opening up my social accounts.

In the search bar, I type in Susanna's name. and she comes up immediately with a blue check mark next to her profile picture. I tap into her feed and find artful pictures of mugs and bowls and vases. She has several hundred thousand followers. I had no idea there was such a market for ceramic.

I hit the MESSAGE button and type out a note.

Hi Susanna! I'm Sunny Low's daughter, Rain. I'm trying to hunt down Jeffrey from that camping trip you guys took before I was born. Do you happen to know him? Or someone who might know how to get hold of him?

Finger hovering over the SEND button, my heart kicks up in my chest. There's always been a small desire to find my father if only to see the man who made half of me. But even as a kid, I was cognizant of the fact that finding him and meeting him was a door I could never shut again.

What if he didn't measure up to the person I had in my head?

And now...what if he isn't even human?

Christ.

Is this really my life?

No turning back now. I hit the SEND button and collapse against the sofa.

I have to tell Gus what I just did. He's going to flip. I bring the tablet back up when a flicker of shadow catches my eye.

Oh shit.

Would Wrath kill a *dieva* just for stealing his car? Technically he doesn't even need the damn thing.

I stand up, trying to keep the slight tremble from my hands as I reach out for the overhead light switch. My gut tells me Wrath won't kill me, but my head says to stop being a fucking idiot. He's killed lots of people since he came here. Who am I to think I'm special? Who am I to think he'd treat me any differently?

But when I flick the light switch and turn to face him, it's not Wrath standing behind me—it's a line of men dressed in wannabe tactical gear, and I recognize the patches they're sporting right away. A circle with a roaring bear and devil horns.

It's the Men Against Wrath.

15

IT TAKES MY BRAIN A SECOND TO CATCH UP WITH MY RACING HEART, AND when it does, it tells me to run for the door even though the men stand between me and it.

Stupid rookie mistake.

One of the burly men reaches out for me and gets a handful of my threadbare t-shirt. I backpedal, and the t-shirt rips up the side. He's caught off guard by it and lets go, and I race around the island, grabbing a knife from the butcher block as a second man comes around to cut me off.

I slice out with the weapon, but the man easily dodges. I swipe again, he ducks, then catches my arm in his meaty grip when he comes back up.

Crap.

I drop the blade and kick him in the fucking balls. He sinks into the fetal position.

"Get her," one of them barks as I jump over the man-baby and lunge for the door.

Someone hooks an arm around my waist and hauls me off my feet. I kick and flail and rage. "Motherfucker! Get the fuck off me!"

A sweaty hand clamps over my mouth and anger burns through my body. Using my elbow, I jab at his face and connect with the hard tissue of his nose.

"Fucking bitch," he howls. Blood runs down his face. He hands me off to someone else, and I start flailing like a fish, trying to dislodge them in any way I can.

That's when a tall, Military Man steps in front of me and back-hands me.

Bright light flares in my vision as the room sways and the coppery taste of blood fills my mouth.

"Get her to a chair," a gruff voice orders, and I'm carried like a limp doll to one of the chairs at my dining table.

The man drops me unceremoniously. Head still spinning, I hear the sound of duct tape being ripped and then feel it being wound around my arms, then my legs, taping me to the chair.

It all happens so fast, I barely have time to register what's happening, and by then, it's too late.

I'm royally screwed. Didn't I promise my mother not ten minutes ago that I'd be careful? Now look at me.

As soon as I'm secured to my own goddamn chair, the assholes of MAW crowd around me. I count five men total. The tall, military man stands at the head of the group. He stares down at me with narrowed eyes, muscular arms crossed over his chest.

There's a gun strapped to his belt and a giant knife in a sheath around his thigh.

I may be in a really, really bad spot right now.

I test the tape by wiggling my arms, but there's no give.

"Listen, darling," the military man says.

"I'm not your fucking darling."

He backhands me again and tears spring to my eyes as a sharp ache rings through my head and in my ears.

That really fucking hurt. I grit my teeth against the rage boiling in my bones.

When the room stops spinning again, and the pain dissipates, I scowl up at him. I'm going to murder him. I'm going to curb stomp all their balls.

I go feral in the chair, pulling and tearing at the tape when the sound of a bullet being racked in a gun pulls me to a stop.

"Let's try this again," the man says.

Blood drips from the corner of my mouth. I poke at the wound with my tongue, then run my tongue along my teeth. All of them seem to be accounted for, but the wound is raw on the inside of my bottom lip.

"If you cooperate," the man says, "we'll let you live."

One of the others, a blond guy wearing camouflage, darts his gaze to the leader as if he's surprised to hear this news.

So has the blond guy been left out of the loop or is Military Man lying to me? The way they're handling me is leading me to believe this might be more than just a shake down.

As my breathing grows shallow, dread creeps up my spine.

I'm taped to a fucking chair in my own goddamn condo surrounded by military wannabes armed to the teeth.

This isn't good. It's not good at all.

"What do you want?" I ask, my voice reedy and wet.

"Tell us why the demon trash wants you."

"How the hell should I know?"

Whack.

My head whips back from the hit. A fresh bloom of pain vibrates through my skull.

The rage grows teeth, and I can feel it coiling in my limbs.

"Try again," the guy says.

"I don't know, okay? Wrath doesn't know either. He's been trying to figure me out. He even brought a witch to the house and—"

"You've been to his house?" the man says.

I clamp my mouth shut. Is that a bad thing? It isn't like I made that choice freely and willingly.

And then it dawns on me...no one knows how to find Wrath.

That's always been one of the big sticking points for the government and the Citizens and yeah, probably even the Men Against Wrath.

So admitting that I know where his house is, is clearly a very big mistake.

"Do you know how to find it again?" one of the other guys asks. This one is dark-haired with a goatee. He gives me second-in-command vibes by the way he stands at the leader's left shoulder like he's ready to step in to protect the other man at a moment's notice.

"Hey," the guy says. "Focus." He snaps his fingers in my face.

"I don't know how to find it again, no. Wrath took me through the sub-dimension."

"The what?" the second-in-command asks.

"Wrath, is it?" the leader says. "You're on a first name basis, huh?"

"Everyone knows his name. It's not like I have special privileges."

The leader pulls back a hand again as if to slap me and I tense in the chair, braced for the blow when the guy on his left grabs him by the arm to stop him.

Did I misjudge this little band of merry men?

The military man, the one I thought was the leader, takes a step back, and the other guy steps forward. I *have* misread them, and worse, I barely noticed the shorter guy, the one with the shaved head and the glinting eyes.

He blended in so he could watch and listen.

"It's a pleasure to meet you, Ms. Low," the guy says. "I'm Ryder. We're not here to hurt you—"

I snort, and pain burns through my face.

Ryder goes on. "We're just desperate for answers and some of us" —he sends a withering look over his shoulder— "have allowed our passion to get the better of us. Will you accept our apologies?"

"Ummm...no."

"Good. Let's start over."

I roll my eyes.

"Can you tell me what the sub-dimension is?" His voice is quiet and even, unlike the military man, all gruff and demanding.

I swallow, lick my lips, and taste blood. "Wrath described it like the space between walls. It's how he poofs in and out."

A murmur goes through the men. This is news to them. Which means Wrath has told me more than he's told most.

Why?

"Do you know how he makes that ability work?" Ryder asks.

"I'm assuming it's just his power. I don't know."

The military man shifts his weight and looks at the blond man.

"Do you know anything about the world where Wrath hails from?" Ryder asks. "We know it's called Alius, but do you know how to reach it?"

I shake my head. "Sorry."

"Do you know why Wrath has taken a liking to you?"

"A fascination, I assume. I'm not anything special."

Ryder nods and casts his gaze to the floor, thinking. The others go quiet. I wiggle my arm in the tape bindings again because sitting still isn't an option.

"What did he tell you when he took you?" Ryder asks.

"About what?"

"Anything."

"I don't know. Listen, I don't have what you want, okay? I have no information that will help you defeat him or send him back to whence he came. I'm just a photographer, a rando girl, and I'd very much like you to untape me from this chair."

Ryder takes a step forward and pulls a long knife from a sheath at his hip. The blade glints in the overhead light and my breath catches in my throat.

"I swear, okay," I say. "I don't know anything."

Ryder slips the blade into one of the many holes in my

borrowed jeans and slices up. I yelp and instinct has me trying to pull away, but I'm rooted in place, helpless and at his mercy.

The pant leg falls away. He drags the blade over the bare flesh of my thigh, sending a shiver of fear down my spine.

"Please," I say.

He crouches in front of me and meets my eyes. His are dead and distant. And it's at this point that I realize his cool, calm, collected voice is just an act. Get the scared rabbit to calm down so he can slit its throat.

"Give me something I can use," Ryder says.

"I don't know what you want." I inhale deeply, trying to subdue the spindly fingers of panic currently squeezing at my heart. "I'm serious. If I had something, I'd give it to you. I just want to go back to my normal life."

Ryder turns the blade.

"Please," I say again.

He puts pressure on the tip of the blade, and it sinks into my flesh, pain radiating out like a starburst. My mind goes numb to everything else, everything but the pain. I hang my head back and cry out, but Military Man clamps his hand over my mouth, squelching my pain.

Pulling the blade back, Ryder drags the bloody tip up toward my core, and terror pounds through me.

"Bet she's fucking the demon trash," Military Man says, his meaty hand still clamped over my mouth.

The pain ebbs and I look up at him, narrowing my eyes. I'm not fucking Wrath, not that it's any of his fucking business.

"Maybe what she needs is a real man between her legs, huh?" Military Man says, his other hand trailing down my neck, down to my torn t-shirt where he takes a handful of my boob and squeezes.

My eyes go round, and I fight at the tape again. The blade comes back to my jeans, and Ryder cuts through the other leg. A chill seeps into the gaping pants, reminding me that I'm not wearing any underwear.

"Ms. Low," Ryder says, his voice still quiet and even, "how do we kill the demon trash?"

I mumble around Military Man's hand, but he doesn't let me go.

The blade hooks into the crotch of my pants, and I immediately go still.

What was I thinking, coming home alone? I should have called Gus, Adam, anyone.

It's in this moment that I realize my normal life is dead. There's no way to go back to it. And not just because of Wrath. Because of assholes like these men who think they can get what they want, when they want it at the expense of everyone else.

They'll never know the fear of being a woman alone in the world. They don't care that the fear a woman feels is only perpetuated by men like them.

They hide behind their mission, pretending to be valiant heroes trying to save the world, but really, they're just bullies afraid of someone more powerful taking over their turf.

Heat flares at my sternum and I latch on to it, hungry for something, anything other than the terror.

The heat builds and grows, flushing my veins with fire.

Military Man curses and yanks his hand back, shaking it out like he's been burned. "What the fuck?"

A strange kind of butterfly fills my gut. Butterflies like firecrackers, popping and fizzing.

A bright red light flashes through the room and the smell of burning plastic fills the air. The duct tape falls away, and suddenly I'm free.

I bring my arms up in front of my eyes, not quite believing it, only to see the duct tape burned along its edges.

The men are scattered around the room, arms up like a shield as the light dies out.

I stand from the chair and find my legs are free too.

Ryder looks from his team back to me, his mouth tightening into a grim line as he brings the blade up.

"There's my answer," he says and charges me.

16

Ryder slashes out with the knife and I leap back, just barely avoiding having the top of my head cleaved off.

He turns the blade so it's parallel with his forearm and swings again, cutting through the thin material of my t-shirt and into the flesh above my right breast.

The pain, the wetness of the blood seeping down my chest, is distant.

The rage is in the driver's seat now, fuel in my veins.

I grab the lamp from the end table and lob it at him. He bats it away and it bounces off the island, smashing on the floor. The glass crunches beneath his boot as he advances on me, and I dart back toward the balcony. Except I stumble right into Military Man who fists my hair and steers me back toward the chair.

I'm not getting back in that fucking chair.

I ram my elbow into his side, only to hit my funny bone on what feels like a bulletproof vest.

The pain is so acute, and so quick, my knees buckle, and Military Man drops me on the threshold of the balcony doors.

"Get her up," Ryder orders.

Military Man groans and bends down as I turn on my back and kick up with my bare foot.

He slaps me away.

"Get control of her," Ryder says.

"I'm trying," Military Man says.

The air crackles.

Military Man straightens. The room goes still. Goosebumps lift on my skin and there's a knowing building in my gut, an electric kindling in my chest.

He's here.

Something shoots across the room and the overhead light shatters, the light winking out, plunging us into silver moon darkness.

I hear the telltale sound of guns being pulled from their holsters, bullets being racked into barrels.

As if a bullet could stop the Demon King.

Military Man towers over me, his gun in hand. "Where is he?" he says, voice low.

"Haven't spotted him—*ahhhh*!"

A gun goes off and then a body hits the floor. The air shifts again and the moonlight flickers like a strobe as shadows flit around the room.

I get onto all fours and scurry back toward the balcony, into open air.

Ryder skirts around the dining table, gun up. Military Man is going in the opposite direction with the blond guy, back by my bedroom door, and the goatee guy is by the bathroom.

The fifth guy is lying on the floor by the island and I'm pretty sure he's dead.

A shadow flies through the air and blond guy lets out a strangled cry, blood splattering against the wall behind him as he crumples to his knees, falling onto his face. He didn't even get a shot off.

The shadow disappears.

Goatee guy looks like he's about to piss his pants.

"Look alive," Military Man says.

You're about to be dead.

One of the shadows coalesces into a human-like form in front of the TV, and I see Wrath's pale, gorgeous face in the swirling darkness.

The men swivel to him, guns aimed, and fire. The loud *pop-pop* makes my head ring, and I instinctively shrink down behind one of my lounge chairs.

The dark silhouette of Wrath goes misty on the edges and the bullets pass right through him.

My TV shatters and sparks and wobbles on its stand.

When the guns click with empty cartridges, the real show begins.

Black mist trails off of Wrath like steam rising from hot pavement as the men fumble with their guns, trying to reload. The shadows sharpen into spears and shoot across the room.

Goatee guy is impaled in the gut. His body jolts from the impact as he coughs up blood.

Military Man ducks at the last second and the spear lodges itself into my bedroom door with a loud, resounding thud.

The last spear shoots across the room, aimed at Ryder, but he's already leapt out of the way, right to my side.

He grabs the back of my shirt and yanks me to my feet, gun aimed at my head.

"Stop," Ryder says, his voice still that menacing calm.

Wrath turns to us, and I catch a barely perceptible wince.

"All right," the Demon King says, "you've got my attention." He takes a step toward the open balcony doors.

"Uh-uh," Ryder warns and pulls me back, closer to the glass railing. "Stay where you are."

Wrath is already through the French doors, but he stops beside my outdoor café table and spreads out his hands. "Now what?"

Military Man edges around Wrath, gun up, but the sights aren't aimed on Wrath, they're squarely on me.

"If she's so important to you," Ryder says, "then we'll do a good old-fashioned horse trade. You get the girl, and we walk out of here alive."

Wrath keeps his hands up, as if those were the only weapons he wields. "You know I can't do that. Not now."

"Why's that?" the military man asks gruffly.

"Because you've already harmed her. You've already put her life in jeopardy."

Military Man frowns, bushy brows sinking over his eyes. "Why do you even care? She's just a girl. Not even a hot one."

Excuse me? If I didn't have a gun trained on my head and blood pouring from two wounds, and pants that are about to fall off, I'd be charging across the balcony to slap that son of a bitch.

"If she's no one special, then why risk your life here and now?" Wrath asks. His face is devoid of emotion. I guess when you know you're invincible, you have no reason to fear an adversary.

Putting more distance between us and Wrath, Ryder guides me back to the edge of the balcony and I bump against the railing. "If she's no one special, then why do you care if she dies? You've already killed so many. What's one more?"

Wrath flexes his jaw, and the first sliver of emotion tells the truth.

He does care.

He cares very much.

"That's what I thought," Ryder says, and then he yanks me by the arm and shoves me over the balcony railing.

I hear Wrath's strangled voice as the sky goes up.

"Nooooo!" he shouts.

My arms pinwheel. People on the boardwalk scream as I plunge for the concrete walk three floors below my balcony.

Will it hurt to hit the pavement?

Will I feel every bone breaking?

On the bright side, this madness will officially end and thinking that almost brings a sort of morbid relief.

I breathe out, exhale at the shining stars and think—*okay. I'm ready.*

And then—

The crowd lets out a collective gasp as strong arms catch me.

The disbelief hits me like a crashing wave, and suddenly I'm sobbing with relief.

Wrath looks down at me, breathing elevated, dark brow sunk into a concerned frown.

He caught me. He saved me. I'm not a puddle of goo and blood on the pavement outside my condo.

Holy shit.

Holy shit.

I clutch him as the emotion overwhelms me. As the realization of how big this is, how real it is, eats away at my bravery and my resolve.

I was just held hostage by five men that were slowly cutting the clothing from my body and—

Wrath pulls me in closer and his darkness envelops us, that rich, spicy night scent filling my nose, easing the panic still knotting my stomach.

The Demon King saved me.

Again.

"Hold on," he tells me, and then the air cracks open, pulling us away.

17

We reappear seconds later in the cool, dark hush of what I think is Wrath's castle. He still holds me close to his body, arms tight around me. His breathing is still fast and rough, and I can hear the rapid beating of his heart through his shirt.

"Arthur!" he shouts as he carries me to a bed and lays me down. He pushes the hair from my face with sure, warm fingers. "Arthur!" he shouts again.

The door opens and light spills in. The silhouette of Arthur appears in the rectangle of light. "What is it?" Arthur calls as he stumbles into the dark and flicks on a lamp. "Oh. Is she—"

My clothing is practically hanging off my body like rags, and there's blood everywhere, running down my leg, down my chest. I can only imagine what my face looks like after getting backhanded so many times by that asshat's meaty hand.

"I'll get some rags," Arthur says and hurries away.

Wrath yanks the collar of my shirt down, assessing the wound above my breast. "Describe to me how you feel," he says, his eyes sweeping over my chest.

My voice comes out squeaky and thick. The tears have somewhat stopped, but the unshed ones are still making my vision blurry, and my throat hoarse. "Sore," I answer. "But I think I'm all right besides that."

Forget the fact that I almost died and that Wrath has officially saved me twice now.

How the hell is it that I'm safer in the hands of a demon king from another world than I am with mortal men?

They've turned on me. All of them. I want to blame it on Wrath, but even before him, would any of those men have thought twice about protecting me? Or not laying a hand on me if I said no?

My head is spinning and my stomach is knotted and I'm just so fucking exhausted.

Arthur returns with several wet rags and a first aid kit. He moves to the side of the bed like he means to take over, but Wrath yanks the towel from his grip and doesn't move. With a gentle sweep of the cloth, he swipes away the blood.

I wince. The skin is tender and raw and it's starting to turn hot with inflammation. I can only imagine what comes after this clean up.

I rest my head against one of the soft pillows and sling my arm over my eyes, blocking out the weak light of the lamp. Even that is making my eyes burn.

"Here," Arthur says from somewhere beyond Wrath, and when I peek around my arm, I see him offering a blanket.

"Take off your clothes," Wrath says.

Normally I'd argue about the villain wanting to disrobe me, but the clothing is almost useless anyway, and it's starting to stick to my skin as the blood dries, causing fresh pain every time I shift and the material pulls away.

Wrath opens the blanket with a snap and drapes it over me.

I slowly do as instructed, carefully yanking my shirt up. Wrath has to help get it past my head and even though I won't admit it out loud, I'm grateful for his help.

Next, I unbutton the jeans and shimmy out of them. Arthur grabs them by the cuffs and pulls them off the rest of the way.

"Tell Lauren to get her some real fucking clothes," Wrath says over his shoulder, "or I will not only denounce her as an ally, I'll rip out her fucking heart and shove it down her throat."

Arthur gives a half bow. "Of course."

"Those exact words, Arthur," Wrath says with bite.

Arthur nods and ambles away.

Looks like I'm not the only one in pain. Of course, mine will heal and fade. Arthur has to live with his forever.

It makes me suddenly sad. It makes me feel like an ungrateful snot. Here I am always bitching about my life, about what I don't have, about the new chaos and stress, and Arthur is dealing with chronic pain every single day, trying to navigate life around it.

I sigh.

Wrath frowns down at me. "What is it?"

"Nothing," I say, eyes heavy.

"That's impossible," he points out. "There is never nothing."

True enough.

"You keep saving me," I answer.

"To the surprise and shock of us both."

"You really think I'm something special."

"Special is a stretch. A thorn in my side is more adequate."

"You heard Emery," I say distantly. She used those exact words to describe him.

Wrath drags the rag over my chest, revealing the state of the wound. "It needs stitches," he says. "But I can likely heal you."

He shifts down the edge of the bed to assess the wound in my thigh, and as he pushes up the blanket, fingers dragging over the sensitive flesh of my inner thigh, I clench up tight, a thrill pulsing in my clit.

"Careful, *dieva*," he purrs.

"What?"

"I can smell you," he says.

"Ummm...What do you mean?"

His eyes flash red. "Your desire."

"What?" I screech, eyes suddenly wide, face painted with shame.

Fuck. How the hell am I supposed to control that buzzing in my core? How the hell am I supposed to ignore the way his touch ignites something inside of me even though I'd rather light myself on fire?

Oh really? an inner voice says. *If that's what you think, you're lying to yourself.*

If I'm turned on by Wrath, what the hell does that say about me?

I don't like it. I really like it.

I want him to keep touching me.

"It isn't like I'm doing it on purpose," I mutter, face still hot. "I don't actually like you."

He gives me a look like he's calling me on my bullshit. "We have that in common then, don't we?"

He nudges my leg open to get a better look at the wound, and wetness spreads between my folds.

I leap off the bed and curse as the wound opens, fresh blood seeping out. I press against the wall, holding the blanket to my chest. I'm right back where I started, naked except for a thin bit of material in Wrath's cool, dark castle.

Why do I keep finding myself in this predicament with him?

He stands, the bloody rag hanging from his hand. "You need to lie down," he growls.

I take in a stuttering breath. "I don't think that's a good idea."

"And standing is a better one?"

My vision swims as I become lightheaded. I sway on my feet and slump down the wall and Wrath darts over to catch me.

Feeling his arms around me again, his hands on the bare flesh of my hips, causes me to let out an audible gasp.

His irises glow brighter and the blackness surges around us. The monster is here, and it makes my belly soar.

"Why are you so stubborn?" he purrs.

"Why are you so infuriating?" I challenge.

He leans in close, his spicy scent overwhelming me. "If I'm so infuriating, then why are you so wet?"

I frown. "I'm not."

"Oh?" He raises his brow as his left hand slips away from my waist. I know what he's going to do before he does it, and my heart kicks up, racing in my chest so fast I worry it might thump right out of my rib cage.

"Infuriating," he says low and throaty as his hand slips beneath the blanket and trails up my thigh.

I close my eyes. I should stop him. I really should. But I don't want to.

It's like I've slipped into an alternate reality, a dream, where I can give in to the Demon King and not suffer any consequences.

So I don't stop him.

His sure, deft fingers tease at my opening and I breathe out.

My eyes are half closed when he brings his hand up and licks my juices from his fingers.

Holy shit.

A needy pulse grows at my core.

I'm in trouble. So much trouble.

"You taste good, *dieva*." His lips are wet with my desire. "Infuriating, indeed," he says, his voice turning into a growl.

"What are we doing?" I ask.

"I don't know," he admits, and that does weird things to my belly.

For the first time since he arrived here, he seems unsettled, and not because of the Citizens or MAW or the government.

Because of me.

Maybe I do hold some kind of sway over the Demon King.

So I give in. I give in to the power and the thrill of it.

I kiss him.

He goes stiff at first, maybe caught off guard by it, but then he gives in too, and his responding kiss turns hungry.

We're both starving.

Ravenous for *something.*

His tongue flicks over my lips, and I part my mouth, letting him in. I moan into him as his tongue meets mine, that delicious caress of him sending a shiver down my spine.

I want more. I've never been so fucking turned on. And I realize maybe I was never better than the fangirls.

Maybe I was always starving for the Demon King. The power. The sexiness. The dark mystery of him.

Now I have him. Now he's mine and no one else's.

He hooks his hands around my thighs and hoists me up against the wall, pressing his groin to my center.

He's hard, so fucking hard and it makes me instantly wetter.

The Demon King wants me too.

His mouth trails to my jaw, down my neck, and the blanket falls away, pooling between us at my waist.

My nipples peak and he takes one into his mouth, his tongue flicking over the tight bud. I hang my head back and exhale at the ceiling, arching into him.

Fuck, fuck, he feels so fucking good.

"How furious are you now, *dieva*?" he mutters and nips my nipple.

I pant. "So...fucking...furious."

The pain from my wounds fades away. I'm not sure if it's the pleasure overriding it, or if he's somehow healed me like he does for Arthur.

"Tell me to stop," he says.

"Do you want to stop?"

He growls and presses forward with his hips, grinding his cock against me. His breathing is heavy, threaded with desire and something that sounds an awful lot like fear.

He's afraid of giving in to me.

"I've been thinking about your tight little pussy since we met in the alley."

I moan at his words and run my fingers through his hair, disheveling it.

"And now?"

He pulls me away from the wall and the room disappears.

There's a rushing noise in my ears as he pulls me into the sub-dimension, then a settling again as we reappear in another room. He drops me on the bed. The duvet is thick and dark and everything smells like him.

Like summer and sin.

He tears the shirt from his body, then unbuttons his pants.

When his cock is free, I let out a little yelp of surprise.

The Demon King is big.

"Get on your knees," he orders.

I'm distantly aware of coming full circle. Of our first meeting in the alley when he told me to bow and I refused.

There's a challenge in his eyes, a desire for control.

If I bow to him now, he won't feel so powerless beside me.

Do I give in?

I burn with the temptation to be submissive before him. I don't know why.

It's all an act, I tell myself as I slide off the edge of the bed and stand in front of him.

A silent moment passes between us as his eyes glow red in the semi-darkness.

I think we're playing a game here, one where we're both the king, swinging for power.

I'll let him have this win.

I sink to my knees and he exhales. "Is this what you wanted?" I ask and look up at him around the hard, thick line of his cock.

The blackness plumes around him and his face sharpens to the monster he is. But for the first time, I'm not afraid of him. I'm not afraid of the villain.

He takes a fistful of my hair and says nothing.

But everything he does, every movement he makes says one word—*yes*.

He wants to feel in control with me. But he's not. He never will be. Because I'm an enigma. I don't know why. I'm still not sure if I believe the possibility that I'm something other than human.

In this moment, I don't care.

There's a gaping hole in my center that somehow feels fuller now.

I drag my tongue over the underside of his shaft, and he hisses. I straighten and tease at the tip, circling the head before I take him into my mouth.

He gasps, his hand tightens in my hair as he guides me over his cock, pumping into me.

I feel him grow harder on my tongue, the head of his shaft throbbing against the back of my throat.

A bead of precum hits my tongue and he stops himself suddenly as he pants in the dark.

He hoists me up and throws me on the bed on my stomach. His hand comes back to my hair and yanks my head back.

"This changes nothing," I breathe out.

His mouth is at my ear when he says, "Oh *dieva*, this changes everything."

And then he plunges into me and my vision goes white.

18

Not even an hour ago, I was falling to my death.

I feel like I'm falling again, but I can't tell if it's the dangerous kind or the divine.

I've never been fucked like this.

It's like my body is coiled up tight, ready to burst. Like if I were a circuit board, all of my lights would be glowing bright.

Wrath pounds into me, his hands on my hips, pulling my ass into him. I can feel him throbbing hard inside of me, the head of his shaft hitting a spot that's never been hit before.

He fills me up, and the sensation of his thick cock is painful and sublime all at the same time.

But I think more than the physical, it's the mental pleasure of knowing the Demon King can't get enough of me. The way he thrusts inside of me, it's like he's claiming me as his, claiming me as his divine retribution.

His hand snakes around my thigh, fingers circling my clit, and the pulse of pleasure grows into a supernova in the center of me.

"Oh god," I pant out.

"Not god," he says as he thrusts.

Close enough.

My arms are shaking, and my thighs are quivering as his fingers circle and flick my clit, the tidal wave of pleasure building and building as he hits deep inside of me.

But then he flattens his hand against my wet center, stealing the pleasure from me. He slows his thrusts.

I moan and tremble. “Stop teasing me.”

“Or what?”

I go down on my elbows and push my ass up so the head of his cock rubs against that delicious spot inside of me.

Or what? Or what?

Or I might scream.

His fingers return to my swollen bud and circle, then flick, then circle again in a tempo that has me jolting beneath him.

“Oh fuck.” My breath is hot against the duvet. “Oh fuck.”

The pressure builds, the thrill weaving through my body like a fire about to ignite.

I can feel the wick flaring, the heat pressing against me as Wrath fills me up.

“Go on, *dieva*,” he says with a quick, ragged breath. “Let me hear you come.”

The orgasm crashes through me and I cry out, body trembling and jolting and burning bright. There is nothing but the sensation, like a symphony, a sublime song surging through every vein, every bone in my body.

Wrath moves with me, riding the wave, then picks up the tempo, thrusting hard and deep.

“Fuck,” he says. “You’re so tight.”

And then his rhythm shifts and he pulls out almost entirely before thrusting back in, deep, deeper, his fingers gripping tightly at my hips as he spills inside of me, groaning low through clenched teeth.

I’m hot at the core, trembling and spent, and filled up with the Demon King’s cum.

How did I get here? And now that I am, do I feel bad about it?

The butterflies in my stomach say no, I don't feel bad one little bit.

He was right—*this changes everything.*

When he pulls out of me, I collapse on my side facing away from him, breathing heavy, eyelids nearly shut. The pain, both physical and mental, of the attack at my condo is a distant memory.

I just fucked the Demon King.

I said I hated him. Detested him. And now I'm in his bed surrounded by his scent, his cum leaking out of me.

I can't believe it and yet...there's a thrum of rightness in my chest. Like a knot has been undone.

A feeling almost like...like I've come home.

Wrath's breathing settles, and I roll over to face him. He's on his back, his hands on his taut stomach. With moonlight pouring in through the windows to our right, I can just make out the sharp, dark lines of his demon mark.

It's complex, intricate with curving lines that wind over his shoulders, across his chest, and then—

There's a very distinct circle at his sternum where the mark isn't black but puckered white like a scar.

If I didn't know any better, I'd think it was an exact match for my birthmark.

Without thinking, I reach out to trace my fingers over it, but he snatches me by the wrist, stopping me. "What is that?" I ask.

Moonlight puts catchlights in his eyes as he looks at me silently.

We just fucked, but the Demon King isn't about to give up his secrets.

With a sigh, I start to rise. "I should go."

His grip on me tightens, keeping me in place.

There's a moment where we're both locked in this dueling

storm of wants and desires, when we both know what we should be doing, and yet can't seem to make ourselves do it.

"Stay," he says, his voice hoarse in the dark.

This is another face-off, an unspoken challenge. He's given me an order. Will I follow it?

I should go. But I don't want to go.

Instead, I slide across the bed to him. He weaves his arm around me, pulling me in, and I rest my head against his chest right over his heart. The steady thrum of it acts like soothing white noise and I'm quickly out, tucked safely into the Demon King's embrace.

19

When I wake, it's still dark and the bed is noticeably empty. It takes me a second to orient myself and to remember where I am. It's Wrath's smell that reminds me first. Not the softness of the sheets or the windows on the wrong side of the room.

I could sink into his smell and never leave. It makes my stomach flutter and my chest lighter.

I wrap the sheet around myself and tiptoe to the door. It's cracked, letting a sliver of golden light shine through.

I'm just about to pull it open the rest of the way when Arthur's voice and my name pulls me to a stop.

"They're saying you kidnapped Rain and therefore have broken the treaty."

I can't see Wrath through the crack in the door, but I can hear his snort of derision.

"As if I would need to kidnap anyone," he says.

What's that supposed to mean? It's not like I begged him to take me, though truth be told, I *did* need some assistance considering the Citizens were trying to murder me at the factory.

"The Army Chief of Staff has filed an appeal," Arthur goes on.

"And what do they think they'll do? Fight me again? As if they are any match for me."

The bite of his tone, the superior tenor of his voice, makes him sound much closer to the villain I imagined he'd be.

My body goes numb.

Arthur moves around the room, and I catch sight of him beside a wet bar along the far wall. Wrath is still out of sight. "Are you any closer to finding it?"

There's a sigh, then, "No. I think the girl is connected somehow, but I don't know how."

"And you thought seducing her would help you figure it out?"

"Mind your tone," Wrath says, and Arthur shifts his gaze to the floor.

"Apologies. It's just...I don't think she knows. Which means she's innocent."

"When has innocence ever protected someone?"

I lick my lips, unsure of how I should feel about this conversation. I'm clearly not supposed to be eavesdropping, and the fact that I'm getting away with it feels both powerful and deceitful.

"And the soldiers?" Arthur asks next.

"They should be ready within a week."

Arthur folds his hands behind his back. "And after that?"

"If I don't acquire the *animus* soon..." Wrath trails off. Arthur fidgets, shifting his weight from foot to foot.

"Can Chaos cross over without help?" Arthur asks.

"I'm not sure, but I can feel him trying."

Wait, *him*? Did he just refer to chaos as a person? Someone from Alius? Does the government know there are more supernatural people trying to get through?

Panic flutters beneath my ribs. This isn't good.

Or maybe...

What's the saying? *An enemy of my enemy is my friend.*

But the very thought of fighting Wrath burns shame through my veins. I said I hated him but now...now I'm not sure how I feel about him. He's been kind to me, which yeah, surprised me. I can't forget that he's saved me twice when—

"And Rain?" Arthur asks.

I hold my breath again. I don't want to miss Wrath's answer.

There's a long pause, and for a second, I worry I've been discovered snooping. If Wrath poofs into the room right now, there's no hiding what I'm doing, but I really want to hear his response.

I want to know how I figure into this, and how he really feels about me.

"The girl stays until I figure out how to use her to my advantage or until I bend her to my will. Whichever comes first."

I clamp my hand over my mouth to tamp down the cry that threatens to escape.

The girl.

That motherfucker.

The euphoria I was feeling earlier turns sour in my gut.

So I'm just a tool he's trying to figure out how to work?

Was he just fucking me to get closer? So he could use my compliance to his advantage?

Tears burn in my eyes, and there's a sharp pang of betrayal in my chest.

I fell for it. Just like everyone else. I fell for the power. I fell for the manipulation. I thought I was somehow special. But ever since Wrath got here, he's looked at all of us like we're inferior to him and demanded we be subservient.

Fire lights in my veins from pure rage.

I should have known better.

He told me to bow, and I finally got to my knees.

Stupid. So fucking stupid!

The rage blooms at my sternum and light shines into the room.

The hell?

I turn to look for a lamp and see none.

"What's that?" Arthur says. "You see that light?"

Shit.

I scurry back into the bed, tangling myself into the sheets. *Calm down. Breathe.* I close my eyes and pretend to sleep and count my breaths, trying to quell the pounding of my heart.

"*Dieva.*"

His voice comes to me in the dark, and my heart beats harder. I open my eyes and find his silhouette against the growing dawn. "Hey," I say in a croak. "You scared me. What are you doing?"

He comes to the bedside and sits beside me, and my damn heart is still ramming against my ribs.

Can he hear it?

"I have something I need to attend to," he says and pushes the hair from my face. The sharp, haughty tone I heard him use with Arthur is gone, but now I know this is all just part of the act.

"Okay," I say. "How long will you be gone?"

"Not long. There are clothes for you in the bathroom and plenty of food in the kitchen. I assume you can tend to yourself?"

I roll my eyes, even though it's still dark in his room. "Obviously."

"I'll be back later. Stay within the walls of the castle." His voice turns dark as he adds, "Behave, *dieva.*"

I snort for grand effect as he sweeps out of the room. "Fine."

Behave. Behave!

I'm going to burn this son of a bitch to the ground.

20

When I'm sure he's gone, I hurry out of the bed and look for the bathroom. I find his closet first, though it's mostly empty. A half hour ago, I would have walked inside and fingered the soft material of his shirts, his jackets, drank in the scent of him.

What an idiot I've been.

I slam the door closed and find the bathroom on the next try. It's massive with white marble floors and a shower stall done in some kind of slick, black tile. There's a rain showerhead about the size of a pothole, and I wish I could take advantage of it.

But no.

I have to get out of here.

Behave.

Ha. He's going to see just why my mother avoided disciplining me the old-fashioned way. Sunny Low had to get clever with her parenting style. When she told me to go left, I went right. When she told me not to stay out after curfew or else I'd be grounded, guess who came home an hour late?

Behave!

I don't care about the consequences.

The clothes Lauren acquired this time are much better. I find a pair of black leggings and a white t-shirt folded on a bench in the bathroom with a pair of white tennis shoes on the floor. There's also a pair of panties that actually fit, though the bra is a sports bra that mashes my boobs to my body.

I'm not complaining. I've pretty much been naked since I got here.

As I'm pulling on the leggings, I pause at mid-thigh where Ryder had cut me open. The skin is completely healed with only a pink slash where the wound had been. I scan my chest and find the same thing.

That's interesting.

I shake my head and resume dressing.

Once fully clothed, I poke my head through the door where I'd been eavesdropping earlier and find the room empty. Taking a deep breath, I cross through it and then check the hallway outside.

Where is Lauren anyway? And is Arthur with Wrath?

What did Wrath have to attend to?

I need to get out of the castle—again—and this time, I have to escape on foot. Even if Wrath recovered his car, I'm not risking stealing it. Luckily for me, I noticed several farmhouses on the way to Norton Harbor. Plenty of places where I can stop to use the phone.

But there's a voice in the back of my head that can't help but wonder if Wrath can find me regardless of where I am. He found me at my condo, though I suppose that's an obvious place to look for me.

I slip out the door at the back of the kitchen just as the sun rises over the treetops. The woods surrounding the grounds is my best bet for coverage, so as soon as I'm clear of the gardens, I run.

When I'm beneath the cool, shaded canopy of the hardwoods, I lean against the trunk of a giant maple, hands on my knees as I suck in air.

I'm not a runner. In fact, I hate exercise. I might need to rethink that now that I'm running from a monster.

If I've oriented myself correctly, I can escape through the woods that will eventually meet up with the main road, and then I should be able to find a house to stop at.

I'm not sure how long it takes me to get through the woods. I alternate between running and walking fast, my throat tight and raw the entire way.

I finally come out of the woods as the sun burns off the dew that's gathered on the grass. In the distance, I make out the rise of a silo and the pitched roof of a barn.

"Oh, thank god."

I close the rest of the distance in a slow jog.

Free-range chickens squawk in the yard of the old farmhouse when I run up to the front porch. I knock and knock on the wooden screen door. The interior door is propped open with an iron stand so I shout, "Hello? I need a phone! Please help."

A man appears and frowns at me. He's sunbaked and wiry with hair that could rival a model's. He's old though, sixties maybe, judging by the deep wrinkles around his face and the gray threading his hair.

"I need a phone," I pant out.

"Your car breakdown?" He looks past me through the screen.

"Something like that."

The man brings me a cell phone a minute later, and I almost laugh. It's a flip phone. "It's nothing fancy," he says as he hands it to me.

"Not fancy will do." I punch in Gus's number and bring the phone to my ear.

"Hello?" Gus answers on the second ring.

"Gus! It's me. I need a ride."

"Rain! Where are you?"

I ask the kind man for an address and he quickly relays it to me.

"We're coming to get you," Gus says, and I almost sob with relief.

"Thank you."

"Hang tight. We'll be there soon."

We hang up, and I snap the phone closed. "Thank you..."

"Tom," the man answers, then, "Are you okay?"

I sink onto one of his metal porch chairs. "Have you not watched the news?"

"Can't say that I have. I don't have a TV."

"You don't have a TV and you're using a flip phone? Have I time traveled?"

He scratches at the back of his head. "I've got no use for smart phones and sitcoms. Plenty around here to keep me busy." He leans against one of the porch columns. "You in trouble, miss?"

I push sweaty hair out of my face. "You know of the Demon King?"

He nods. "I've heard of him."

"Well, he's after me, and I just escaped his house. He lives right down the road."

The man frowns and looks down the road as if he can spot Wrath. "Can't say I've ever seen him in the neighborhood."

"There's literally a castle that way." I point to the woods I just emerged from.

The man chuckles. "I'd know if there was a castle around here."

"What? What is happening? You've never seen the giant castle literally a mile down the road?"

He just gives me a confused look.

Could it be more magic? Wrath has witch connections. Maybe the castle is shielded in some way too.

It would explain why the men from MAW were literally torturing me to get a location.

Tom waits with me on his front porch for a good half hour before a black SUV slows down out front. The chickens squawk and trundle out of the way as the SUV eases in off the road.

"I think that's my ride," I tell Tom.

He takes off his baseball cap. "Well, it was a pleasure meeting you, Rain. If you ever need the use of a flip phone again, you know where to find me."

I laugh. "I hope for your sake you don't ever see me again."

He smiles a closed mouthed smile and looks at the cap in his hand.

"Rain!" Gus shouts.

"Gus!" I thud down the three porch steps and race across the yard, slamming into Gus's open arms when we meet up. I drink in the smell of him. It feels like it's been forever since I saw him. Days, weeks. Too long.

"Thank god," he says in my ear. "I was so worried about you." He pulls back, but keeps his hands on my arms as if afraid to let me go. Adam climbs out of the SUV's driver's seat, hands on his hips. He nods a hello to Tom, who is still standing at the top of the porch steps.

"You were at your condo last night and you didn't call us? And then you fell over the balcony and the Demon King saved you?"

"Wait, how do you know all that?"

Gus frowns at me. "It's all over the news, babe. Like, *all over* the news."

"Have you been with the Demon King since last night?" Adam asks.

My face pinks just thinking about what I did last night, but I quickly bury the memories and leftover feelings. "I've actually been with" —I was about to say Wrath, but I'm acutely aware that every time I say his name, everyone around me looks like I've just called the pope by name— "the Demon King since I left your factory."

Gus's eyes go wide. "Shut the fuck up."

Eric and Sanjay climb out to surround us like guards. I don't miss the guns strapped to their hips.

"Where did he take you?" Adam asks.

"He—" I look over my shoulder at Tom. He's got a shoulder leaning against the porch column again and his baseball cap is back in place. I told Tom where Wrath's castle was. I could easily tell Adam, but...

What is stopping me?

I want revenge, don't I?

He was using me, looking to take advantage of me in any way he could.

But I can't seem to get the words out. I'm not ready to give up the Demon King. Maybe it's because I want to gut him and burn him myself, not hand him over to Adam and his team.

There's a little voice in the back of my head that says that's not even close to the reason.

"Can we just get out of here?" I ask. "I have this feeling that the Demon King can find me wherever I go. Maybe Eric can strengthen his barrier or whatever."

"Of course." Gus steers me into the backseat of the SUV. It's got two rows of seats in the back, so plenty of room for all of us to climb in.

I wave goodbye to Tom and he waves back. We need more nice people like him in the world, willing to help a stranger without a single question as to why.

As soon as the SUV is moving down the road in the opposite direction of Wrath's castle, I lean into Gus's shoulder and thread my arm through his, taking his hand in mine. "I'm so glad you're here."

"Same," he says. "Are you okay? Did the Demon King hurt you?"

Does betrayal count? Not that I plan on revealing those details to Gus. Or anyone.

"Oddly enough, no. In fact, he helped clean me up after the attack at my condo."

"What attack?"

"MAW?"

"They were there?" Sanjay asks from the backseat.

I nod. "That's who threw me over the balcony. Some guy named Ryder wanted to know where they could find the Demon King."

Adam makes a disgruntled sound deep in his throat. "Ryder Carrigan. Ex-military. Dishonorable discharge."

"You know him?" Gus asks.

Adam slows for a turn. "The guy is bad news. He's one of the founding members of MAW."

Sanjay frowns. "How come we've never heard of him?"

"Because that's the way he likes it," Adam says. "Did you give Ryder a location on the Demon King?"

"I didn't have one to give."

Adam makes eye contact with me in the rearview. "But you were there. What did this location look like?"

I shrug and look out the window, feeling caged in suddenly. "It was really big. Regal. Lots of oil paintings on the wall."

"Really?" Sanjay leans over the seat. "That surprises me. What were the paintings of?"

"Old white men."

She rolls her eyes. "Also doesn't surprise me."

They give me a reprieve from questioning after that. It takes nearly forty-five minutes to reach the factory again, and I see Adam has upped his security. There are more guards out front and a locked gate that we have to be let past.

Gus sticks by my side as we go in through one of the side doors, and I'm ready to ask for a hot shower or a hot meal or both when Adam turns to me, muscular arms crossed over his chest.

"I know you've been through a lot, Rain, but time is of the essence."

Ugh. I wrinkle my nose.

"Okay."

"Would you be willing to discuss the Demon King and everything you witnessed while with him?"

"Sure. But maybe later?"

"How about in thirty minutes?"

Gus squeezes my hand. I can't tell if it's him dropping a hint to say yes or if he's just trying to be supportive.

Am I in trouble here?

"I guess I can do thirty minutes," I say.

"Good. Eric, call Hansen. Set it up."

"Wait, who's Hansen? Set up what, exactly?"

Gus grimaces in an apologetic way. "So I know you're probably tired and could use a spiked half-and-half right about now, but how do you feel about meeting the president?"

"President? Of what?"

"Of the United States?"

"Oh shit," I say, and Gus nods.

21

I have a mini panic attack just thinking about the seriousness of meeting the President of the United States.

In the Low house, our Madame President is holier than the pope.

Naomi Wright was only forty-seven years old when she was elected president. She has a master's degree in English from Yale University and a PhD in political science from Harvard. She founded two non-profit organizations before her twenty-fifth birthday and went on sabbatical for a year so she could photograph remote corners of the world.

My mom loves Naomi Wright and I love Naomi Wright and now I'm going to meet her.

Could this get any more insane?

But what the hell does she want with me?

I guess I can fill in the blanks, but she's going to be sorely disappointed when she realizes I don't have much to contribute to the ongoing war against Wrath.

Sanjay helps fill me up with coffee and the jolt to my veins is welcomed and needed. Eric makes me peanut butter toast, and

Gus slices up an apple while I sit at one of the tables in the cafeteria.

"So what exactly happened when the Citizens showed up?" I ask.

"Darren happened," Sanjay answers, her face contorting with anger.

I look at Gus.

"Apparently Darren got greedy," he explains. "He was shooting for two birds, one stone. He gave the Demon King the info he was looking for hoping to score the big payout, while also using you as bait."

"He let the Citizens into the factory," Eric fills in.

"That little weasel. Pitch died because of him!"

"We lost several other members of the team too," Sanjay says.

"I'm so sorry, you guys."

"It happens when you're in this line of work."

Eric and Sanjay hold up their cups of coffee in salute.

"Still, it shouldn't have happened." And it was partly my fault.

When will this end? I still feel like I'm living in a nightmare.

"Here," Gus says and sets down a plastic bowl adorned with cute sloths. The apple is sliced neatly inside.

"You guys are amazing," I say just as Eric grabs the toast from the toaster and slathers it in peanut butter.

"You're the belle of the ball, babe." Gus takes a giant bite out of my toast when Eric sets it down in front of me. Peanut butter globs to the corner of his mouth.

"I'm not," I insist and dab at his mouth with my napkin. "But I'll pretend I am for food and caffeine to be delivered straight to my face."

Sanjay has her butt resting against the next table over, her hands resting on her belt. "So you have to tell us...what was he like?"

I think for the rest of my life, I will be constantly faced with this question.

And just the suggestion of Wrath makes my stomach knot and my insides light up. "He was as you'd expect."

Gus snorts. "Come on. That's a cop-out answer."

They're all staring at me now, waiting, ready to hang on my words. I realize that even if a person hates Wrath, they're still fascinated by him the same way people are fascinated by true crime and car accidents.

It's the mystery, the puzzle, the spectacle.

I think I better understand the way we consume everything about him. In our internet, social media world, beauty and power travel faster than anything else.

But I'm not used to the attention. Like I'm some prophet of God, the only one with the inside scoop. It feels unnatural, ill-fitting.

"He was...snarky," I admit with a smile. "Super intense though too." I suck peanut butter from my thumb. "Beyond that, he was actually..."

I trail off, the toast still clutched in my hands.

"He was what?" Gus prompts.

I was going to say *kind*, but that's not the right word. Not when he literally had me by the throat pressed against a wall. Not kind, but not vicious either. At least not toward me. Everyone else definitely got the bite of his teeth, metaphorically speaking.

But however I'd describe that, I can't admit it to these people, not when they've risked their lives for me. I don't want them thinking I've switched sides. Because I haven't. Wrath just got inside my head. And sleeping with him was a minor misstep. A moment of delirium.

Thank god no one knows about it.

"He was arrogant," I finish, because that's also true. The asshole is captivating, and he knows it.

Sanjay nods like she'd been expecting something like that and Gus plucks a slice of apple from my bowl. "Sometimes arrogant is sexy," he muses.

I frown at him.

"What?" He shrugs. "Confidence is hot."

He's not wrong. I'm also *not* admitting that.

They let me finish my snack in peace, and by the time I've popped the last bite of apple into my mouth, Adam is there, summoning me.

"Get ready," he says as we all catch the sound of some far-off humming.

"What is that?" I ask, because none of them seem to be on alert.

"Chopper," Eric answers and hurries for the door.

Gus smiles. "Come on." He grabs my hand and yanks me to the door, down the hallway. The *whump-whump* sound gets louder, closer. When we push through one of the access doors and spill into a parking lot, the helicopter is circling above, sending a gale force wind down around us.

I bring my arm up, shielding my eyes as the helicopter finally lands. Instinctively, I duck.

"This is insane!" I shout at Gus.

"I know!" He leans down and kisses my forehead. "Good luck!"

"You're not coming with?"

"I wish. I'm not special enough to meet the president."

"But—" *Neither am I.*

Standing beside me, Adam goes rigid and puts his hand up to his forehead in a salute just as a man dressed in full camouflage runs up to us.

"It's a pleasure to meet you, Sergeant Stone," the man says to Adam.

"Pleasure's all mine, Sergeant Hansen."

Once the pleasantries are over, Sergeant Hansen turns to me and holds up a weird harness he's brought with him. "I've been instructed to ask that you wear this."

"What is it?" I side-eye Adam. He seems just as surprised by this as I am. I'm not sure if that's a good sign or a bad one.

"It's witch-made," Hansen says , and points at the dagger-like object in the center of the harness. Its end is a rounded point, and while it's shaped like a blade, the material it's made from is dull. "This thing apparently helps shield you from the demon. It goes here." He taps at his sternum.

This feels sketchy all of a sudden. Wrath might have whisked me away to his castle, but he never forced me to put on a magical object. How am I to trust a stranger? Now that I know there's more to the world than just Wrath and his dark magic, I have to be careful with who I trust and what I allow them to give me. It's hard saying what this object will do—fry my uterus?

Now I sound like one of those conspiracy theory nutjobs.

Adam holds out his hand. "May I?"

Sergeant Hansen freely gives it, and Adam turns the center object over, inspecting it. When he looks over at me, I see nothing to warrant suspicion on his face. "I know of Sergeant Hansen," he says. "I would trust him with my life. It makes sense they'd have a witch on their team, and it makes sense that they'd want to protect your location if you're meeting the president."

I really appreciate Adam's logical side in this moment. I was getting ready to tell this soldier to fuck off, but Adam makes a lot of good points.

"If I refuse?" I say to Hansen.

"I'm sorry, Ms. Low, but I'm not allowed to transport you to the president without wearing the shield."

I figured as much, but it was worth a shot. "All right. How do I put it on?"

Adam holds it up so the back of the dagger object is facing me. "Arms through here," he says, and I slip into it. The harness winds around my back where two little clips lock into place.

"Good?" Adam asks.

There's no sensation, no rush or tingling. I expected to feel something. "I guess I'm good."

"Let's be on our way then," Sergeant Hansen says. "The president is ready for you."

Adam puts his hand on the small of my back and ushers me forward.

"Are you coming?" I ask him.

"Yes."

A rush of relief floods through me.

Adam puts his hand on top of my head and forces me to hunch as we approach the helicopter. There's nothing on the side of it to indicate it's a helicopter sent by the president. It's plain black with no markings.

Someone throws open the side door and a man appears wearing full military gear. He salutes Adam and Adam salutes back.

"Climb in, Ms. Low," the man says and offers me his hand for a boost up. I take it and he yanks me inside, depositing me into a bucket seat in the back. He straps me in like I'm a toddler in a high chair, then slides on a headset, adjusting a microphone so it curves toward my mouth.

When he speaks next, I hear him through the headphones. "These are to protect your ears while in flight and to allow us to communicate with one another. Any questions?"

"Umm..." My heart is racing and my hands are shaking and I feel like I've been tossed into a washing machine. Everything is happening so fast. "No," I answer.

Adam drops into the seat beside me and clips himself into the buckles. When his headset is in place, he turns to me and says, "Everything is gonna be all right, Rain."

"I believe that you believe that's true," I tell him as Sergeant Hansen takes the seat across from us and pulls the door closed. "But I'm doubtful."

Adam's team, along with Gus and Sanjay and Eric are gathered outside. As the helicopter leaves the ground, my stomach drops to my feet. Everyone waves goodbye like I'm off on a Caribbean vacation or something. Not on my way to meet the President of the United States because I'm immune to a demon who wants to use me to his advantage.

I take in a deep breath as the factory disappears from my sight and it's nothing but treetops and sky.

"Oh shit," I say, and everyone chuckles, their voices sounding directly in my ears. Adam reaches over and takes my hand, and I almost cry with relief. Adam isn't a guy that shows affection easily. I know this because Gus complains about it all of the time.

The fact that he's given me this kindness means more than I can ever express.

"Tuck in, ladies and gentlemen," one of the pilots says. "We should arrive at our destination in approximately forty-five minutes."

Oh god.

I'm going to meet the president in less than an hour?

What does she think I can do for her?

I guess I'm going to find out.

22

We land in an open field just beyond a cluster of army green tents. There's lots of activity outside, men and women in black tactical gear and soldiers in camouflage bustling from here to there. I count five tents in varying sizes. One of them is open on all sides with two giant tables beneath.

On the ground, Adam helps me out of the helicopter as the engine is cut and the rotors stop spinning. We're greeted by another soldier with broad shoulders and close-cropped dark hair. He salutes Adam and Adam salutes back.

"This way," the man says and leads us out of the field to the biggest tent in the center of the cluster. He holds back the door flap for us and ushers us inside. It's quiet and artificially lit, giving it a sharp, sterile feeling.

There's a table in the center, and more tables set up along two walls of the tent where several monitors silently play news footage and surveillance video, though I can't tell what location they're scanning.

Wrath's face flashes on the news with a headline that reads, *"Demon King Breaks Treaty."*

When the tent flap is closed behind us, Adam and our guide go rigid and salute the room.

I glance between both of them, stuck in the middle like a duck out of her pond. Am I supposed to salute? Also, what are we saluting?

Then a figure at the far table turns around, and I nearly choke on an inhale.

Naomi Wright, President of the United States, is looking at me with interest and warmth. Her dark hair is twisted up and clipped with a tortoise shell clip. Pearls dot her ears and hang around her neck, but her trademark navy blue blazer is gone and the sleeves of her white blouse are rolled up to the elbows.

There's a moment where I consider bowing to her. I won't bow to Wrath—or at least I won't outside of the bedroom—but I would most definitely bow to the president.

I'm saved from any of the awkward second-guessing by her bright smile. "Rain," she says. "How good to meet you. Come. Sit." She gestures to the chair to her right as she takes the chair at the head of the table.

I walk across the tent and sit down, heart pounding. I lick my lips, clear my throat, and say, "I'm such a big fan of yours. Like you don't even know. In our house, you were practically a god. My mom loves your work from your year of travel. She raves about it all of the time and—"

The president laughs, and the fine lines around her eyes scrunch up as she does. "Well, thank you. That means a lot coming from a Low woman. Your mother is world-renowned. She's a talented lady."

"She might keel over when I tell her you said that."

"I would love to meet her someday."

"You'll be meeting a corpse." I hear the words only after they come out of my mouth. Such an idiot! "I mean...I took that joke too far. I'm sorry. I'm nervous."

The president reaches over and takes my hand in hers. "It's okay. You've got a lot going on these days."

I snort.

Someone brings us both a cup of coffee in mugs with the presidential seal on the side. Steam rises from the dark liquid. I like mine with oatmilk, but I'm not about to get picky in the presence of the president.

"So let's talk, Rain."

"Yes. Of course. Sure, Madame President."

"Please, call me Naomi."

I laugh nervously. I'm on a first name basis with the president and the villain.

How is this my life? Just a few days ago I was taking photographs of a bratty seven-year-old, and now I'm in some secret, remote location with the leader of the free world.

My mom once wrote an article for Click magazine, and she talked about her Disaster series where she photographed landscapes after a natural disaster. "Anything can change in an instant," she said. "Everything and anything. And nothing can make you feel so small, the universe so big, *as sudden change*."

Mom was right. She was so right.

"I know everyone is interested in your connection to the Demon King," Naomi says.

"I wouldn't call it a connection."

She continues on, "But I'm more interested in who you are."

I turn the coffee mug on the table, staring at the ripples in the liquid. "I'm nobody, really. I don't know why I escaped that confrontation with Wr—the Demon King. I didn't do anything to get away. I swear it."

Naomi smiles, but it's a closed mouthed smile, and I get the feeling she's already got her own feelings and theories on this.

"Would you mind meeting a friend of mine?" she asks.

I look around the room. There are at least a dozen people in here. "Sure."

Naomi gestures with two fingers and the tent flap opens again, letting in stark daylight. A woman walks in. I only catch her silhouette at first and the shiny rings on her left hand. When the ten flap closes again and the contrast in light evens out, I finally get a good look at her face and have to bury a gasp.

There are three scars running from her forehead down the right side of her face. Three even scars that look distinctly like claw marks. They're healed now, the skin puckered white, but looking at her still makes me want to cringe just imagining the pain she must have gone through while she healed.

"*Zievata*," the woman says and gives a slight bow. When she comes back up, her wide, puffy lips are pursed in an expression of mild annoyance like she doesn't want to be here, like she has much better things to do.

"Rain, this is Sirene," the president says. "She's a witch."

A week ago, I had no idea witches existed, and now I've met three in a span of twenty-four hours. I guess when you get pulled into a world of the supernatural, you're bound to start seeing more of it. Like when you decide you want to buy a red car—suddenly there are red cars everywhere.

"Nice to meet you," I say.

Sirene nods at me, but stays at the end of the table, one hand wrapped around the other wrist.

"Sirene isn't just any witch," Naomi says. "She's familiar with Wrath."

I look at her again with new eyes. "Really? In what way?"

Did they sleep together too? She's extremely beautiful with big, bright eyes and a slight build. Much more attractive than I am, if I'm honest. The thought of her with Wrath sends a streak of jealousy through me. I don't want to share space with another woman who has known him that way.

I want to be the only one.

Goddammit. No. That's not what I want. I don't own him. And he doesn't own me.

It's not like we're exclusive boyfriend and girlfriend. Just the thought of that makes me feel stupid and weak.

"I come from Alius," Sirene answers. "A long time ago."

"Whoa. Seriously? So how does it work? How do you get here? Is there really a gate? Some mystical portal between worlds?"

Sirene grumbles low in the back of her throat. She doesn't answer me.

"I've asked Sirene here to see if she can read any magic on you," Naomi says. "It might help inform us of why you're immune to Wrath and why he now wants you."

My heart thumps hard in my chest. Up until this moment, everyone has suggested there might be more to me than first meets the eye. Magic. Special immunity. Even something inherited through my father.

I've been avoiding thinking about it as much as possible and still failed spectacularly at it. There's a nagging feeling in the back of my mind, a shadow that's screaming at me that if I look at it more closely, I'll realize everything I thought I knew about myself is wrong.

Sirene comes over to me and puts her right hand, palm up, on the table. "Give me your hand," she says.

I feel like I'm being shoved down the plank, the cold, choppy water promising my demise.

Everyone is silent and staring at me, including the President of the United States.

If I bolt, will they let me go? Doubtful. I'm like a rogue missile. They're either going to figure out how to guide me or shoot me out of the sky regardless of what I want.

As much as I respect Naomi Wright, I'm starting to worry about my own autonomy now that I'm on everyone's radar.

Whatever answers Sirene gives us, I'm worried about the lasting consequences.

I reach over and slip my hand into hers. Her cold fingers curl around me, sharp, pointed nails biting into flesh. She pins her green eyes on me and on an intake of breath, they flash brighter with magic.

I jerk, caught off guard, but her grip is strong.

The soldiers around the room tense up, ready for what, I'm not sure. Are they here to protect me or protect against me?

Goosebumps rise on my arms as the air grows charged.

My heart thumps harder as my stomach swims.

What if she finds something? What if...

She pulls away suddenly and drops my hand unceremoniously.

"Well?" Naomi asks.

I'm worried I won't hear Sirene's answer over the pounding of blood in my ears, so I focus on her mouth.

"I didn't sense any magic."

I practically melt into the chair, I'm so damn relieved. "Thank god," I say to the ceiling and then scrub my hands over my face.

It's like I've been running a marathon and have just now crossed the finish line. I can relax. I can stop worrying and wondering.

"Nothing?" Naomi asks, her brow furrowed.

"No. Nothing." The silver rings on Sirene's fingers flash as she pulls her hand back. "The girl is a red herring."

"Hey!" I say, and then, "What?"

"You know, something that is misleading or a distraction."

"It's not like I meant for this to happen."

"The light in the initial video was probably just a camera malfunction," Sirene says and snaps her fingers at one of the men behind her. "Can I have a cup of coffee?"

"So you're telling me" —Naomi leans into the table— "that Wrath's interest in Rain is a mistake? That he's been duped?"

I don't like how they keep insinuating that I'm playing some kind of game. I didn't want this.

"That's exactly what I'm saying," Sirene answers.

A murmur goes through the room as people start whispering to one another.

"Okay," Naomi says, her gaze unfocused. "Okay, so..." She pushes away from the table and starts to pace back and forth in the tent.

I'm not special.

I was just in the wrong place at the wrong time.

This is what I wanted, isn't it?

So why does it feel like I've been gutted? Why does it feel like something has been ripped from my body?

"Madame President," a man in full military uniform says, "we could still use her to our advantage."

"I'm not a chess piece," I say, and Sirene looks at me down the straight line of her nose.

"What are you suggesting, General Briggs?" Naomi asks.

"He's suggesting you use her as bait," Sirene answers.

"That didn't exactly turn out well the last time," I say to Adam, but no one seems to care what my opinion is.

Naomi holds up her hand, as if she's a teacher trying to silence a rowdy student, but this is my life we're talking about.

"He can't be killed," I say. "Using me as bait would be pointless."

"He *can* be killed," Sirene says.

"He...what?" The churning of my stomach turns to knots, and suddenly I'm sick with dread. "How?"

"Magic. And a blade."

I swallow hard. "If you already know that, then you don't need me."

"We can't get close, Ms. Low," General Briggs says. "But perhaps you could."

I lick my lips, but my tongue is suddenly dry, raw. "Are you saying...you want me to kill him?"

Holy shit. They're insane. And I'm in fucking trouble.

"I can't do that."

"That's probably true," Sirene says.

"Rain," Naomi starts, but I no longer care that I'm sitting

beside the President of the United States. Not when they're suggesting I risk my own life against Wrath, no less.

"I'm not doing this." I shove the chair back, and several of the soldiers shift, blocking the president from me. Adam comes up behind me and puts a hand on my shoulder, grounding me, reminding me of who I am and where I am.

"It's okay," he says beneath his breath.

Naomi tells the soldiers to stand down and they fall back. "Rain, can we take a walk?"

I look at Adam over my shoulder. "I'll come with you," he says, and knowing he'll be there, I nod.

The tent flap is pulled open for us and Naomi ducks out first. The air is cool for the middle of the summer, and I wonder if there's rain on the horizon. I'm not even sure where we are, or what state we're in, and even if I did, I haven't checked the weather in a while. I used to check it almost every day to prepare for photo sessions.

So much of my normal life has completely fallen by the wayside. In fact, I still have photos to finish processing from my session before the last.

Naomi leads us away from the tents and down a dirt road. There's a strip of grass and weeds down the center of it, and we keep that between us as we walk.

"You're in an impossible situation, Rain," Naomi says. "And I don't envy you."

Several soldiers follow us, but they keep their distance. Adam is at least ten paces behind us.

"I know what we're asking of you seems not only dangerous, but outlandish, *impossible*."

I fold my arms over my chest. "I'm a photographer, and you're asking me to kill someone."

"Not someone." She tips her head to look at me. "A bad guy. An infiltrator. A *demon*." She laughs to herself. "When I ran for president, I thought I understood our enemies. Terrorism. Foreign dictators. Political opponents. I had no clue what I was getting myself into."

"I suppose it's made worse by the internet turning Wrath into a celebrity."

She slides her hands into the pockets of her navy blue chinos. "I'm not surprised by it. The mundane things, the things that matter like green energy and infrastructure, they aren't pretty."

Pretty like Wrath. Not just pretty—*otherworldly gorgeous. A work of art.*

"Are you worried at all about where he came from? This Alius? Do you know about it? How did you even find Sirene?"

Naomi keeps her gaze trained straight ahead. "I wish I could tell you, but it's classified."

That's another sentence I never thought I'd hear someone utter within earshot.

"Someone that works for Wrath," I start, "she suggested there's more going on. I don't know what, but I got the impression that Wrath might just be the beginning."

Naomi nods. "We've had to cover a lot of ground in a very short amount of time, but we're learning, thanks to people like Sirene. Right now we're working to identify others like her who are magical or who have knowledge. It's a work in progress, of course, but in the meantime, we need to deal with Wrath before he gets too far ahead of us."

Deal with him.

Kill him.

I huff out a breath and continue walking. I don't know how long this dirt road is, but I have half a mind to follow it to the end. Maybe leave my problems behind and see what new life I can find at the other end.

"Is there more you know about Wrath?" I ask. I think she knows I'm looking for an excuse, any excuse to follow through with their request.

I know he's the villain. I know he's done bad things, killed people, but even knowing that, the thought of ending him just makes me want to...*break*.

"We think he's building an army," Naomi answers. "And he's planning something big."

"How do you know?"

"We have surveillance on him," she answers. "He's been busy."

"I don't think he's building an army. I mean..." I trail off as a memory jars my train of thought. When I was listening at the bedroom door, Arthur and Wrath said something about soldiers. Something about them being ready within a week.

Oh crap. If Wrath stages a bigger confrontation, if it's more than just him facing off against the military, he really could take over the country. Put a throne at the White House and make us all bow at his feet.

"Do you know how to find him again?" Naomi asks.

I look across the field as the breeze shifts and the wildflowers sway. That field would make a perfect spot for a family session. Several days ago, I hated my job, and now I long to have the camera back in my hand if only to feel normal again.

I want things to be normal again. I want to stop worrying about magic and demons.

"I don't think I'd have to go to him," I answer. "I think he'd come to me."

"Really?"

I nod. "When I was attacked at my condo, Wrath showed up to save me. And when I stayed at my friend Harper's, he found me there too. I think he can find me wherever I am. Somehow."

"I suppose it's a good thing you're wearing the harness Sirene made."

I run a finger under one of the straps. "I suppose so."

We keep walking.

"So this blade..." I start. "How sure are you that it'll work?"

"The blade was crafted with Sirene's help," Naomi explains. "She assures us it'll kill Wrath."

"Easily? Quickly?"

"I believe so, yes. The main thing will be wounding him so he's weakened. Then my team will come in to mop up."

Mop up. Like it's a ketchup spill at a diner.

"What if he figures me out? What if he tries to possess me?" I look over at her. "What if I miss?"

"I have faith you won't."

Wrath's words come back to me. *She stays until I figure out how to use her to my advantage.*

He might not have been plotting my murder, but it wasn't like he cared what happened to me in the long run.

Wrath is merciless. Powerful. Domineering.

I have no doubt that if the roles were reversed, he'd take me out without a second thought.

For a brief moment, I thought maybe he did care about me in some weird, twisted way, but now I realize his heart is dead—if he has one at all. He's a monster from another world and he's on a mission. He was planning to use me however he could, while fucking me to make me pliant. Because he thinks I'm just a weak, mindless girl who worships him. A *dieva.*

The fire reignites in the hollows between my ribs, and I drop my arms, hands tightening into fists.

Wrath wants to use me. The general of the fucking Army wants to use me.

But what do I want?

I don't want to worry about fanatics chasing me or trying to kill me.

I don't want to worry about a sinfully sexy demon appearing in my bedroom to—

I want him to be gone. But he's never going to let me go. He thinks he can use me, and no matter what I say or do, he's not going to believe that I'm no one special.

Which means, if I want my old life back, I have to fight.

I have to face off with the villain.

"Okay," I say.

"Okay?" Naomi echoes.

I nod. "I'll do it."

She comes to a stop and faces me. "Rain, I don't think you know just how much your country needs you right now, and how grateful it is to have you."

It feels like a bullshit line. "I just hope I don't screw it up."

"Don't worry." She reaches over to tenderly squeeze my arm. "We'll have your back the entire time."

23

We return to the cluster of tents but go inside a secondary tent. This one is mostly empty save for a few chairs, a table, a mirror, and a metal clothing rack. There's a single shirt hanging from it.

Two hard-shell briefcases are open on the table, revealing their contents. It looks like a bunch of surveillance equipment.

Naomi sits in one of the chairs while Sergeant Hansen preps the equipment. Sirene is there too, but she stands beside the mirror, one arm folded over her middle, the other hand curled along her jaw, eyes assessing me.

"We'll put a wire on you," Naomi explains, "so that our team can step in should you need it."

Blood rushes to my cheeks. I hope Wrath keeps it PG. I hope he doesn't mention what we did.

"Sirene?" Naomi prompts.

Sirene waves her hand in the air and mutters something beneath her breath.

"Good?" Naomi asks, and Sirene nods. "You can go ahead and remove the harness, Sergeant Hansen."

He comes around behind me and unclips it, and the harness slides off my arms.

"Is this okay?" I ask before removing it entirely.

"Sirene has put up a shield around us," Naomi says. "So the harness is redundant."

Hansen sets it on the table, then picks up a tiny object from one of the briefcases. "This is a microphone," he says and then goes to the hanging shirt. "It'll be threaded through here." He opens one of the ruffles along the collar and threads the microphone into place. It's certainly more discreet than what I pictured.

When he's done, Hansen pulls the hanger from the shirt and holds it up before me. They all stare at me, waiting.

I guess I'm stripping in front of the President of the United States. No biggie.

I pull my t-shirt off and toss it to the table. Hansen opens the collar for me so I can stick my head through, then my arms. He checks the microphone again before flicking on a device in the briefcase. A screen embedded in the case's shell lights up.

"Testing one, two, three," he says, and the screen dances with the audio.

"We good?" Naomi says.

Hansen nods. "We're good. Here, Rain." He holds up the harness once again. I guess my Sirene barrier doesn't travel with me. Pity. The harness is already feeling like a collar.

The president stands and makes her way to the door. "Now let's go get that blade."

As we cross the clearing, I catch a shift of shadows out of the corner of my eye.

My heart leaps to my throat, and I let out a strangled cry.

Everyone is immediately on alert.

"What is it?" one of the soldiers asks as he trains his gun on the surrounding woods.

"I..." I swallow the lump rising in my throat. There's nothing there. "Sorry. I thought I saw shadows."

"Scan the perimeter," the guy says, and the soldiers fan out.

"Sorry," I say to the president. "I'm just—"

"Where are you, *dieva*?"

His voice comes to me like a fever dream.

I dance to the side as if he's behind me. There's no one there.

"Rain?" the president says.

There's an itch between my shoulder blades, right where my birthmark lies.

"When I find you, *dieva*," Wrath says, "I'm going to make you pay for this."

"Fuck," I say and leap to the side again.

"What's happening?" Naomi asks.

Sirene steps in front of me and snaps her fingers in my face. "Focus."

"What? I'm trying...I keep hearing him."

"Has he found her location?" Naomi asks as her secret service agents tighten in around her.

"I don't think so," Sirene answers, narrowing her eyes, "but I think there's a connection open between them."

"How?" I ask, voice shaking.

Sirene purses her mouth. She doesn't answer.

That might explain why I saw Wrath in the factory my first night there. He came to me then too, but was nowhere to be found after.

"He's trying to find me," I decide, and Sirene nods.

I rake my teeth over my lip as the soldiers return to us. "All clear," one of them says.

"Let's get this going," I say. "The sooner he's gone..."

"The sooner he's gone the better," Naomi finishes. "Come."

We go to the tent that's open on three sides. Adam is there with the general and another man that is vaguely familiar. They're standing around a table.

When we approach, they step back, and I get a better look at the third man. He's sun-kissed, hair coiffed, and body toned. His black suit probably cost more than my condo, and when he smiles at me, it's like looking into the sun.

It takes me another second to pinpoint him. It's Harper's dad, Niles Caldwell.

"Rain," he says and offers me his hand. We shake. His grip is firm and energetic. "It's nice to see you again. I wish it was under different circumstances."

"Likewise," I answer, because it's the polite thing to do. I've never liked Mr. Caldwell, even though I barely know him. He's just always rubbed me the wrong way. "I didn't think I'd be seeing you here."

He slides his hands into the pockets of his expensive trousers. "I've been by Naomi's side since this demon infiltrated our country." His expression darkens. "I wouldn't miss this for the world."

"Take a look at this, Rain," Adam says and nods at the table.

I find another rectangular hard-shell case open in the center with a blade nestled in thick, gray foam inside. The dagger isn't as big as I thought it'd be. More of a steak knife.

"This is it?" I ask.

General Briggs nods and gently pulls the weapon from its foam nest. The blade is made of some kind of metal that's nearly black so even as he turns it this way and that, the blade barely shines in the light.

"You'll wear a sheath on your forearm," Briggs says, "so it'll be easy to access the weapon when you're close enough to the demon."

My stomach churns just thinking about it. "What if he finds the blade before I get to it?"

"Don't let him touch you," Briggs says, leveling his hooded gaze at me, as if he's insinuating that I'm some simpering woman who can barely control herself around Wrath.

Well, I did end up in his bed.

But no. That was a lapse in judgment.

"Give me your arm," Briggs says.

I hold it out and shove up the sleeve of the borrowed blouse. Briggs straps a black nylon sheath to my forearm, then slides the blade carefully inside. When he tugs the sleeve back down, the blade and the sheath all but disappear.

Clearly they chose this blouse for this reason, to hide all of the things we'll use against Wrath.

Why do I suddenly feel a thread of shame? Like I'm betraying him?

I don't like it. Maybe he really has messed with my head, like some kind of twisted Stockholm Syndrome.

"Now what?" I ask.

"Now you wait while we prepare and get into position." Briggs gives a quick nod to Hansen, who hurries away. "Care to join us?" he says to Adam.

"If you'll have me," Adam answers.

"We can always use more men like you, Sergeant Stone. Suit up."

Adam starts moving away, but I grab him by the arm. "Can I talk to you for a sec?"

He eyes Briggs and Naomi over my shoulder, almost like he's waiting for permission. He must get it, because he says, "Of course," and leads me away from the tent, but not far enough away that we're out of sight.

My birthmark itches again, and Wrath's voice sounds in my head. "Oh the things I'll do to you, *dieva*."

Son of a bitch.

Hands on his hips, Adam says, "What's up?" as I fidget in front of him, trying to shove away the demon in my head.

"Can you like...I don't know...talk me off the ledge? Because I'm sorta starting to freak out, and usually it's Gus that I go to when I need someone, and he's clearly not here and—"

Adam smiles, and I see the light of it in his eyes. "Gus is good at alleviating stress and anxiety."

"I wish he was here right now. No offense."

"None taken."

"It's just...I didn't sign up for this, you know? I'm no killer."

"But Wrath is." All of the joy is gone from Adam's face. The soldier with a mission is back and he has a really good point.

"Yeah, that's true."

Adam puts his hands on my shoulders and gives me a light squeeze. "You can do this, Rain." For someone usually so detached and emotionless, the conviction in Adam's voice almost catches me off guard. He believes in me. Adam, badass soldier, leader of a demon resistance, believes in me.

So why don't I believe in myself?

"I'll be there if you need help," Adam goes on. "So will Sergeant Hansen and several other well qualified soldiers."

"Adam," I say, almost like a whine.

"Yes?" he says.

There are so many things I want to say but don't know how.

I slept with Wrath. He saved me. Multiple times. I feel an odd sort of connection with him.

And this...this doesn't feel right, but I don't know why and I don't know how to stop it, and even if I admitted any of that, Adam would never look at me the same again, and while we're not exactly best friends, I want his respect.

Adam is a good guy. I see that now. And my best friend is lucky to have him.

I just want this to be over so everything can go back to normal.

"Rain?" Adam says, frowning.

"It's nothing. Just nerves, ya know?"

He gives me a quick nod but the frown stays. "How about some practical advice."

"I'd love some."

He takes my hand and guides it to the bottom of his rib cage. "Feel this?"

"Yeah."

"When you're ready to take the shot, aim up from here. Up beneath the rib cage and straight through the heart. Okay? It's unlikely you can get through the ribs, so don't stab *at* the heart."

"Okay. Thanks."

He pulls away. "You've got this, Rain. You're about to save the world."

I snort. "You better throw me a party. I want karaoke and party hats."

He laughs as he jogs away, leaving me alone beside the tents, a magical dagger strapped to my forearm, and a whole lot of doubt churning in my gut.

I spend the rest of the afternoon pacing around the field. I don't know how long it takes to get a team of soldiers ready, but apparently several hours because by the time we pile into several black SUVs, the daylight is fading beneath the tree line.

We take the dirt road out of the hidden location and bump along. The president, along with Senator Caldwell, has already been whisked away on the helicopter, with plans to listen in on the audio from some remote location.

My heart won't stop hammering in my chest.

My knee jiggles as we drive, and I can't stop tugging at the sleeve of my blouse.

Sirene sits next to me. Adam is in the passenger seat with Sergeant Hansen behind the wheel. This is all happening so fast.

"So," I say to Sirene, trying to fill the awkward silence, "you're from that other world? Alius?"

She turns to look at me but says nothing.

I bury a shiver. Sirene makes me squeamish. She's intimidating as hell. Is it a witch thing? Maybe knowing they can do magic makes them scarier? Kat was intimidating too, but not like this.

"How long have you been here?" I try instead.

"A long time," Sirene answers.

"How did you get here?"

"A traveler."

"What's that?"

"A person who travels."

I grimace, feeling Sirene's weariness chafing. I may be stubborn, and sometimes yes, a bit standoffish, but generally speaking, I'm a likeable person. And Sirene clearly does not like me.

"How long have you been working for the government?"

"A long time," she says again.

"Ooookay," I say. "Do they not teach you conversation skills in Alius?"

She looks at me again, and I swear her eyes flash. "In my world, they teach you worthwhile skills, like how to cut out tongues of pretty little girls."

I snort. "*Dieva*."

She goes rigid beside me. "What did you say?"

"*Dieva*? Am I pronouncing that wrong?"

"Where did you hear that?"

She turns in her seat, back pressed against the car door, eyes narrowed.

"It's what Wrath calls me. Why? He said it means 'little girl.'"

"That's not what it means."

I sense Adam and Hansen's interest piquing.

"Okay, so what does it mean?"

She inhales through her nose, nostrils flaring before she answers, "It's a term that denotes ownership over something."

I grumble. “He was lying to me? Of course he was. I shouldn’t be surprised. What a prick.” I shake my head and brush it off, but Sirene is still staring at me. “What?”

“I don’t think you understand, *little girl.*”

“Okay, then *make* me understand.”

“In Alius, calling *dieva* means you’ve claimed someone as yours. It is an unbreakable oath. It means that when a person has called *dieva,* they will do anything in their power to protect what is theirs.”

Adam shifts in his seat, tilting his head our way.

“In Alius, lesser men have gone to war over *dieva,*” Sirene says.

“Lesser men?”

“In all of my years, I have never seen Wrath or any of the royal line call *dieva.*” There’s a flash of emotion on her face, something that looks an awful lot like jealousy. “They’ve never wanted something that badly.”

A shiver races down my spine, and I swallow hard around a lump quickly growing in my throat. There are firecrackers in my veins and fizz in my lungs.

Wrath has claimed me as *his.*

The fizzing warmth sinks between my legs, and I get a flash of Wrath fucking me, of him filling me up, of him taking a fistful of my hair—

I clench my teeth as I hear the echo of his voice in my head. *Oh dieva, this changes everything.*

24

It takes us nearly two hours to return to Norton Harbor by car, and by then, it's well after dark. As usual, Norton is lit up and partying despite the fact that it's a Sunday night. Hansen skirts around downtown Norton and starts heading south. We finally pull over along the curb on the edge of town. There are no houses way out here, only fields and woods.

"Here?" I ask.

The whole point of this is to face off with Wrath, but this feels like the wrong place for it.

"You'll get out and walk from here," Hansen instructs. "Head toward Riverside Park."

Riverside Park. I almost laugh. It was just a few days ago that I was doing a family session there, chasing Josiah the demon child.

Now I'm facing off with a bigger demon.

"So when I get to Riverside, then what?"

Hansen eyes me in the rearview mirror. "Go to the fountain and start walking south and take off your harness. Be sure to toss it into the bushes, somewhere out of sight. We'll retrieve it later. Once the harness is off, keep walking. We'll track you as you progress through the park. Depending on how long it takes the demon to come to you, if you make it to the end of Riverside, circle back, but don't go north of the fountain. Understood?"

I nod. "And when he comes?"

"Say whatever you need to say to get close," Hansen says.

"Then use the dagger the way I showed you," Adam adds.

He says it like it'll be easy.

"Okay. So...should I get out now?"

They're all looking at me, half their faces highlighted by the soft amber glow of the dashboard, the other half hidden in shadow.

"Whenever you're ready," Adam says.

I give one quick nod, inhale deeply, and then open the door.

The sooner I get this over with, the sooner I can go back to my normal life. Whatever that is now.

Riverside is usually dead this time of night. Most tourists stick to downtown and Harbor Day Park alongside the lake. Riverside is for kids and picnics and family photo sessions. It has the most gorgeous fields that border federal land on the south side of the park. I've done countless photo sessions here.

I enter the park by the row of sculpted hedges and make my way to the fountain, heart racing the entire way. Even though I'm still wearing the harness, I feel exposed, vulnerable, and if I'm honest, excited.

Not because I'm supposed to stab Wrath, but because—

He claimed me.

I don't know how I'm supposed to feel about that. Probably not like I'm on cloud nine.

Probably not like I've been given a crown.

But...it probably just means he sees me as property to do with as he pleases. I should have asked Sirene for more details, but I was already embarrassed by the topic in front of Adam. I don't want him thinking I've jumped ship.

Have I?

My hands shake at my sides as the fountain comes into sight. There's a lamppost just beyond it casting a halo of light. Spray from the water glitters in the air.

It's getting harder to breathe, my heart is beating so fast.

When the plain cement footpath gives way to the designed cobblestone of the fountain pad, my hands turn slick with sweat. The government wouldn't send me into the middle of a fight with a defunct weapon, would they?

This has to work.

And the thought of it working makes me want to vomit.

If I manage to pierce his flesh, send the blade to his heart...

He'll be gone.

I nearly sob thinking about it.

Once I pass the fountain and head south as instructed, I pull my arms out of the harness and twist it around, unclipping it. When I hit the next footpath and the foliage crowds in around me, I toss the harness to the underbrush.

Blood rushes to my ears. My heart is beating so hard, I can feel it in my tongue.

Fuck, fuck, fuck.

What am I going to say if he shows up?

Oh the things I'll do to you, dieva.

I ran from him—again. Is he going to be pissed? Maybe I'll—

The hair lifts on the nape of my neck. I get the distinct feeling a spider is crawling over my back.

I still in the middle of the footpath.

He's here.

The Demon King has come for me.

25

"Why do you keep running from me, *dieva*?"

As soon as his quiet, smoky voice finds me in the semi-darkness, goosebumps pop on my skin and a shiver rolls down my spine.

But there's a surge of adrenaline, too, that leaves me a little giddy.

Being around Wrath is like being caught in canyon rapids. It's a rush of exhilaration and fear. And maybe like with white water rafting, being with Wrath is like toeing the very thin line between living and dying.

"You keep giving me reasons to run," I say, my back still to him.

My heart is thudding in my chest and in my head. If I turn around now, he's going to see my hands shaking.

Will he be able to make out the shape of the dagger strapped to my forearm?

The air snaps and I suck in a breath, knowing what's coming.

Wrath reappears in front of me shrouded in black mist. "What reason did you have this time?" he asks with a thread of sarcasm, as if no reason could ever be good enough.

"You've been using me." If I latch on to that, embrace the anger, then I can do what I need to do.

If I become the rage, maybe I can ignore the desire.

"How so, *dieva*?" He takes a step. "You seemed happy to be in my bed."

Fucking hell. Everyone on the comm system now knows I screwed the Demon King. Embarrassment flares in my cheeks. Thank god for the darkness.

Does Wrath know they're listening? I have the distinct feeling he just moved a chess piece on the game board, a move that has blocked me in.

I decide dodging is better than confronting it. "What are you even doing here? What do you want with me?"

"Come with me, and I'll tell you."

I snort. "I'm not going anywhere with you." I put as much conviction in my voice as I can, just so Adam and the rest of the team know I'm serious.

I haven't fallen for the dark power of the Demon King.

I'm not under his spell.

Wrath takes another step, and a ray of moonlight illuminates half his face. Every time I look at him, his beauty catches me off guard. Every. Single. Time.

Focus.

"Why side with them?" he asks.

The way he lifts his chin makes me think he knows Adam and Sergeant Hansen and the rest are somewhere in the surrounding woods.

"Why side with you?"

He comes closer still. There's now three feet between us. He's close enough to touch if I reached out with my hand, but maybe not close enough to stab through the heart.

"I don't care about your power," I say, trying to distract him.

"You think this is about power?"

"Isn't it?"

He takes a step to the left, keeping the same distance between us. His head is bowed, the moonlight rimming him in silver. "No, *dieva*," he says. "This is a tale as old as time."

I lick my lips. "What do you mean?"

"It's a story of revenge."

"I don't understand." He's circling me now, and I follow his movements. I don't want him at my back.

"And I don't trust you enough to tell you," he answers.

That catches me off guard. I'm a trustworthy person, goddammit. I don't tell secrets. I don't stab people in the back.

Well...except for Wrath apparently. Maybe he's not so far off.

"I thought you were looking for something?" I ask.

"I am."

"And have you found it?"

He stops, and I stop with him. He lifts his head and looks over at me through a lock of hair that's fallen over his forehead. "I think I have, yes."

I get the distinct impression he means me.

"I don't have magic," I blurt. "I'm not who you think I am."

He frowns.

"Sirene tested me," I say.

His expression darkens, and his eyes dart to the woods. "You saw Sirene? Is she here?"

So she wasn't lying about knowing Wrath.

"Why would she be here?" I ask.

Wrath turns back to me, eyes narrowed. "You've brought friends with you, *dieva*. Did you think I wouldn't notice?"

A breath stutters up my throat as the darkness kicks up around him like a storm cloud blotting out the moonlight.

The night goes silent and still like a jungle when a predator stalks through.

All of the men and women that are part of Naomi's team might be highly trained soldiers, but I think they know, whether consciously or subconsciously, that here, now, next to the Demon King, they are very clearly prey.

I backpedal when the darkness takes on the shape of men.

The *norrow.*

The shadows solidify, and the enslaved soldiers dart across the field like specters from a nightmare.

Grown men, trained to kill, scream in the night.

Bullets fly and the gunfire flashes in the dark.

Wrath charges me, his face shifting to the sharp monster he hides beneath that beauty. And when his eyes flare red with a predatory glow, I can't help but scream.

26

WHEN IT WAS JUST ME AND WRATH, IT WAS EASY TO FORGET ABOUT THE monsters he controlled, about the dark magic he possessed, and the monster he can become.

He manipulated me into believing maybe he wasn't as bad as I first thought.

I grew complacent, lulled by the beauty and the power.

But now as he bears down on me, I can't deny it any longer.

Wrath is the villain.

And I am his enemy.

The darkness sharpens around him as I reach for the blade hidden in my sleeve. The hilt is easy to find beneath the gauzy material, and I wrap my hand around it, sliding it from its sheath. The black metal barely glints. It's a weapon as dark as Wrath.

More gunfire sounds from the woods, and I have a split second to wonder about stray bullets when Wrath slams into me.

The darkness swallows me up.

I can't let him win.

Tightening my hold on the blade, I angle it between us and shove up beneath his rib cage just like Adam taught me.

Wrath roars as something hot and wet runs down my arm, soaking the material of my borrowed blouse.

There's a moment of triumph—the blade worked, I did what no one else could do—and then—

Blinding white pain.

Pain that lances through me like a thousand needles burns at my nerve endings like a wick lit by a match.

I scream.

I scream and scream and scream.

Wrath grabs hold of me because I'm falling, falling—

"Rain!" he shouts. His darkness caresses my skin and the pain ebbs to something manageable.

Tears blur my vision as I look up at him. "What's happening?" I pant. I can't catch my breath. I can't seem to fill my lungs and everything aches.

"I don't know," he answers, his arm held tight beneath his ribs. He's still bleeding, but the knife is gone.

I hear movement in the brush, and then several glowing red dots appear on Wrath's chest.

"Fire!" someone yells.

Wrath grits his teeth and the air snaps as he disappears. Bullets *pop-pop* through the night.

"Wait!" I scurry up but keep my head down. "Stop!"

Pop.

A bullet hits me in the shoulder, throwing me back. Blood soaks through my shirt.

I've been shot. Fuck, I've been shot!

I clutch at the wound as if I can keep the blood from gushing out of me. The pain comes several seconds later and throbs through my shoulder and down across my chest. I have to grit my teeth from crying out.

Wrath reappears next to me, paler than normal and coughing up blood.

Holy shit.

There's a matching bullet wound in his shoulder.

I look down at my torso at where the initial pain radiated from and see blood slowly staining my shirt. I quickly yank the hem back to reveal a gaping stab wound right beneath my rib cage.

Holy fucking shit.

"Stop shooting!" I yell as Wrath collapses on me. "I'm wounded! We're somehow connected!"

The soldiers go quiet.

My breath wheezes out past wet lips as Wrath's weight falls on me.

"Rain," he says, voice hoarse.

"No," I say to him. "Don't *Rain* me. You're the bad guy here!"

"Rain," he says again, teeth clenched now as he wraps his bloody hand around my wrist.

"What?"

A dozen red dots appear on my chest.

Fuck.

"Get down," Wrath grits out.

Oh god. This can't be happening.

"Please!" I cry out.

"Stop firing!" Adam yells.

But Adam doesn't control this team, and no one listens to his order.

The *pop-pop* of bullets fills the night.

I'm the enemy now.

They think I'm the enemy.

I'm going to die. I'm going to die standing next to the Demon King, and the entire world is going to think I was somehow his accomplice, and Gus and my mom—

No.

No. Fuck that.

How dare they turn on me!

I'm seething. Filled with fire. Boiling with rage.

I may not be a heroine, but I'm not the villain's pawn either.

A sharp breeze cuts through the field and a roaring sound fills my head.

My hair flies around my face.

Bright red light flashes in the night and fire kicks up, eating away at the grass, spreading out like a ripple in a lake, consuming everything in front of it. Voices shout as the soldiers run.

Smoke plumes in the air, embers raining down around us.

And it isn't until Wrath shouts my name that I realize...

I'm floating.

Panic cuts through me, and I scrabble at the air. Wrath grabs hold of my arm and yanks me down into his grip.

"We have to go," he yells as the roar of the fire builds, flames licking up the surrounding tree trunks.

"But—"

"Rain," he says, pinning me with his gaze, "they will kill you."

The reality of it finally seeps in and tears burn in my eyes. "No," I say.

"Yes."

He's right. He's fucking right.

They were going to kill me before the fire, before Wrath...was that Wrath? I've never seen him use that power before and—

What is happening? My head is pounding and I'm so cold, I'm shivering.

"Come with me," Wrath says as he grits his teeth. There's violence painted across his face in splatters of blood and murder in his eyes. "*Dieva.*"

I look around the clearing. It's only a matter of time until they put the fire out, until someone gets a shot lined up and...they want Wrath dead. And all they have to do to take him out now is kill me.

They wanted to find his weakness, and now they've got it.

My world shifts, and I lose my balance. Wrath winds an arm around my waist.

"Come with me," he says again.

The way he looks at me, it's with panic and hope and fear and *desire.*

No one has been able to get to him until now.

No one other than me has been able to get beneath his skin.

And I think he's afraid. But more than that, I think he's a little bit captivated too.

It's in this moment that I realize I've become an enigma to him, just as much as he is for me.

In some weird, twisted way, we're equals.

And now I can't walk away. I can't run away.

But still...he's giving me a choice.

And I already know what the answer is.

"Okay."

The Demon King tightens his hold on me as the air cracks open and he pulls us away.

27

We crash to the ground in the alley where we first met.

Everything is coming full circle, apparently.

"What's wrong?" I ask when Wrath falls to his knees. "We have to get back to your house. We'll be spotted here."

It's only a matter of time until someone recognizes Wrath, or hell, me, and word spreads. I have no doubt Naomi and her team can get more soldiers here within minutes.

"I can't," Wrath grits out. Pain is etched around his eyes.

"Why not?"

"Because I've been stabbed, *dieva*," he says sharply. "And shot, apparently."

"Well, so have I. Apparently. But you don't see me collapsing to the ground."

He looks up at me, eyes narrowed, face sharpening. The monster is throbbing in the bright red of his irises, but the blackness that usually trails off of him is growing paler by the second.

Something is very, very wrong.

Is he dying? Because of me?

I can't let that happen. I can't look at the reasons too closely either, otherwise I might scream or cry.

"Can you get us to my building?" I ask and get my shoulder beneath him so I can help get him to his feet.

"Yes."

Before I even have time to prepare, he pulls us away again. We collapse into the hallway outside my condo. "Come on." We stumble down the hallway to the door marked 404. I knock loudly. "Mrs. Mulhang! It's Rain. I need your help."

Wrath leans against the doorframe, blood still dripping from his wounds. He's not looking good.

"Mrs. Mulhang!"

The door yanks open. "What is—oh. Rain?" Her eyes dart from me to Wrath before she slides her glasses on. "Oh dear." A silky green kimono robe is tied tight around her petite frame. Her hair is mussed like she just crawled out of bed. What time is it anyway? I don't even know.

"I need your car," I say quickly.

"My car? But—"

"Please, Mrs. Mulhang."

She cups her hand around her mouth, and whispers, "That's the Demon King."

"I know."

Wrath grumbles, his arm held tightly over his midsection.

"I need your car. Please. I'll owe you big time."

She frowns at me but nods. "Give me a second." I watch her shuffle down the hallway to a ceramic dish that sits on the hall table. She plucks the key fob from it and brings it back. "Here. There are two wool blankets in the trunk. Put them over the seats. I don't want blood stains on my leather."

"Of course." I'm so relieved I want to kiss the woman. "You have no idea how much this means to me."

She frowns. "I hope you know what you're getting into, dear."

I look over at Wrath hunched against the door, and the sight of him vulnerable, bleeding, dependent on me...it makes me want to burn down the world to save him.

We leave Mrs. Mulhang and take the elevator down to the garage. I send up a silent prayer, hoping we don't run into anyone. When we get down to the garage, we find it blissfully empty and quiet.

I spread out the blankets on both bucket seats and then get Wrath into the passenger seat. I hurry around to the driver's side. My own pain is just a dull ache now, and my wounds have stopped bleeding, so I guess that's a good sign.

"Hold on," I tell him as I tear out of the parking garage.

28

I DON'T KNOW HOW IT WORKS, BUT I FIND THE CASTLE EASILY AND PULL down the winding driveway, going much faster than I should.

When I come around in front of the house, gravel sprays behind my tires. I slam on the brakes, slide to the left, and finally come to a stop.

"You are a horrible driver, *dieva*," Wrath mutters, slumped over in the passenger seat.

"Shut up. I got you home in one piece, didn't I?"

"Debatable."

As I come around to the passenger side, Arthur runs from the house. "What happened?" he asks and shoots me an accusatory look. Shame festers in my gut.

With Arthur's help, Wrath climbs from the Audi. "Where's Lauren?"

As if summoned, Lauren appears in the doorway. "What the hell happened to you?"

"I'll fill you in while you heal me," he says.

They can do that?

"And her?" Lauren gestures to me with a dismissive wave of her hand.

Wrath looks at me over his shoulder. There's still blood splattered across his face.

"Looks like Rain has been keeping secrets from us."

"Excuse me?" I say.

"She has the *animus*," he says, and Arthur and Lauren look at me wide-eyed.

"The what?"

They ignore me.

Lauren makes a face like she just smelled something rancid. "How did she manage that?"

"I don't know," Wrath answers as Arthur helps him up the stairs.

"What the hell is this *animus* anyway?" I ask.

Hands on her hips, Lauren says, "The *animus* is a part of the trine of the Demon King's power. It was stolen from Wrath a long time ago and he wants it back."

"What?" I shout. "I don't have power. A witch tested me. She didn't find anything."

"Sirene was lying," Wrath says.

"Why would she do that?"

"Because Sirene wants the *animus* for herself." He groans as Arthur gets him in the door.

"Why?"

"When a royal demon is given the title of king, he inherits the Triad of Power," Lauren explains.

"Okay."

She lifts a finger. "One, the *oculus*. The ability to control minds."

"Has he been controlling me this entire time?"

Wrath snorts. "Would that make you feel better about what we did, *dieva*?"

"Two," Lauren goes on, "the *dominus*. The ability to hold dominion over other demons. And lastly, the *animus*."

"Which does what?"

"Think of it like this," she says. "The *oculus* is the king's scepter. The *dominus* is the king's throne." She narrows her eyes at me. "And the *animus*, that's the king's crown. It's called the Hellfire Crown."

I suddenly feel a little woozy. "Why?" I suspect I already know the answer.

"Because it burns whatever it touches."

No. No. I don't buy that. That sounds absolutely insane. Me, in possession of the Demon King's crown?

I don't believe—

The light.

The fire.

The heat at my center.

The constant, familiar rage.

The way I immediately reach for the heat, the urge to burn.

That's been with me since birth.

The fiery Aries, my mom always said.

No. Please, for the love of god.

"I'm sure you can put two and two together," Lauren goes on. "Wrath came here for his crown, and he'll do whatever it takes to get it back."

I'm so fucking screwed.

SINFUL DEMON KING

1

I'M A FUGITIVE IN MY OWN DAMN COUNTRY, AND I'VE TAKEN REFUGE IN the villain's castle.

How the hell did I get to this place? Oh right, I apparently possess the Demon King's Hellfire Crown, and now he wants it back.

I sit up in the bed I've been given in Wrath's castle and scrub at my face, groaning into my hand.

There are online Wrath fan clubs and demon devotees chasing sightings of him all around the world. Literally thousands of people who would kill to be where I am, living in a house with the Demon King close by, in possession of the one thing he wants...but those people are idiots.

Living with Wrath is like living with a serpent. It's all fun and games until someone gets bit. And that someone will be me.

My bedroom door bursts open, and Lauren, one of Wrath's demons, barrels inside.

"Can you please knock?" I say, pulling myself up against the mammoth headboard.

Even though it's still dark in my room, I swear I can see her eyes rolling. She crosses the room, grabs the thick velvet drapes and yanks them open.

I grimace as I bring my arm up to shield my eyes. "Was that really necessary?"

She stands in front of the bank of windows, the light blooming around her so she's nothing but a dark silhouette. "It absolutely was."

It takes my eyes a few seconds to adjust. I'm not sure how much sleep Lauren needs as one of the lower-level demons, but she looks ungodly good for it being so early in the morning.

Her blond hair is neatly plaited in a French braid, the tail hanging over her shoulder. There's fresh makeup on her face, but not a ton. She's been blessed with perfect, fair skin. Is that also a demon thing? Because if so, I'm clearly not one of them. I eat take-out, and the next day my face is like a poppy field—red blooms everywhere.

It's still a mystery, who and what I am to Wrath. He said I have the *animus*, the Hellfire Crown, but it doesn't take a genius to figure out that a normal human shouldn't be able to hold that much power.

Which means...

Nope. Too early in the morning to go down that road. I'll cross that whole you-might-not-be-who-you-think-you-are bridge after some coffee.

"What do you want?" I ask Lauren.

"Wrath told me to wake you up."

"If he told you to eat glue, would you?"

"Yes," she answers without hesitation.

While 'king' is literally in his name, sometimes I forget how easily he commands people and how quickly they jump.

I'm an exception. I think maybe the *only* exception. But that doesn't stop the fiery rage from rearing its head whenever Wrath *tries* to tell me what to do. Or the lust that chases after it.

I don't know what it says about me that I like fighting him every chance I get. And I like seeing what he'll do.

Last time we got into a tit-for-tat, we ended up in his bed.

I get a flash of his hands digging into my hips, of his cock banging into me, and I'm suddenly pulsing with need.

He brings out the worst in me, turns me mindless and horny as fuck.

Lauren scoffs. "Can you not control yourself?"

"Excuse me?"

"Listen, cupcake—"

"What's with all the nicknames?"

"Most supernaturals have better senses than humans. Demons, vampires, shifters."

"Okayyyyy."

"Okayyyy," she sing-songs, parodying me, then bugs out her eyes.

Oh shit. "Nooooo. Are you telling me...*all of you can smell me like Wrath can*?"

"Yes. Every time you get all horny fangirl over the king. So stop being a whore around Wrath."

I put my hand to my forehead, blood pulsing through my cheeks. "Oh god."

"You're welcome."

That explains what Dane the vampire was referring to when they visited the castle. He asked if they were interrupting something, and at the time I'd been fantasizing about what Wrath could do with his hands on my body.

Fuck.

Wrath then proceeded to stab him with his dark magic, told him to be respectful.

My face warms again, but for a different reason this time. Was the Demon King defending my honor?

Pfftt. Fat chance of that.

"So how do you stop that?" I ask, wrinkling my nose.

"I already told you. Stop being a—"

"I'm not a whore, goddammit."

Lauren screws up her mouth. "Could have fooled me."

I grit my teeth, nostrils flaring as I suck in a breath, anger igniting at my sternum.

Lauren takes a step back. "Calm down." She holds up her hands. "I was only joking."

The room fills with more than morning light. It's a pulsating bright orange glow. I catch a glimpse of myself in the tall, gilded mirror across the room and a shiver runs down my spine.

My eyes are glowing.

I dart across the room and paw at my face as my irises ebb from bright, fiery orange back to their normal shade of hazel green. "What is that?"

"The *animus*, I'm guessing," Lauren says behind me.

"My eyes have never done that." I turn back to her, and she flinches away. "Why are they suddenly glowing?"

She summons some of her usual bravado and crosses her arms again, long fingers curling around her toned biceps. "Probably because of Wrath. Being around him has likely unlocked the power."

It's becoming more and more impossible to deny the truth—I do have some kind of magic, and worse, it's not mine.

It's the Demon King's.

"I don't want it," I tell Lauren.

"Good. Because *he* wants it back. And he's—"

"Going to do whatever he can to get it. I know. I know. But I don't plan on putting up a fight, okay? My entire life, my temper has always gotten me into trouble. Maybe giving back the crown will take some of the anger with it."

I don't entirely understand all of the animus's characteristics, but it definitely responds to the rage most often. It makes sense that a power literally called *Hellfire Crown* would be tied to rage.

My anger management issues have always been a handicap I

desperately wanted to be rid of. I'm more than happy to give it back. If only we can figure out how to do it.

Lauren gives me another onceover before making her way to the door. "The king has instructed that I get you food. Arthur made a quiche. It's in the fridge. Now you know where to acquire said food so my job is done."

My stomach growls immediately, as if it's been waiting for the promise of food before speaking up. A quiche does sound positively divine. And it immediately makes me think of my best friend, Gus, and Collie's Tea Shop. We usually have breakfast there a few times a week, and quiche is a favorite. And now...

I hope Gus doesn't hate me. I hope he understands why I left with Wrath.

It was just the night before that I was asked to kill Wrath by none other than the President of the United States. And Gus's boyfriend, Adam, along with a bunch of other soldiers, were supposed to have my back during the confrontation.

Until we all found out that I was connected to Wrath. When I'm hurt, he's injured. It's his only weakness.

I'm his only weakness.

That's when the soldiers turned on me, trying to kill me to kill Wrath.

I had no other choice but to leave with him, but will Gus understand that? God I hope so.

With Lauren gone, I head into my bedroom's attached bathroom. Flicking on the overhead light, I peer closely at my eyes again in the vanity mirror.

Wrath's eyes glow red sometimes.

Now mine do too. A different shade of color, but they glow nonetheless.

What the fuck does that even mean?

"Who are you?" I say to my reflection. It's like looking at a stranger. Nothing has changed about my face, and yet...something is different. I don't recognize myself, and yet I oddly feel more like myself at the same time.

There's still a voice of dissent in my head that's trying to come up with every excuse under the sun.

Maybe being around Wrath has warped me. Maybe I've entered some kind of twilight zone. Maybe Wrath is using his power to control me. Lauren said one of the powers the king possesses is the ability to control minds.

The *oculus*, she called it.

I want to believe any one of those reasons, but deep down, I know the truth.

Somehow, someway I have a piece of Wrath's power flowing through my veins.

"You just have to figure out how you got it," I tell myself. "Then get rid of it."

It's like the flu or a head cold. I'm in the misery right now, but eventually I'll get better.

Eventually.

And speaking of getting better.

I lift the hem of my t-shirt to assess the wound in my stomach, the one that I accidentally inflicted on myself when I stabbed Wrath with a special witch blade.

My skin is still a little tender and flushed red, but the wound has healed. There's no indication that I was sliced open at all.

It really is a miracle. All of it.

I get dressed and then head downstairs. Might as well face the music. Except on my way to the kitchen, after peeking into several of the sitting rooms, I don't spot Wrath anywhere. Disappointment sinks in my gut.

As much as I hate him, I also can't get enough of him. I'm back to being a teenager, doing some minor stalking of her crush, hoping for just a glimpse of him around the corner.

I'm losing my goddamn mind.

It might be fucking complicated, but in simple terms, he's

turned me into a horny devil, and I just have to resist him and his allure long enough to disentangle myself from his royal power.

Never thought I'd be making a plan for *that* reality.

I find the kitchen empty and go straight for the industrial fridge. The interior glows with a sterile white-blue light when I open the door. I spot Arthur's quiche in a red ceramic dish. It's nestled amongst a bowl of fruit, a head of broccoli, and some takeout from Par House.

The quiche is homemade and somewhat fresh, but greasy restaurant leftovers sounds delicious. I'll just quickly see what it is.

When I pop open the Styrofoam lid, I find a few veggie sushi rolls and a spring roll.

"Ewww." I wrinkle my nose at it. I prefer a California roll drenched in soy sauce.

"Planning on stealing my leftovers, *dieva*?"

I yelp and spin around, nearly losing the Styrofoam container.

Wrath stands in the center of the kitchen in nothing but loose black pajama pants.

Oh fuck.

He's a vision of pale morning. Like ice frost on tree leaves. Like hot breath condensing in the winter air.

His black hair is wet and raked back from his forehead. Water droplets still cling to his skin and glisten in the light.

I want to lick them off.

One by fucking one.

"*Dieva*," he says, a hint of a smile pulling at the corner of his fuck-me mouth.

"Huh?" My gaze trails away from the sweeping black lines of his demon mark on his chest, down to the hard line between his hip and pelvis. A shadowed line that goes down, down—

I can see the press of his cock against that soft black material. Can make out the swell of the head, the ridge around it and—

"*Dieva*," he says again, louder this time.

I blink. "Sorry. What?"

"If I'd known you'd turn into a horny little girl at the sight of me shirtless, I would have put on more clothes."

That snaps me awake.

Son of a bitch.

I've never been accused of being horny so many times in one day. But yet here I am, and here it's true.

I set the takeout on the counter. "That is...not what's happening here."

"Oh?" Wrath comes around the kitchen island and advances on me. I take a step back. "You were just staring at my cock."

At the mention of his cock, my gaze sinks again involuntarily.

"Was not."

He disappears.

The air catches in my throat as I stumble back.

Right into him.

His hands come to my shoulders, and he spins me around, pressing my pelvis into the edge of the counter as his groin presses against the swell of my ass.

I sputter out a breath.

He threads his fingers into my hair and yanks my head back, exposing my throat.

"You're such a filthy liar," he says, his mouth at the rapid beat of my heart.

I swallow loudly as his other hand sinks down the curve of my belly, down between my legs, cupping me over my shorts.

I'm in so much trouble. I pretty much challenged him to prove me wrong, and now he's doing just that.

I groan as he nips at my neck with sharp teeth, causing me to jolt against him. He tightens his hold on me, cock now hard at the seam of my ass.

A very weak, very hopeless rational side of me is faintly calling out, *this is a game! He's playing you! He needs you complicit!*

But that sweet, sweet summer child has no hope of getting my attention.

Not when the Demon King is slipping his fingers around the hem of my shorts, in past the seam of my panties, and then sends those fingers sliding down my wet folds.

I close my eyes and descend into the madness of the pleasure. He presses closer, the counter digging into my hip bones.

I can't pretend I don't like every single part of this.

Especially not when I'm dripping wet, and I know he can smell me.

He yanks my shorts down, taking the panties with it. Is he going to fuck me right here?

Should I try to stop him?

I'm distantly aware that he's practically lording over me right now, proving just how powerless I am when he turns me to lust, but I can't seem to care.

He bends me forward onto the counter, pressing my cheek to the cool granite, exposing my ass to him and my wet pussy. A second later, the heat of his cock nestles into my opening but stops before entering me.

"How about now, *dieva*?" His voice is rough and hoarse. "Horny now?"

"Nope," I pant out.

"Then I'll stop."

"Go for it."

He growls, his long fingers still tangled in my hair.

Now I'm calling his bluff.

We stay locked there for several seconds, neither one moving, his cock *right there*, throbbing at my opening. It takes everything I have, every ounce of willpower not to arch into him and push back, sink him deeper.

"You drive me mad, *dieva*," he admits.

His hands go to my hips and a traitorous moan escapes me. The head of his cock swells at my opening.

I shouldn't be here, mindless for more of him, the fucking Demon King, and yet there's nowhere else I'd rather be.

I chose my side.

There are no heroes here.

"Admit it, *dieva*," he says. "Put us both out of our misery." He pushes in deeper, hard as a fucking rock.

"Why won't you?"

Because the Demon King won't admit to his weaknesses. Especially not me.

He pulls out, and the heat of his throbbing dick disappears.

"No! Okay. Okay," I whine, a little breathless, totally mindless. "Fuck me. Okay. I admit it."

My clit is pulsing, my inner walls clenched up tight. I can't take it any longer.

I think this might be the only time he takes an order from me.

He drives into me. My hips bang painfully against the counter's edge, but I don't fucking care.

The pain and the pleasure make up a sublime duo. I'm soaring. Fucking flying as the head of his cock hits deep inside of me.

"Oh fuck," I moan, my breath condensing on the counter.

When I feel him grow harder at my words, there's a burst of power at the center of me. Like kindling finally catching fire. The rush of heat spreads through my entire body, and my head sways like I'm caught in a wave.

I imagine it's what it feels like being high. Otherworldly. Divine.

Wrath fucks me harder, faster.

I can't help the loud, high-pitched moans that escape me as the pressure and the pleasure build.

I couldn't control myself if I wanted to.

The orgasm comes hard and fast, burning through me like a forest fire.

My skin goes flush, my blood hot in my veins as the flood of pleasure beats through me.

Wrath groans as I try to curl into myself, nerves flickering with sensory overload.

And then his tempo shifts as he lets out a loud, raw groan.

The Demon King comes inside of me.

His hold tightens on my hips as if he's saying *mine*, as if he's proving on some base level that this was his decision, not mine.

For the second time in so many days, I fucked the Demon King.

The realization feels like a crown itself. Like I've conquered some unconquerable land and come out the other side of it a motherfucking victor even though he was the one who initiated it, trying to prove a point.

When he pulls out of me and steps away, I practically melt into a limp doll on the counter, his and my juices leaking out of me, down the backside of my thighs.

Holy shit.

What just happened?

And why do I feel like maniacally laughing?

When my soul returns to my body, and sensation returns to my legs, I step back and shimmy my shorts up.

When I turn to face the Demon King, his eyes are glowing vibrant red.

There's no glory on his face. No cocky grin.

This emotion, foreign as it is, as subtle as it is, almost looks like fear.

His shoulders rise and fall with quick breaths, his pale chest now coated in sweat instead of water from the shower.

"You've healed," he says, ignoring what we've just done.

"Yeah." I nod at his stomach, the flat plane of it, the defined ab muscles. Every line of him is fucking art. "You did too."

He levels his glowing gaze at me, as if there's more he wants to say.

And I want to hear it. God help me, I want more of him. I want all of his deep secrets. All of his inner thoughts. I want more than just his cock and his cum.

"You can have the leftovers," he says and turns away.

"What?"

"Eat, *dieva*," he orders and disappears around the corner.

I blink after him for several minutes, trying to make sense of it all.

I splash cold water on my face and hang over the sink as the beads of water drip from the end of my nose.

He makes my head spin. He makes me feel out of control but in the most exciting way. Is this what it feels like to succumb to drugs?

Because I'm starting to worry I need an intervention.

I swipe the water away and take a deep breath and then sit at the kitchen island. I finish off the Demon King's leftovers, telling myself the entire time it's because I'm hungry and not because he ordered me to eat.

2

The veggie sushi and spring roll are better than I expected. Once I'm done eating, I explore more of the castle. Around every corner, I swear I can feel and smell Wrath, but he's never there. I'm beginning to crave that spicy, winter scent of his. Like a cup of hot chai tea on Christmas morning.

It shouldn't be comforting and familiar, but somehow it is.

I find a library eventually and marvel at its sheer size. It might be bigger than the public library in Norton Harbor. There are two levels. The second opens in a loft that's accessible by a winding metal staircase. I go up and down it several times like I'm Belle in *Beauty and the Beast*. The scenario fits, I suppose. I'm held prisoner (sort of) by a monster in a castle.

I'm not free to go. And I know he would find me if I ran.

The *animus* connects us in some way, and I have to wonder if my vision of him my first night in Adam's factory was in fact real. If he found his way to me without knowing how to physically come to me because of Eric's witch barrier.

I pull a few leather-bound books from the library shelves and flip through their pages. I smell something sweet and sugary on the pages, but I can't read the language, so I put the books back.

There are no rom-coms here. No self-help books about living your best life.

Pity, I could use some of both right now.

I leave the library and wander down the next hall. When I come to a room that actually looks like a normal room with a sectional couch and a flat screen TV attached to the wall, I expel a contented sigh.

I need normal right now.

Does the Demon King have a subscription to any of the streaming services? Because I could totally go for some Netflix and chill.

I plop on the couch and grab the remote from the heavy iron coffee table. It takes me a second to figure out how to work the system, but I eventually get to live TV and land on a news channel.

"Another mass shooting has been reported," the news anchor says.

It immediately makes me sick to my stomach. It seems like there's one every day of the week. When will we ever stop killing each other?

I flip to the next channel and frown at the sight of my face plastered on the screen.

"What the hell?"

The headline reads: *Rain Low in Demon King Confrontation.*

The news anchor comes on, with my picture scaled down on the upper right-hand side of the screen. It's an image they stole from my mom's social media, one she took the year before on a hiking trip we went on in the Adirondack Mountains. My hair is windswept, my face pink from too much sun. But I look happy.

The funny thing is, my entire life I couldn't wait to settle down and actually live in one town longer than a year. But ever since I settled in Norton Harbor, I've been hungry for adventure. I've been wondering if maybe my mom was right, if maybe I'll always be perpetually dissatisfied. Always trying to fill an unnamable hole.

"We're approaching twenty-four hours since Rain Low was reported as missing," the news anchor says. "But is that what really happened? We go to Ken in the field who might be able to shed more light on the situation."

The footage flips to Ken—a man in his thirties with black hair and thick glasses that are putting up a valiant effort to take over his face. "Thank you, Melissa. I'm here in Riverside Park on the outside of Norton Harbor where witnesses say just last night, there was a massive showdown between Wrath and our military forces. And if you look behind me, you'll see part of Riverside Park was destroyed in a rogue fire. Was it Wrath? Or was it Rain? I have an eyewitness here to tell us more."

Ken steps to the right, and the camera pans with him. An older woman comes onto the screen, graying blonde hair curled back in a poufy up-do. "Mrs. Thompson, tell the viewers what happened last night in the park."

Mrs. Thompson's small eyes widen to the size of dewdrops as she leans toward the microphone. "I was out walking my dog, Mr. Fuzzles, when I heard shouting. Like a dummy, I went toward the sound and—my god." Her wrinkled hand goes to her chest as she shakes her head. "I saw Rain Low in the park with that devil. At first I thought they were necking—"

"Oh please," I mutter at the TV.

"But then I saw her go—" she makes a stabbing motion, teeth gritted "—and I don't know how she did it, but it looked like she actually stabbed him! It was like the devil was in pain, and then all hell broke loose, and there was shouting and yelling and then BOOM." She makes an explosion with her hands. "There was light and fire, and the park started burning."

Ken pulls the microphone back to himself. "Did you see what happened to Rain? Or the Demon King?"

Mrs. Thompson shakes her head, and not a single hair moves

out of place. "Right after the explosion, there was a bunch of shooting, and I high-tailed it out of there. It's unfortunate what's become of this town since the devil moved in. I never had to worry about taking Mr. Fuzzles for his nightly walk!"

Ugh. I flip the channel, feeling a little ill, only to land on a different broadcast with a man and woman behind a news desk.

"Rain Low—hostage or demon sympathizer?" the woman says. "I'll tell you which—she's proven she does not care about our country. We have reports that she's chosen the Demon King over our own soldiers time and time again."

I lurch off the couch. "That's not true!"

The man nods. "It's unfortunate, Bridget, but women in particular are incapable of fighting his dark power." He turns to the camera and looks directly into the lens. "Men, if you're out there listening, you gotta protect your wives, your daughters, your sisters, and mothers. The devil is here, ladies and gentlemen, and he's here to corrupt the women in your lives."

"As if we're simpering idiots who can't control our ovaries," I say and punch at the OFF button on the remote.

This time, when the rage comes, I notice it right away.

Light shines across the room, and it's definitely not sunlight.

I scurry over to the glass door of the entertainment center.

There's literal fire lifting off my shoulders, much like Wrath's dark mist.

And my eyes are flaring in the glass.

As soon as I lean in close to inspect, the light disappears.

The power is like water through my fingers, there one minute, gone the next.

I stand there watching my reflection as if I might catch some hint, some more proof. What more do I need?

I feel like everything I thought I knew about myself has suddenly evaporated.

I have magic.

I have power.

Why does it make me so fucking terrified?

Raised voices pull me from my reverie. I follow the sound only to find Wrath stalking down the hallway, Arthur, stooped, following behind, trying to keep up.

"They've formally requested you return her safely to the president," Arthur is saying.

"Tell them I formally fucking decline," Wrath answers.

I meet them at an intersection of hallways. "What's going on?"

Wrath scowls at me as he stalks past. Now I'm the one hurrying to catch up. He's well over six feet and towers over all of us. He's put on clothes since he fucked me earlier and is now clad entirely in black. I can just make out the twining lines of his demon mark peeking out from beneath the collar of his shirt.

I have a sudden urge to run my fingers over it, feel his skin beneath mine, and then have to tamp down a shiver that threatens to shake my shoulders.

Fucking demon.

Arthur says, "General Briggs is demanding your safe delivery back to them."

I laugh. "That's rich, considering they tried to kill me."

Wrath turns down another hallway. "They wouldn't be trying to kill you if you hadn't shouted from the top of your lungs that we're connected."

"Hey, I was being shot at. I wasn't thinking clearly."

"Your lack of preparation and forethought must be legendary."

He turns into another room. I'm finally starting to recognize some of the rooms within the castle, and this one I think is Wrath's favorite. It's the most lived in and smells the most like him. It's also the room that houses the best bar and the best stock of liquor.

Predictably, Wrath goes to the bourbon and pours himself a glass.

"You're an asshole," I say.

"I've been called worse."

"I fucking hate you."

Back to me, he says, "Is that supposed to hurt my feelings? Do you have any idea of where I come from? What I've faced?" He slings back the drink, then slams the glass down again.

"Am I supposed to feel sorry for you?" I blurt out before I can think better of it.

I really wish I'd thought better of it.

Arthur tenses up and steps aside.

Wrath disappears in a crack of air.

Oh shit.

When he does that, it's like the dark shape of a great white shark has just disappeared into the depths below you. You might not see him, but you know he's there, waiting for the perfect moment to attack.

I look to Arthur for help, but he has his head bowed, his hands folded in front of him.

Arthur owes me nothing. He owes Wrath his life. He's not going to come to my defense.

Wrath reappears in front of me in a swirl of black mist. His eyes are flaring up. I'm learning that the red glow can be an indication of desire and rage. Just like with me.

We are more alike than I want to admit.

The black mist lashes out almost like it's an entity of its own.

I'm thrown back, slam against the closest wall, then slide down to the floor.

I quickly roll onto all fours and climb to my feet, only for Wrath to be there, taking a fistful of my hair. Instinctively, I grab at his wrist, trying to take some of the pressure off. He gets in close to me, and I hold my breath, regret a bright thing in my vision. "You would cower in the face of my enemies," he says.

My nostrils flare as my nose fills with his spicy, cool scent. The sensation running through my veins is familiar now. Desire. Excitement. Exhilaration. As if being manhandled by Wrath is some kind of sick foreplay.

I don't know what to do with this constant push and pull of hate and ecstasy.

I'm close to embracing it. Damn the consequences. Forget about the guilt and the shame.

Because the truth is, I've never felt so damn alive.

I run my tongue over my bottom lip, and Wrath's eyes dart to the movement. His jaw flexes as he grits his teeth.

If Arthur wasn't in the room, I think we might be fucking again on the nearest piece of furniture.

I want to rip his clothes off and ride him until he comes inside of me, until his fingers leave bruises on my skin.

If I'm not careful, Arthur might not even stop me.

Get it together, Rain.

With his hand still in my hair, I say, "You have enemies?"

He blinks, lets me go, and shifts away. I quickly fix my hair and scratch at my aching scalp.

Goddammit, I love it when he pulls my hair.

"Why do you think I've been searching for the *animus*?" he says.

I'm not sure if that's a rhetorical question or not, so I say nothing as he returns to the bar and refills his glass. He likes to drink, I'm realizing, but I've never seen him tipsy or drunk. I wonder how much liquor it takes to soak a demon.

I'd very much like to find out.

"I am losing my grip on my throne," he admits.

"Wait...what?"

The liquor sloshes into the glass as he gives another generous pour. Diffused sunlight shines in around him from the nearest window, turning his dark edges hazy.

Him admitting this to me...is this some kind of tactic to earn my sympathy?

I look to Arthur, but his weathered face is turned away from me, his thoughts distant.

"It won't be long," Wrath says, "and I'll lose the throne entirely, and if that happens…" He turns his head, his face now in profile highlighted by that hazy, gorgeous light.

I wish I had my camera.

I wish I could capture him this way, vulnerable, but still dark against the light.

"If that happens?" I prompt.

His shoulders rise and fall with a breath, then he brings the glass to his lips and drinks down the amber liquid.

I almost lean in, waiting for his response when he comes up for air.

What happens?

Who are his enemies? Is one of them this Chaos I heard him and Arthur talking about the other night?

I suppose someone with a name like Chaos, they're predisposed to being an enemy.

But I never get the response because the sound of a bell dinging through the house pulls Wrath's attention away.

"That should be Ciri," Arthur says and hurries away.

"Who's that?"

Wrath frowns at me. "Do you ever stop asking questions?"

I grumble in the back of my throat and come up next to him at the bar. "Do you ever not act like an asshole?"

He turns his head, eyeing me. "I would kill lesser men for such insolence."

"Good thing I'm not a man."

He snorts and pours a third round of liquor.

"Are you an alcoholic?"

His dark brow arches sardonically.

I asked another question.

"Can you be an alcoholic with all of—" I gesture at his to-die-for physique "—all of this?"

"If you're asking whether or not I can get drunk, the answer is yes, but not on this." He tips the glass before slinging it back. "This just takes the edge off." He sets the glass aside and puts his hands on the bar top. Hunching over, he closes his eyes, dark lashes fanning over his pale cheeks.

More of the demon mark is exposed as his t-shirt slouches on his broad shoulders.

Everything about him is so deliriously masculine. So fucking hot.

"Do you have edges that need to be taken off?" I joke.

He looks at me through a lock of dark hair that's fallen forward. His eyes brighten and flare red. "When I'm around you, every edge feels like it could cut."

Holy.

Holy good god.

What am I supposed to make of that? Is that a good or bad thing?

Don't believe a word he says. He's playing you.

But is he? After we fucked in the kitchen, that look on his face...it was like he was afraid of me. And maybe not because of the power itself, but because of the power I seem to hold over him.

I snatch the glass and give myself a splash of bourbon, then sling it back. The alcohol burns all the way down and warms my belly with a delicious fuzziness.

"That makes two of us," I say.

The corner of his mouth lifts.

Arthur comes in and announces, "Ciri has arrived."

Wrath straightens, the amusement and the warmth gone from his face in a blink.

I turn with him and stand by his side, and for the first time, I think it's exactly where I should be.

Ciri is a slight woman with wavy black hair and horn-rimmed sunglasses covering her eyes. She's wearing an elegant pants suit that reminds me of the fifties with its nipped waist and Peter Pan collar.

"Hello, my king," she says and gets down on her knees when Wrath turns to her.

It must be exhausting having to bow to him every single time you cross paths with him.

I'm glad I don't have that problem.

"Ciri," he says. "A queen in her own right."

"Really?" I blurt out.

Arthur holds out his hand for her, and she kindly takes it, rising to her feet once again. "I'm known in Saint Sabine as the Queen of the Oracles," she explains.

Saint Sabine is the nearest big city. It's known by some as the New Orleans of the east coast because of its distinct architecture, its wrought iron balconies, and its eclectic music scene.

"You must be Rain?" Ciri says as she crosses the room on loud, clacking heels.

"Hi." I give her an awkward wave.

She stops several feet away and curls her hand around her hip as she assesses me from behind the darkness of her sunglasses.

Is she sensitive to light? I don't think she's a vampire. I didn't get that impression when Wrath spoke of her.

Ciri pulls the glasses away, giving me my answer.

Her eyes are pure white.

For a second I think she must be blind, but then she laughs and says, "Don't worry, child. They won't bite."

I guess she must see my shock.

"Ciri is a traveler," Wrath answers. "She's the one who helped bring me here to your world."

Sirene mentioned a traveler too when I asked her how she got here.

"Travelers control the gates between worlds," Wrath explains.

"Worlds? Plural? There are more?"

"There are infinite worlds," Wrath says drily like it should have been obvious.

"Indeed," Ciri says. "But not all are easy to access, and the traveling magic has been damaged for a very long time. But let's not wander in the weeds. We're here for you today."

"*We*?" I look around her and spot no one else. "Do you have the *norrow* too?"

"Something like that."

Ciri lifts a hand, two fingers giving a *come-hither* gesture.

A girl in a gauzy white gown appears on Ciri's left, directly in front of me, and she's *floating*.

I yelp, lurch back, and realize that I've retreated behind Wrath.

He looks down at me, cowering behind the line of his shoulder, and some foreign emotion flickers in his eyes. My stomach warms.

"She won't bite either," Ciri says.

I lurch away from Wrath, embarrassed and oddly annoyed by him even though I was the one cowering.

"What is she?"

Her billowy white dress undulates in a phantom wind.

"She's an Oracle. They're spirits from Alius that can see and predict the future," Ciri says. "As a traveler, I can communicate with them regardless of which side of the gate I'm on."

I examine the girl more closely. In any other context, I'd think she was a ghost. Her hair is white and as fine as silk so it lifts and floats easily in her phantom wind. She has the same colorless eyes as Ciri, and her mouth is set in a grim line.

Does she have a mind of her own? Does she detest being summoned?

I suddenly feel sorry for her.

Ciri utters two words that are foreign to me and the Oracle closes the distance between us. She stops with only a foot of distance between us.

Wrath edges closer to my side.

"What can you tell us about her?" Ciri asks the Oracle.

The Oracle blinks, bright white lashes flitting over pale cheeks. "She is not what you think she is."

I frown. "What does that mean?"

No one answers.

The Oracle gets closer, and her scent fills my nose. It's like a match struck in a cave. Wet stone and sulphur and darkness. The back of my throat itches and my vision tunnels until everything beyond the Oracle is a blur, like a fingerprint smudged on glass. Every muscle in my body clenches up, and I grit my teeth so hard, my jaw aches.

"Someday," the Oracle says, "she will rain."

"Rain!" Wrath is in front of me, concern pinched between his brows. His hands are on either side of me, shaking me.

"What? What's the matter?"

The Oracle is gone, and Ciri stands behind Wrath, her hand at her chest.

Wrath whirls around, black mist lifting from his shoulders. He is a vision of darkness and rage. "What the fuck did you do to her?"

Ciri flinches back and holds up a hand as if that will keep the raging Demon King at bay. "She was in no danger."

Within seconds, he's surrounded by several of the *norrow*. They flank outward like well-trained soldiers.

The shadows swirling around Wrath sharpen into a dozen blades.

"My king," she says with a shaky tenor to her voice. She starts to sink to her knees.

"Stop!" I shout. The shadow blades freeze mid-air. "I'm all right. See?"

Wrath turns to look at me with those bright red eyes, and even I flinch. His jaw flexes as his gaze sweeps over me, assessing for himself whether or not that's true.

"I'm okay," I say quietly.

The *norrow* disappear. The blades retract and Wrath disappears.

Ciri and I brace.

He reappears right in front of Ciri and grabs her by the throat and lifts her off the floor. Her pointed heels scrabble for purchase as she fights at his grip.

"I know what you're doing," he says.

"My king," she chokes out.

"You're playing both sides. I don't like it."

"No, I—" Her eyes bug from their sockets. She chokes back a strangled breath and starts again. "Every path has... a...destination."

"The destination," Wrath bites out, "is that I will be the victor. I will wear the crown. Not her. Not Chaos. I will. And if you forget that again, you won't be bowing at my feet, Ciri. You'll be nothing but bones in the earth. Do we understand one another?"

She nods quickly.

"Wrath!" I say. "Let her go!"

He drops her unceremoniously, and she falls to a heap on the floor. I rush to her side.

"Are you okay?"

The air snaps behind me, and when I check for the Demon King, he's already gone.

"I'm fine," Ciri says, but her voice is raw and reedy.

"I'm sorry he did that."

She rubs at her neck where a bruise is quickly coloring her skin.

"I wasn't worried, child," she says with a laugh, but there's real pain and anguish in it.

I help her up. "You should be."

"I already know when I will die, and it isn't here, and it isn't today." She clears her throat and smooths back her hair.

"Okayyyy. Well...good then?"

Her gaze darts around the room, then she leans in conspiringly. "What did she tell you? The Oracle?"

It's all fuzzy in my head. "I don't know. She just said my name."

Ciri frowns. "That's it?"

"Did you guys not hear her?"

"No. And you froze up like you'd been shocked, and your eyes went white."

"Really?" I guess that explains why Wrath went berserk. "That's not normal for your Oracles?"

Ciri shakes her head. "They don't physically interact with people on this side. It drains too much energy from them. *Usually*." Her thoughts go distant as she considers something.

"What is it?"

"Nothing it's just...she almost seemed energized by your touch. It's like..."

"Like what?"

She looks over her shoulder again with her colorless eyes. I see the moment she shuts down and the hard-to-read sophisticated woman returns.

She picks up her sunglasses from where they fell to the floor and slides them back on the wide bridge of her nose. "It will get worse before it gets better," she says. "Remember that when you think you'd rather die than be where you are."

"Well that leaves me feeling cozy," I say. "What about the *animus*? Isn't that why you're here? To help me figure out how I got it or why I have it? And how the hell I give it back."

She levels out her shoulders, straightens her spine. "If you want to know more about how you came to be in this predicament, I'd start by looking at the beginning."

"Meaning?"

"Your birth."

Heels clacking on the hardwood, she leaves me.

I stare after her for a long time, trying to figure out what just happened and what it all means.

And why Wrath acted the way he did.

I know he wants his crown back.

And I don't want it.

But...hearing him say it was his in that way, with a complete disregard for how I'd feel about it irritates me. And when I'm irritated, it makes me want to dig in my heels. Sometimes it's not about the outcome so much as it is about the fight for me.

That fiery Aries.

But no. It doesn't matter. None of it matters. Because the crown, the power, it was never mine to begin with.

Ciri is right about one thing—I think I need to have a chat with Sunny Low.

It's high time I meet my biological father and try to figure out if me being in possession of the *animus* has anything to do with who my father is.

Please dear god let him be human.

3

I GO ON THE HUNT FOR WRATH AFTER CIRI LEAVES.

That man needs a cell phone, and this castle is too damn big. I shout his name through the hallways after an hour of searching all the nooks and crannies, except it's Lauren's attention I get.

"Stop yelling through the damn house," she says as she leans casually against the doorframe of the room she just slithered from.

"I can't find him."

"He's in the stables."

I make a face at her. "There are stables? With horses?"

She just stares at me blankly, pretty eyes blinking like I'm the stupidest creature she's ever encountered.

"Where would I find the stables?"

She nods in the opposite direction. "Go that way until you come to an exterior door. Go outside and to the right."

"Thank you."

"Whatever."

With a massive roll of her eyes, she heads in the opposite direction.

I follow the hallway until it breaks to the next. Here I look left and right. This hall sits on the backside of the house. Giant arched windows overlook one of many landscaped gardens. I spot an exterior door to the right and hurry through it, coming out on a stone pathway that winds through the garden and then back through the woods.

A couple of gray squirrels chase each other across the ground then scurry up a tree. A chipmunk darts past me on the path, nuts packed in its mouth. Birds chirp from above.

With everything that's been going on, I haven't been able to fully appreciate this place. Who would have thought I'd find myself living in a fairytale? Except I'm not living a fairytale life with Prince Charming.

I'm filthy fucking the villain instead.

Ten-year-old me would be so disappointed.

I shake my head and keep walking.

Eventually, the path gives way to rolling green grass and I spot the stables in the near distance.

As I walk up to the open bay door, I hear horses whinnying inside. I find Wrath at the front of a stall that houses a massive black horse. The horse is ducking her head out through the half open door, soaking up Wrath's attention.

His pale hand runs down the horse's muzzle, and her eyes turn heavy and half closed.

I know how she feels.

I know how it feels to want to melt beneath his attention.

"You disappeared," I say.

He keeps petting the horse.

"Why did you do that to Ciri?" I come up beside him. "You could have killed her."

His hand goes still on the horse's muzzle and her eyes shoot open. I can almost see her disappointment.

"I'm sorry, *dieva*," he says. "Did I give you the impression that I only meant to scare her? My intentions were to kill her."

I try to ignore the way that admission makes my stomach a little ill.

"Is that a habit of yours? Killing your friends?"

He turns to me. "A king has no friends."

I scan his face for any hint of emotion, but there's none to be had. He is stoic as usual. I want to poke and pick at him and bring down his walls. I don't care what the emotion is, as long as it's something.

"Sirene told me what *dieva* really means," I say and immediately regret it. I'm afraid of where this conversation might go, and what it means to have it. This isn't what I came out here for, and yet, now that I've opened the door, I'm eager to walk in.

"Did she?" His face is still expressionless.

"She said it doesn't mean *little girl*. It's a term that denotes ownership."

He snorts. "Clearly Sirene has been speaking out of turn."

"Is that not what it means then?"

The horse takes a loud clomping step closer and nudges his shoulder. He reaches out absently to pet her again. He gives in to her so easily, an animal.

I want him to give in to me too.

"*Dieva* means different things to different people," he answers.

"So what does it mean to you?"

"It's a promise."

"What kind of promise?"

"That I protect what's mine." A flicker of something appears in his eyes. Not rage. Not anger. But something akin to it. Begrudging loyalty maybe.

I believe what he says, but I don't think he likes admitting it.

"And am I?" I say quietly. "Am I yours?"

He grits his teeth. A tendril of black mist lifts from his shoulder. It glitters in the diffused light like crushed obsidian.

"No one wants to be mine, *dieva*," he says, shrouding the earlier emotion in a dark scowl.

"Why not?"

He takes a step toward me. Then another. The black mist suddenly engulfs me, and I backpedal, slamming into the next horse stall.

The only light in the darkness is Wrath's pale face.

"You wouldn't survive in the dark," he says, voice low and menacing.

Somehow this conversation has turned from the theoretical *them* to *me,* and I realize that he always intended it to be about me. Not some stranger. Some random person off the street.

He means *I* wouldn't want to be his.

I wouldn't survive his cold, dark heart.

I want to prove him wrong.

Summoning a breath, I lift my shoulders. "I don't think you have any idea what I'm capable of surviving."

His dark magic writhes in the air, and it drives out the heady scent of hay and animal, overwhelming me instead with its cool, crisp sweetness.

The darkness shoots out and presses against my throat, forcing my chin up. A surprised yelp punctuates the unnatural silence, and I find it hard to fill my lungs again as the shadows restrict my throat.

Wrath hasn't moved a muscle, and yet I'm pinned against the wall, fighting for air.

His expression is blank, as if he doesn't care. As if this outcome has no effect on him.

But I fucking know it does.

"Is this all you've got?" I choke out.

There's a pinch of annoyance at the outer corners of his eyes. "You don't want to play this game, *little girl.*"

He's probably right.

My inner voice is screaming at me to stop being an idiot.

But—

"Maybe I do," I bite out, the instinct to prove myself to him overriding my good sense.

He laughs through his nose. "You will regret this."

The darkness expands, pulsating outward like the blast from a nuclear bomb. The air crackles as the shadows solidify taking the form of the *norrow*, the six of them.

Oh shit. I forgot about them.

The shadowmen shoot forward, barreling into me. It's like a thousand needles piercing my flesh. Like nettles coursing through my veins.

The scream that rends from my throat is involuntary and pain filled.

The *norrow* grab hold of me and yank me off my feet, throwing me back. I slam into the opposite row of stalls, teeth clacking painfully together as I crumple to the concrete floor.

The coppery tang of blood fills my mouth. Wrath runs his fingers over his own lips, and they come away red with blood. He scowls at it.

"Have you had enough, *dieva*?"

Rolling to all fours, I say, "Is that all you've got?"

Something slams into my side. A rib cracks. Pain shoots through me as I'm tossed back. The shadows blot out the light as I blink blindly upward, waiting for the pain to subside, trying to catch my breath.

I try to sit up, but the shadows press down. It's like a boulder has been set on my chest. An unmovable force.

"How about now?" Wrath's voice is no longer measured and calm. There's pain there and impatience.

A sense of déjà vu comes over me. We're playing that game again, that push and pull game where he tempts me and I tempt him but instead of fucking this time, we're fighting.

And I think for us, they're one and the same.

The darkness kicks up again. "Tell me to stop, *dieva*," he says. I can no longer see him, but I can hear him just as plainly as if he were speaking directly in my ear.

He's everywhere. Overwhelming me.

He knows exactly what he's doing.

I might not be king, but I have the crown and part of the Demon King's magic. That means I can do something about it.

The heat and the power burn quickly this time. I don't even have to think about it as it roars through me.

One second I can't breathe with the *norrow* pressing closer, and the next second—bright, fiery light shines through the stable.

The *norrow* let out a primordial roar as the light burns through them, devouring them.

When the light and the darkness dissipate, it's just me and Wrath again.

It takes me some effort to get up, and I have to use one of the stalls for leverage as I climb to my feet. My side is aching; it's getting harder to breathe by the second, and there's still blood in my mouth.

But I'm not about to back down.

Wrath stands in the middle of the aisle, hands hanging casually by his side. There's no expression on his face. No emotion. He just watches me from his lofty height, silently assessing. Despite our supposed connection, he appears untouched, save for the blood dotting his bottom lip.

"Now what?" I say, a little cocky.

He bows his head.

A flash of triumph lights in my gut. I try to bite back a whoop because I don't want to be too cocky. Not yet anyway.

But then—

When Wrath looks up again, his eyes are burning brightly.

"Oh *dieva*," he purrs, "you have so much to learn and far too much to lose."

He lifts his hand and snaps his fingers, and suddenly, the stable is filled with *norrow*.

Not just the six I usually see him with.

Dozens.

Their dark shapes soak up all the light. The horses whinny and stomp in their stables.

Across the expanse of the stable, in the sea of darkness, Wrath's pale face stands out in stark relief. And there's a devilish grin on his sinful mouth.

I've grown too cocky.

All it took was Wrath fucking me to make me forget who and what he is.

He's the villain.

And I'm just prey.

"Take her," Wrath says.

And the tide of dark soldiers charges me.

I have a stupid second of confidence where I think maybe I can take them, and I reach for that now familiar heat of power.

But I'm not fast enough. I'm not trained. I don't know the first thing about winning.

The *norrow* swarm me. My side flares with pain again and I let out a screech.

They take it as an opening, and soon their darkness is surging down my throat, filling my lungs, drowning me in it. There's no air to breathe, and no air to take in. I'm lost in the darkness.

I'm drowning in it.

And Wrath...

I get a flash of him as the *norrow* bury me.

A flash of him walking away.

4

I WAKE WITH A JOLT.

Everything is dark.

For a panicked minute, I think I've been possessed and have joined the ranks of Wrath's dark army.

I guess the president was right—Wrath *is* building a weapon.

It's only when I feel the softness of the sheets beneath me, and stretch out my toes beneath the blanket, that I realize where I am. I'm back in my room in Wrath's castle.

And a second later, Wrath's voice rasps from the shadows.

"Did you learn your fucking lesson?"

I startle, not realizing he was there, and then press my hand to my chest. My heart is racing. "You're an asshole," I mutter for the billionth time and pull myself up against the headboard.

"You keep saying that as if you hope it'll change." His pale face finds a sliver of moonlight, and a shiver rolls across my shoulders. "They call me ruthless for a reason, *dieva*. I'm not here to be your friend."

I scrub at my face. I surprisingly feel all right considering the *norrow* consumed me to the point I was knocked unconscious for... what, a few hours? If it's dark beyond the castle, it must have been.

"If we're not meant to be friends, then why do you keep fucking me?" I challenge.

I almost feel the drop in the barometric pressure as soon as the words are out of my mouth. It's like I've just put chum in the water and realized I forgot the fucking shark cage.

Wrath darts across the room, yanks me from the bed and throws me up against the wall. His arm comes across my throat, forcing my head to the side just so I can find a hollow of space to breathe.

He lords over me, a beacon of darkness and rage.

I might have the *animus*, I might burn with the hellfire of it, but Wrath might be my match in temper.

I'm not playing in the little leagues here. I keep forgetting that.

This isn't some guy I met at a bar. Or someone Gus set me up on a blind date with.

He's not even a man.

He's a demon from another world. A king without his crown.

The villain.

A thrill shivers over my scalp as he leans his weight into me, proving just how weak I am next to him, both in strength and in determination.

Because when I find myself in these predicaments with him, my primal bitch wants to bend over for him, bare myself, let him do whatever the hell he wants to me.

"I fuck you, *dieva*," he says, "because you like it."

I swallow, feeling the first sink of pressure to my clit.

I moan and writhe, and he tightens his hold. His mouth comes to the shell of my ear, and with the barest touch of his lips, I'm ignited with desire. I must be going mad. I'm losing my damn mind.

My nipples bud under my shirt. My clit throbs.

"I fuck you, *dieva*," he whispers, "because I can."

He's right. Curse him for being right.

I would let him do just about anything to me.

The breath catches in my throat and I sputter to get it back.

Wrath lets up just a fraction, showing me mercy, and I seize the opportunity.

I shift beneath his hold and kiss him. It takes him by surprise, and he drops his hands.

That's all I need.

I wrap my arms around him, fingernails digging into his scalp.

And then—

He lifts me up, and I wrap my legs around his waist, feeling the dig of his cock at my center.

He might pretend there's nothing between us, that this is all me and my weak lady desires, but I know he's fucking lying.

I know it by the press of his hard-on.

I know it by the way he can't stop himself either.

His tongue meets mine as the kiss deepens, as the kiss turns hungry and burning.

I moan into him, and he groans back, the sound reverberating through his chest.

He's as mad as I am.

We're both fucking mad.

He turns to the bed and throws me back, then pulls his shirt off over his head. I scurry out of my pants, then my shirt, and he's on me again, growling into me as our mouths collide.

I am lost in the chaos of it, in the mindlessness. There is only my body, the driving need to fuck, to glow with the pleasure of it.

Somehow, my panties are torn off, my bra tossed aside, and Wrath's mouth sinks to my breast, sucks my nipple into his mouth, and bites at the bud.

I cry out into the darkness as his cool, spicy scent fills the room.

He winds his arm around my hips, lifting my pelvis to him. He's naked too, cock hot and throbbing at my opening.

"Fuck me," I pant into the dark.

"I'll fuck you when I'm ready." He nips at my breast again and I jolt beneath him.

I grab a chunk of his hair and yank hard. "Fuck me goddammit."

There's a burning desire so potent at my core, I think I might ignite from the inside out if he doesn't light the match.

He teases at my opening, and I buck beneath him, coaxing him in.

Teeth gnashing at my earlobe, he says, "I am in charge here, *dieva*."

I wrap my legs around his waist and roll him over. "If that's what you need to think."

The head of his cock hits at my clit as I straddle him. I rock against him, and his eyes roll back.

I fucking knew it.

He brings his hands to my hips, forcing me still. But I can feel the throb of him at my slick channel.

I shift forward, and the slide of his dick against my clit is damn near mind-blowing.

"*Dieva*," he says into the dark.

"Yes?"

His grip on my hips tightens, and he lifts me up just enough to get beneath me.

"I am your king," he says.

Chest heaving, body buzzing, I answer, "I bow to no one."

"You bow to me." His eyes glow red.

I've never felt the hollowness at the center of me so acutely.

"Say it." His hands press harder, fingertips practically bruising bone as the head of his cock swells at my opening.

I'm not sure what I'm giving him by giving in.

What is the cost?

And do I fucking care?

I want to be filled up by him.

The building pressure is so intense, I'm practically crawling out of my skin, flush and quivering, whimpering with the need. Is it me or the *animus* battering down my inhibitions, the crown desperate for its king?

I can say one thing and do another.

I know he's playing a game. I can play it too.

"Fine," I say. "You are my king."

"Good girl," he says and then shoves his cock inside of me.

5

He lets me ride him through waves and waves of pleasure. Let's me rock against him, hitting my clit just right every time he slides in and out of me.

I've already given up whatever it was he wanted, so he lets me hold the reins.

We are loud and frenzied in our fucking. Both of us.

Every nerve ending in my body fizzes like a firecracker.

There is nothing other than here, now, and the hard, rough drive of Wrath's cock inside of me.

If I didn't believe in other worlds before, I do now.

Because I feel like I've been transported to some other plane.

When the orgasm comes, it's like a hurricane. Like I've been swept off the earth. Like I am weightless and burning hot, carried off on a gale wind.

As I cry out, Wrath tightens his hold like he's holding on for dear life. He roars loudly, tenses up, drives deep.

I swear I feel the intense heat of his cum filling me up.

Mine, he says.

Mine, I echo.

He'll be dripping out of me later, the proof of the pleasure I milked from the Demon King one drop at a fucking time.

When the wave is over, and I quiver through the aftershocks, I look down at Wrath, coated in sweat, and find his eyes, two burning embers in the dark.

Butterflies arch through my belly.

He lifts me off of him and we collapse onto the bed together.

I'm lost in the delight of it all. Maybe a little drunk on it.

I'm never going to tell him how he makes me feel.

I can't tell him that there's this familiar warmth burning through my chest that feels awfully close to *like*.

I don't like him.

I can't like a villain.

The mattress shifts as Wrath gets up. For a blind, stupid second, I reach out for him as if to keep him there.

Thankfully, his back is to me, and he misses the slipup. I yank my hand back.

I hear the bite of a zipper somewhere in the shadows as he gets dressed.

"I'm starting to wonder if I should carve a notch in my bedpost every time we fall into bed together."

I'm goading him. He knows it. I know it.

He grumbles somewhere by my bathroom.

"I hold the power, *dieva*," he says. "Don't forget that."

I snort at the ceiling. "I have your handy little crown. Don't forget *that*."

"You possess what was stolen from me."

I lean back on my elbows. "It's not like I snuck into your world and stole it for myself. I didn't choose this."

There's silence in the shadows of my room. I have to fight the urge to flick on the bedside lamp.

"I will have the *animus* returned to me," he says finally.

"Obviously," I say before I can think twice about it. I don't know what giving it back entails. How long have I had it? How did

I get it? And does it have anything to do with my biological father?

There are still so many questions and too few answers.

"As soon as we can figure out the *how*, then yes, you can have it back. I don't want it," I say oddly wanting to please him.

The Demon King appears by my bedside and towers over me, shirtless, jet-black hair damp from our fucking. His dark demon mark winds around his shoulders, across his chest.

He puts fists on the edge of the bed and hunches toward me. His mouth is inches away. Without thinking, I bite the edge of my lip like I'm staring at a tasty snack I know I shouldn't eat.

In this position, every fiber of muscle in his arms stands out. Thick, corded muscle. Every inch of him is a miracle. A sight to behold.

If I had my camera, would he let me photograph him?

When the crown is his, will I ever see him again?

Maybe I want a memento to remember the wild ride.

"I think you're lying," he says quietly. "I think you like the power."

"Oh? Maybe I'll prove it to you."

He waits.

"I think we should go see my mom and figure out how I came to possess the *animus*. Ciri said if we can figure out how I got it, we can figure out how to take it away."

He thinks this over for a few seconds and then pushes away from the bed. "All right. Where is your mother now?"

"Scotland. Somewhere. Not exactly sure where."

He crosses his arms over his chest.

"Can you put a shirt on?" I say.

He looks down at himself. "I'm sorry. Am I too distracting?"

I slide out of the bed, still completely naked, and put my hands on my hips, forcing my boobs out. "I don't know. Am I when I'm like this?"

Gaze hungry, he drinks in the sight of me. I slide two fingers between my legs, and they come away slick with our mixed pleasure. I drag my tongue over the tip of my finger and close my eyes, moaning. "Mmmm. It tastes so good. Maybe I'll go for another round by myself and—"

His hand is suddenly wrapped around my wrist. My eyes snap open to find him just inches away, his gaze burning into me.

There's a rumble deep in his throat. He sucks one of my fingers into his mouth, his tongue sliding over the tip. The sensual feel of it causes me to gasp in surprise.

"You possess the Hellfire Crown and yet you still dare to play with fire." His teeth sharpen along with his face, the monster coming out to play. He bites my finger, piercing flesh, and I hiss in pain as he laps up the blood.

A replica of the bite appears on his finger, an echo of the connection between us. But Wrath ignores it.

"Do not vex me, *dieva*. Or I'll take the next bite out of your ass."

"Do you promise?" I challenge because damn if I don't want to get burned.

He reaches around me and grabs my ass cheek, squeezing hard, then gives me a smack. I yelp as an echoing thrill pulses in my clit.

"Why don't you bend me over and do that?"

He gives me a cross look. "Get dressed, *dieva*." He steps away and retrieves his shirt, slipping it on over his head. "Well go on," he says when I haven't moved.

Body buzzing, chest tight, I find my clothes in a ball on the other side of the bed and slip into the bathroom. I quickly dress and catch my reflection in the bathroom mirror before leaving.

Damn. I look like hell. Like I've just rolled out of bed hungover and...well, *fucked*.

What exactly did Wrath do to me in the stables? Was it all for show or will there be consequences?

Even though I'm enjoying this intense energy between us, I don't want to find out somewhere down the road that I was naïve and gullible, especially not when he's gutting me with his dark magic, trying to carve the *animus* from my bones.

A shiver makes my shoulders shake, and I hunch forward over the counter, inhaling deeply. Gus tried talking me into yoga last year to help me deal with some of the stress of my job, but I barely made it through one class. I don't like the slow movements. I like speed and intensity.

I can just hear my mom in my head: *All that Aries fire!*

I could really use those breathing techniques right about now though.

I could really use Gus too.

Another pang of guilt and heartbreak comes over me, thinking of my best friend. When this is all over, how will Gus feel about me? Knowing that I ran away with the villain?

I'm stuck in the Demon King's castle, fucking him around every corner and liking it more than I should. The thought of admitting that to Gus makes me want to vomit.

I just need to figure out how to give Wrath his power, and then we can go our separate ways, and I'll purge him from my system like an illicit drug.

It might be hell, but I'll make it through.

And then he'll be someone else's problem. Not mine. And I can focus on my own life again.

A dark shadow flits through the bathroom. A second later, Wrath appears behind me, leaning casually against the white tiled walls, arms crossed over his chest. The black mist trailing off of him blurs his sharp lines, making him look as though he's stepped right out of some divine renaissance art.

"What's wrong?" he asks, but I can't tell if he's asking because he's concerned or if it's something else. Can he feel my emotions too? Just how deep does this connection go?

"Nothing," I say. "I was just thinking."

"About what?"

I'm not going to tell him the truth, so I come up with something on the fly.

"If you're hurt when I'm hurt, why weren't you knocked unconscious when you sent your demon horde against me?"

"It seems pain is only echoed when blood is spilled."

"Interesting."

"Very."

Wrath could turn the *norrow* on me again and walk away unscathed.

A burr of fear sticks in my chest. At what point will I have gone too far? And as long as I possess the crown, does that line even exist? Would he let me get away with just about anything?

"How do you plan to find your mother?" he asks me. "I have to know a location to travel to it."

"If I had a phone, I could call her."

"Where is your phone?"

"Last I saw it, it was at the factory. Hard to say at this point." I turn the faucet on and splash cold water on my face. When I come back up, water dripping from my nose, I find Wrath staring at me through the mirror.

When he looks at me like that, I can't help but feel like a wick that's been lit. Not with a match, but a stick of dynamite. Two ends, both burning, both about to blow.

I take in a settling breath. *Focus, Rain.*

"If we can get to my condo, I have an old phone I could use."

He nods and pushes away from the wall. "Then we'll go to your condo."

"Aren't you afraid of being seen? I'm sure Naomi has my place watched around the clock."

He stops a few inches from me. "Hiding will make us appear weak. We'll carry on as if nothing has changed."

It must be nice to have no fear. Even before the Demon King arrived on our soil, there were still a thousand and one things to worry about in this world. I might not be as anxious or afraid as some people, but I still have to check my surroundings at night, lock my car doors behind me, and park beneath streetlights.

Now, knowing I possess the *animus*...

Nope. It's not mine, and I don't intend to keep it. No sense using it like a crutch when I've gotten by without it.

I dry my face on a black towel hanging on the rack, then turn to him.

He holds out his hand for me.

"Oh, we're going now?"

"Is there a better time?"

Probably not.

I slide my hand into his, and the second our skin touches, that now familiar jolt courses through me. It's like the crown knows it's found its rightful place.

It's these little touches that sometimes do me in. When it's nothing but skin to skin contact for no other reason than to touch.

Touching is more than fucking.

It's something more intimate.

Hand firmly in his, he tugs me into his side, tucking me protectively beneath the crook of his arm. My body warms. I have to check my reflection just to make sure I'm not glowing. I look normal.

I look...happy.

Does he feel this too? Or is it just me?

Am I falling for the trap of his beauty and his power?

"Ready?" he says.

I glance up at him. There's no indication on his face that he feels anything at all.

I nod because I don't trust my voice.

We just fucked, but his arm around me is about to unravel me.

He tightens his hold and pulls us away.

The state of my condo catches me off guard. I forgot about the fight that ensued last I was here when the Men Against Wrath taped me to a chair and tried to torture information from me about Wrath.

The TV screen is spiderwebbed and the stand is crooked so the TV sits at an angle like it could tip over at the slightest gust of wind. Broken glass crunches beneath Wrath's boots. I'm barefoot, so I skirt the mess, angling for my bedroom door.

There are no bodies here, but old blood is splattered across the walls and dried in puddles on the floor.

It's a grim reminder of who and what Wrath is.

He was the one who saved me from the Men Against Wrath.

He is merciless. Brutal. Violent.

Gloriously powerful.

And right now, he's standing in the middle of the wreckage of my condo, and I can't help but watch the way the moonlight finds his face, paints it in shades of silver and blue.

I hurry to my bedroom, slip on a pair of shoes, then grab my back-up camera. I flick it on and silently send a prayer that the battery still has some juice left in it.

It does, so I dial in the settings I think I'll need based on the lighting conditions and come back out to the living room.

Wrath doesn't notice me pointing the lens at him, and I snap a picture, the click of the shutter pulling his gaze to me.

I snap another.

He scowls at me.

I hit the button again and a breath gets lodged in my throat.

Even through the viewfinder, I know that last shot will be something haunting.

"*Dieva*," he says with a growl.

I pull the camera back and flip through the images on the screen.

My mom has always talked about the euphoria she feels when she gets The Shot. When she's on location and the light is perfect and everything comes together to capture magic through her lens.

I've never felt that.

Photography for me was always just a job. I knew how to operate a camera, how to shoot, how to find the light and get the shot.

But never *The* Shot.

I used to think my mom was exaggerating. Or that I didn't have the talent. Or that something was broken inside of me, that I couldn't connect to the art like she could. Like I couldn't truly see the beauty in the world.

Wrath's face, half highlighted by moonlight, that pinch of exasperation between his eyes, the glint of wetness on his lips, sends a shockwave of excitement through my limbs.

Every portrait photographer I've ever met says that it's the eyes that can make or break a shot.

Wrath's gaze in the image has caught a pinpoint of light while his irises flare red.

Wrath's eyes are piercing at the best of times, downright volcanic now.

There's a burn of tears in my sinuses.

I'm immediately embarrassed by the reaction, but there's no sense trying to hide it.

I've never felt this way before about my art. I've never gotten The Shot.

Family photography was never my thing, and that's because I never had a subject quite like Wrath. Full of darkness and power. If the eyes are the window to the soul, Wrath's gaze is the window to an abyss.

It's haunting and electric. It's hard to look away from the image.

I immediately want to post it online. Blow it up and hang it over my mantle.

This is the kind of memento that might haunt me for the rest of my life. I can just see a ninety-year-old me in a nursing home clutching a photo of Wrath to my chest, the paper curled along the edges, creased in the middle.

"*Dieva*," he says again, quieter this time, more of an exasperated warning than anything.

"Sorry." I swallow, lick my lips. "I couldn't help myself. It is my job, after all."

He gives me an indecipherable look.

I set the camera aside and go in search of my old cell phone. I find it in a bin in my closet. When I come back out into the living room, Wrath is holding a pair of World War II binoculars in his hands.

"Those were my great-grandfather's," I say absently while hunting for my phone charger.

"What were they for?" He holds them up in the light.

"Finding and shooting Nazis."

Wrath grumbles. "Chaos."

"What?"

"It was Chaos that started World War II."

"You could say that again."

He sets the binoculars down and plucks a seashell from the shelf. It's one I collected when Mom and I stayed in Florida.

I spot the charger on the kitchen counter and plug my phone in. The screen lights up with the low battery symbol.

As I stand there waiting for it to turn on, my brain finally picks up on what Wrath said, dislodging the conversation I overheard between him and Arthur the other night.

"Hold on a second. Whenever you talk about Chaos, it sounds like you're talking about a person."

He turns the shell over in his hand. "Chaos is my brother."

"Wait...what?!"

He returns the shell to the shelf.

"You have a brother? Named Chaos?"

"Yes."

"And?"

"And what?"

There are so many questions running through my head that it's hard to make sense of where to begin. I run my hand through my hair and pace the room. "You and Arthur were talking about Chaos getting *through* and...you told Ciri that you would wear the crown, not Chaos. So...Chaos is your brother, and he...he's trying to take your throne?"

Wrath remains as stoic as always, but I can hear the anger and the fear in his voice when he says the one word, confirming my suspicions. "Yes."

"I don't understand. Why is he trying to get through? To find the *animus*?"

"Yes."

"So he...me...oh god." I have to sit down.

The couch squeaks when I plop onto the cushion and prop my elbows on my knees, hands buried in my hair. This is worse than I thought.

But really...I can't be surprised, right? Wrath and Lauren and Arthur have hinted that there's more than Wrath, that he's been searching for the *animus* because of a threat to his throne, and to our world because of it.

What was it Lauren said to me the first time I was in the castle?

You don't even know what you stand to lose or how hard Wrath is working to save this entire world.

If Chaos started World War II...

"Why?" I say. "Why did your brother start a war here? Why is he trying to take the throne? What does he plan to do if he gets through?"

"Wars are inevitable," Wrath answers as he flips through one of my self-help books. "My brother and I represent two sides of a coin. I may be ruthless, but I rule with order. Without order, there is chaos. But without chaos, what is order? Does one exist without the other?"

He puts the book back and comes over to the sofa, hands loose fists by his side. "But I am weak without my crown, and he knows that. He poses a threat to my world and to yours. The more chaos he breeds, regardless of where it is, the stronger he becomes. I just need to hold him in check."

I look up at him. "So that's why you're here. Why you're looking for the *animus*. To save us?"

He turns away. "Do not look for redeeming qualities within me, *dieva*. You will be disappointed with what you find."

Down on the boardwalk outside my building, a group of people laugh and cajole each other. They have no clue that just three floors up, I'm having a life-altering conversation with the Demon King while he riffles through my belongings and mementos.

"You're still trying to stop him," I point out. "And by stopping him, you'll help stop more chaos from entering our world."

The line of his jaw runs parallel to his shoulder as he turns to me. "Chaos is already here."

I frown. "I thought you said he was trying to get through."

"Physically," he says. "But his power has been slithering through the gates for decades. Likely you've felt the rise in the disorder, the sense that a volcano is building, about to erupt."

I have. I can't deny that. The news has been awful. The world is a dumpster fire. The mass shootings. The global disasters ignored by the people in power. The bickering politicians. The non-stop violence, mayhem, and...*chaos*.

"He's been getting through," Wrath says, "because without the *animus*, I grow weak. The weaker I am, the harder it is for me to balance him out. We only work together when we are both in check."

"So how did he get through back in the 40s?"

"It was an oversight on my part. Once Chaos was safely back in Alius, Ciri sealed the gate with my help. Of course, the longer the gate was closed, the harder it was to open again. And I've heard travelers have been hunted on your side. Witches who knew what Chaos had done wanted to make sure he couldn't do it again. With

Chaos gone and the gates sealed, your world stabilized again after the 40s, but when I lost the crown...."

He trails off and looks out the window, limned in faint, hazy moonlight.

"You never did tell me who took your crown."

"Chaos did." He looks at me across the living room, eyes starting to burn in the dim light. "I trusted him, and he betrayed me."

The Demon King might be ruthless, but I'm coming to realize there are a few things he sees as unbreakable—loyalty and honor. He has his own set of rules, and he controls the throne with them.

They might be cruel rules, and we all might disagree with them, but at least he has them.

"Why didn't he keep the crown for himself then?"

"At the time, he couldn't."

I frown at him. "I don't understand. I have the crown, and I'm clearly using its power. Why couldn't he?"

"Now you know why you've caught my attention, *dieva*. You are an anomaly. You shouldn't be able to use the *animus*, let alone contain it. Your first brush with it should have incinerated you."

That's an image I don't want burned into my brain.

"So does that mean by simple elimination that I'm not human?" The question makes my heart thud loudly in my ears.

"If I had to guess, I'd say yes."

Deep breaths. Deep breaths.

It's not like that should surprise me at this point. I'll get to the bottom of my lineage, somehow, someway.

"So Chaos took the crown, but he couldn't use it. What's the point of it all then?"

"It's true that in a *typical situation*," he levels a penetrating look at me, meaning I'm *not* the typical situation, "you need all three powers to master all three. But without the full triad of power, I grow weaker by the day. Chaos might be able to overpower me soon enough and then he'll take *dominus* and *oculus* from me. And if he gets all three, I will no longer be king."

A shiver races up my spine. Both at the mention of royalty and at the thought of someone named Chaos ruling anything.

"Do you not get along with your brother?"

Wrath turns away from me as he considers the question. "We got along once."

"And then he became too power hungry?"

He bows his head and says something low and beneath his breath. Something that sounds like, "Or perhaps I did."

"What did you say?"

My phone lets out a chime, signaling it's finally charged enough to turn on.

Wrath ignores my question and stares out the window. Figures.

I grab the phone and hit the power button, and the screen flashes. "You talk about the triad of power like they're actual objects. Is that true?"

"When not claimed, they are." He plucks one of my crystals from the bookshelf and holds it out in his hand. It's the large chunk of amethyst I bought at last year's fine arts & crafts fair. The purple stone glitters in the light.

"Each trine of power is no bigger than this stone. They're all black and carved with the old language. There are many legends of how they came to be, but the one I like best is that they were gifted to the first Demon King by our father god."

He tosses the crystal up into the air and catches it again as he walks toward me. "When a demon becomes king, there is a ritual where he takes on the power of the stones and he absorbs them."

"Have demons always ruled your world?"

"Yes. We are the most powerful. Vampires and witches like to argue against it, and they've certainly tried to overthrow us, but they've failed every time."

"How long has the triad existed? How long have there been kings?"

He keeps tossing the crystal and catching it again. "I'm the twelfth king. There have been kings since the beginning of recorded history."

"Did you guys just learn how to write or something? Twelve... that's not a lot."

When he catches the amethyst this time, he stops, fingers curling over its sharp points as he looks at me. "I've been king for over six hundred years."

The room sways. "Six hundred? Are you kidding?"

"I don't *kid*," he says with a sneer, as if the very idea is beneath him.

My voice is shrill when I ask, "Exactly how old are you?"

"Does it matter?"

"Ummm...yes."

"My father died in my two-hundredth year. That's when I became king."

"That makes you...eight hundred years old?"

He doesn't confirm it, but I can see the truth in his eyes.

No wonder we're powerless against him. Not only does he possess the kind of magic that only used to exist in our fiction, but he's older than our country. By a lot. To him, we must all be idiotic children.

I can't imagine the sheer weight of eight hundred years of living. Or six hundred years of ruling.

"What was your father like?" I ask, wondering if I even want to have this conversation.

It was a lot easier to think of Wrath as nothing more than a villain when he had no past, no family. When my imagination could fill in the blanks, when I could tell myself a story of how the wicked Demon King sprouted from a puddle of black ooze in some dank cave.

He must have the same thought, because the gaze he cuts to me is withering. "We're not doing this, *dieva*."

"Doing what?"

"You're looking for ways to humanize me." He returns the amethyst to the shelf. "And I refuse to give them to you."

I scowl and cross my arms over my chest. "Is that so bad? To want to hope that you're more than what you appear to be?"

"Oh, I am more." In a blink, his face contorts to the monster. The sharp cheekbones, the glowing eyes, the teeth that remind me of a vampire's fangs, the kind of teeth that could sink into flesh and chip away at bone.

In the next blink, he's back to that ethereal, pale beauty as he skirts around the couch, black mist rising in the hazy rays of moonlight.

"Fine," I say. "Then let's talk about Chaos. He stole your crown, hid it away and now..."

"Chaos has more patience than I do. He knew that if he hid the crown from me, the longer I was separated from it, the weaker I would become. He just had to wait. And now..." He sighs and presses his fingers to his eyes.

It's the first time I've seen him portray any kind of apprehension.

"Now, without the *animus*, I fear that if it came to it, Chaos could beat me."

"Really?"

"Yes, really."

He seems so unbeatable though. Untouchable.

The fact that he's worried about facing off against his brother has me worried too. And I have the one thing he needs to keep his brother in line, to stop Chaos from starting another world war.

I cross the room and come to stand beside Wrath. His back is to me now, as if that one unguarded moment was too much. I reach down and take his hand in mine. He doesn't pull away.

"You will get your crown back," I say. "I'll make sure you get it back."

He looks over at me. There's an emotion pinched between his eyes, one I haven't seen before, one that looks incongruous on his sharp, beautiful face.

Hope.

"I will hold you to your word, *dieva,*" he says quietly. "Don't make promises you don't intend to keep."

"I intend to keep this one."

His mouth turns into a grim line, but he nods once and pulls away.

I immediately miss the line of him next to me, the feel of his hand in mine.

"How do we find your mother then?" he asks.

"That shouldn't be too hard." I return to check my phone and find the screen lit up with an old background photo of me and my mom in a sunflower field.

I navigate to messenger and tap on Mom's name to call her.

It rings and rings and rings.

When she doesn't pick up, I end the call and tap out a message. *Call me as soon as you can.*

I'm just about to darken the screen, when a notification for my social account catches my eye. That's when I remember I messaged Susanna, one of my mom's friends from the fabled camping trip.

I tap to my direct messages and find Susanna's replied.

So good to hear from you, Rain! I do remember your mom. We haven't spoken in a very long time. I hope she's doing well. I remember Jeffrey, yes. In fact, we had a show together a few years back. He's a sculptor now. Here's the last phone number I had for him. Good luck!

My stomach drops.

Wrath comes to stand beside me. "What is it?"

"I think...well, I'm just now realizing that this is the phone number for my biological father." I laugh nervously. "A little part of me knew that if I really wanted to meet this man, I could figure out a way to track him down. But once the door is open—"

"It cannot be closed."

"Exactly." I bite at my bottom lip. "What if he's a big douche bag? An asshole? What if he doesn't want to speak to me?"

Wrath's face hardens. "He has no choice in the matter. He will speak."

"We're not going to threaten my biological father."

"We will if it gets us what we want."

"*Wrath.*"

He scowls. "Fine. We will not threaten your father. Does that appease you?"

There's a flash of warmth in my chest, the good kind. I think I just won something I didn't realize I needed to win.

He gave in to me!

"Yes, consider me appeased," I answer and try to bury the smile that wants to plaster itself on my face.

"Don't get cocky," he mutters.

"Who me? Never."

I hear him snort as he saunters away.

My finger hovers over the phone number. I have no idea where Jeffrey lives or what time zone he's in. He might be sleeping.

Before I can second guess it, I tap at the number and initiate the call.

I put the phone to my ear as it connects on the other end.

Shaking, hand sweating, I pace back and forth in front of the refrigerator. My heart is beating so fast, I can feel it in the back of my throat.

The phone rings once. Then twice. I consider disconnecting and pull the phone away from my ear.

No. I have to do this. I have to figure out how I got dragged into this nonsense.

I have to find out if—*if I'm not human.*

"Hello?"

I think my heart stops beating the second I hear the gravelly voice on the other end of the line.

"Hi," I blurt and then panic because I didn't give a second thought to what I actually wanted to say once I got this man on the phone.

There's silence for a beat, and then Jeffrey says, "Can I help you?"

"Hi. Yes. Sorry." I close my eyes and take in a deep breath. When I open them again, Wrath is standing in front of me, arms crossed over his chest. His presence is almost like a balm, soothing my nerves.

If I can stand in the same room with the Demon King, then I can have an actual conversation with my biological father.

"Hi," I say again, "my name is Rain Low, and I think you knew my mother—"

"Sunny," Jeffrey says. I can almost hear the smile in his voice. "Wow. Yeah. How is she?"

"She's doing well. In fact...I wanted to talk to you about her, if you had time? There's something I wanted to ask you."

"Oh." I can hear him breathing through the phone as he considers my request. I can only imagine what he's thinking. Sunny Low's daughter calls him over two decades later after a wild summer romp.

Is he making the connections? Did he ever wonder? Or did he leave Mom that summer and never give their tryst a second thought?

"Sure," he finally answers. "I can chat now."

"This would be better in person," I say and then hold my breath. I know I'm asking a lot of a complete stranger damn near in the middle of the night.

"Now?" he says a little taken back.

"Yes. If it's not too much trouble."

He's quiet a beat, and then, "Hell, I suppose. I'm in the studio.

And I don't sleep much. Do you know where I live? Are you in town or something?"

I look at Wrath. I have the best kind of transportation this side of the multi-verse or whatever. "I can get there pretty quickly if you give me an address."

He rattles off an address in upstate Vermont in the mountains.

"It's kinda hard to find if you don't know where to look," he says.

"Don't worry." Wrath is already surrounded in black mist, ready to carry us away. "I'll manage it."

Jeffrey chuckles to himself. "I guess I'll see you soon then?"

"Definitely."

We disconnect. I slide my phone in the back pocket of my jeans and then race to the kitchen sink and splash cold water on my face.

I never pined for a father. I knew it could have been cool to know him, considering how much my mom liked him, but I never felt a father-sized hole in my heart.

But now, the very thought of meeting him has me shaking and nauseous.

Bent over the kitchen sink, sucking in several deep breaths, I try to quell the rising tide of nerves when I feel Wrath's presence behind me.

"I'll be with you," he says quietly. "You have no reason to worry."

"I know. It's not that. It's—"

What if I'm not human? What if I'm a demon? I don't have the demon mark like Wrath and Lauren and Emery, but maybe it's hidden or—

Everything is changing and shifting beneath me, and I don't know what to hold on to.

Wrath pulls me upright and forces me to face him. "You need answers. I need answers," he says. "The safety of your world might depend on it."

I nod weakly. "I know. I'm fine. I can do this."

His sudden kindness, the way he's gentle with me, has me feeling all sorts of weird things in my belly. Maybe there is a softer side to the Demon King that only a very select few get to see.

Maybe he's not as bad as I thought.

"Show me the address on a map," he says, turning us both to business. Focusing on the tasks will help.

When Wrath has a lock on the location, I duck into my bedroom and shove a few more things in a bag. I want my clothes and my shampoo and toothbrush. Apparently, I'm officially moving in with the Demon King.

I never wanted a roommate, and certainly not a demon one.

At the last second, I wrap my back-up camera into a sweater and shove it to the bottom of the bag, ignoring the look Wrath gives me. There will definitely be more pictures in his near future whether he likes it or not.

He is a haunting subject, one I want to document.

"Ready?" he asks.

"As I'll ever be, I suppose."

He holds out a hand for me, but I ignore it and step into his side. He doesn't hesitate and quickly wraps his arm around me, holding me close.

Now I can breathe easier.

The darkness kicks up around us and carries us off.

6

WRATH DROPS US AT THE END OF JEFFREY'S DRIVEWAY.

Whenever we reappear somewhere through the sub-dimension, there's always this sound that reminds me of a superhero's cape snapping in the wind.

But Wrath has no cape, and he's no superhero.

It's dark here. Crickets and other nighttime creatures sound in the night. The moon is waning, making the darkness heavier.

I was never afraid of the dark as a kid, but I was afraid of the dark woods. I had a wild imagination and thought there might be monsters lurking just past the tree line, waiting for the perfect moment to attack.

How ironic is it that I'm now standing in the dark with something, or rather *someone*, worse than the monsters in my childhood imagination? I certainly never dreamed the monster would look like Wrath.

We follow the dirt driveway through dense woods before the landscape opens up to a field and a cabin nestled at the back of the property.

The cabin is dark, but a second outbuilding several yards from it glows brightly.

Jeffrey mentioned he was in his studio.

Wrath is the first to start forward. I hesitate, trying to prepare myself to meet a man that might share half my DNA.

Wrath stops at the top of a gently rolling hill in the field. I can't see his face with the moonlight and the studio glow at his back, but I can hear his voice perfectly.

"Come, *dieva*."

I surge ahead.

The closer we get, the more I can smell marijuana in the air. Piano music filters out into the night.

We come up on the outbuilding where two large windows look in on the studio.

A man with broad shoulders and graying blond hair tied in a bun uses a chisel on a tall marble slab. There's a joint hanging from the corner of his mouth, smoke curling around his squinting eyes.

The marble is slowly taking the shape of a person, and when the man steps to the side to examine some fine detail, I can see the face of what he's sculpting.

It's a Romanesque woman draped in sheer fabric. Somehow, by some magic, Jeffrey has managed to sculpt each fabric crease in the hard stone.

The figure's mouth is open like she's taking a deep breath, and the fabric yawns over her thin lips.

It's absolutely gorgeous. I think this is my favorite thing about art, how something can be created from nothing and make you feel something so potent, it's almost magic.

"Are you ready?" Wrath asks.

"Will you know if he's supernatural?" I ask him.

Wrath looks at the studio and inside at Jeffrey. "I'll know if he's a demon. If he's something else, depending on what it is, I'll smell it on him. Vampires I know the scent of. Witches are harder to parse. Each witch line smells a little different."

"Okay." I lick my lips. "If he's a demon, wouldn't we know if I was?"

Wrath regards me. "You would think, but everything about you, *dieva,* has been unprecedented."

I shiver in the summer heat.

"I guess we should get this over with then." I take a quick, deep breath and knock on the studio door.

Tools clatter to a table inside and then footsteps come near.

When Jeffrey pulls the door open, the weed hits me along with the scent of pine and whiskey.

"You weren't lying," he says to us. "Did you fly here on a helicopter?" He looks from me to Wrath, and his façe falls. "Oh. Well...that explains it." Some of the cheerfulness has disappeared from his face. The Demon King will do that to a person.

"I didn't realize you knew the demon."

Wrath scowls. I can't help but note the way he says *demon* like he's removed from it. Like he isn't one.

Wrath gives me an almost imperceptible shake of his head.

The relief is nearly palpable.

Jeffrey isn't a demon.

But that only brings up more questions.

"Come on in," Jeffrey says and pulls the door back.

The building is air conditioned, and as soon as I step inside, I have to rub my arms to ward off the sudden chill.

Wrath stands beside me, dwarfing both Jeffrey and me.

In his giant castle, with its soaring ceilings, it's easy to forget just how tall he is. Hell, I'm 5'7" and I feel like a five-footer next to him.

"Welcome to my studio," Jeffrey says. He's wearing a denim apron, the front pockets full of tools. Bits of marble are caught in his graying beard. Black framed glasses slouch on his wide nose.

I look for similarities in our faces and see none. The panic sets in.

"This statue you're working on," I say as I circle it, "is incredible."

"Thank you. It's a commissioned piece. It'll be shipped out to France middle of next month. Still lots more to do." He crosses his arms over his chest. "So what can I do for you, Rain? You said you wanted to talk about your mom?"

"Yeah. I've heard so much about you from her. When you guys all camped together...it's one of her best memories I think."

I sense Wrath circling the room behind me. Jeffrey's eyes stray from me to him and then back to me.

It's hard not to track the Demon King when he's around.

"Your mother is an incredible woman." Jeffrey picks up a steel flask from his work bench and unscrews the top. He takes a swig, then offers it to me.

"No thanks."

He caps it and returns it.

"So... there's no easy way to say this..."

Wrath goes still behind me. Jeffrey's gaze darts to him again.

"So I'm just going to say it. I think you're my father."

Jeffrey's attention jolts back to me. "What?"

"I'm sorry to spring this on you. I wish my mom would have told you a long time ago. I don't know why she didn't. That was her choice, of course. But now...now things are complicated, and I need to know more about my birth and you...my biological father. I mean...maybe you can shed some light on who you are? Like...maybe—"

"Hold on." He lifts his hands, his thick brow sunk over his glasses. "You think I'm your father?"

I nod and surge on. "My mom found out she was pregnant with me right after the camping trip, and you were the only person she was with."

Jeffrey leans against the workbench and puts the heels of his hands on the edge of the counter. "Rain...I—"

"I know this must come as a shock to you."

"That's not it."

"Oh?" I pause, frowning. "Okay. Then what is it?"

Wrath is closer at my back now, hovering like a protector.

"I'm sorry, Rain," Jeffrey says, "but I can't have kids."

My mouth drops open. I blink at the man. My brain stutters to a stop.

"You...*what do you mean*?"

He pushes away from the counter. "I had pediatric leukemia. I've been infertile since I was twelve years old."

I'm hot all over, but numb. I can't feel my legs.

"I'm sorry," Jeffrey goes on. "I did care for your mother a great deal, but I knew she wanted kids, and I knew I couldn't have them. I thought I told her that, but maybe I didn't. It *was* a whirlwind."

I backpedal and slam into Wrath. His hands come to my arms, steadying me.

"No," I say.

"*Dieva*," Wrath says quietly.

"I...you...I mean..."

Pediatric leukemia? *Infertile*?

"I'm sorry you came all the way out here," Jeffrey adds. "If I'd known that was the reason—"

I swallow hard and hold back the tears that are now threatening to spill over. "It's okay. I'm sorry I bothered you," I manage to get out right before I bolt through the door and out into the night.

I stumble into the woods. I'm directionless. The branches tug at my hair.

Tears stream down my face. What the fuck is happening?

I feel like a tree that's been ripped from the ground, roots and all. I have no anchor. Nothing makes sense anymore.

Thunder rumbles overhead and a drop of rain splatters on my forehead.

Stumbling into a clearing, I find Wrath standing in the weak moonlight as thick clouds roll in. Black mist plumes in the air around him. He's a vision of dark beauty, and I'm snotty and sobbing and—

"*Dieva*," he says again.

"What is happening?" I shout as the rain starts to fall.

He says nothing, and I huff out a breath, hands on my hips.

Suddenly he's beside me, but I don't flinch. I'm used to him disappearing and reappearing with no notice. I'm no longer afraid of the monster at my back and the threat of his dark power.

I'm not sure what that says about me, that I believe myself to be safe in the presence of a demon.

The rain slides down his face, flattens his hair. Somehow, he looks even more gorgeous soaking wet. It makes me ravenous for a meal I didn't realize I needed and wanted.

There's been this gnawing hunger at the center of me for a very long time, one that's only satiated when Wrath is around.

Now that I know the taste of him, I'm not sure I can ever give him up.

"Why me?" I ask him.

"I don't know," he admits.

"It could have been anyone that got the animus, and yet here I am. Like getting struck by lightning." I wave vaguely at the now dark sky.

"No," he says.

"No?"

"Not just anyone."

I frown at him.

"As I told you, the *animus* would kill most who possessed it the way you do. So no, you're not just anyone. You're the only one who can tame it, apparently."

And me, he doesn't say, but I think we both know it to be true.

No one can stand up to him the way I can.

"What happens after?" I ask. "When we figure out how I got it, what happens after?"

"I take it back."

"And then?"

The grim line of his mouth tells me all I need to know.

"I am a king," he finally says. "I have a duty."

What did I think he'd say? Did I think we'd save the world together and then ride off into the sunset? Maybe retire to the beach and sip margaritas? Maybe he'd stay in Norton Harbor and we'd move into a condo together and pretend to be normal?

The rain picks up. I'm thoroughly soaked now and starting to shiver as the temperature plummets. Wrath frowns at me as thunder cracks closer to the field causing me to flinch.

"Come," he says and holds out his hand.

"Where are we going?"

"Home."

Home. As if we belong there together. As if it belongs to us both.

I slip my hand into his as lightning bolts through the sky, sending silver light across the clearing. The beat of electricity crawls down my spine, and the Demon King pulls me into him.

I finally feel like I can breathe. Like I'm exactly where I'm supposed to be.

I was wrong, I realize as Wrath's shadow magic kicks up around us, somehow defying the driving rain.

Wrath's castle isn't home. It isn't where I want to belong.

It's right here, tucked into his side, surrounded by his darkness.

Everything is changing and nothing makes sense, but the one constant?

The one constant is Wrath and the familiar feel of him.

How the hell am I ever going to let him go?

7

We reappear in my bedroom at the castle. Water drips from us onto the rug with a loud plop-plop.

Wrath doesn't let me go right away, and I don't make a move to step back.

I shouldn't like being surrounded by his arms or his scent.

I shouldn't like being the only person who can get this close to him.

I shouldn't, but I do.

I like it very much.

I tilt my head back and look up at him. There's worry in his eyes.

It's an echo of what I feel, like this should be wrong, but it doesn't feel that way.

I'm supposed to hate him, and he does infuriate me but—

Wrath lifts his hand to my face, his pale fingers pulling away a wet strand of hair from my jaw. I shiver beneath his touch. He then lifts the strap of my bag from my shoulder and sets it aside.

There's no storm here, several states away from Vermont, but the air is charged nonetheless.

I rake my teeth over my bottom lip as the tide rises in my gut. I can't get enough of him. I can't stop this endless churning of desire any better than I could stop the night from falling. Does he feel it too?

Or maybe it's just the *animus* for him, power calling to its king.

His hand cups my jaw, the cold pad of his thumb brushing over my wet bottom lip.

I'm ignited in the span of a breath, and though I can't see my reflection, I can tell by the shift in Wrath's expression that my eyes are glowing.

"*Dieva*," he says, pulling the name out like a prayer.

I'm still wet with his cum from the last time we fucked, but I could always take more.

My heart thumps in my chest. "Yes?"

"Will you really do anything within your power to return the *animus* to me?"

The open plea on his face almost breaks me. It could all be a ploy to win my trust, but I don't think it is. Wrath might be ruthless, but he's always been straightforward.

Giving him the *animus* means I might have to give him up too, but he was never mine to begin with, and neither was the crown.

"Of course," I breathe out. "You have my word."

His eyes are a red mirror of my own, and then he kisses me. Hard and fast. We break to inhale then crash into one another again as he drives me back to the bed, tearing off my wet shirt in one quick pull of his hand.

We bang into the bed post as Wrath's tongue finds mine with a delicious slide of heat. I'm throbbing between my legs and soaking fucking wet. Wrath yanks off his shirt and picks me up with barely any effort, his hands at my ass.

We're locked together like that in sensuous heat when the door to my room bangs open, and Lauren saunters in.

We stop kissing, and Wrath looks over at the intruder around the tangle of my wet hair. "What?" he barks.

"Never thought I'd catch the mighty Demon King with his pants down," Lauren snarks.

The growl that rumbles in Wrath's chest reverberates through me. He sets me down carefully and then disappears in the next breath. Reappearing behind Lauren, he's shrouded in darkness and fury. Two *norrow* jolt around him, grab Lauren by the arms and slam her to the floor.

She barks out a yelp as her face is smashed against the wood.

Wrath descends on her, his knee pressed between her shoulder blades.

When he speaks, his voice is like the blade of a knife drawing over stone. "I grow tired of your insolence."

She wiggles beneath him as the *norrow* disappear to whatever limbo they live in when Wrath isn't using them as weapons. "You're risking everything," she says, breath fanning over the hardwood floor. "And for what? Some whore?"

I fold my arms over my chest and scowl. "I'm allowed to embrace my sexuality," I argue, though truth be told, I'm kind of a whore for Wrath. Not going to lie. I don't know where it's coming from or why, but when he puts his hands on me, I'm pretty much mindless, nothing but buzzing lady parts.

"The *dieva* is right," Wrath says. "In fact, I like when she embraces her power."

"You do?"

He rises to his feet and yanks Lauren upright by her hair. He guides her over to me. "Bow to her," he tells her.

"What?" Lauren and I say in unison.

"You have a decision to make," Wrath tells Lauren. "You either die or you bow. You have five seconds."

"You have got to be kidding me," she says.

"One." Wrath lets her go and she stumbles forward.

Lauren scowls. "I'm not bowing to her."

"Two."

"Wrath," I try, "this really isn't necessary."

"Three."

Lauren rights her shirt and smooths back her hair. "She's no one. Nothing! Without the *animus*, she's just—"

Wrath levels her with a glowing red glare. The darkness builds around him, the edges sharpening into blades. "Four."

"All right! Fine!" She sinks to her knees in front of me. "Happy now?"

"Now stay there."

"What?"

"You get up when she tells you to get up."

"Um..." I look at him over the top of Lauren's head and mouth, "What are you doing?"

"She needs to know her place," is his answer. "And you need to know yours."

His words hit me like a bomb. Is he saying...that I even *have* a place? The crown was stolen, my power borrowed from him. I have no place.

And yet the idea is intoxicating, even if it is temporary.

But I think there's more to it. I think this is some kind of test, and I know I want to pass it.

I'm still shirtless in just my bra and soaking wet jeans, but I straighten my shoulders and spine and walk a slow circle around Lauren feeling mightier than I have any right to be.

"Why do you hate me so much?" I ask.

She snorts.

I look at Wrath. "Could I ask you to kill her?"

Wrath clasps his hands behind his back. "Yes."

I don't plan on it, but it's good to know what my options are. I'm no villain, after all, but I do think Lauren has been hating on me for stupid reasons.

"Answer the question," I say.

Lauren inhales. "He can't keep his hands off you. For months, people have fawned all over him, and he's barely batted an eye, and now you come along and he's losing his damn mind."

Well shit. They say pride is a dangerous emotion, but damn if it doesn't feel good.

I look across the room at Wrath. There's nothing on his face to hint at how he feels about this accusation being thrown in his face, but the fact that he isn't denying it makes me feel like a goddamn legend.

"What do you care?" I ask Lauren. "Because it's sounding an awful lot like jealousy."

"I'm not jealous."

"Aren't you?"

Wrath slowly circles her, and her attention immediately wanders to him. She can deny the jealousy up and down, but the way she tracks him whenever he's in the room tells me all I need to know.

I don't blame her really. Until I got here, she had him all to herself. And whether or not she wanted him in her bed is irrelevant. I've clearly disrupted whatever it was she had before. It's why she's willing to risk his anger when she speaks against him. She's hoping she can talk sense into him. She wants him to return to what he was before me.

"You'll cost him something," she says to me. "I don't know what it is yet, but it won't be anything good."

When I catch Wrath's eye again, he's staring at me in that distant yet penetrating way he has. Does he think Lauren might be right? Is he worried?

"Get up," I tell her.

Mouth pursed tightly, she climbs to her feet and waits.

"Go." I give her a tip of my chin.

"I did come here with a purpose other than to be made into a doormat," she says.

Wrath stands in front of me now. "Go on."

"Arthur is hearing word that the government is looking to make a declaration against you. Because of *her*. They think you're perverting her or something."

Well, she certainly wasn't wrong about me mucking things up. Clearly my being with Wrath locked away in his castle is stirring up some shit that wasn't in the Save the World plan.

Wrath looks at me over his shoulder. "*Dieva*, how would you like to go on a date with me?"

"What?" I say with a nervous laugh because I'm not entirely sure he isn't joking.

"Let's show them how little we fear them." He starts for the door. "Let's show them where you stand. Lauren, book Par House tomorrow night for eight."

"Wait! I didn't pack for a date night." I only tossed leggings and t-shirts into my bag.

He stops at the door and considers something, then, "I'll request Kat take you shopping tomorrow. She can shield you so you're safe when I'm not with you. Will that suffice?"

The Demon King is letting me go shopping with a witch for a date night?

He's making it harder and harder to hate him.

"Yeah, that will be fine."

He gives me a nod. "I'll set it up then. Goodnight, *dieva*."

"Goodnight."

When he's gone, Lauren turns to me and narrows her eyes. "I bet you like him parading you around."

"I'm not a Mardi Gras float."

She looks me up and down. I'm still in my black lace bra, hair soaking wet. "Could have fooled me." Then she turns on her heel and marches out the door.

8

KAT AND EMERY PICK ME UP THE NEXT DAY A LITTLE AFTER NOON. I HAD thought it would only be Kat, so Emery is a welcome surprise. The first time we met, Wrath stabbed one of her friends, but she was still warm and kind to me. In fact, she helped talk me off the ledge and had been the first one to suggest I look into my birth.

"Hey!" Emery climbs out of the black SUV and wraps me in a hug. "I didn't think we'd get to see you again so soon. How are you?"

"I've been better. I've been worse."

Kat comes around the SUV to join us in the driveway. "You look better. You're practically glowing. New skin care or something else?" She arches an eyebrow and gives me a devilish grin.

I get the distinct impression that while Kat isn't Wrath's biggest fan, she wouldn't judge me in the least for sleeping with him.

I think Kat might be the type of person to take what she wants and needs, regardless of the opinion of others.

I dodge answering because I'm not about to dish on my demon

sex life just yet. "Thank you guys for agreeing to take me out. I think I need this more than I realized."

"We're happy to provide a day of normalcy," Emery says. "When you're dragged into the supernatural world, those days become fewer. But they are needed. Don't forget that."

Kat puts her hands on my shoulders. "I'm tasked with shielding you so you won't be recognized. Are you ready? It won't hurt."

"Sure. Go for it."

Something sweet blooms on the back of my tongue and perfumes the air around us. Kat's eyes glow bright green as my face warms, and the warmth spreads over my body.

"There," she says. "That should do."

"Kat always amazes me," Emery says, eyeing me.

"That's it? I don't feel any different."

"Check your reflection." Emery nods at the driver's side mirror.

I duck down and see someone that looks like me, but only vaguely. My nose is sharper, my lips thinner. All of my freckles are gone, but my skin is still fair, my eyes still hazel.

"Wow." I paw at my face. "It's like an alternate reality version of me."

"I've also given you a bit of a personal shield," Kat explains. "We shouldn't have any trouble."

"It's like being invisible without being invisible." I smile up at her. "You could sell this. It's amazing."

"Ahh." She huffs out a breath. "Too much work. Too much trouble. Come on. Wrath has only given us two hours and we have a lot of ground to cover."

Kat climbs into the backseat of the SUV.

"I can ride in back," I say.

"Don't be silly." Kat folds her long legs in behind the driver's seat. "I like feeling like I'm being chauffeured around. Emery will attest to that."

"She does."

"See?" Kat's bright red lips spread into a grin. "Now get in. Chop chop."

Emery drives and takes us to one of the upscale shops in Norton Harbor. It's a place I've entered only once with Harper. The only thing I could have afforded at the time was a pair of underwear. And I'm not the type of girl to shell out fifty bucks for panties.

"Here?" I say and wrinkle my nose as Emery lets the SUV parallel park itself.

"What's wrong with Ocean and Glass?" Kat asks from the backseat.

"The price tags?"

Kat waves away my concerns. "Wrath is paying. He didn't give us a limit."

"Are you serious?"

"It pays to fuck rich men," Kat says and Emery bursts out laughing.

"You laugh but you know it's true too."

The SUV expertly gets us into a spot, and Emery shuts the engine off. "I'm not going to lie. The money is a perk."

"Rhys is the richest man on the eastern seaboard," Kat explains. "Emery still hates taking his money, but he has plenty to give out. Trust me."

I grumble to myself. "I'm suddenly feeling like a hooker."

"Hookers only fuck for the money." Kat sits forward between the seats. "Are you only fucking Wrath for the money?" She lifts a brow at me as if she already knows the answer.

"Is there a right answer to that question?"

"Both answers are the right answer. Don't let anyone tell you otherwise."

Inside Ocean and Glass, we're greeted immediately by a saleswoman dressed in a sleek black pants suit. Her curly hair is pulled tightly into a ponytail, and the poufy tail bobs back and forth as she makes her way toward us on stilettos. She beams when she sees Kat.

"Hey Kat! Lovely to see you! It's been a while."

"It has," Kat agrees. "Apologies, Shauna. It's been wild the last few months."

"No need to apologize. I'm glad to see you now. What can I assist you with today?"

Kat motions to me. "We're here to outfit our friend for a date night."

"Ahhh." Shauna claps her hands together. "My favorite occasion to dress for. Is it formal? Casual?"

I look to Kat because I honestly don't know. Did Wrath give her instructions? We're going to Par House, which straddles the line between casual and upscale hipster.

"Let's say casual sleek," Kat decides.

"I didn't even know that was a style," I mumble to Emery.

She smiles over at me and then whispers, "Kat is several hundred years old. She knows all of the styles. *Literally*."

I look at Kat with new interest. She doesn't look a day over twenty-six. Everything about her is flawless. I guess I shouldn't be surprised that she's several hundred years old. I should stop being surprised by anything I learn about the supernatural world.

Shauna shows us to the fitting room and then with Kat's help, gathers several outfits for me to try. I start with a pants suit much like Shauna's, but I don't have her long, lithe form and I end up looking like a licorice stick that's been soaking in a puddle for too long.

Next, I try a bright red dress that is too big in the waist. Then another dress that droops on my boobs.

I try on so many outfits, it makes my head spin. "Tell me again why I can't just show up in my leggings and a t-shirt?"

"Think of this as a sort of coming out party," Kat says, her arms crossed over her chest, eyes assessing me in an emerald green dress with a long skirt. "The whole world will be watching you. You best look the part."

I check out my ass in the mirror. I've always liked my butt. It's nice and plump. "I get that, but what exactly *is* my part?"

Emery holds out a black dress to me. It's made of faux leather that is buttery soft between my fingers. "The part of a queen."

I give a very unladylike snort but disappear back into the dressing room.

The leather dress fits perfectly, the soft inner layer skimming my hips, nipping in at the waist. I turn around for a mirror check and damn near whistle at the sight of my ass covered in leather.

"This is the one," I say.

"Well show us," Kat demands.

I come out, and the girls' eyes get big as they scan the look.

"You're right. This is the one." Kat claps once. "Now accessories. Shauna, what do you have for statement jewelry?"

Shauna and Kat disappear to the front of the store just as Emery's phone rings. Rhys's face appears on the screen, and Emery smiles down at it. "I'm gonna step out to take this."

"Sure. Of course."

I wander back out to the main floor to check out their shoe collection. I find two girls huddled together, staring at one of their phones.

The audio is down low, but I can make out screaming and then a loud OOOHHHH! from a crowd.

It sounds familiar somehow. I get a little closer.

"Can you *even*?" the dark-haired girl says to her friend.

The clip starts over. "No," the shorter girl answers. "I would die."

"He's so fucking hot."

My ears start to burn with realization. I think I know who they're referring to and what clip they're watching.

"I don't mean to be nosy," I say.

The girls look up.

"Is that Wrath?"

The dark-haired girl grins. "It's from a few nights ago when he saved Rain from falling to her death."

Hearing the girl refer to me catches me off guard until I remember I'm disguised with magic. They don't know who I am.

The shorter girl has the phone in her hand, so she turns it around to show me the clip that's on a repeating loop. The video starts with a girl laughing at the phone's camera, then there's shouting from above.

Wrath's deep voice cuts through the night as he shouts, "Nooo!"

Then he's suddenly standing on the sidewalk, people shrieking and darting from him as his shadowy magic writhes in the air like ink. His eyes are burning red.

"Holy shit," someone says near the phone, and then the camera pans up just as I'm shoved over the railing.

My stomach drops as if I'm experiencing the plummet all over again.

Wrath holds out his arms. The dark-haired girl shrieks in front of me, clearly ready for the climax of the scene. "It's so fucking hot!" she whispers as Wrath catches me.

It's over within seconds.

It didn't feel like that when it was happening.

"See what I mean?" the dark-haired girl says, her eyes bright. "Rain has got to be the luckiest girl on this planet."

I practically snort. The only reason that clip exists is because the Men Against Wrath tortured, beat me, and then tried to kill me. In my own damn house.

The shorter girl nods. "I'd take Rain's place in a heartbeat."

"Why would you say that?"

They both give me a blank stare.

"What if he's horrible to her behind closed doors?"

The dark-haired girl takes the phone and freezes the video on

Wrath. "Look at his face." She turns the phone around. "He's desperate to save her."

A lump forms in my throat.

When I was shoved over the railing by Ryder, the leader of MAW, all I could see was the night sky above.

All I could think was: I'm going to die.

I had no way of knowing what Wrath was doing or what he looked like.

Until now.

Because he does look desperate. He looks panicked and afraid.

He had no idea at the time that I had the *animus,* so it couldn't have been only the connection or the power.

"Rain!" Kat calls.

The girls look from Kat to the phone then back to me. They frown in unison.

I hurry into the back. I'm not prepared to have a conversation with two strangers about what it's actually like being with the Demon King.

I'm beginning to think maybe I've had it wrong this entire time.

Maybe the Demon King isn't as black and white as I first thought.

9

KAT, EMERY, AND I FINISH OUR SHOPPING WITH A HALF HOUR TO SPARE, SO we stop for a cup of coffee. I try really hard to be present for the conversation—I could learn a lot from these two women about the supernatural world—but my brain is now stuck on a loop of the video clip and the look on Wrath's face as he watched me plummet over the railing.

Emery and Kat drop me off at Wrath's house in the afternoon with a promise to get together again soon. Before they leave, Kat removes her spell and my face returns to normal.

It's almost a relief.

I don't cross paths with anyone inside the castle as I make my way to my bedroom. I take an extra long hot shower, then doze off for a while, then pace my room, then take another hot shower.

My stomach is full of butterflies.

The Demon King is taking me on a date, and I can't fucking wait, and it terrifies me.

When I'm finally dressed, my hair dry and left wavy, my makeup on, I make my way downstairs.

Wrath is waiting for me in the sitting room I've decided to call the Bourbon Room, since I always find him drinking there.

Tonight it's no different. There's a tumbler of bourbon in his hand, but when he turns to me as I enter the room, he sets the liquor aside and drinks in the sight of me instead.

The expression on his face is not unlike the expression I saw in the video.

It's an expression that looks an awful lot like desperation.

His nostrils flare and he licks his lips.

"You look nice," I say, trying to cut the tension.

A tailored black coat hugs his body the way I wish I could. The material skims the swell of his biceps, the hard line of his shoulders. A stiff, pointed collar stands like a shield around his neck. He's got on a V-neck black t-shirt tucked into black jeans with a black leather belt around his waist.

A few sweeping lines of his demon mark peek out of the V-neck.

His hair is still damp, but he's combed it back and set it with a pomade that has a slight sheen to it beneath the ceiling lights.

My fingers itch for my camera.

I want to immortalize him. He's too much. Too much beauty to look at all at once.

I want to hold the vision of him in my hands so I can savor every detail.

"You look lovely as well," he says, his voice a little husky, a little thick.

I fidget with the long necklace Kat picked out for me. The chain is delicate gold with a sharp spiked charm hanging from it. "I'm not really a dress kind of girl."

"Oh *dieva,*" he says, "I disagree."

My belly warms, and I can feel an echoing heat flaring in my cheeks. "So we're going to Par House, right?"

He nods. "My favorite place this side of the sub-dimension."

"Oh?" I raise a brow. "Did you just make a joke?"

He smiles. It's the first genuine smile I think I've seen on him since we met. It's openly happy. No snark or arrogance behind it.

"I can find levity from time to time."

"I like it when you surprise me."

"Challenge accepted." He holds out his elbow for me, and I gladly step into him.

The darkness sweeps in around us. The next instant, we're in the alley behind Par House where it all began, where we first officially met. Twinkle lights glow against the night sky.

Wrath goes to the metal door on the back of the restaurant and pulls it open. Instantly, we're greeted with the familiar clatter of the innards of a restaurant. Dishes clanking against each other, waitstaff yelling at the kitchen staff, the sizzle of food and the pop of frying oil.

I step inside into the hallway that runs parallel to the kitchen just as a waitress comes bustling out. She's got two plates in hand and rocks back on her feet just moments before smashing into me.

Anger is the first emotion on her face, and then she sees Wrath behind me. "Oh! Wrath! Didn't see you there."

"Good evening, Rosa," he says. "My table ready?"

"Of course. Always." She smiles awkwardly beneath the fringe of dark bangs as big hoop earrings swing from her ears. "Seat yourself," she says and picks up her pace. "I'll be back around to take your order in just a second."

Wrath's hand goes to the small of my back and guides me down the hall the way Rosa disappeared. I've been to Par House a handful of times before. They're well-known around town for their sushi and tempura with their house miso sauce. My stomach growls with anticipation.

The second we step out of the hallway and into the main restaurant, several people turn to us, and it doesn't take long for the awareness to spread through the room.

Thankfully, the Demon King has been here many times before, and most of the people at the Par seem totally accustomed to looking up from their platter of fried vegetables to see the Demon King walk in.

Hand still on my back, Wrath guides me to a booth in the far corner. He gestures for me to slide in, so I do. He takes the seat on the opposite side, the one that faces the door.

The soft golden light coming from the pendant that hangs above our table softens some of the hard lines of Wrath's face.

If I didn't know who he was, I might be tricked into thinking he was just a guy on a date with a girl.

There are already menus on the table, so I flip one open even though I'm pretty sure I already know what I want. "What are you ordering?" I ask.

"Veggie sushi," Wrath answers.

I recall the leftovers in the fridge. "Do you eat anything else?"

"I like order, remember? It also means I'm not typically a risk-taker. Besides, I like the veggie sushi here."

"Do you not like fish?"

"I believe in your world I am what you would call a vegetarian."

My eyes widen. "Are you serious?"

"Yes."

"The mighty Demon King doesn't eat meat? Is it like an ethical choice or something?"

Though I sense people whispering around us and watching every move Wrath makes, his attention is firmly on me.

"Still trying to find redeeming qualities, are you *dieva*?"

"I've always liked the villains who brake for deer."

He laughs and the sound is so unaccustomed, I nearly wet my new black lace panties with glee.

"Meat makes it harder for me to travel through the sub-dimension. It weighs me down."

"Womp womp. I like my version better."

He smiles at me across the table.

Rosa quickly appears with a tablet in hand, a stylus poised over the screen. "What can I get for you guys?" Her attention lingers on me, and I have to wonder if the Demon King has ever dined at the Par with a woman.

I'm totally going to ask him now.

Wrath folds his hands on the table. "I'll have the usual."

She smiles and nods and taps in the order on her tablet. "And Rain?" She glances up at me.

So she knows who I am. Does everyone here know? Being adjacent to the Demon King has thrust me into the spotlight I suppose.

"I'll have a lavender margarita and an order of the perogies."

"Good choices all around." She makes note of my order. "The drinks shouldn't take long. I'll have the kitchen put your order at the top."

"Thank you, Rosa." Wrath rests against the booth and spreads an arm over the back. I catch Rosa watching him.

A burr of jealousy is firmly lodged in my chest.

Fucking hell.

"Thanks, Rosa," I hear myself saying, clearly dismissing her.

Wrath shoots me a look. Rosa nods, smiles, and scurries away.

"Jealousy does not become you," Wrath comments.

"And gloating doesn't become you, Demon King."

He laughs.

Damn if I don't love the sound of it.

The streaming radio switches to an upbeat pop song and it immediately makes me feel giddy.

"So." I fold my hands on the table.

"So." His irises are their normal stormy gray, no hint of a red glow in sight, but his eyes are glinting just the same.

Is the Demon King in a good mood?

"When's the last time you were on a proper date?" I ask.

He tilts his head, giving me a look that says he knows exactly what I'm doing.

And to my surprise, he lets me do it.

"A very long time," he answers.

"How long are we talking? A decade? A century? Two centuries?"

He sighs and looks away. "Nearly six hundred years."

Rosa returns with our drinks. Wrath has ordered a tumbler of what looks like scotch or bourbon. My margarita is a shade of pale lavender with sugar crusted on the rim.

"Your order should be out soon." Another table waves her down, pulling her away.

"Six hundred years, huh? And here I thought my track record was growing stale. Who was the lucky girl?" I take a tentative sip of my margarita. Oh it's damn good.

"She was my betrothed."

I nearly spit out my drink and catch it at the last second, clamping my hand over my mouth. The Demon King was engaged? That territorial flare returns.

Wrath frowns.

Are my eyes glowing?

An older man at the table over from us bugs out his eyes at me, so I'm guessing that's a yes. I quickly look away.

"*Dieva*," he warns.

"Sorry. You just caught me off guard."

He sips at his drink.

"You have to elaborate," I say. "What happened to the woman you were supposed to marry?"

"I killed her."

"You *what*?" Good thing I wasn't drinking again. "Why?"

"She betrayed me, and as king, I cannot abide by that. I needed to send a message to those under my rule, and those who had contrived to overthrow me with her help."

It takes me several seconds to digest this information. There's so much to unpack here, but the one question running through my head is one I can't stop myself from blurting out.

"Did you love her?"

Wrath's gaze flicks up to mine. There's a heaviness on his face, an invisible wound that has never healed. "Yes."

He was betrothed to a woman he loved, and she tried to help overthrow him.

I don't want to feel sorry and yet...I do. I really fucking do.

He must see it on my face. "Don't," he says.

"Don't what?"

"Do not pity me."

"I don't."

"Lies."

With a sigh, I fall back against the booth and turn my drink in my hand. Condensation is starting to collect on the glass, and it runs down to meet my fingers.

"Is everyone always trying to take your power from you?" I ask.

"Many have tried, yes."

Has anyone ever seen him as anything other than an adversary? Someone to beat in order to steal what he possessed?

I can't help it—I do pity him. First his soon-to-be wife betrayed him, and then his brother.

It just proves my earlier suspicion—loyalty and trust are paramount for him because so few have proven to have both.

I make myself a vow right then and there to never break my promises to him. I'm not going to be like those people. I'm not going to break his heart.

Rosa arrives with our food not long after, and I immediately dig in. I didn't realize how hungry I was, and diving into Wrath's past has made me ravenous. I'm not delicate about devouring my food either, but Wrath eats his sushi with chopsticks like he's some kind of civilized human being or something.

Somehow, we settle into companionable conversation, and Wrath tells me about his favorite meal as a child (lentils and fresh vegetables yuck) and I describe Mom's homemade lasagna in great detail. I haven't had it in months.

When Rosa checks in on us and I lift my glass to indicate

another margarita, Wrath snatches the glass from my hand and says, "No, Rosa. Water only."

"What? Why?" I whine. "Those are really good margaritas."

"And you're very drunk," he points out.

"Am not."

He frowns at me with the kind of exasperation that should only be reserved for petulant children.

"Fine," I say with a groan.

"Being inebriated is a liability," he says. "And we're not in the position to be reckless."

"We. Is there a 'we'?"

The question snuck out on me, but it's too late to take it back.

The furrow between his brows deepens, and when he frowns like that, eyes narrowing, his slate gray eyes look like knives that could cut.

I inhale and lick my lips, wishing I could return the words to my mouth and hide them behind my teeth.

Because I want there to be a *we*. I'm falling hard and fast, and it doesn't make any fucking sense, but here I am and there he is looking at me like I just dragged a tornado inside his house and let it loose.

"*Dieva*," he says, voice low and throaty.

"It's okay," I start, but his attention cuts away from me to the front of Par House, and his frown sharpens to a razor. Immediately he's shrouded in black magic, and my skin erupts in goosebumps.

I turn in my booth just in time to see several dark figures hurry through the restaurant, all dressed in tactical gear. And they're coming right for us.

Wrath goes still while my heart lurches to my throat.

"What do we do?" I whisper across the table.

"We do nothing," he says, his eyes still on the soldiers.

"Are you kidding me?" I reach across the table and take his hand. His gaze strays to our connection for a split second. "Take us out of here!"

"No."

"Why not?"

He yanks his hand back.

The wait staff disappears into the kitchen, and the diners lurch away from their tables and file out the door. So when the soldiers surround our booth in a neat semi-circle, it's just us and them.

"Ms. Low," the man at the front says, his voice muffled through his face mask, "step away from the booth slowly. We're here to take you home."

"I'm sorry?" I say. "I'm not going anywhere with you."

"Ms. Low, we're under orders from the United States Government to get you to safety."

"I'm not in danger."

"Ms. Low," he starts.

"No." I stand from the booth, and all of the soldiers go on alert, barrels pointed right at me. "You all tried to kill me. I'm not any safer with you than I am with him." I nod vaguely at Wrath who still sits in the booth as if we're not under threat. He's as vulnerable as I am. I'm sure these soldiers know that if they kill me, they kill Wrath.

"We're not leaving here until you're under our custody," the man says, changing tactics.

I cross my arms over my chest. "Then I guess you're not leaving."

The man says into his headpiece, "Permission to move?"

That's probably not a good sign.

"Soldier," Wrath says, "you have three seconds to leave this place."

The soldier's eyes flick to Wrath as the darkness kicks up around us. The *norrow* are coming. I can feel them like a spider along my spine.

Old me would be panicking at the impending danger, but there's a little voice rising in volume in the forefront of my mind and it's saying: fuck this.

Power roars through me in a blinding crescendo. Several glass sconces pop and shatter on the wall. Plastic condiment bottles melt to nothing. The wood frames of the booths catch fire and burn. And I am filled with an elation so pure, I'd almost think I'd left my body.

"I'm not going anywhere with you," I say, and when a hand closes around mine, and I look over at Wrath, I realize I have to peer *down* at him.

Because I'm floating again.

The rest of the soldiers fall back, eyes wide behind the shields of their thick helmets.

"It's all right, *dieva*," Wrath says as he squeezes my hand.

Whatever magic holds me in midair quickly fades, and I plumet back down. Wrath catches me around the waist, lessening the impact when I meet the floor again.

I don't know how I did that, but now is not the time for questions. I want the soldiers to think I knew exactly what I was doing. They don't want me safely returned. They want to use me.

Wrath takes me by the hand again and pulls me toward the rear entrance. But before we leave, he calls out to the soldiers. "Do not forget you were warned. You have Ms. Low to thank for your lives. I would not have been so merciful."

When we burst out the back door, I hang my head and shout at the sky, "That was amazing!"

I'm drunk on power and lavender margaritas, and I don't know why I ever wanted to return to my normal life.

This is fucking amazing.

I turn a circle around Wrath, head a little swimmy, as he starts down the alley where we first met.

"Don't get cocky," he admonishes.

"I'll do whatever I want. And also, every time you say that word I think about your dick."

"Filthy mouth for a filthy girl."

I smile big. "And when you talk like that, I'm immediately horny and wet."

"I'm aware."

"Oh?" I quirk a brow. "So why don't you do something about it?"

"Are you trying to manipulate me into fucking you?" There's a flash of amusement in his eyes.

"Yes. Is it working?"

He snatches my wrist and yanks me into him. I've been spinning since we came outside, and I stumble on my feet until he steadies me. His nostrils are flaring, his jaw flexing as he grits his teeth.

I grab him by the cock and find him hard. His eyes slip closed as he growls low in his throat. "I see," I say up to him, "that the answer is yes."

When he opens his eyes next, they're glowing red, and it makes me even wetter.

We're both drunk on power and something else that I think we're both afraid to name.

"Will you bow to me this time?" I say, and I know he knows exactly what I'm asking for.

He wraps an arm around my waist and pulls us away from the alley. We reappear with a snap of air on a rooftop deck at the castle.

The wind whips across the open space, but the air is warm and humid.

Wrath lets me go once the world stops swaying and takes a step back. "Take your clothes off," he orders, his irises still molten red.

Oh fuck me.

I don't hesitate.

I unzip the dress and pull it down around my waist. My hair cascades down my back. I shimmy my hips to pull the dress off the rest of the way, and Wrath's gaze is on me the entire time, though he doesn't move an inch.

The bra is easy to unhook, and I let the straps slip from my shoulders and hold it to my chest with my arm. "Was that a yes?" I ask. "I want to hear you say it."

"I know you do."

God, he knows just what to say to get the better of me.

I let the bra go. My nipples bud.

Wrath takes in a deep breath.

I hook my fingers into the waist of my panties, wiggle my hips and slowly slip them off. Naked, exposed, I rock back my shoulders, one hand on my hip. I've always been a little soft around the hips, not particularly narrow at my waist. There was a time I was self-conscious about it, but not anymore.

And besides, the way Wrath devours the sight of me, eyes flaring brighter in the darkness, makes me feel like I might be the most beautiful woman he's ever seen.

There's a brief flash of satisfaction in my chest, and then Wrath disappears, and my clit immediately throbs at the thought of him coming for me.

When he reappears, he's inches away, and his dark magic surrounds us, perfuming the air with spice and heat. He walks me back to the railing, and the cold stone on my ass tears a hiss from my throat.

Overhead, a few bats swoop at the air while an owl hoots in the distance. The Demon King slowly drops to his knees in front of me. I inhale sharply, a fluttery feeling overwhelming my lungs.

"Is this what you wanted, *dieva*?" he asks as he nudges my knees apart. A few minutes ago, I thought the night was warm, but now that I'm naked and beneath the weighty attention of the Demon King, I'm chilled and quivering.

"Yes," I breathe out.

His touch is delicate as his fingertips trail up my sensitive inner thigh inching closer and closer to my wet center.

The anticipation drives me wild. I'm shaking, panting, and when he reaches my wet slit, he slides his fingers over me.

I exhale with pleasure and writhe against the stone, waiting for him to reach my swollen bud.

When he leans in, I tense up, so damn ready for his mouth to be on me.

But he decides to torture me instead and sends a jet of warm air over my needy clit.

I moan at the sensation and try to arch into him, but he's not letting me get away with it. Not yet.

"You smell so good, *dieva*," he says, sending butterflies tearing across my stomach.

"I bet I taste just as sweet," I challenge and reach out for his head as if I really think I can push the Demon King's face into my mound.

He easily dodges me and smacks my hand away. "You wanted me on my knees. Now that I'm here, let me do as I please."

I whine. I can't help it. I'm wound up tight, every nerve pulsing for release.

"You're torturing me," I mutter.

He slides two fingers closer to my opening and I widen my stance for him.

"Every second I'm in the same room with you is torture, *dieva*."

"That can't be true," I say.

"I don't lie," he points out and then he pushes two fingers inside of me and sucks my clit into his mouth.

Knees going week, I collapse against the stone railing.

"You taste so fucking good." He laps me up, drinks me down. His tongue is absolute bliss on my pussy. I won't survive this. I won't survive him.

I'm already trembling at the knees and restless. Like my skin is too tight, my nerves too volatile.

Like I could burn into the night.

Wrath fucks me slow and steady with his fingers.

I pant and tangle my fingers in his dark hair.

"You are amazing," I say and mean it even though it's insane and wrong.

He makes me feel so fucking good.

My breath quickens as the point of his tongue flicks at my clit and the pressure builds at my core.

"I'm already close," I say because I don't want to reach this crescendo without him.

He slows his rhythm, and I tense up, trying to hold the orgasm at bay.

Not yet. Not yet.

"Wrath."

He pulls away but keeps his fingers inside of me. My juices coat his mouth, and he runs his tongue over his bottom lip, savoring it, his eyes burning bright red.

"I want that cock inside of me."

He stands in front of me, fingers still buried to the knuckles in my pussy. "Do you now?"

"Yes."

I shiver at a cool breeze and Wrath's darkness slithers over my tight nipples, driving away some of the ache.

"Wrath. Don't make me wait."

"Try that again."

Eyes heavy, I try to focus on his face. What does he want from me?

And then I know.

"My king." I suck in a heavy breath. "Will you please fuck me?"

His eyes glow brighter. "Good girl."

I fumble at his belt. When I get it undone, I slide my hand inside his pants and squeeze at his hard-on through his boxer briefs. His eyes roll back in his head as he hisses through gnashed teeth.

"That's what I thought," I say.

He growls and when he opens his eyes again, they glint like embers.

"I don't know what to do with you," he says.

"What do you mean?" I'm frenzied. "Fuck me. That's what you do with me."

He grabs me by the wrist to stop me. "You make me feel out of control, *dieva*."

I go still beneath his gaze. His confession is a jolt of electricity to my chest, and my heart pounds beneath my ribs.

I'm breathless and empowered and so fucking ravenous for him.

"Me too," I admit.

We stare at each other in the night, and some unspoken vow is made right then and there.

Whatever this is, it's messy and savage, and it doesn't make sense, but fuck if it doesn't feel so damn right.

We both make the decision at the exact same moment to give in to it.

Our mouths crash into one another, needy and feral. His tongue finds mine easily, and slides over me, filling my mouth with my own taste. I drag my hands through his hair as he tears off the rest of his clothes, his cock thick and heavy between us.

I grab hold of his shaft and he groans loudly against my lips.

"You're so fucking hard," I pant out.

"You make me so fucking hard." He drives me back against the railing and hooks a hand around my thigh, lifting my leg for him.

The throbbing head of his cock finds my opening, forcing a carnal gasp from my throat. "You're dripping wet."

He's right. I can feel it coating my inner thighs.

"Stop torturing me." I kiss him again. "Fuck me."

With a deep inhale, he shoves inside of me, and I cry out as he fills me up. I wrap my arms around him, holding on for dear life as he fucks me hard and fast and almost angrily, like he's pissed it feels so good.

Sweat glistens on his chest, muscle and bone twining as he works at me.

The pressure builds and builds, and as I reach the peak, as Wrath's cock throbs inside of me, it's almost like I can feel him reaching that pinnacle too. As if we're joined fully, completely, connected in every imaginable way.

"Don't hold back, *dieva,*" Wrath says through gritted teeth. "I want to hear you come loudly and without restraint."

I will gladly give it to him.

He pinches my nipple between thumb and forefinger sending a delicious flare of pain through me.

"Go on." He pinches harder, then shifts forward, putting weight on my pelvis, causing friction to build between us.

"Fuck, yes...just like that."

He keeps the pace, driving into me, and then—

Firelight flares across the rooftop as the wave hits me all at once, rolling, crashing through me.

I hang my head back and cry out at the darkened sky, every ounce of pure satisfaction pours through me and then out of me as my body convulses beneath him.

Wrath drives deeper, spilling into me, his answering gasp sounding at my ear, a hot pant of breath sliding like a delicious flame down the curve of my neck.

When he collapses against me, sweaty and spent, I can't help but delight in the Demon King being absolutely satiated by me. I had no idea sex could be so empowering.

We stay like that, locked together for several long seconds as the aftershocks of the orgasm shiver through me.

When Wrath finally straightens and pulls out of me, he remains close and wraps his arms around my waist. The dark mist of his power follows and soon I'm enveloped by him and his magic.

There's a snap of air and a tugging at my sternum as his power carries us from the roof to his bedroom.

"Come," he tells me, but this time the command is only meant to pull me into his bed. I climb in without hesitation and make room for him. He slides in next to me and draws me into his chest.

Resting my ear against him, I listen to the steady thud of his heart as his fingers trail absently over the soft flesh of my hip.

"What's Alius like?"

His intake of breath is a little raspy, a little tired. "It's a lot like this world, just with more magic."

"Are there s'mores?"

He laughs, the sound reverberating through his chest. "No. We don't have marshmallows."

"Tragedy. How big is it? Your world?"

"Similar in size as well."

"Do you rule as king of one country or—"

"I rule the world."

I can't help but sink into that realization, let my mind wander over what that must be like. I knew he was a king, but to rule an entire world?

"How do you manage all that? If the world is the same size, how do you rule over all of it without losing territory to revolts or whatever?"

"Well, we've grown beyond the medieval era."

I can hear the laughter in his voice.

"I'm being serious."

"All right." His hand comes up and plays with my hair. I don't know if he realizes he's doing it, but I try not to make any sudden movements so he doesn't stop. "Several demon princes help me maintain control, along with the lords. I'm usually on good standing with the vampires as well, and I've given several titles in exchange for their loyalty."

"This place sounds like the mafia but with supernatural creatures."

He laughs again. I love the sound of it. It's a rich, deep sound that reminds me of a crackling fire.

"The mafia has its place and for what it does, it does it well," he points out.

"I suppose." We grow quiet, but he keeps stroking my hair, and the soft caress of his long fingers is making me sleepier by the second. "Do you miss Alius?"

"When I'm alone, yes. I miss it very much."

"And when you're not alone?"

"Depends on who I'm with."

I sense our dance around the things left unsaid. I want to ask him—what about when you're with me?—but I'm too tired to summon the courage. And the Demon King is too stubborn to admit to having a weakness for anyone.

But the way he shifts and pulls me closer, the way he tilts his head into me and takes in a deep breath of my scent tells me all I need to know.

I think we're falling for one another. Me, Rain Low, a nobody photographer from a little tourist town and the Demon King who rules an entire world.

I don't want to look too closely at it. I don't want to poke at it, at the fragile shell of it.

I'm too afraid it'll break.

10

When I wake in the morning, I find the bed empty beside me, but I can still smell Wrath. I can smell him on the sheets and on my skin.

Toes curled, I stretch beneath the covers and smile at the high ceiling as sunlight lengthens across it. There's a weird feeling fluttering in my chest and in my belly. If I didn't know any better, I'd almost think I was falling in lo—

"Good, you're awake."

I yelp and tug the sheet close to my chest until I realize it's Wrath standing at the end of the bed somehow looking hot as hell in the early morning hours. His black hair is damp and raked back. He's wearing fresh black jeans and a black t-shirt. I don't know how someone can do only one color at all times and still look like he stepped from a dark divine dream.

"Do you ever sleep?" I ask with a grumble.

"Rarely," he admits. "Demons don't need sleep like mortals do, and especially not the royal line."

I let out a humph and then collapse back against the bed. "Must be nice to be a demon king. I guess we can cross demon off my list of possibilities then because I love my sleep." I close my eyes. "Wake me in an hour."

"Absolutely not. Get up. Your phone has been making a noise."

I blink at the ceiling again. "My mom!" I lurch from the bed only to realize I'm still naked, and my clothes are on the roof.

Wrath's eyes ignite at the sight of me, but he quickly tamps it down. Apparently when the Demon King is on a mission, he's serious about it and nothing will get in his way.

He disappears then reappears with my bag from my room. "Here. Get dressed and come down. I've had Arthur prepare coffee for you."

I groan with delight just thinking about it. "I think I love you."

His face goes cold and blank. "*Dieva*," he warns.

"It's a figure of speech. I still hate you, don't worry." Except thinking about last night, about his gentle touch as I drifted off to sleep has me doubting everything.

"I'll be down in a minute," I say.

With a snap of air, he's gone.

I sigh at the empty spot he just inhabited and then scrub at my face. I hadn't intended for those three little words to mean anything at the moment.

Shaking it off, I get dressed and clean up as best I can in the attached bathroom then make my way downstairs. I take the main hall to the Bourbon Room and find Wrath outlined in sharp daylight in front of one of the gigantic windows. This room has become the main gathering room for us, but I also wonder if I can find him wherever he is just like he can find me.

Sometimes, when I think about him, there's a noticeable thrum at the center of me as if we're connected by some invisible string.

"Good morning, Rain," Arthur says at the coffee bar.

"Good morning, Arthur." I join him as he fills a white mug with coffee that's so dark, it might rival Wrath's magic.

"How do you like your coffee?" he asks.

"Do you have oatmilk creamer?"

Arthur frowns. "No, I'm sorry. Lauren likes almond milk and—"

"Add oatmilk to the shopping list, Arthur." Wrath's voice cuts in like a blade.

"Of course. I'll get some right away." Arthur pulls his phone from his back pocket and makes a note in it.

I watch Wrath, trying to catch his eye. He just chastised me for joking about having feelings for him, and now he's altering the grocery list for me? The Demon King is making sure I have my coffee creamer on hand.

I can't figure out this man.

I can't wrap my head around this life I find myself inhabiting.

"Almond milk will do for now," I answer.

Arthur nods and retrieves the carton from the mini fridge. There's also honey on the bar and a jar of sugar along with several bottles of flavored syrup.

I can't imagine the Demon King takes his coffee any special way. This must be for Arthur and Lauren.

And speaking of which—

"Where is Lauren, anyway?"

Arthur cuts his gaze to me and widens his eyes in the universal expression for *shut the fuck up*. He does that a lot.

Wrath is still at the window. "She's run off like a petulant child."

"Oh. What happened?"

Arthur gives a little shake of his head.

Sorry, Arthur, I'm nosy. I really want to know.

"She and I are having a disagreement," is what Wrath says.

"What sort of disagreement?"

Arthur nearly keels over. I suppose when you've been living with the Demon King for months you know better than the oblivious photographer when to keep your mouth shut.

But also, I'm immune to Wrath. For the most part, anyway.

"She doesn't like that I'm fucking you," Wrath answers.

My face pinks immediately, and when I look at Arthur next, his head is bowed, his gaze downcast. Arthur was trying to save me some embarrassment.

Could this man be any kinder?

But also…I'm in deep on this one now, and I'm not ready to backtrack.

"Do you not make it a habit of fucking random girls?"

Wrath's eyes shift to me.

He's been adored by over half the female population since he arrived here. I've seen the crowds outside Par House and the Demon Devotees in Norton Harbor just clamoring for a sighting of him.

If he wanted to fuck any of them, he could, at anytime, anywhere.

Women have practically been throwing themselves at him since he got here. Men too.

My guess is he could fuck someone in the middle of Par House, and no one would bat an eye.

So has he?

Have there been others besides me?

He comes over, towers over me, blocking the sunlight behind him in all his dark glory. "Are you jealous, *dieva*?" he asks.

There's a noticeable edge of smug pride in his voice.

Fucking hell.

Well yeah, I am.

It came out of nowhere, and I don't like it, but those are the facts.

Fat chance of me admitting to it though.

"Just wondering if I should be worried about STDs is all. We haven't used protection. I mean…I have an IUD, so hopefully I won't be inseminated with demon spawn." I laugh nervously, realizing I've galivanted myself into a conversation I didn't mean to have with the Demon King.

I clamp my mouth shut as he peers down at me.

"I carry no disease," he says almost like he's offended by the very notion. "I'm immortal, after all. And don't worry, *dieva*. I only impregnate those I mean to."

The way he says this, I can tell he's trying to poke at my jealousy, rile me up.

And it's working, goddammit.

"Does that mean you *have* impregnated someone before? Probably an innocent virgin in Alius, I assume?"

He narrows his eyes. "I wouldn't subject an innocent virgin to such misdeeds."

"What does that mean?"

He takes a step closer and hunches forward, bringing his stormy ocean eyes level with mine. "Impregnating someone with demon royalty is rough, brutal fucking. Not many could handle it."

My nipples are immediately peaking under my shirt. I didn't put on a bra, and the Demon King's gaze sinks to them before flicking back to my face.

I could handle it.

That's what I want to say.

Forget the demon spawn. I just want the brutal fucking.

His nostrils flare, irises bleeding to the bright red glow.

I rake my teeth over my bottom lip as I sense a very clear wetness spreading between my legs. I'm throbbing now, and Wrath's jaw is flexing as he takes another step toward me.

And then Arthur clears his throat.

And I realize he's still standing there, coffee cup in hand.

Wrath turns away, and I take the coffee and scurry over to one of the couches. I don't know what it is about Wrath that makes me lose my ever-loving mind around him.

"Arthur," Wrath says as he rifles through some papers on his desk, "give Rain her phone."

"Right." Arthur grabs my phone from one of many cabinets around the room. "Here you go."

When I brighten the screen, I find a few alerts for my social accounts and then a message from Mom. I tap into it to read.

Baby, you're not going to believe this! I just saw Tatiana on TV with the president!!!! With my hero Naomi!!! Call your mother back!

"Wait…what?"

Arthur and Wrath turn to me.

"What is it?" Wrath asks.

"My mom…there's this woman who used to be her best friend. Her name was Tatiana. She was on that camping trip? Mom just said she saw her on the news with the president."

Suspicion immediately comes to Wrath's face. "Which channel?"

"I don't know. She didn't say."

"Arthur," Wrath says.

Arthur is already moving across the room. He pulls back the double doors on a tall cabinet to reveal a flat screen TV hung inside. Retrieving the remote from a drawer, he flicks on the TV and quickly finds a recent news broadcast.

The banner across the bottom reads: *Madame President discusses latest Demon King strategy.*

But it's not the broadcast that matters.

It's not the words coming out of Naomi's mouth that send a chill through my body, one that sinks bone deep.

Standing just behind her, and to her left, is a woman I immediately recognize from my last meeting with the president.

But I don't know the woman as Tatiana.

I know her as the witch, Sirene.

Sirene who came from Alius, who created a blade that could kill Wrath.

"Oh shit," I breathe out.

"Is that the woman your mother knows?" Wrath asks. "From the summer she was impregnated with you?"

"I don't know. Maybe?"

Shit shit.

This can't be good.

Anger pinches between Wrath's dark brow. "Fucking Sirene," he mutters.

"What does this mean? Maybe my mom is mistaken—"

"We need to see your mother." Wrath stalks over to me.

"Now? I haven't even had my coffee."

"Now, *dieva*."

"All right fine." I gulp down three glugs of coffee and wince at the burn, then tap out a quick message to my mom though I hesitate on what to say.

Should I go with the truth? *Hey Mom, I'm about to pop up in your kitchen halfway across the world with a Demon King in tow. Don't panic!*

Instead, I go with: *Wrath and I need to see you. Can you send me your address?*

The three dots immediately dance in the message screen as she types.

The address pops up a second later.

Then: *How are you getting here? And you're coming with* him*?*

There are no italics within the messaging app, but I can definitely tell she's thinking with italics when she says *him*.

The Demon King.

I'm taking the Demon King home to my mother.

No big deal. Right?

It takes us less than a second to reach Scotland. We stand in an emerald green field, surrounded by rolling hills on one side and a lake on the other. There's a little white cabin in front of us with a red tin roof and a red front door.

"I guess this is it."

The air is wet and chilled. I didn't come dressed for Scottish weather.

We walk up to the front door, and I rap on the nicked wood with my knuckles. Mom pulls the door open before I even finish knocking. She's harried and wide-eyed, several wispy strands of hair fluttering around her face.

"Rainy baby!" She looks from me to the Demon King then back to me. "He's real. I can't believe he's real."

"Oh he's definitely real."

"I mean...I've seen you on TV," she says to him with a nervous trill of laughter. "But to see you in person, my god." She waves her hand up and down, gesturing at the length and breadth of him. "I mean...baby. Have you looked at him?"

I snort. I've done more than look, Mom.

She folds her hands over her chest. "He's a work of art."

"Don't tell him that, Mom. It'll go straight to his head."

Wrath scowls at me and I give him a smirk.

"Well come in from the rain." Mom laughs at her own joke. My name has always been a source of endless puns.

I step inside the cozy cabin, but Wrath has to duck into the doorway. In the castle, he's just taller than me. In the cabin, he's unnaturally big.

We come in on a small kitchen with a worn table in the middle. Mom's things are piled on top of it. Cameras and lenses and photography magazines. She has a few sheets of proofs of the Scottish landscapes jammed in between some contracts and bills.

It reminds me of my childhood, this cozy chaotic space that smells like my mother, like patchouli and lemongrass.

The deep sense of missing her hits me out of nowhere and tears sting in my sinuses. Without thinking, without considering what it might look like to the Demon King, I wrap my mom in a hug. "I missed you."

"I missed you too, baby." She rubs my back the way moms do.

I linger in her arms longer than I normally do, and it's her that ends the hug. "Okay," she says, "please update me on everything because I've been hearing all sorts of things that have been freaking me out. There was a woman on the news saying you were in the middle of an altercation with—" she waves at Wrath again "—him, and there was a fire and he kidnapped you? I knew you'd already been with him though, so that likely wasn't true and you know how the news can be." She rolls her eyes.

"Don't worry about me. I'm fine," I say bypassing the truth. I *was* in an altercation. I stabbed Wrath. And then the park burned. But I don't want to get stuck in the weeds here. There will be plenty of time to explain it all to my mom later. After I've figured out the mess that has become my life.

"Tell me about Tatiana," I say.

"Oh!" She claps her hands together, and several silver bangles slide down her forearm, clattering together just above her peony tattoo. "Can you even believe it? After all these years? I had half thought she was dead. She would reach out from time to time to see how you were doing and—"

"Wait...she did?" Wrath edges closer to me.

"I mean...it was just an email here and there," Mom clarifies.

I pull out my phone and search the internet for recent coverage of the press conference. It's easy to find an image of Sirene. "Is this Tatiana?" I ask.

Mom nods. "She hasn't aged a day. I don't know how she managed it."

I look over my shoulder at Wrath. There's an unfamiliar expression on his face.

Worry, maybe.

"Mom," I say, "tell us everything about Tatiana. From the first moment you met her, to the last word you spoke to her."

"What—*everything*?"

"Yes, everything."

When she frowns, it brings out the deep wrinkles around her eyes. "Well, all right. But this requires a pot of tea. Wrath...Mr. Demon King, is that what I should call you? Do you drink tea?"

I snort. "Yeah right—"

"Yes," he answers.

"You do?"

"Is that so hard to believe?" he says frowning at me.

Mom clutches at my arm. "His voice is even better in person. Like crushed velvet on your skin."

"Mom!"

"What? Oh don't look at me like that. I've photographed rock stars, for Pete's sake! Naked!"

"Mom!"

She screws up her mouth like I've massively disappointed her. Forget that I've been spending the last several days with a villain.

"The naked body is the purest form of art," she says.

"I agree," Wrath says.

"Oh my god. I can't believe this is happening." When I scowl at him, he remains expressionless, but I know he's doing this just to get beneath my skin.

"I'll put a pot on," Mom says. "Baby, you want coffee instead?"

"Yeah. I'll make it."

Mom busies herself pulling out tea bags from the cupboard. I grab the coffee pot to fill it at the tap. The faucet's pressure is low, and the water trickles out. As I stand there waiting, my mother muttering to herself at the cupboard, tea bags in hand, I look over at Wrath still standing near the table.

It's always just been my mom and me, and we're so familiar with inhabiting the same space that the silence is always comfortable and our movements around a room natural and fluid. We are a well-oiled machine, Mom and me. Wrath is a dark cloud in the bright cottage kitchen with Sunny and Rain.

It's so ridiculous that I almost burst out laughing.

Instead, I smile at the Demon King when he catches my eye, and for the briefest of seconds, I think I see the corner of his mouth twitch like he wants to return it.

There is nothing I like more than seeing his stoic, kingly demeanor crack.

When the pot is full, I get the coffee maker ready after finding a bag of ground coffee in the cupboard above. When the machine hisses to life, I drop into a chair at the rickety table. "Sit," I tell Wrath.

The hint of a smile is gone from his face now, and when I give him an order, he curls his upper lip at me. He parts his mouth as if to correct me of my insolence, but then Sunny Low is turning to him, and the ruthlessness is immediately buried.

"Have you tried Henley & Sons tea, Mr. Demon King?"

Leave it to Sunny Low to dismantle the overbearing power of the Demon King by asking him about tea blends and calling him Mister.

"Wrath," he corrects her. "And no, I haven't."

"Well, you'll love it. They're master tea blenders, Henley and his sons. I once went on assignment in Sri Lanka during a harvest. Changed my outlook on teas. It's still harvested by hand, did you know that?"

"I did not."

Oh this is a delight.

And the fact that Wrath is entertaining my mother by being civil has my chest warming in a very funny way.

The coffee pot gurgles and lets out a puff of steam. Mom gets the kettle on and starts rooting around in another cupboard. "Oh, baby, I have to tell you what I recently tried out. It's the next best thing."

"Mom."

"What?"

"Let's talk about Tatiana."

She stops looking for whatever this next best thing is and turns to me. The bangles on her arm slide back down to her wrist. "Okay. Sure. Sorry. It's just been a while since we've been together. We need to catch up!"

"I know. And we will. But maybe when you come home?"

She heaves a sigh. "Fine." She takes the chair next to me then glances at Wrath. “Come join us Wrath! People hovering make me nervous. Sit.”

He takes the chair on my left side, and the old wood creaks beneath the weight of all that muscle and sinew.

Mom readjusts the flowy fabric of her brightly colored ruana. “So...Tatiana...I’m not even sure where to start.”

Over the years, I’ve heard many, many stories about that fabled camping trip and sometimes the details changed as the edges of the memories blurred over the years. I’m hazy on the facts.

“How did you meet Tatiana?”

“Well...” Mom’s gaze goes far away as she digs up the memories. “We had already been hiking for a few days when we ran into her on the trail. She had no bag, no provisions. She said she’d been out there with a friend, and they got separated, but she didn’t seem scared. I always thought that was brave of her to be out in the wilderness with no supplies and be totally calm about it.”

Mom laughs to herself. “But that was Tatiana for you. She was afraid of nothing.”

The kettle starts to steam on the stove.

“Anyway, we brought her into the group. We insisted. She stayed in my tent with me, and we became fast friends. She was an odd one, but you know I love odd people, baby. The odder the better.”

“It’s true,” I tell Wrath. “We once spent a weekend with a troop of circus performers. If you want to have some interesting conversations, find yourself a bearded lady.”

Mom laughs loudly. She has one of those big, bold laughs.

“Please,” Wrath says, “go on.”

I’m not sure if he’s eager to hear the rest of the story or if he’s trying to avoid a tangent into circus culture.

Mom continues. “I’m not sure there’s too much more to tell. Tatiana was with us for the rest of the trip, and then we shared an apartment together for a while after. In fact, she’s half the reason I was sane enough to get through the surprise of finding out I was pregnant with Rain.

"I had wanted children, but in a vague, far-off kind of way, you know?" She looks at Wrath and nods her head, prompting him. He doesn't respond, but Sunny Low isn't affected by a one-sided conversation. "Anyway, she was with me all through the rest of the pregnancy and for several weeks after I had Rain. She moved eventually, said she had other things to tend to. But she'd call out of the blue in the beginning and say, 'Is she raining yet?' That was our joke and—"

The chair squeaks loudly as Wrath sits forward. "What did you say?"

"Oh...it was our joke? That's where I got Rain's name, from Tatiana. 'She'll rain,' she used to say. I suspected Rain might be an Aries while I was pregnant, and an Aries can go one of two ways—absolute rage or crying because she doesn't get her way. So yes, she rained all right." She leans back against the chair, laughing to herself.

Wrath looks like he wants to murder something, and my heart thuds harder beneath my ribs.

"What is it?" I ask him.

"It's not *rain*," he says with a bite to his words. "It's reign. As in 'rule.'"

"What do you mean? My name? It's Rain, as in from the sky and—"

"Perhaps that's what your mother intended, but it's not what Sirene was referring to."

Mom frowns. "Who's Sirene?"

The tea kettle lets out a low whistle and she gets up to remove it from the burner.

"We think Tatiana might actually be a witch named Sirene," I tell Mom.

She clicks off the stove. "Witch, huh? Well." She sets the kettle on a cork trivet. "I guess I'm not surprised. I've met plenty of witches in my day. I never really doubted they were who they said they were."

"Did Tatiana ever say she was a witch?" I ask.

"No. Never."

Wrath shifts, and the chair complains again. "Did she ever do anything out of the ordinary? Anything that might have looked like magic?"

"No, I'd remember that."

"Did you have sex with another man during that time?" Wrath asks.

"Hey!" I reach across the table and whack him on the arm. "Not cool."

He glares at me. If I were anyone else, I'd probably be a puddle of meat on the floor right about now.

"Rainy!" Mom scolds me. "We don't hit people."

Oh if she only knew.

Mom pours boiling water into two teacups. "To answer your question, no, I wasn't with anyone else. I would have told Rain if I had been. There's nothing wrong with not knowing the father of your baby. We're all sluts in our own way." She laughs again to herself.

"God, Mom." I scrub at my face. She's always had zero filter, and I got used to it a long time ago, but this is different. This is in front of the Demon King. I don't want him unfairly judging her.

But when I look across the table at him, his gaze is far away.

"What are you thinking?" I don't like that look on his face.

Just as the earl grey starts perfuming the air, Wrath rises from his chair and makes his way for the door.

"Where are you going?"

"To find Sirene."

"Have you gone mad?"

"I believe so, yes. Every single day I think so." He gives me a pointed look from the door. "Ms. Low," he says, hand on the door handle, "I appreciate your hospitality. I wish I could stay for tea, but we really must be going."

"Is everything okay?" Mom asks.

"It's...complicated," I say because what else am I going to do? Things *are* complicated. There's so much I want to tell her, and so much I keep back. I don't want to worry her. I'll deal with this myself.

"Someday soon we should chat about Jeffrey," I say as Wrath pulls the door open, and a cool rainy mist flies in around him. "I think you should reach out to him again."

"Did you talk to him?" Mom asks, the excitement thinning her voice. "Did you tell him?"

I give her a quick hug. "It's a long story." It's not. It's a short one. But it might destroy her, and I don't have time to pick up her pieces. Not when I'm holding on to mine for dear life.

"Baby, should I come home?" She brushes a lock of hair away from my face and tucks it behind my ear. "I can come home early."

"No. I'll be fine." I nod at the impressively tall demon. "I have the best bodyguard this side of the sub-dimension."

He sends a withering glare my way, causing me to smirk at him.

"All right." Mom squeezes my arm. "I have another two weeks here and then I'll be home."

"Sounds good." I kiss her cheek and then follow Wrath out the door. "Love you, Mom."

"Love you, baby."

Wrath and I head out into the mist. He stalks across the emerald green field, his clothing shimmering with glistening drops of rain.

"Where are you going?"

He doesn't answer, and I have to quicken my pace to keep up with his long stride.

"Wrath!"

He looks at me over the line of his shoulder. "Something foul is afoot."

"Okay, Edgar Allan Poe."

The line of his dark brow sinks in annoyance.

"Talk to me."

He stops at the top of a knoll. "Do you remember your promise to me?"

"Which one?"

"*Dieva*." He growls out the word, frustration pinched at the corners of his eyes.

I sigh. "The crown. That I'd happily give it to you."

"Yes."

"What about it?"

He looks away from me, toward the lake. Droplets of rain cling to his eyelashes and coat his mouth in a sheen. Something is bothering him, but I don't know what, and all I can think is I want to reassure him, take away his worry.

I want it so badly, it makes my chest ache.

"Wrath?"

He blinks, swipes the rain from his face, and pulls me to him. "We need to see Sirene."

"I think that's a—"

He pulls us away from Scotland and deposits us back in the castle in the Bourbon Room. The sensation of traveling through the sub-dimension is just a shiver now, like a kiss of air. It's no longer the same jarring, spinning discomfort from my first time.

"—that's a bad idea," I finish as he lets me go. "Do you even know how to find her? I mean...she's working for the president and—"

"It won't be hard. Be ready." Then he's gone.

I sigh and drop into one of the leather side chairs.

I don't know what he's thinking, but I suspect he has a theory, and it leaves my gut all knotted up.

Something is wrong.

I just don't know what.

11

As I wait for Wrath, I fill up on some of Arthur's quiche and scroll through my phone. I had turned off notifications the day before, so when I check my social accounts, I find a kajillion hearts and comments and messages.

My social accounts have swelled in size. I now have millions of followers.

"Well shit," I mutter to the screen.

I worked so damn hard on my social media presence before all of this only to get absolutely nowhere. Now I'm famous for fucking the Demon King. Figures.

Now if only I had time to capitalize on this new fame. What would I do with it? Start a merch store? I can just see the t-shirts now.

I fucked the Demon King, and all I got was this lousy t-shirt.

Coffee cups that say, Villain Fucker and Proud.

Keep Calm and Fuck a Villain.

Okay, I might actually buy that coffee cup.

Since I don't have anything better to do while I wait, I decide to take a quick peek at the comments and then fall down a rabbit hole.

There is so much fan art of Wrath and me.

One artist whose style is dark and slick has digitally painted us in an embrace, skeins of dark mist wrapping around us.

And the way Wrath's looking at me in the painting...

Holy shiz, one person comments, *can I be this girl pls?*

Someone has tagged me in a comment: *@RainLow how big is the demon D? Asking for a friend.*

These people wouldn't know what to do with Wrath in bed. Hell, I still don't. But gods do I enjoy it.

I go to the next comment. *If I were Rain Low, I'd be making that demon king my daddy.*

I snort and nearly tap a like for that one. If I called Wrath Daddy, he'd probably wring my neck.

But it'd be fun to see the look on his face right before I take my last breath.

I keep scrolling through my notifications then pop over to my messages. I find similar things in my inbox and then, several swipes down, I see Gus's name.

A flash of panic tightens in my chest. What if he's messaging to yell at me?

There is a lot of shame and guilt festering for the decisions I've made, and the one person I don't want to think less of me is my best friend.

I tap his name.

Babe, he wrote, *Adam told me what happened. Fuck the president. Fuck her soldiers. I'm so sorry you're going through this. We found your phone here, so I don't know if you'll get this message, but if you do, please let me know you're all right. XOXO*

Tears are welling in my eyes by the time I get to the end of the message.

He isn't mad at me.

I think deep down I knew he wouldn't be, but the very small possibility had me avoiding even looking.

I quickly tap to reply.

I'm okay, I write. *Just confused. So much has happened. I can't wait to tell you about it.*

I hit send.

Within seconds, the three dots appear as Gus types back. I can't help but hold the phone tighter, smiling at it like a fucking goon.

I miss him so much.

THANK GOD, is his first response. *Where are you?*

The Demon King's dark den.

Shit really?

Well, I might be exaggerating. It's actually bougie as hell.

Not surprised. He isn't hurting you, is he?

Sweet, sweet Gus. I could kiss him. *No,* I say. *I'm good. Really. How's Adam? The team?*

Adam is good. Babe, he's gutted about what happened. And he's worried about you.

I smile again as a rogue tear slips out of the corner of my eye. I swipe it away. Adam really is a keeper. I feel bad for not giving him a chance before all this.

It sucks, I tell Gus. *I can't believe they were going to shoot me just to kill Wrath.*

It's fucked up. So...you really are connected to him?

Apparently.

And so much more.

With my plate clean, I set it in the sink and pace to the window. Wrath has been gone all day, and I haven't seen Arthur or Lauren either, but I still get the distinct impression I'm being watched. It makes me wonder where the *norrow* go when they're not here. Can they just hang around without you knowing they're there?

I've been meaning to ask Wrath, but I'm not so sure he'd tell me.

What are you going to do? Gus asks.

I look out the window as I consider how to respond. We have a plan. Figure out how I got the *animus* so I can give it back. But every time I think about it, it leaves me feeling hollow and wrecked.

I tell Gus as close to the truth as I can get: *I honestly don't know.*

"*Dieva.*"

The sound of Wrath's voice in the room sends a shiver down my spine and butterflies fluttering in my stomach.

Every time he returns to me, it's a goddamn relief.

I imagine this is what a woman felt hundreds of years ago when her husband's ship appeared on the horizon.

I shouldn't feel this way.

Not about the villain. I shouldn't be so damn giddy that he's here.

"Hi," I say.

"Who are you talking to?" He nods at the phone clutched in my hand. There's an edge of suspicion on his face.

"Gus."

"I see." His expression softens just a fraction.

"Why?"

The hardness returns. "Because you are skilled in making bad decisions."

I blow out an exasperated breath. "Yes, and one is standing right in front of me."

"Funny, you weren't saying that last night."

My face pinks. Goddamn him. I flash back to him plowing me and immediately feel an answering tingle between my legs. The corner of his mouth ticks up.

I level my shoulders. "Do I have to remind you of which one of us was on their knees?"

The distaste that comes across his face is like a golden ray of sunlight to me. I love it when I can get beneath his skin.

"On my knees, perhaps," he says, "but devouring what was mine."

A breath gets stuck in my throat. I'm not sure if he's referring to me or the *animus*, or if there's no distinction at this point, but I secretly like him calling me his.

I want to be his. But I don't want him to know that.

"You keep telling yourself that," I challenge.

He disappears.

Crap.

I back toward the wall because if he gets behind me—

Too late.

His hand wraps around the back of my neck, fingers punishing as he whirls me around and slams me against the wall.

"As long as you hold the *animus*," he says, "you *are* mine."

"Am I?" I wiggle beneath him. His groin presses against my ass. There's no mistaking the hardness of his dick, and there's no denying that every single step we take in this dance makes me fucking wet.

Wrath's voice sends a shiver down my spine. "Why do you insist on provoking me?"

"Because I like seeing what you'll do."

"Liar. You do it because you like it when I dominate you. It makes your refusal to bow even more ludicrous."

He's got a good point.

"Are you kink shaming a girl?" I say. "That's not very nice, Daddy."

I'm so going to get burned for that one.

He spins me around. There's fire in his eyes. "You like to play games, *dieva*, but you don't know the rules."

My heart is thudding in my ears, and I can't seem to catch my breath.

"I don't need to know the rules when I'm favored to win." Now I'm just talking bullshit, but the bite that comes to his teeth, the flare of his red eyes sends a delicious flash down my belly right between my legs.

He's right. I do like being dominated by him. I don't know why. My entire life, I've been in control of every single thing. I have never, ever given up control.

Until Wrath.

It's almost liberating in some fucked up way.

The darkness kicks up around him, blotting out the daylight. Two thick skeins rise like ribbons, undulating in the air. They arch out then snatch me by the wrists, effectively bolting me to the wall.

Wrath steps back.

My clit is buzzing now, and I'm so wet, I can feel it dripping into my panties.

"Get on your knees," he says.

Um. No.

We have a long standoff with nothing but our eyes.

The darkness exerts pressure on my wrists, forcing me down. There's no option to fight it. I'm on my knees within seconds.

Wrath stalks toward me.

I could probably get out of this if I put up some effort. And I think Wrath knows it too. I don't control this wild power at the center of me, but it's never let me down when I absolutely needed it.

But right now...it doesn't come calling, because I don't want it to.

My chest is heavy with excitement. My pussy is throbbing. Fuck if this isn't getting me off. He knows it. I know it. He and I keep giving in to one another in so many fucked up ways. We're falling down the rabbit hole together with no care as to what we'll find at the bottom.

Wrath unbuttons his pants. When the zipper slides down, it reveals a very clear bulge in his black boxer briefs.

He crouches in front of me and pushes the hair away from my

face. "The little girl wants to play games. Maybe *Daddy*—" he says the word on a husky rasp "—should teach you a lesson."

Oh fuck.

Okay apparently I like this Daddy play because I'm buzzing now.

Wrath straightens and dips a hand inside his boxers, pulling out the heavy weight of his cock. He strokes it once, twice as he steps closer.

"You're always running off that mouth of yours," he says. "Why not put it to good use?"

I look up at him as the darkness ribbons around us.

"Open up, *dieva*."

I rake my teeth over my bottom lip.

"Go on."

I know the instant my own eyes flare with hellfire. It rims him in fiery light.

I am the candle in his dark night.

He drags the head of his cock over my lips and then stabs at my mouth.

I finally give in and open my lips for him and he shoves inside of me.

The second my tongue glides over the underside of his shaft, he's groaning low in his chest.

He slides out, back in and puts his hand on the wall above me to keep himself upright.

He's so big, so fucking hard I have to breathe through my nose so I don't choke on him.

The head of his dick swells at the back of my throat when he pumps into me, and it doesn't take long for pre-cum to coat my tongue.

He works at my mouth, lost in the pleasure of it, of me.

He pulls at my hair, angling my mouth to him as he grows harder, harder, fucks my mouth faster, faster.

Tears stream down my face as we lock eyes. His burning bright red, mine bright with hellfire.

He growls, the rumble deep in his chest as his cock throbs and hits the back of my throat.

"Fuck, *dieva*," he says on a reedy breath and then the darkness plumes around us as he spills his pleasure down my throat.

He groans, pumps again, and I swallow it back, every drop of him.

His come tastes like night. Sweet and coppery.

He exhales loudly, one hand still buried in my hair, the other holding him upright.

When he finally pulls out of me, his gaze locked on my swollen, red mouth, I think he realizes he made a mistake. He meant to teach me a lesson, but all he did was prove how lost he is in me.

A scowl comes to his gorgeous face, and then the dark shackles yank me to my feet as he steps into me and yanks off my pants, my panties. "Wrap your legs around me," he orders, so I do.

He shoves inside of me so hard, a bite of pain flashes through me before the pleasure of being filled up chases it away.

The darkness retracts from my wrists and Wrath's red gaze meets mine. "Hold on to me, *dieva*," he says and fucks me against the wall. I'm already dripping wet, wound up tight.

I'm ready to go in a second as the friction builds between us, rubbing against my swollen clit.

"Fuck," I moan out. "Fuck, you feel so good."

He pinches my nipple through my shirt, and I hiss, wishing it were off. But there's no time for that. I'm flying close to the sun now.

"Come for me, *dieva*." As the darkness twines around us, he pinches harder, sending a jolt of pain through my breast. "Let me feel that pussy clench around my cock."

His words stoke the pressure and soon I'm riding the wave, the bright sensation blinking through my nerves, causing me to arch, to jolt, to flinch through the orgasm.

When the wave crests over the other side, I collapse against the wall, eyes closed.

"Look at me."

I open back up to him and find his gaze penetrating, searching for something on my face.

I don't know what he's looking for or if he finds it, but suddenly he's kissing me.

It's a slow, sensual kiss, his tongue sliding over mine as he exhales through his nose, long and low, almost a sigh.

I hold him tighter and drink in that heady wintertime scent of him.

I don't want to let him go.

I don't want him to leave.

When he breaks the kiss, he rests his forehead against mine, and we breathe hard against one another.

We're drowning.

We both know it.

And I'm not sure if either of us knows how to swim in these choppy waves.

I don't know what happens if we stop fighting it and let the water rush in.

Tears burn in my eyes. I'm in trouble. So much fucking trouble.

We stay locked together much longer than we should, so when he pulls out of me, our juices have turned sticky.

I'll have a mess to clean up later.

Wrath steps away, tucking his cock back in his pants. "Don't call me daddy ever again."

I make a sound. It comes out like *PAH*. "I will not make that promise."

He grumbles in the back of his throat. "You drive me mad, *dieva*."

"I know." I give him an innocent smile, and he rolls his eyes.

After fetching my clothes, I dress and follow him out of the kitchen and to the Bourbon Room. At the bar, he pours drinks for two. He slings his back, sweat still gleaming on his collarbone along the lines of his demon mark where his shirt is pulled away from his body.

I think the most telling thing about our relationship is that we can do what we just did and then fall back into a comfortable existence as if what we did was totally normal.

That's how I know we're drowning.

How I know we're losing air.

"Did you find Sirene?" I ask and sip from the bourbon.

"I did." He pours another.

"And?"

He downs his second round and winces at the burn. "I need to know the truth, but I'm afraid I'm not ready to hear it."

"What does that mean?"

Worry comes to the creases around his eyes. He's not looking at me. His gaze is far away, his thoughts even farther.

"Wrath."

"Don't forget the promise you made to me."

I lick my lips. The bourbon has driven away the taste of Wrath and I almost mourn it.

"I won't," I say quietly.

His shoulders rise as he takes in a deep breath. He still won't look at me.

"Wrath?"

"Come." He holds out his hand, blinking out of his reverie.

"Okay. I guess we're doing this?"

He's silent, guarded. It makes my stomach knot up.

The worry from earlier returns. Something is wrong. Something is troubling him, and he won't tell me what.

I sling back the last of the liquor and cough at the heat. Then I slip my hand into his and let him carry us away.

12

When we reappear outside of what looks like a miniature version of Westminster Abbey, I know we've arrived at Sirene's.

The gothic stone house is very much her style, I think, even though I don't know her well. Smoke spirals from the chimney, and several birds chirp from the tangled vines of an old wisteria bush that is clinging to the stone archway around one of the entrances.

"Now what?" I say to Wrath, but I don't get his answer before one of the heavy wooden doors creaks open and Sirene steps out.

Several blades are strapped to her waist on a black leather belt. Tall black boots probably hide more. Right now, she is the perfect vision of a warrior witch from another world, a fairytale land.

Hands loosely balled at her sides, she steps out from beneath the shadows of the wisteria. "Took you long enough," she says to Wrath.

"As if I'd waste my time searching for you," is his reply.

"And yet here you are."

I swear I hear his teeth crack, he's scowling so hard.

It occurs to me that there's a long history here between these two that I don't understand, the details of which I'll never fully know.

Were they together?

The very thought makes me sick to my stomach.

I'm turning into a jealous, possessive bitch over the Demon King, and I don't know what that means.

I wish I could blame it on his dark magic, his mind control capabilities, but I know that's not it.

That's not it at all.

"Well go on," Sirene says and crosses her arms over her chest. "We all know why you're here."

But now that we are, Wrath is silent. I can't tell if he's contemplating his words or trying to decide how he'll gut Sirene.

I step in front of him. "We're here about the *animus*."

"Yes," she says.

"And my mom."

She tilts her head, her braid sliding over her shoulder. "How is Sunny anyway?"

"So you did know her."

"I think you know the answer to that."

I take another step. "You were there when I was born?"

"Mewling fat little baby you were."

"The *animus*...how did I get it?"

"Ask your boyfriend," she challenges.

The air cracks and darkness swoops in. Sirene is suddenly surrounded by the norrow, six of them in all. She doesn't flinch.

I hold up my hand to Wrath, asking him to wait.

She's baiting us. I need to know the answers as much as he does.

"I want *you* to tell me, Sirene," I say. "Or should I say Tatiana?"

She flinches at the name my mother knew her by. Did she want to be that person? Does the name mean something else to her?

I guess we're all trying to be something we're not, taking refuge behind the masks that hide who we really are.

Sirene steps forward, and the *norrow* echo her movements, stalking her like prey. She's not the least bit bothered by it.

"Chaos stole the *animus* from Wrath," she says, "but he was never powerful enough to hold on to it, so he gave it to me for safe keeping."

Sirene comes to a stop in the middle of the dirt driveway. "I knew a traveler on the other side powerful enough to get me through to your world. I thought I'd just shove the animus in some dark hole, even though it was an awfully risky plan. What if some idiot happened upon it? What if *this* idiot—" she nods at Wrath "—found his way here and reclaimed it?"

The *norrows'* edges blur, pluming into dark mist.

Heart thudding in my ears, I say, "Tell me what you did with it."

She smiles. "While searching for said dark hole, I stumbled upon your mother and her camping party."

My mouth is suddenly dry.

"An idea started to form."

I sense Wrath coming up behind me.

"Did you tell her the fables of the Demon King's power?" she says to Wrath. "Where they originated?"

"He told me of the father god."

Her gaze cuts back to me. "Yes, but did he tell you the whole story?"

I glance at him over my shoulder. His face is unreadable, his eyes locked on Sirene.

"No," I say to her. "I don't think he did."

"They say the *animus* was carved from the dark heart of the father god, that it was the *animus* that truly held his dark magic."

I frown at her. "Okay, so? I don't know what this has to do with me."

She smirks at me. "Power of that magnitude can do a great many things."

I can smell Wrath now, his dark winter scent wrapping around me as he comes closer.

"Power of that magnitude," Sirene goes on, "could create life."

It's as if the world goes still, and all I can hear is the loud thumping of my heart and the roaring rush of blood in my veins.

My stomach drops. I backpedal and stumble into Wrath, and he grabs me by the shoulders, keeps me upright.

My voice wobbles. "What does that mean?"

"It means..." Sirene says, her mouth curving into a devilish grin, "you don't *have* the *animus*. You *are* the *animus*."

The air crystalizes in my throat. I can't breathe. Wrath's grip on me tightens as my knees give out.

No. This...no. *No*.

"You're lying," I choke out.

"Am I?" Sirene's eyes dart to Wrath behind me. "I'm pretty sure he knew before he brought you here."

I look back at him, but his gaze is on the witch. "Did you?"

When he looks down at me, there's a pinch of something foreign between his brows. Something that looks like regret.

He *did* know.

That's why he's been acting so distant.

"But...how...how do I give it back to him?"

"You're not listening," Sirene says. "You can't give it back. There is nothing to *give*."

I find renewed strength in my legs and straighten and yank out of Wrath's grip. I look between him and Sirene. "What does this mean? Tell me right now. How do we fix this?" Cold sweat breaks out across my forehead. "How does he get the power back to defeat Chaos?"

"Go on." Sirene cocks out a hip and curls her hand around it. "I'm sure you can figure it out, Demon King. Tell her what she'll have to do."

I look to Wrath. There's a hardness to his expression now.

"Tell me," I say.

"You'd bind yourself to me in blood and oath."

"Forever and always," Sirene adds. "No backsies. No cancellations. No loopholes. Bound to him for however long you live and breathe. I'm sure the *animus* will just love that."

Fear burns in my chest. My vision tunnels. It's like I'm trapped, the world narrowing around me.

Bound to him forever? With no control over my own life?

No one has ever told me what to do. Not even my own mother.

If I bound myself to the Demon King, I would always be subject to his control. Even with the *animus*, I'm not more powerful than he is.

I'm hot all over and numb and shaking and—

"I can't do this," I say. I look to Wrath, pleading. "Please. I can't do that."

"He can't make you," Sirene says. "A blood bond has to be consensual."

There's a brief flash of relief in my chest, until I realize who and what I'm dealing with.

The Demon King isn't the type to take no for an answer.

He came here with a mission. He's not just going to give up.

"Please," I say again.

He takes a step toward me, and I flinch away.

Sirene's trill of laughter sends the birds flying from the wisteria in a flap of wings.

"I can't do this," I tell him.

He grabs me by the arm and yanks me into his side. To Sirene he says, "Do you understand what you've done?"

"Of course I do." The amusement is gone from her face now, and the scar puckers around her eye as she narrows her gaze. "Your time is coming to an end, Demon King. Tick-tock."

There's a snap of air as he pulls us away from Sirene's stone house. When we reappear at the castle, he drops me unceremoniously on the couch.

Something is breaking between us.

"I'm not binding myself to you," I say.

He goes to the bar and pours himself a drink and adds a drop of something from an amber vial tucked in one of the bar's drawers. He tips his head back, pours the drink down his throat. When he swallows it back, he hisses and bows, hands flat on the bar top.

Sirene might have said he can't make me bind myself to him, but I know him well enough by now to recognize he is ruthless, merciless, and clever enough to find a way around the rules.

I go to him. "Wrath."

"What would you have me do?" He's still bowed, his gaze downcast, dark hair hanging over his forehead.

"There must be some other way."

"You think I haven't thought about that?" When he turns to me, his face has sharpened, hinting at the monster.

"How long have you known?"

He sighs and runs a hand back through his hair. "I started to suspect after we visited Jeffrey. Even if he would have been a demon, it wouldn't have made sense that you, a halfling, could hold the *animus*."

"Why didn't you tell me?"

"Because I worried how you would react. Much as you are now."

"I'm not binding myself to you."

"You made me a promise," he throws back at me. "Or did you forget?"

"That was before I knew! There has to be some other—"

Without warning, the monster surges to the surface, his face contracting to the sharp demon that lurks beneath. "There is no other way!"

Goosebumps erupt on my skin. "Don't do that."

"The *animus* is mine by right."

"I'm not property to be owned."

"You *are mine, dieva*!"

"I am not yours!"

I bump into the sofa and Wrath presses closer. The sharp lines of the monster has faded, but his eyes are still crimson. "I might need your permission," he says, his voice low, "but there are plenty of ways for me to get it."

His hand circles my wrist. "I'm asking nicely, *dieva*. It will be the only time I do."

My gut knots as tears sting my eyes. I can't bind myself to him. This is all...everything is happening so fucking fast.

I have a life.

I *had* a life before him.

He's asking me to bow to him. Forever.

Taking his side in a fight against the government is one thing —they were trying to kill me—but aligning myself with him for the rest of my life? That's not fair.

I can't. I won't.

The power answers my call and roars through me like a forest fire blazing through dry kindling.

Wrath hisses and drops my wrist as smoke curls from his hand. His skin is charred around the fingertips for a brief second before his body heals itself.

"*Dieva*." His voice is edged in warning.

"I will not bind myself to you."

The scowl disappears from his face as he takes in a deep, settling breath, nostrils flaring. His expression is cold, eyes distant.

"That's an unfortunate position to take," he says, "for a little girl who has so much to lose."

Dread snuffs out the rage. "Don't you dare—"

The air snaps and he's gone.

"Wrath!"

The tears are immediately welling in my eyes as the panic takes hold. "Shit. Shit. Where's my phone? Wrath!"

I finally find it and tap on my mom's name. "Hey baby," she answers. "Everything all right?"

"Is Wrath there with you?"

"What? No. Why?"

There's nothing I can say or do to help keep her safe. There is no lock that can keep him out other than something witch-made, and my mom is all the way on the other side of the world.

"Just...run if you see him."

"What? Baby—"

I end the call and tap at Gus's name. The phone rings and rings and rings.

I pace the room, hand at my forehead, heat burning through my veins.

What am I supposed to do? What *can* I do?

"Pick up. Pick up."

The phone stops ringing, and I hear an intake of breath on the other end.

"Gus?"

"Do you think you can reach him before I snap his neck?"

Fuck.

"Don't do this," I say.

"You gave me your word."

"I didn't know—"

"I don't fucking care."

"*Please.*"

The line cuts out.

"Fuck!" I run from the room and down the hall and out into the driveway. The Mustang is parked near the garage, and I yank open the door, slide in behind the wheel, and punch at the ignition button. The engine roars to life.

I hit the gas and tear down the driveway and barrel into the street.

With a squeal of tires, I point the car toward Norton Harbor and Collie's Tea Shop. Back where it all began.

13

THE MUSTANG COMES TO A SCREECHING HALT OUTSIDE COLLIE'S WHEN I slam on the brakes. It's a miracle I didn't get pulled over. It's a miracle I didn't wrap the car around a tree in my rush to get here.

I'm too slow compared to Wrath. I can't just come and go as I please and I've wasted so much time driving here.

I hope I'm not too late.

Please, Gus, be okay.

I yank open the heavy door and charge inside.

When the door slams shut behind me, I wince.

Even though it's the middle of the afternoon, there's no one inside save for Gus and the Demon King.

The music is off. The steamers silent.

It is eerily still.

Gus is sitting at one of the round tables by the front counter. There are no bruises on his skin, no blood marring his face. He's unharmed—for now.

Wrath stands just behind him and to the left. "Sit, dieva," he orders.

I'm so keyed up, my heart is practically thumping on the back of my tongue.

I scan the shop, trying to find us an exit, a weapon, anything.

But this is the Demon King I'm dealing with.

Unless Gus has a witch blade hiding in one of the tin canisters on the counter, we're out of luck.

"Sit, *dieva*," Wrath says again, this time with more venom.

I sit at the table across from Gus.

"I'm sorry," I say to my best friend.

"It's okay," he says back.

It breaks my heart knowing he means it. Even though his life is literally hanging in the balance, he doesn't blame me.

Sometimes I think I don't deserve Gus. I should have warned him. He should have stayed behind Eric's witch barrier until this whole thing blew over.

I should have done more to protect him.

One by one, the *norrow* take shape around us until Collie's Tea Shop is overwhelmed with their primordial scent.

Gus doesn't flinch, but I notice the way his hand shakes on the table.

"Rain has something that belongs to me," Wrath tells Gus. "Or rather, she is exactly what I need."

Gus's gaze is questioning, but how the hell can I explain this? How can I make him understand what's at stake?

"If you want to live, I suggest you convince her to do what needs to be done."

"And what's that?" Gus asks.

"He needs me to bind myself to him," I answer.

Gus snorts. "I'm not going to talk my best friend into doing that."

One of the norrow darts across the room and slams into Gus. The chair teeters back and he slams to the floor.

I leap out of my chair, but Wrath is suddenly behind me, hand on my shoulder, forcing me to sit back down.

"How could you do this?" I say up to him, tears blurring my vision.

The fear is visceral, the panic sharp.

This is no longer a game.

Wrath bends down, his mouth at the sensitive flesh of my ear. "You've forgotten who I am, *dieva*."

I scowl. "I'll never make that mistake again."

Gus's hand appears on the table as he uses it to leverage himself back up. Blood is dripping from his nose when he stands upright, and he swipes it away with the back of his other hand.

"Are you all right?" I ask.

"I'm okay." He gives me a weak smile and rights his chair.

"Gus, I—"

"Do what you have to do, all right?"

A tear streams down my face. It's getting harder and harder to breathe. The rage has abandoned me, leaving only despair in its place. I can't do anything with that.

The last few days, I allowed myself to fall under Wrath's spell. I allowed myself to believe that I was somehow special, that I could escape his violence and his cruelty.

I wanted to believe that I could make him different than he was.

And now I'm suffering the consequences of it.

"I've been patient, *dieva*," he says as he paces the shop. "I've allowed you to get away with far more than anyone else." He cuts his gaze to me. "I've been merciful. I require only one thing of you in return. It's a simple thing, really."

"It's the rest of my life," I say. "There's nothing simple about that."

"Your life was never yours to begin with," he points out. "You have *always* been *mine*."

The thrill that runs through me when he says those words makes me want to vomit.

What twisted reality have I stumbled into that when the villain calls me his, I want it to be true?

But I'm not his in the way I imagined. He sees me as nothing more than a tool, something to be used to wield more power.

I stand up from the table and ball my hands into fists at my side. This probably won't end well, but I have to go down swinging if I go down at all.

I will *not* go down on my knees.

I can do this.

If I'm really to believe that I am the *animus*, then I have to believe that I *am* the power.

It's not like water that runs through my fingers. It's the blood in my veins, the marrow in my bones, the breath in my lungs.

The reality of it feels too big and yet...when I reach for the power now, it comes with no effort at all, dawning like a sunrise.

It was never tethered to the rage. The rage and the anger and the frustration were just the easiest doors for me to open until I could learn the power is my strength.

The fiery Aries like my mom always said.

Strong and determined and so fucking done with this.

Golden light bursts through the room.

The *norrow* shriek and burn into embers.

"I will not bind myself to you," I tell Wrath. "You will not force me to make this decision."

There is no one else in this whole fucking planet who can stand against him...except for me.

His features sharpen into the monster.

"You will regret this," he says.

And then the air snaps, and he's gone.

I whirl around. I can feel him, but I can't see him and then—

He slams into me. I fly through the air and crash into the piano. The keys let out a discordant twang.

I'm up again, just in time to duck as Wrath swings at me. I'm in over my head in a fistfight, but if I can summon the fire—

Wrath backhands me. I slam to the floor, the air knocked out of me. He appears above me and takes a fistful of my shirt, yanking me to my feet as I gasp for oxygen.

"How about now, *dieva*?" he asks, an echo of his earlier words when he was fucking me against the kitchen counter.

My how far we've come.

"Fuck you," I choke out.

He narrows his eyes. "You'd like that, wouldn't you?"

I catch sight of Gus just beyond the line of Wrath's shoulder. There's a cast iron skillet in his hand and it's cocked back like a baseball bat.

"I think you'd like it more than I would," I argue just to keep Wrath talking as Gus edges closer.

His face contorts, his mouth twisting into a menacing grin.

Several tendrils of dark magic lift from his back, sharpen into spears.

One shoots out with a clear target in mind.

"No!" Fire burns through my hands. Wrath lets me go, smoke curling from his body.

It's not enough time to stop the dark spear from impaling Gus.

"No! Gus!" I catch him as he falls, blood eating away at the white of his shirt. "Fuck. Gus."

His eyes are wide, panic dilating his pupils.

"It's okay. It's going to be okay."

There's too much blood. I don't know where he was hit or how bad it is.

I have to get him out of here. I have to—

Several skeins of dark magic rise around us.

I have to get us out of here. I have to go. I have to get Gus to safety and—

There's a rushing in my head, a pressure in my veins and in my bones, then a tearing snap and—

Blackness. A surge of wind. A sudden jolt.

When I open my eyes, Gus and I are on the concrete floor of the cafeteria at the factory.

My stomach knots as my vision sways.

Gus coughs. "Rain," he croaks. "What...how—"

I lurch to my feet. My hands are slick and red with his blood.

I'm vibrating. My veins are fire. I can't see straight.

"Fuck," I pant out as my stomach revolts.

"Rain!"

My vision tunnels as my stomach empties and I gasp against the forceful retching.

I think...I think I just traveled through the sub-dimension.

Holy shit.

"Rain!"

I can't breathe. I can't breathe. Everything hurts, and I can't see straight and—

"Rain!"

The darkness swallows me up.

14

I WAKE NESTLED INTO GUS'S SIDE, HIS HEART THUMPING BENEATH MY EAR. His scent—the sweetness of his cologne and the earthiness of tea—hits me next and immediately makes me feel like I'm home.

There's a lamp lit in the far corner of the unfamiliar room, and beneath the arch of its glow is Adam.

His eyes meet mine.

I come to awareness quickly and forcefully. I sit up and look down at Gus, scanning his body. He's paler than normal, but he's breathing fine and there's tape and gauze on his naked shoulder.

"Is he—" I start.

"He'll be fine," Adam answers. "He got hit in the shoulder. Sanjay and Eric patched him up."

I brush one of his stray curls away from his face. I didn't lose him, but the fact that I could have makes me want to scream and rage.

How could he? How could Wrath do this?

I disentangle myself from Gus's side and climb over him slowly so as not to wake him.

Adam sits forward as I cross the room. He props his elbows on his knees and folds his hands together.

"Hi," I say, voice low.

"Hi."

There's a mismatched wingback chair sitting kitty corner from him, so I take it and tuck my legs beneath me.

We sit in silence for a beat and then both start talking at once.

"So listen," I say.

"Rain, I have—"

We laugh and trail off.

Adam starts again. "I have to apologize for what happened out in the field. Rain..." He takes a deep breath and runs his hand over his buzzed hair. "You never should have been the target. I'm sorry that you were and that your country put you in the position of choosing between them and your life."

I shrug and try to play it down because I'm just thankful to be here, and grateful to have him. "It's not a big deal."

"It is."

I rest my head against the curved wing of the chair. The navy-blue upholstery smells like my grandmother's house, and it immediately makes me think of Christmas and sugar cookies and silver garland.

A wave of emotion comes over me, and I close my eyes against the bite of tears. "I was worried you'd hate me," I tell Adam.

"Why would you think that?"

I snort and wave my hand in the air. "You know, I chose the villain."

Adam shakes his head. "I served in two tours. You think those terrorist assholes saw me as the hero?"

"Well, no but—"

"I wouldn't side with the terrorists, don't get me wrong. But sometimes...the things our country does to get the job done...you wouldn't look at us as the heroes. There's always two sides to a story."

It hurts how much I believe that. “You are wise and far too kind, Adam.”

He laughs and rubs his hands together, the dry skin rasping in the quiet. “If my mama heard you say that.” He whistles. “‘Boy, get your head out of your ass!’ That was her favorite saying. In fairness, I did have a couple of years in my teens when I was being a dipshit because I didn’t want to admit I was gay.”

“We’re all dipshits as teenagers,” Gus says as he stretches on the bed and then dissolves into a trail of curse words as pain etches into his features.

“Hey, take it easy!” Adam hurries over to him.

“I’m fine.” Gus sits up and grimaces again.

“You are not fine. You were stabbed.”

“You stab me almost every night with that dick.”

I burst out laughing. Adam sighs and rolls his eyes.

God I love these two.

With Adam’s help, Gus comes over and Adam deposits him in the chair.

“How are you?” Gus asks as Adam wraps one of the throw blankets around his shoulders.

“I’m...okay.”

“That was badass what you did.” Gus rests his head against the back of the chair and Adam, standing beside him, absently runs his fingers through Gus’s unruly curls. “That was some next level voodoo shit you pulled off.”

“I don’t even know *how* I did it.”

“If you’re connected to the demon,” Adam says, “does that mean you also have his abilities? That might explain it.”

They don’t know about the *animus*. Should I tell them? I know I can trust Adam and Gus, but I don’t want to endanger them any more than I have.

“I seem to have some magic, yes.”

“My mother would need a fainting couch if she were alive to hear this,” Gus says.

I smile thinking of Gloria. "She always wanted magic to be real."

"Apparently, we just weren't looking hard enough."

"So now what?" Adam asks. "What do you need from us? Is—"

I will find you, dieva.

His voice in my head is like a length of silk dragging over my bare flesh.

I can't help but shiver.

I have a moment of panic before I remember he likely can't find me if I'm inside the factory. Eric's witch barrier will stop him.

Gus frowns at me. "What's wrong? You have a look on your face."

Do you hear me, dieva*?* Wrath says. *You will beg for mercy, and you will find none.*

There's a sickness churning in my stomach. I'm both terrified and filled with guilt.

Why does it feel like I've betrayed Wrath?

I've done what I promised him I wouldn't. I'm no better than his betrothed or his brother.

But he left me no choice. He forced my hand.

I don't know if I can answer him the way he can speak to me, but I'm not about to try. It'll be better if I just keep my mouth shut.

But I have to do something. Wrath is right—I can only hide for so long, and at his age, I'm sure he's made an art form out of being patient.

"I need to talk to Sirene," I tell Adam. "Do you think you could find out how to get hold of her?"

"Sure. It shouldn't be hard to make it happen."

"Thank you."

Thinking about what I might have to do to survive this has me wanting to crawl into bed and never get out.

I don't want to do any of this.

Why the fuck did he have to go after Gus?

There's only so much I can take, so much I can turn a blind eye to.

Wrath did the unthinkable, and he left me no choice.

If he'd cared for me at all, he never would have threatened my best friend. But to him, Gus is just collateral damage. Insignificant. And to me, Gus is everything. Wrath should have known that. He shouldn't have crossed that line.

But he's the villain, my internal critic points out. *What did you think would happen if you told him no?*

Adam gets up from the chair. "I have to touch base with my team first, and then I'll work on getting you Sirene."

"Thanks Adam."

He kisses Gus goodbye. "Rest. You hear me?"

"Aye, sergeant."

Adam blows out an exasperated breath and then leaves.

"So," Gus says once we're alone, "are you going to tell me what's *really* going on?"

"It's complicated."

"Of course it is."

With a sigh, I scrub at my forehead and stall. Maybe Gus deserves to know the truth, considering he was almost killed because of it.

"I'm sorry that he did what he did to you," I say.

He waves dismissively. "It's a story to tell my grandkids."

"Gus." I level him with a stare.

"*Babe*," he says mocking me. "Don't worry about me, all right? Spill the tea."

"Fine. But if I'm going to tell you all of this, I need a drink."

He grins at me and nods at the cabinet beside me. "I might have something in there."

I open the door and pull out a bottle of Patron Silver.

"Well well well," I say. "The good stuff, is it?"

"It sounds like a good-stuff scenario."

He isn't wrong.

I spot a stack of red plastic cups on a shelf and get up to grab two.

Gus pours us each a shot, and we clink glasses.

"To besties," I say.

"To besties."

We drink the liquor back, wince and laugh together.

"I've missed you and I love you," I say.

"It's only been a few days. And I love you too. Now tell me everything."

So I do.

I tell Gus every gruesome, unbelievable detail. Including the part where I fucked the Demon King. Not once, not twice. Many times.

When I finish, he just looks at me with a blank stare.

We're both three shots in, our eyes glassy now.

"Say something." I snap my fingers in front of his face. He blinks.

"I don't know where to start." He pours another shot and slings it back, then chases it with a splash of sparkling water. "You're some kind of immaculate conception from some dark god's heart? A dark god from another world?"

"See?" I hold up my hands. "Ridiculous. Ludicrous. Absolutely outrageous."

"And you fucked the Demon King!"

"Shhhh!" I look over my shoulder just to be sure we're still alone. No one has come in or out since Adam, but it's always hard to say who might be listening.

"What?" Gus frowns at me. "So what? Who cares? You're allowed to roll with the devil."

"Everyone in this entire factory is trying to kill him. So I think they'd be judging me if they knew the truth."

"They might be actively trying to kill him, sure, but half of them would also be actively trying to fuck him if given the chance."

I drop back into the chair, laughing but also a little too drunk.

"So was it good?"

I meet his curious gaze. "Fucking spectacular."

"I knew it. If I wasn't in pain, I'd be giving you a standing ovation."

I lean forward again and take a sip from his can of sparkling water. The tequila is making every move exaggerated. I really should have eaten before I started guzzling Patron.

"So you have the Demon King's crown—"

"Not have. Am. Are? Is? I *am* the crown."

"Right. And the Demon King wants it back, but in order to have it—*you*—he wants you to bind yourself to him for the rest of your life."

"That about sums it up."

"You know what that sounds like to me?"

"What?"

"It's like the demon version of marriage. He wants you to be his queen."

I freeze up. "Ummm...*no*."

"Yes."

"He doesn't want someone to reign—" I get an immediate flash of Wrath's theory about my name "—by his side. He wants to control the power so *he* can reign."

"If you say so."

"Are you taking his side?"

"You know me. *C'est la vie*."

"This isn't a burnt biscuit or an unexpected medical bill. This is a demon from another world. One who is relentless and violent and—"

"Fucking dynamite in bed apparently."

"Gus!"

"What?" He's laughing now, tears glistening in his eyes. "I'm just saying!"

I really have missed him. So damn much. Being with Gus is my safe space. I feel more like myself when I'm with him.

A shadow darkens the doorway. "Rain?"

It's Sanjay with Eric at her back.

"Hey guys! Hi." I try to pretend I'm sober.

"Are you two drunk?" Sanjay asks, eyeing the half empty bottle of Patron between us.

"Sorta," Gus admits.

"Possibly," I say.

Head down, Eric comes into the room. He's got an old friend in his hands—the witch-made harness that should shield me from Wrath.

"Adam saved it for you," Eric says, avoiding my eyes. "I will admit it's a magic I don't know or understand, but I believe it to still be active."

"But I'm in the factory. Do I need it? Isn't your barrier up?"

He frowns at himself. "It is but—"

"This is just another preventative measure. Just to be safe," Sanjay adds.

With a sigh, I take the harness from him and put my arms through it. Sanjay comes up behind me and clips it into place.

It's either I wear this for the rest of my life and stay locked away behind a witch barrier, or I face the shitstorm of my life and find a way out of this.

But none of those options leaves me feeling rosy and bright.

"Adam has an update on Sirene." Sanjay comes further into the room and caps the bottle of Patron.

"Hey!" Gus whines.

"You're injured. Alcohol thins the blood. You shouldn't be drinking."

"Oh shit, that's a good point," I say. "Sanjay is right. No more Patron for you Gus."

Sanjay goes on. "Adam is finishing up with something right now and has asked us to bring you to the control room."

"Okay. Sure." Fuck this is really happening. Why am I suddenly panicking?

"I'll come with," Gus says.

"Adam asked to speak with Rain alone," Sanjay says. "And to tell you to get back into bed."

"Ugh. Fine."

I help him back into the bed and tuck the blanket around him. "Good?"

"TV remote?"

I spot it on the cabinet and retrieve it for him. He flicks on the flat screen attached to the wall across from the bed.

"Better now," he says.

I wish I could do that. When was the last time I just laid in bed with guilty pleasure TV?

I was always hustling before Wrath, thinking that I was working toward something, even though I didn't know what that thing was.

Now I wish I would have taken more time off just to relax.

"Love you, babe," Gus says.

"I love you too."

Sanjay and Eric lead me out. We're in a part of the factory that I didn't get a chance to see before, but the walls are still prison gray, the floors scuffed concrete. There isn't much about it that's different.

We eventually reach the cavernous main room where the metal stairs wind up to the control room. Adam is there at the table, a map spread out before him. Tommy is hunched beside him.

"Rain!" Tommy says and comes over to give me a hug in the wide span of his arms. He smells like stale cigarettes and motor oil, and his hug is like the squeeze of a boa constrictor. It makes me like him even more.

"Hi Tommy. Nice to see you again."

"Likewise. Likewise." Then he says something in Russian and chuckles to himself.

Adam rolls up the map. "Have a seat, Rain."

I plop into one of the metal chairs. "So you found Sirene?"

"I did."Adam tucks the map into a cubbie behind him as Sanjay sits in the chair beside me. Eric hovers by the door.

"So what did you want to talk to me about?" I ask.

Adam crosses his thick arms over his chest and sucks a breath in through his nose. I sense the others sharing a look between one another.

"What is it?"

"I don't have particulars," Adam says, "but I suspect Naomi and General Briggs have commissioned Sirene to take some desperate measures to eradicate Wrath."

My heart kicks up. "Okay."

"I've made it very clear that if your life isn't protected at all costs, I will personally destroy them."

Some people are full of bravado and not much action. They say lots of things that sound serious and grave, but when it really comes to follow through, they shrivel up like old fruit.

Not Adam though. I can tell by the grit of his teeth, the narrowing of his eyes that he means what he says, and he has the courage to follow through with his promises.

"You didn't have to do that."

"This isn't up for debate," Sanjay adds. "We want you to know that what happened at Riverside Park was not something we supported."

Tears spring to my eyes. "I really appreciate that. Thank you."

"With that said," Adam goes on as he starts to walk around the table, "Sirene has asked to speak to you alone. No soldiers. No General Briggs. No president. Just you and her."

I lick my lips. I'm no match for a witch from another world, but what other choice do I have? I think Sirene has her own agenda, but I can't forget the fact that she literally helped make me and was my mom's best friend at one point in her life.

I don't think Sirene wants me dead. But I don't exactly feel good about the plans she *does* have for me.

She will reign. Those were Sirene's words once upon a time.

What exactly does she think I'll do? Overthrow Wrath?

Never. Not in a million years.

But something does need to be done about him before he hurts someone else I care about.

"I'm okay with seeing her alone," I say. "Just tell me when and where."

Adam gives a quick nod. "We're to meet her in two hours on the side of the road in the middle of nowhere. I don't like it, but Tommy and I used remote surveillance to check out the location, and there's nothing there to warrant suspicion. But it's entirely up to you what our next move is."

I give a quick nod. "I'm good with that. I trust you."

"Then we'll leave in a half hour. The drive will take us over an hour just to reach the destination. Everyone good?"

The team gives him a nod of acknowledgement, and then Adam unfolds his arms and waves his hand. "You're dismissed."

The others leave. Adam checks a notification on his phone.

"Can I ask you a professional question?"

"Of course," he says, his attention still on the screen.

"What would you do if you were in my position?"

He finally looks up, his dark brow furrowed over his eyes.

"If you were in enemy territory," I go on, "with your back against the wall and the enemy was closing in..."

"I'd go down swinging."

"Even if it hurt people?" I don't think he knows that the 'people' I'm referring to is Wrath. I can't shake this feeling that I'm betraying him even though he literally threatened the life of my best friend.

Would he have followed through with the threat on Gus's life? Will I ever know?

Why did he have to do it? *Why*?

Or was this always our path? Maybe I wanted to believe he was better than he was.

"Our goal as a soldier is always to minimize casualties," Adam explains, "but sometimes the risk is worth it if the outcome is better. Does that make sense?"

Betraying Wrath is worth it if the outcome is the one I want.

But where do I go from here?

I'll still have the *animus*...or *be* the *animus*. Maybe Sirene will have a solution for that. She said I'd reign, but what did she mean by that all those years ago? Did she literally think I'd go to another world and rule the throne?

Fuck no. I'm not doing that. What I want is to go back to having quiche and tea at Collie's with Gus and enjoying my life.

Isn't it?

There is a festering seed of doubt at the center of me that I can't seem to push down.

I just have to focus on dealing with Wrath. Then I can figure out the rest later.

I walk over to Adam and give his forearm a squeeze. He looks down at me. "Gus is lucky to have you. And by extension, me too."

He smiles. It almost looks bashful.

"I mean it. Thank you."

"Of course, Rain. We're going to get you through this."

I believe that he believes it. But I'm not so sure.

15

The drive to Sirene's secret location seems like it takes longer than an hour, and I find myself dozing in the back seat next to Sanjay.

When we finally pull over onto the rocky shoulder, I look out the window to find we're surrounded by nothing but trees.

"This is it?" My voice is thick and groggy.

"These are the GPS coordinates Sirene gave us." Adam puts the SUV in park but leaves the engine running.

"Is Sirene supposed to meet us or—"

A figure steps through the trees up ahead, and Sirene comes into the beam of headlights. She's wearing a tight-fitting black outfit with several gold buttons up the front and thick suede at the shoulders. Her hair is braided over her shoulder, partially obscuring the three claw marks on the side of her face.

She cocks out a hip and crosses her arms over her chest, waiting.

Adam turns in the driver's seat. "Sirene wouldn't allow us to wait for you, but we'll be nearby if you need us. I can give you that much."

"Thank you." I move for the door handle.

"Rain?" Adam stops me.

"Yeah?"

"If you sense any kind of trouble, you run."

Running won't save me, but I don't tell him that.

I give him a nod and then open the door.

The gravel of the dirt road crunches beneath my feet as I walk over to Sirene. The wind kicks up, tossing hair in my face.

"I wasn't sure if you would come," she calls.

"I'm running out of options," I say.

She smirks. "Wrath has a way with that, doesn't he? Closes you off, makes you feel divine and hollow all at the same time."

The way she speaks about him, like she knows what that feels like, makes my stomach knot.

I think they were together at some point in their long lives, and the jealousy tightening like a band across my chest is both shocking and foreseeable.

"He hurt my best friend." I come to a stop a few feet from her.

"He's done worse."

My heart beats a little harder. She's baiting me, and I'm biting. I have to. "Like what?"

"Walk with me, and I'll tell you." She gestures with her hand to a hollowed path in the forest.

No time like the present I suppose. "After you."

She crosses over the road's shoulder and steps onto the path, and it's almost like the forest swallows her whole. There's plenty of light from the SUV headlights, but I can barely make out the line of her shoulders or the sweep of her hair.

I follow her and the outside world disappears. It's a quiet hush that comes over me, like the background noise has been shushed.

Now I can hear only the croak of tree frogs and crickets in the underbrush and the panting of my breath.

The air is colder too, mistier.

"What is this?" I gaze around.

"It's a barrier."

"It's incredible. Eric's barrier doesn't feel like this."

Sirene snorts. "That's because Eric is a diluted witch bastard with very little power."

"Hey. I like Eric."

"Given the chance, I might too, but those will still be facts."

We keep walking deeper into the forest until we come to a large stone mausoleum. It's straight out of a Halloween movie with its columns reminiscent of ancient Greek temples, arched iron door, and stained-glass windows.

It's no resting place for a single person, either. It's big enough to house a dozen if I had to guess.

Sirene waves her hand in front of the iron door and a loud clank sounds inside. When she looks over her shoulder at me, her eyes are glowing green.

"Come on, Hellfire Girl." She yanks the door open by a heavy ring. The metal groans and creaks, the bottom corner scraping over the stone.

Inside, it's even bigger than it seems outside with one central room with a frosted glass ceiling held together with ribbing of rusted iron. More stone columns surround the central room. There's one other door opposite the entrance, but it's made of stone and not iron. Almost like it's there for show and not functionality.

"What is this place?" My voice bounces around and comes back to me. The air is dank and cold.

Sirene crosses to the middle of the room right beneath a medallion at the center of the ceiling. It looks like a compass rose but with eight arms instead of four.

"In Alius, they're called *porta limina*. Portal of worship."

I shiver.

Sirene paces across the room. “In Alius, the demon race is revered like royalty whether or not they have a title, but the higher ranked, like Wrath, are worshipped like gods. After all, as you know, our legends tell us that by being king, he is worthy of the power of the Dark Father God.”

She stops and looks up at the medallion. “The portals are constructed across Alius by lesser beings, and they worship there, hoping that Wrath or another of the royal line will come to them and bestow them favor or power or gifts.”

“Does it ever work?”

She looks at me over her shoulder. “Like with your gods, the humans keep worshipping and the demons keep ignoring.”

That does sound familiar. My mom has always been spiritual, always searching for greater meaning and higher powers. Not me. I’m too impatient for that.

“So why is this place, one of your *portas*, here in our world?”

Sirene finally turns to face me. “Because they can be used as portals.”

The hair rises along my arms. “Between your world and mine?” Sirene nods. “But I thought you needed a traveler for that?”

“Oh you do. You need both. And usually you need demon blood too, but I suspect with you, that won’t be necessary.”

The goosebumps lift higher on my skin. “Why would you want to open a portal?”

She looks me right in the eyes as she says, “To bring Chaos over.”

16

"Fuck you." I turn for the door, but it's gone. "Goddammit. Let me out, Sirene!"

"Listen for a minute."

I run my hand along the wall, looking for a break in the illusion. "I'm not solving a problem with a bigger problem."

"You only know the side of the story you've heard from Wrath, and we both know how good he is at manipulation."

I always went back and forth on whether or not he was manipulating me or if I was just really good about ignoring all the red flags.

My fingers find nothing but smooth stone on the wall. I'm not getting out of here until Sirene lets me out. "Okay." I turn back to her and cross my arms over my chest. "Tell me the whole story."

She taps at the scars on her face. "This is from Wrath."

I frown. "Why would he do that?"

"Because I tried to stop him."

"From what?"

"Destroying an entire town."

A lump forms in my throat. Should I be surprised by this? The fact that I'm not makes me question my moral compass.

"I'm listening."

"One of the demon princes formed an alliance with a vampire house to overthrow Wrath many, many years ago." She turns away from me and walks to the stone doorway opposite me. "Wrath was planning to decimate the entire town that the demon prince ruled. Chaos and I disagreed with that strategy. Fear is a powerful motivator for obedience, but it can backfire."

She tilts her head, thinking. I can only see half her face—the half with the angry white scars. "But as king, Wrath didn't have to wait for approval, and he sure as hell wasn't going to listen to us. So he did it anyway."

I inhale sharply. "He destroyed the town?"

Sirene looks at me. "And everyone in it."

That motherfucker.

That vile, violent motherfucker.

Of course he destroyed a town.

He's a fucking villain.

Even though I know all of these things, even though I know who and what he is, I still feel like vomiting hearing this story, thinking of all of those people.

"He'll do the same here," Sirene says. "You've defied him now. There will be no escaping him."

I know she's right. I'm not stuck between a rock and a hard place. I'm stuck between a fucking volcano and quicksand. No one in our world is equipped to stop Wrath.

But is the only answer summoning his brother? The very same demon that had a hand in starting WWII?

"There must be some other way," I try, but Sirene shakes her head.

"You think I wasn't exactly in your shoes all those years ago? You think I wanted to help steal the *animus* and shove it into the belly of a new ageist?"

"Hey!"

"And then have an argument with the *animus* all those years later?"

"I'm a living, breathing person. Quit referring to me like I'm an object."

"I wanted there to be another way," she goes on. "Any other fucking way would have been preferred."

I sigh and pinch the bridge of my nose. "So say I help you bring Chaos over. Then what?" I look up again. "He wants the *animus* as much as Wrath does. And I'm assuming the throne too?"

Sirene's mouth twists into a sinister grin.

"What?"

"How would you feel about screwing over not one demon but two?"

I narrow my eyes at her. "What are you getting at?"

Stone grinds against stone behind me. I turn in time to see Ciri step into the mausoleum.

"I think you've met the Queen of the Oracles," Sirene says.

Once Ciri is through, the doorway disappears again. She comes over to me, her white eyes hidden behind dark Jackie O sunglasses. Her hair is neatly combed back in a chignon. "You don't look well," she says.

"No shit."

"Do you remember what I told you?" She takes my face in her hands, making me feel like a child in an auntie's grip.

"'It will get worse before it gets better,'" I repeat, and she nods. "He threatened and then stabbed my best friend. And my mom—"

"We've protected your mother," Sirene says.

"How?"

"Magic, of course." Ciri brushes a lock of hair behind my ear. "Now listen."

"I am," I say with a growl and a flash of gold reflects in the lenses of Ciri's sunglasses. She takes a quick step back.

"Careful now." Ciri clasps her hands in front of her. "We are not your enemy."

I inhale, trying to clear away all of the frustration building in my sternum. "I'm sorry. It's just...I'm stressed out, and I don't know who the fuck to trust. Didn't you bring Wrath here? Now you're double crossing him?"

"I did bring him here, yes," she says. "We all have a part to play in this. And I made no allegiance to him. He knew that. Why else would he threaten me and accuse me of playing both sides? He wasn't wrong. I know what needs to happen, and that's why I'm here."

That's all I want. I want to get through it and get to the other side with all of my loved ones intact.

"I'm not going to be responsible for starting WWIII," I say.

Sirene shakes her head. "It won't come to that. We won't let it."

"All right." I lean against one of the stone columns and fold my arms. "Then let's hear it. Let's hear your brilliant plan."

"Chaos is the only one strong enough to take the *oculus* and the *dominus* from Wrath," Sirene says. "That's why we need him."

I'm pacing the mausoleum now trying to make sense of all of the moving pieces. I know everyone involved in this has something different to gain, but I'm still not sure what Ciri and Sirene want.

"So you want to summon Chaos," I say, "so he can take the rest of the dark god's powers from Wrath, thereby weakening him? And then what?"

"Then we destroy Wrath," Ciri answers.

"And Chaos?"

"We'll destroy him too," Ciri says.

My mouth goes dry at the thought. Two demon brothers gone just like that. Can we really do it? I think Sirene can. I'm not sure what Ciri is capable of, but there's no doubt she's a badass bitch.

And on top of that, she clearly knows more about the future than she's letting on.

"Who will take Wrath's place? I'm assuming someone needs to."

She will reign.

Please don't say me. I keep thinking it over and over again.

"There's a prince," Sirene says and my shoulders sink with relief. "One that would rule fairly and justly."

But as she speaks, I sense Ciri giving her a pointed look, as if there's more they aren't saying.

But do I really care who rules Alius? No. There's just one little problem...

"And me? What about the *animus*?"

"We can't get around that," Sirene answers. "And a ruler must have all three aspects of power. But a prince can't and won't be able to overpower you. Not like Wrath. If you bound yourself to him, you would have your freedom. You could do as you pleased."

I stop pacing to look over at her. "So I could go back to my normal life?"

She nods.

The idea is appealing. With Wrath, there's this overwhelming feeling that if I bowed to him, if I bound myself to him, he would control me and rule me. We are not equals. That will never change.

This whole time, I've been searching for a way to return to my life, and I think this might be the closest I can get, considering my life was never mine to begin with.

That's a whole other thing I need to deal with someday, the fact that everything I thought I knew about myself was a lie. The fact that I was an immaculate conception from a power stolen from a dark god from another world.

Just thinking about it makes my head spin. It sounds too ludicrous even for a fantasy book.

But right now, I need to deal with Wrath and Chaos. I can't bury my head in the sand anymore. It's no longer an option.

I need to do something, and this might be the only something I *can* do.

"Can either of you give me something to assure me Chaos won't run amok? I don't want to be responsible for another world war."

Sirene looks at Ciri.

"I can give you something." Ciri raises a hand and a second later, an Oracle appears. There are no distinguishing features to tell me if she's the same girl as the one who visited me at Wrath's castle. Her gauzy white dress is the same. Her skin is pale and shimmery. When she edges closer, I catch the scent of wet stone and a struck match.

She stops when she's a few feet away. Her dress hovers over the stone floor.

"Through Chaos, there is order," the girl says. "Through order, there is peace. Through you, there is redemption."

She comes closer still, and her scent fills my nose. "You are the only way. So you must do as you must and do it quickly."

My eyes burn looking at her, so I blink for a reprieve, and in that fraction of a second, she's gone.

I stumble back and suck in a breath like I've just been shoved out of a dream. My head is suddenly pounding, my stomach swimming.

"Did you get what you needed?" Ciri asks.

I lick my lips. "I don't know. Maybe?"

You are the only way.

It still feels like my hands have been tied, but if I put my faith in anything, it has to be in the belief that this is all happening for a reason and that I will get through it.

I can set things right.

"So?" Sirene says.

"Tell me what to do."

The witch's face lights up, her scars wrinkling as she smiles. "Let's get to work."

17

As Sirene and Ciri prepare the portal, Wrath comes to me in my head.

Dieva, he says, *I can't feel you.*

He's probably just playing games again.

In my head, I think, Dieva *is busy right now. Fuck off.*

There she is, the mighty Rain. Surly and fierce. My two favorite characteristics.

Shut up. I'm going to destroy you for what you did.

You think so, do you? Tell me, dieva, *what do you plan to do? You think your mortal soldiers can stand at your back and save you from me? I will decimate them.*

His voice is louder in my head, stronger.

Sirene points at something on the gate and Ciri nods.

I don't know how long we've been in this mausoleum. It feels like seconds and hours all at the same time.

And how do you plan to stop your brother without the animus*?* I ask.

There's only silence in my head now, and my heart aches at the void.

Wrath has me all twisted up. Clearly, he's been brainwashing me. The sooner I can get this over with, the better.

"Rain?" Ciri says over her shoulder. "We're ready for you."

I rise to my feet and meet them at the gate. A year ago, I never would have believed a fake door might actually open a portal to another world. But now it's as real as the clothes on my back.

"What do you need from me?" I ask.

"Your blood," Sirene says, not missing a beat.

Of course.

"Give me your hand."

I hold it out for her, and she produces a knife and drags the blade over the soft flesh of my palm. I hiss from the pain and flinch, but Sirene holds me tightly as the blood wells in the cut.

"Now what?"

"Put your palm to the stone doorway," Ciri answers.

"That's it?"

She nods. "I'll take care of the rest."

"*Dieva*!"

We all go silent at the sound of Wrath's voice.

"Did you guys hear that too?" I ask.

Sirene's eyes narrow. "Apparently his ability to track her is stronger than I thought."

"He's really here?"

"Keep going," Sirene orders us, and then with barely any effort, she scales up one of the stone columns and peeks out through the glass domed ceiling.

With a deep breath, I step up to the doorway and press my palm to the cool stone. Pain radiates out through the cut as pressure is applied to it.

"He has a witch," Sirene reports. "Rhys Roman's witch, I think."

Kat is helping Wrath?

I like Kat. I trust Kat. If she's taking his side...

Doubt settles in my gut. But then again...she doesn't know that

Wrath threatened my best friend. If she did, would she still be helping Wrath?

"What's Kat doing?" I ask.

"Trying to bring down the barrier."

Panic tightens like a band across my chest.

"Step back." Ciri puts a hand on my shoulder and yanks me away from the stone gate.

"Maybe we should wait—"

"Absolutely not." Sirene climbs down the column. "We have a job to do. We'll do it."

Ciri lifts her arms above her head and whispers foreign words beneath her breath. The ground trembles.

"*Dieva*!" Wrath shouts again. "When I get my hands on you, you will beg for my mercy."

"Fucking hell," I say beneath my breath.

"It won't come to that," Sirene promises me even though I don't think she has it in her power to make such a promise.

The gate pops and light pierces through the stone.

My heart rams in my throat, thumps in my head.

I'm putting my trust in complete strangers, and I don't know if I'm making the right decision, and what if Chaos is worse than Wrath?

Sirene said Chaos wanted to stop his brother from destroying that village in Alius, but...Chaos started a fucking world war and...

Fuck, I don't know what to think or believe, and I think it might be too fucking late anyway.

More light shines through the mausoleum as the stone doorway melts away, and a portal takes shape with a ripple of energy.

A dark figure appears in the light.

I squint against the brightness as the figure steps through.

Ciri drops her arms, panting, and the portal disappears with a crackle of air.

When my eyes adjust, I look over at the man standing in front of the doorway.

I don't know what I expected Chaos to look like, but it isn't this, and seeing him sends a shock of relief through me.

He looks like an English professor. A hot one, sure, but nowhere near as intimidating as Wrath. I can immediately see the similarities between them though. The chiseled jaw, the sharp cheekbones, the knowing gray eyes. But his are hidden behind round, tortoiseshell glasses.

He's wearing a heather gray henley that hugs his biceps and skims his waist.

I can only imagine what he looks like with it off.

Hot English professors might be my new weakness.

Wait, what? Nope. Not going down that road.

I can't forget this man is a demon whose name is literally Chaos.

He takes two steps down from the gate and looks over at me.

My heart is hammering against my ear drums. I'm finding it hard to catch my breath.

"Rain, I presume?" he says with a slight accent that sounds British to my ears.

"Hi." I wave awkwardly.

He tilts his head, his eyes sweeping over me. "You're gorgeous." He looks over his shoulder at Ciri. "You didn't tell me she was gorgeous."

"Does it matter?" I ask, half joking.

"I suppose not." He takes another step, but when he comes within a few feet of me, he stops and his attention wanders beyond the mausoleum. "My brother is here, and he's close to getting in."

"Sirene said you could help defeat him," I say.

"I can." He smiles, flashing perfect white teeth. He has an easy, casual way about him, like he's had all of these conversations before and knows just where they're going.

Maybe I was wrong about him not being intimidating. Every

word that comes out of his mouth makes me doubt that assessment even more. I get the distinct impression he's five steps ahead of me already.

"Wrath told me you started World War II. I hope you don't have plans to do it again?" I laugh nervously.

A pinch of regret appears between his brows. "An unfortunate accident."

I snort. "That's one way of putting it."

"It won't happen again."

"What about all of the shootings? The chaos in our government? The unrest?"

I hadn't planned on confronting him, but now that he's here, I can't seem to stop it.

"What is light without darkness?" he challenges.

"It's too much darkness."

"Is it?"

Sirene comes over and nearly steps between us. "We don't have time for this. I can feel the barrier crumbling. Wrath will get in and soon."

"Let him come." Chaos is still staring at me, dissecting me with his eyes.

"Wait, you want to fight him now?"

"What better time?"

"I can't. I'm not ready."

"You don't have to do anything."

"Sirene," I try. "Was this part of the plan? I didn't want to have to be here when they went toe to toe!"

Dieva, his voice sounds in my head causing me to flinch. *I'm coming for you.*

"I can't do this. Poof me out of here," I tell Chaos.

"If we're to take my brother, I need you by my side. Come." He winds his arm around my waist and tugs me into his side. "We'll face him together. A united front."

The hair along the nape of my neck lifts at his touch.

There's a crackle in the air, and Sirene grumbles beneath her breath.

"What is that?" I ask.

"That," Chaos says down to me, "is the barrier crumbling."

A second later, Wrath appears in front of us, and his gaze immediately goes to Chaos's hand curled around my waist. Rage etches itself into the fine lines around his eyes.

"Brother," Wrath says.

"My king," Chaos answers.

My shirt is rising and falling to the rapid beating of my heart. My stomach is in knots.

This is all part of the plan, so why the fuck do I have the urge to vomit?

"I've called *dieva*," Wrath says. "So I will ask nicely, just this once, that you remove your hand from her."

Chaos looks down at me again. "You called *dieva* for this little one?" With his other hand, he brushes away a lock of my hair, and Wrath growls as darkness rises from his shoulders.

"The *animus* is already yours by right. So why go to the trouble?" Chaos asks. "Unless..." He takes a chunk of my hair and yanks it, baring my neck. "Unless there's more to her than just the power?"

"If you hurt what's mine," Wrath says, "I will reach down your throat and pull out your fucking spine, brother."

"That's what I thought." Something sharp flashes in Chaos's hand. I realize too late that it's a blade.

"NO!" Wrath shouts, his face sharpening, twisting into the monster as he lunges.

But he isn't quick enough.

Chaos sinks the blade into my back, and everything goes white.

18

THE WORLD BLINKS. DARKNESS. LIGHT. PAIN. DARKNESS AGAIN.

The stone floor is cool against my cheek, but my back is white hot with pain, my shirt soaked with blood.

Wrath and Chaos are a cloud of darkness as fighting ensues.

I can't feel my legs.

Sirene comes into my line of sight. "Rain. Rain? Can you hear me?"

I blink and a tear escapes the corner of my eye, runs over the bridge of my nose.

What have I done?

What have they done?

Ciri's warm hand comes to my neck, her fingers searching for a pulse. "Her heart is weak. Fix this."

Sirene grumbles in the back of her throat. "This isn't my area of expertise."

"I told you this would happen, and you assured me you could manage it," Ciri whispers.

"I am. Just give me a second."

Ciri knew I'd be stabbed? They let this happen? I try to speak, but my throat is dry and everything is impossibly cold now.

Am I dying?

I guess if I'm dead, I don't have to deal with all of this bullshit anymore.

Something loud thuds against the mausoleum wall. Wrath roars. Several *norrow* take shape around the room, and Chaos faces off with them.

I catch sight of Wrath. He doesn't look good. He looks like he's fucking losing.

All because of me.

His skin is paler than normal, and blood is dripping from the corner of his mouth.

Fuck. Fuck.

They knew this would happen?!

How the fuck does this fit into the plan? I move my lips trying to get the words out, but my voice is scratchy and too quiet.

Sirene presses hard against the wound in my back, and I cry out, nerves lighting with excruciating pain.

Wrath roars an echo of pain as my vision spins.

Chaos grabs his brother by the throat and lifts him off his feet. With his other hand, he tears the shirt from Wrath's body and claws at his demon mark.

The mark glows red. The *norrow* screech and quiver, their forms dissipating like smoke.

"It's happening," Ciri says from above me. "Chaos is taking the *oculus*. Whatever you gotta do, Sirene, you do it now."

"I'm fucking trying!"

A sharp pain echoes through the connection between me and Wrath.

We lock eyes across the room.

He's losing.

All because of me.

No. No no.

There's a hollowness carved out of the center of me, seeing Wrath vulnerable.

And a terrifying thought burns through my skull—there's a sick feeling in my gut seeing Wrath in danger, the same sick feeling I had when I knew Gus was in danger.

Oh hell. Fuck. Fuck.

I can't breathe because of the panic. I can't think straight because of the fear.

I can't lose Wrath.

I hate him. I loathe what he did to Gus.

But...

Fuck.

I can't let anything happen to him.

I'm shaking now and burning hot.

"Sirene," Ciri says. "Are you—"

Light burns in my field of vision, and Sirene hisses as smoke curls from her hand.

I'm suddenly flush with the power of the *animus.*

The pain fades away.

Wrath needs me.

The Demon King needs me.

Power crashes through me.

Chaos turns to me, his mouth gaping open.

"Let him go," I say.

Chaos drops Wrath to the floor and turns to me. There's a small stone in the palm of his hand.

I think it might be the *oculus.*

The power to control minds.

When he stole the *animus* from Wrath, he couldn't hold on to it. That's why he gave it to Sirene. But now? Wrath is weakened, the triad of power split. Can Chaos take on the power now?

The stone glows in his hand.

"We're just one stone away," he says and steps toward me. "Let's bind ourselves together and take the last from him."

I laugh. "That was never part of the plan."

I don't exactly know what the plan is at this point. Everyone is keeping secrets. Everyone has their own idea of how this should go down. And I'm fucking sick of it.

Flames lick up my hands. I can feel the kiss of their warmth, but it doesn't burn.

"Give me the *oculus*, and maybe I'll let you live," I say.

He smiles at me and undoes the top buttons on his shirt, baring his demon mark.

"When I took the *animus* from my brother, I wasn't strong enough to hold on to it." His demon mark glows bright red. "I made sure not to make that mistake again."

He presses the stone to his sternum, and the demon mark flares golden. He grits his teeth, tendons sticking out of his neck as he tenses up against the power burning through his body.

The air crackles around him, and light flickers like heat lightning.

Chaos hangs his head back and roars at the ceiling, hands fisted at his sides. The glass dome spiderwebs and cracks and then glass is raining down around us.

I throw my arm over my head, glass cutting at my skin.

When I come back up, Chaos is panting, head bowed. Then he starts to laugh.

Shit.

He levels his shoulders and lifts his head, his eyes glowing red.

Several *norrow* take shape around him. But they're not poised to attack him. They're lined up like soldiers at his side.

"My brother has ruled long enough." Chaos looks over at me. "His time has come to an end. Will you join me, Rain? We would be mighty."

Blood drips from a cut on my nose as sweat beads at my temple. Wrath never gave me the choice to join him. He never asked. He demanded. He expected me to fall in line.

But even still, the thought of joining Chaos instead leaves me hollow and cold.

"No fucking way," I answer.

Chaos smiles at me with his polite professor's smile. It makes my blood run cold.

"Very well." He flicks his wrist to the *norrow*. "Kill him."

"NO!"

I know from experience that the *norrow* are fast. Faster than my legs can carry me.

I don't think I can reach Wrath's side quickly enough.

I can't let the *norrow* take him.

The air pops. My skin grows taut. There's a flash of light and darkness and a forceful shift of my body.

Suddenly I'm standing in front of Wrath, arms raised.

The Hellfire Crown has come out to play.

And she is not taking any shit.

My feet leave the ground as the room burns bright orange.

Wrath is mine.

He is as much mine as I am his.

I can't deny it any longer. I hate him, and I want to murder him for hurting Gus, but he. Is. Mine.

And no one, not Sirene, not the president, not Chaos or the *norrow* is going to take him from me.

A loud WHUMP sounds through the room as fire plumes around us. The *norrow* shriek. Their darkness crackles along the edges like burning wood. With a collective scream, they burn off into embers, and the heat of their destruction warms my skin.

When my feet hit the stone floor again, I'm breathing heavily, but I feel like I could go another ten rounds.

Adrenaline is pumping through my veins and energy coils in my bones.

But when the smoke clears, Chaos is gone.

19

"WHERE DID HE GO?" I TURN IN A CIRCLE.

Wrath uses the stone wall to lift himself up. There's blood dripping from his nose and from the corner of his mouth. The skin around his left eye is purple and black with a mottled bruise.

"Are you—"

The monster comes to his face, and he darts across the room to Ciri taking her by the throat. He sways on his feet, but his grip is tight.

"Wait!" I shout and come to a stop beside him. "Don't hurt her."

Where the hell is Sirene?

Ciri's face is contorted in pain as Wrath lifts her off her feet. "It's okay, Rain," she chokes out. "Today is the day I die."

"You betrayed me," Wrath grits out.

She smiles down at him. Her sunglasses are gone, and her white eyes almost glow in the smoky half-darkness. "I did what I had to do."

"Wrath," I try and put a hand on his shoulder. "Please."

"You can't control her," Ciri says. "So stop trying."

Wrath's expression sharpens even more. "I am the fucking king!"

"And you are no longer the most powerful person in the room."

His eyes burn bright red.

"Wrath—"

CRACK.

Ciri's neck snaps, and her head goes limp in Wrath's grip.

"What the fuck! You can't just—"

He drops her like a sack of trash and rounds on me, eyes still burning.

"You're fucking next." His hand wraps around the back of my neck. He lifts me off my feet and slams me on the ground, kneeling beside me. Pain shoots through my body as a dull ache pounds through my head. I wiggle beneath his grip, but his strength is greater than mine, and he's caught me off guard.

"Kat," he calls, and the distinct sound of stilettos on stone comes into the mausoleum.

"You can't really expect me to bind her?" comes Kat's voice.

"Did I ask for your fucking opinion? We had a deal. Or will you betray me too?"

Kat sighs. "Very well."

Something sweet perfumes the air, and then my arms are tugged behind my back and locked into place. There's a phantom sensation of being tied up, but there's no pressure on my skin, no rope or bindings.

"Can I go now?" Kat asks.

Wrath grabs me by the bicep and yanks me to my feet.

Despite being summoned to battle, Kat looks like she was prepared for a night on the town in a bright red dress that hugs her curvy body. Her dark, wavy hair curls around her face, and her puffy lips are painted in the same shade of her dress.

"I'm sorry, Rain," she says with a frown. "Rhys ordered me to. I am bound to do his bidding."

I'm not sure if I should be offended or not. Kat owes me nothing, but whatever happened to girl solidarity? I guess when you're battling with supernatural forces, the lines are a little blurred.

I decide to keep my mouth shut, and Kat just gives me a quick nod and turns around and leaves.

Darkness wraps around me and Wrath. He gets in close to my side, his hand still wrapped around my arm as he pulls us away from the mausoleum. We reappear outside of the castle, but Wrath collapses when solid ground appears beneath us.

I stand by awkwardly, my hands still bound behind my back. "I'd help you, but—"

He looks up at me with a sneer. "You've done enough, *dieva*."

Arthur and Lauren come out, and I have a distinct sense of déjà vu. It's Lauren that helps Wrath up.

"Chaos has the *oculus*," he tells her.

"Fuck," Lauren says. "Her fault, I assume?"

Wrath ignores her. "Is everyone here?"

"Who's everyone?"

Arthur nods. "We were unable to locate the prince you spoke of. If he's on this side, we can't find him."

Wrath curses beneath his breath.

"What is going on?"

Wrath turns on me and bears down on me. The monster hasn't come out to play, but the way his eyes glow red is warning enough. "You keep your fucking mouth shut. Do you understand me?"

My heart is a staccato beat in my ears.

"Just kill her," Lauren suggests.

"I would if I could," Wrath says.

He would? Of course he would. I've betrayed him. I've crossed the uncrossable line with him.

The guilt is sour in my stomach now, but it's threaded with rage.

"You hurt Gus!" I yell at him. "You knew what I would do! You gave me no choice!"

Without thinking, I reach for the fire of the *animus*. But the call goes unanswered.

A lump forms in my throat when I realize just what a binding means. I don't have access to the power. I'm pretty much fucking useless.

Wrath takes my jaw in his hand and squeezes. Pain shoots through my bones. "I'm going to make you hurt, *dieva*," he says as he gets in close to my mouth, his breath hot and spicy as it spills down my neck. "I'm going to make you pay for what you've done."

The threat slivers down my spine and lights a flare of heat between my legs. The fuck?

Wrath notices. Of course he fucking does.

The smile that comes to his face is full of darkness and sin. "That's what I thought."

He takes me by the arm again and drags me into the house. Lauren and Arthur follow. We go down a hallway, then another, then down a set of stairs.

We enter into a large hall and stop on a landing that puts us on a stage at the head of the room. Several torches flicker from stone columns. Iron chandeliers hanging from the ceiling fill the rest of the space with golden light.

And when I take in the sight, the air gets lodged in my throat.

The hall is easily the size of a football field and filling the hall as far as the eye can see are men and women and dozens and dozens of the *norrow*.

There must be thousands here.

An army.

Holy shit. Holy fucking shit.

When Wrath shouts across the room, his voice booms with command and echoes back to us.

"Prepare yourselves," he says. "We're going to war."

EPILOGUE

Wrath barely looks at me as he instructs Lauren to get me *out of his sight.* Actual words.

I'm led to a cell in the depths of the castle. Using an iron key that hangs around her neck, Lauren unlocks my arms from behind my back, but binds them again in front of me. "You know, you might be the stupidest person I've ever met."

"You might be right," I mutter.

The cell has one window at ground level. Bubbled glass inlaid with iron bars lets in a few rays of early morning light.

"Hopefully Wrath can figure out a way to kill you and get the *animus* so we can finally be done with you."

"You'd love that, wouldn't you?" I circle the small room. There isn't even a bed. It's just an uneven stone floor with a dusting of dirt and pebbles.

Lauren crosses her arms over her chest. "Obviously. You've been nothing but trouble since you showed up."

"As if I had any choice in the matter."

"You had a choice," she points out. "And you betrayed him."

Yes. As everyone keeps reminding me.

"Can you just go? I'm tired."

Lauren rolls her eyes, but leaves me in the dark, cool silence.

I pace the room for a while, looking for any kind of weakness, but of course there's none to be found. The window is solid, the iron bars firmly cemented in the stone foundation. The door to the cell is thick wood and strapped in more iron.

I try using Wrath's power to travel through the sub-dimension—I've used it twice now, so I know I can do it—but nothing happens no matter how hard I try.

Probably because of the binding. Kat's magic is strong, and I don't know the first thing about breaking it or even if I can.

As the daylight fades again, I find a divot in the stone floor and curl into it on my side. I have no blanket, no pillow. Just the clothes on my back. I shiver as the light fades. I slip in and out of sleep.

Sometime in the middle of the night, Wrath comes to me.

I see the outline of him against the weak moonlight at the window.

I know he knows I'm awake, but I say nothing. There's nothing to say.

"Why did you do it, *dieva*?" His voice echoes around the cell and slithers over my skin. A chill lifts the hair along my arms.

"Why did you threaten my best friend?" I counter. The rage builds in my gut, but without the *animus*, it's just useless emotion.

"Is one man really more important than an entire world?" he asks.

I pull myself upright. "Yes."

"You don't believe that. Not really."

"Is power really more important to you than life?"

"Power is life. Life is power. They are intertwined."

"I never wanted the power," I admit.

"You think I did? You think I chose this life? To rule?" He stands and the sandy floor grits beneath his boots. "I do what I must because it is my duty. It is in my blood, much as the power is in yours. And yet, you keep running from it because you are afraid."

He's suddenly in front of me, crouched before me. The barest hint of moonlight skims half his beautiful face. "You may be powerful," he says, "but you are a coward."

I bite at my bottom lip, feeling a sting of tears.

Because he's right.

I am so fucking afraid.

I'm afraid of who I am and who I'm meant to be. I'm afraid of losing who I thought I was and becoming something else.

But most of all, I'm afraid of how he makes me feel, how ravenous I am for him despite all of the horrible things he's done.

Even now, hands magically bound, locked away in a dank cell, I want him to touch me. I want to get lost in his molten eyes and burn beneath his scorching touch.

I hate him and I fucking love him.

No sense hiding from it any longer.

I would scorch the earth for him just the same as I would for Gus.

"I asked you nicely to bind yourself to me," he says. "And you denied me." His eyes flare in the dark. "I won't ask nicely again."

A tear escapes from the corner of my eye. I quickly swipe it away. I don't want him to see my pain.

"You will bind yourself to me," he says, his voice thick and hoarse with something that sounds like heartache, "or I will destroy everything you've ever loved."

I believe him.

I believe him, and it kills me.

There's a crackle of air, and I immediately sense the void he's left. But he pops up again a second later, and a thick, warm blanket is draped over my shoulders, driving the chill away.

"If I say yes now, will you unbind me and get me out of this damn hole?"

He laughs through his nose. "Oh *dieva*. You think you've suffered enough?" He crouches in front of me again and traces a finger over my cheek. His touch ignites me. I close my eyes and sink into the feel of him as my heart kicks up and butterflies fill my belly.

"Your suffering has only begun."

His touch disappears and then he's gone.

And the chill immediately returns.

VENGEFUL DEMON KING

1

I'VE LOST TRACK OF THE NUMBER OF DAYS I'VE BEEN LOCKED IN THIS dungeon in the depths of the Demon King's castle.

For the first week, using a rock I'd found on the ground, I'd gouge a line in the slick black stone wall when the sun dipped below the horizon.

When I made it to day thirteen, I got so pissed, I threw the rock and now I can't find it.

Doesn't matter, I suppose.

Maybe Wrath will let me rot in this cell for an eternity.

Eternity.

My stomach suddenly wants to revolt, but it's damn near empty.

Wrath and I are connected. I was born of the *animus*, one third of the Demon King's power. If he can live forever, does that mean I will too?

Oh god.

I can't be trapped in this godforsaken hole forever.

My own sobs echo back to me when I curl into a ball in the corner and wrap my blanket around my shoulders.

Wrath came to me the first night I was in here and brought me this blanket.

It's the only time he's come.

There's a clank somewhere in the depths of the dungeon. I've come to recognize the sound of the main door being unbolted and opened and like Pavlov's dog, my stomach growls.

A few seconds later, I hear the distinct sound of Arthur's shoes shuffling over the gritty stone floor and then his face pops up in the cut-out in the wooden door of my cell.

I immediately smell food.

The dungeon might be old-fashioned, hollowed out from ancient stone, but someone took the time to install electricity down here and soft rope lights run the length of the hall along the floor. As Arthur unlocks my cell door and enters, the low lighting casts him in eerie shadows.

"Morning, Rain," he says.

"Good morning, Arthur." I make a show of stretching like I just woke up from the best night of sleep.

On my second day down here, Lauren was instructed to add metal cuffs to my wrists, much to her delight.

They look like iron bracelets etched with runes.

Now when I stretch, they thunk down the length of my arms and gouge skin as they do. Lauren wouldn't tell me what they were for, exactly, but I suspect it's just another measure to bind my power because when I've tried to use the *animus*, the runes glow and the cuffs burn.

"I have fresh clothes for you today," Arthur says. "And quiche."

My excitement is so acute, I damn near weep.

Arthur has been making sure I have clean clothes and a basin of soapy water every few days so I'm not a total feral beast in this dank cell.

And he seriously makes the best quiche.

"What kind? Quiche, that is." As if I'm going to be picky about it.

"Broccoli and ham."

I want to kiss the man.

Back slightly stooped, he comes over to me and hands off the tray. There's a permanent frown between his brows, and new lines of pain etched around his mouth.

"How are you, Arthur?"

"I'm okay." He stands back, clasps his hands.

"You don't look okay."

He's sheepish when he laughs. "The pain is worse today, is all. I overdid it yesterday."

I set the tray on the stone ledge by the window. "I thought Wrath was healing you?"

Arthur was in a bad car accident years ago and damaged his back. He has an electrical implant that's supposed to help with the chronic pain, but even that can only go so far.

Wrath's magic was helping him get by beyond what modern science could do.

"The Demon King doesn't have much power to spare these days," Arthur admits.

The guilt is immediate.

I helped Wrath's brother, Chaos, steal that power.

And because of it, Wrath is weak and Arthur is suffering.

"I'm so sorry, Arthur," I start. "I didn't—"

"No. No." Arthur holds up a hand. "The pain is mine and only mine. Please don't hold guilt over me."

I purse my lips and give him a nod.

"So beyond the power, how is he?" I ask.

Arthur casts his gaze to the floor and exhales, not quite a sigh, but almost. "The Demon King is..."

I lean forward, hanging on his hesitation, hungrier for the details about Wrath than I am for the actual food.

The truth is, I'm starving for him in a way that makes me want to claw out of my skin. I'm restless for him.

I didn't think it was possible to want to love and murder

someone all at the same time, but the Demon King has proven me wrong.

He tried to force my hand, make me bind myself to him, and when I refused, he hurt my best friend.

I'll never forgive him for it.

But I don't know how else to punish him either. We are linked because of the *animus*, or rather, because I *am* the *animus*—the Hellfire Crown, one third of the Demon King's power.

If he bleeds, so do I, and vice versa.

I can't punish him physically without physically wounding myself too.

But something tells me the bruises I've left on him are not the kind you can see.

"The Demon King is what? Tell me, Arthur." My voice is quiet and desperate and the echo of it fills the hollowed-out crevices of the cell like a ghost.

"I've never seen him like this," Arthur admits.

"Like what?"

When he finally looks at me, there's worry pinched in the aged lines around his eyes. "Broken."

It's a punch to the gut. A knife to the chest.

I did that.

I did that.

He made me do it.

He gave me no choice.

My frustration burbles up, barbed and burning, and the magical cuffs around my wrists glow bright red.

The metal heats up, runes etched into it glowing brightly.

Then the metal singes my skin as a snap of electricity jolts down to bone.

I yell out and fight at the cuffs like I always do, like this time will be any different from the two dozen other times I tried to use my magic. Like this time maybe they'll come off.

They don't.

The pain reverberates through me and settles at my breastbone. It's a deep ache that will last an hour or so, if I could tell time down here.

Arthur frowns at me.

I shake out my arms, then press my hand to my sternum as if I can massage away the pain. "And Chaos? Dare I even ask?"

"Chaos has been busy."

I curse into the shadows. "What kind of busy?"

"He seems to be working with Naomi now."

"The president is working with the Demon King's brother?"

Arthur nods. "You know the saying. 'The enemy of my enemy—'"

"'Is my friend,'" I finish.

"Precisely."

"Great." I pace the length of the cell. It takes me all of two seconds. "What about the state of the world?"

"Oddly enough," Arthur says, "things have quieted down. We haven't had a mass shooting in over three weeks. A new record since they started recording those stats. And the political unrest has seemed to settle too."

This should be good news. So why does it feel like a shoe about to drop?

"Does Wrath have a theory as to why things have settled?"

"Chaos can bring order just the same as he can cause chaos. He and Wrath are two sides of the same coin, in a way. They represent both."

"So Chaos is what, giving us some zen magic?"

"I guess you could say that."

"Until he decides to flip the switch."

I don't know enough about Wrath's brother to know what his plan is. Maybe Wrath doesn't know either. But it would be in Chaos's best interest to have our government on his side while he fights his brother, and how else could he prove his value than through the tempering of our country's unrest?

It makes Wrath look like a hurricane in comparison.

"Has he...Wrath...has he said anything about me?"

I hate how desperate I sound, but I wouldn't ask anyone other than Arthur. I know he won't judge me.

Arthur frowns. "No, I'm sorry."

I exhale, shoulders dipping. "It's okay. I mean, that's what I expected but if he had plans to murder me, I just wanted a heads up."

"He won't," Arthur says maybe too quickly. "Whatever he means to do with you, it won't be that."

"Because he can't," I point out. "I'm sure he wishes he could."

"I'm not going to pretend to understand what goes on inside the Demon King's head," Arthur admits, "but one thing I do know? He has no weakness but you."

There's a sharp sting in my eyes that feels an awful lot like tears.

I want to go to him. I wish he would let me. We could torture each other, scream at each other, then fuck each other until we were spent.

The reality of our relationship feels like a chain around my ankle, one I'll never escape.

I should embrace it. Stop fighting it. I just wish he wasn't so much of...

A villain.

"Do you think he'll ever let me out of this hole?" I ask Arthur.

"I don't know, Rain."

I nod and collapse against the back wall. "Thank you for the food. You're the bright spot of my day, Arthur."

He smiles a closed-lip smile. "I wish I could do more."

"I know."

He ambles over to the door, grabs my empty tray from yesterday, and then clanks open the lock with his key.

I think it says something that Wrath sends Arthur to attend to me when I could so easily overpower him, especially now that he's suffering from constant pain again.

The Demon King knows I won't fight Arthur—I've got too much of a soft heart. And I think he knows deep down that I won't run. I can't. There's nowhere to run to.

Arthur gets the bolt open and then slips out of the cell. The lock clanks again as he shuts it. "I'll see you tomorrow."

I go to the tray of food and eat it standing at the window ledge. Looking through the old bubbled glass is like looking through a dream. The world outside is hazy and swirled, but the dark shape at the edge of the garden is distinct, nonetheless.

The Demon King is stalking through the garden from the house to the stables, if I had to guess.

It's the first time I've caught sight of him since he ordered Lauren to drag me down to this hole and my heart thuds loudly in my chest reminding me that even when I want to hate him, I don't.

I'm suddenly buzzing.

I drop my fork and wrap my hands around the iron bars inlaid in the windowsill as if I can get closer and get a better look. He's in profile to me and I can just make out the hard line of his mouth and the tension in his shoulders.

Look at me.

Look at me.

I'm so desperate for his gaze that a choked cry escapes my throat.

The Demon King stops.

His body goes rigid, hands balling into fists.

He looks my way, to the window to my cell.

Can he see me through the glass? Can he hear me?

The scowl that comes over his face is sharp enough to cut.

I think my heart stops beating for several seconds as we stare at each other across the expanse of the garden, through the thick, swirled glass.

He is not a dream.

The Demon King is a nightmare come to life.

His eyes burn bright red for a half second before he turns away from me and disappears from sight.

2

Even though I was born with stubbornness stitched into every fiber of my being, going on a hunger strike is absolutely out of the question.

For one, I like food.

And two, Arthur is a damn good cook.

I eat the entire slice of quiche and then mop up the crust crumbs with the tip of my index finger. If I was a free woman, I'd be going for seconds, damn the calories and the thick hips.

I set the tray at the door and then begin my nightly ritual of absolutely fucking nothing.

I pace for a while. Then do some push-ups which I suck at. Then I play this other game I invented called Reach for the Rock.

There's a sharp, black stone just out of my reach in the hallway outside the cell. I spotted it after I threw my first rock and lost it. But no matter how far I reach, I can never put my fingers to it.

It keeps me busy though.

Sometime later, sweating and angry—I want that fucking rock—I grab my blanket and wedge myself into the back corner of the stone cell. There's this semi-comfortable spot where the stone dips in a way that is the perfect cup for my back.

Ahh, it's the little things, right?

I'm going to go insane down here.

I doze sitting up.

I don't know how long or what time it is when I wake.

But I'm sure that I'm not alone.

There's only the glow of the inset lights outside my cell, but I can make out the void of a dark shape in the far corner of my prison.

"Are you really here?" I ask him.

"Does it matter?"

The sound of his voice is like a drag of silk over my skin and I'm immediately shivering in my blanket.

"I think it would," I say.

There's the glint of something in his hand and at first, I think it's a blade, but then I realize it's a glass. He takes a sip. I hear the distinct sound of ice clinking together in the dark.

"Then yes," he says, "I am really here."

His speech is slow and slurred.

"Are you drunk?"

"Very much so," he admits.

"I didn't think you could get drunk."

"I had to go to considerable effort to manage it." He takes another long drink and then comes forward. The shadows writhe around him like living things. He sets the glass on the window ledge and takes another step, but he's unsteady on his feet.

Hugging the blanket to my shoulders, I rise to stand in the corner unsure of where this is going, afraid of where it could, excited that it might go somewhere, anywhere at all.

I am a glutton for punishment. That's never truer than when I'm in the same room as the Demon King.

Maybe I'm going to hell for all of this. If there *is* a hell.

Maybe I'm already there.

I want to sink into the fire. Feel the heat of it, *of him*, on my skin.

"What do you want?" I ask him.

"I want you to obey me."

I snort. The sound echoes in the cavern. "I won't. Not ever. But I think you know that."

He collapses against the wall. "I suppose I do."

"So what do you really want?"

He bows his head. His chest rises and falls. He says nothing for the longest time and my heart hammers at my eardrums.

Thud. Thud. Thud.

"I want to know what to do with you."

My stomach fills with butterflies.

I think this might be the most telling thing that's ever come out of his mouth.

What he really wants to do is force me to do as he wishes—bind myself to him, bow at his feet, obey him—but he can't.

Wrath is a king and no one has ever defied him, and yet the power he holds over me is scant, barely power at all.

"Why did you hurt Gus?"

He comes closer and steps out of the shadows.

In so many days, I somehow forgot what it was to look him straight in the face.

As soon as his pale beauty is in front of me, the air catches in my throat and I have to gulp it back.

"I've never had the luxury of being merciful," he admits.

"Gus is my best friend."

His gaze finds me in the dim light. "And I've never had the luxury of a friend."

"I was your friend."

"No, you weren't."

"Yes, I was!" My voice rises and bounces off the stone. "I wanted you. I wanted this." I wave my hand between us. "I wanted it all."

"Tell me, how does it taste when those lies roll off your tongue? Sweet like honey? Bitter like anise? Or maybe they taste like nothing at all. Maybe you are immune to them entirely."

"Don't do that."

"Do what?"

"Don't pretend that I'm the bad guy here. I was willing to do whatever it took to help you and—"

He looks down at me, down the sharp slope of his nose. "Everything except for the one thing I fucking needed."

"You wanted me to bind myself to you forever. And you didn't even give me the time to consider what that meant."

"We didn't *have* time, Rain."

Him using my real name is like a slap to the face and I shrink back from it.

He always calls me *dieva*.

I thought it meant little girl, but it's actually more like a promise, a promise to protect that which he's claimed.

It became a term of endearment. And the loss of it is the same as being gutted.

Tears immediately well in my eyes and I wish I could use my newfound power to blip out of sight.

I don't want Wrath to know he can get to me with something so easy as calling me by my name.

"It wasn't a killing blow," he says, low and beneath his breath.

"What?"

He meets my gaze again and the first hint of red fire is flaring in his irises. "I've spilled enough blood in my lifetime to know how to spill only what I need. Your friend wasn't in any danger. Not really."

For some reason this makes me even angrier. "So you did it just to scare me into doing what you wanted."

"That's precisely what it was."

"You're an asshole."

He crosses the distance between us, his face morphing into the monster. "No, I am a king!" His voice booms through the cell and echoes down the hall. "I do what I must! And you're just a stupid little girl who sacrifices so little to have so much."

My own rage burbles up my throat.

Fuck him and fuck his arrogance.

Without thinking, I grab his abandoned glass from the windowsill and smash it against the stone wall. I'm left with a long, pointy shard in my hand.

He looks at it, then looks at me, his mouth twitching.

Staring him right in the fucking face, I drag the sharp end of the glass over the pale underside of my arm.

The pain is acute. White dots burst in my field of vision and I grit my teeth against it as my skin splits open and blood wells out.

Wrath's eyes narrow to slits as his jaw flexes.

It may be dark in the cell, but even in what little light there is, I can see the mirroring wound on his arm, his blood dripping to the stone floor and pooling in the divots.

When I bleed, he bleeds.

"Maybe I'll just slit my throat so I can finally be done with you," I say.

"You're too fucking stubborn."

I bring the shard to my neck.

His eyes pinch tighter, his chest rising with a quick breath and then absolute stillness as he holds it in.

I'm not sure if I'm bluffing. Or if I'm tempting the connection between us and the power of the dark father god burning through my veins.

Can I die?

I'm the *animus,* one third of the legendary dark god's power.

Maybe there's no such thing as death for me.

But I like seeing the mighty Demon King flinch.

Grip tight on the shard, it cuts into the palm of my hand and across the meaty parts of my fingers. I'm a mess. Blood is already pouring down my hand, down my arm, dripping from my elbow.

I move to pull the glass over my throat.

The Demon King snaps his hand out and grips me at the wrist, stopping me.

"Don't," he says.

There is the barest flicker of panic in his voice.

I don't know if it's for me or for him. Or maybe both. Maybe it's impossible to unsnarl us now.

"Let me out of this fucking hole."

He takes another breath, but his grip remains on my wrist, fingers circling me like a vise.

"Why did you refuse me?" He gets in close, overwhelming me with his size and the sheer power of his body. "I would have protected you."

A sob threatens to escape from my throat, so I clamp my teeth, trying to catch it before it does.

The most painful thing is, I believe him.

I think if I'd agreed to bind myself to him, he would have kept his promises. I would have had him in my bed every night. I would have had his dark power at my side. I would have ruled on a throne beside him if I'd wanted.

Every man and woman and demon and vampire would have bowed at my feet, jealous of what I had and they didn't.

"Why did you refuse me?" he asks again. "Tell me."

I have nothing to hide. And even though I hate the idea of him thinking of me like *a stupid little girl*, I want him to trust that what comes out of my mouth is always the truth, despite what he may think.

"Because I was afraid, just like you said."

He runs his knuckles down the side of my face, a featherlight touch, but he leaves a trail of blood on my skin. It's hot at first and cools quickly in the dank air of the cell.

"And now?" he asks.

"Now I'm terrified."

"Do you want to know a secret?" he whispers.

"Yes."

"So am I." He pulls my hand away and wrenches the glass from my grip. It plinks into the shadows when he tosses it aside. "I'm terrified of being weak," he admits. "And I'm terrified of how I feel whenever you're not by my side."

I shiver as his hand comes to my throat. "And how's that? How does it make you feel?"

"Like I've been cleaved in two." He tightens his hold, fingers punishing me for making him feel the way he does.

I've laid him low.

The mighty Demon King.

When I walk out of this cell, I will be ten feet tall.

I grab hold of his hair with my bloody hand and yank him to me. Our mouths collide. He bites at my bottom lip, drawing blood and hissing when an answering wound must come to his mouth.

I taste the coppery tang of our blood.

He wraps his arms around me and lifts me up, pressing me against the stone wall as he tears the shirt from my body.

The material rips loudly in the chamber and the sound tangles with the echo of our pants, our groans.

We are famished for something that cannot be bought.

His mouth comes to my neck, his sharp teeth dragging over my sensitive flesh. I moan and instinctively curl away from the pain, but he is relentless. He nips at me again and I jolt beneath him, rocking against his crotch.

There is a considerable bulge there.

Grabbing the center of my bra, he rips the material from my body, exposing me to the chill air. More blood drips from his mouth which covers me in splatters as he hoists me up, capturing my nipple in the heat of his mouth.

His tongue slides over me, drawing me to a peak and the pulse of the pleasure scorches down my belly and sinks into my clit.

The Demon King might not know what to do with me outside of this cell, but he sure as hell knows what to do with me now.

Anchoring me to the wall, he rolls my other nipple between his fingers, sending a shot of pain and pleasure through my nerves.

I cry out in the dark.

I want him inside of me.

Right fucking now.

I squirm beneath him, trying to get my hand between us so I can pull him out of his pants.

I manage to snag the waistband and yank them down and his cock hangs heavy and thick between us.

When I take him in my fist, his eyes slip closed as his Adam's apple sinks on a deep, guttural groan.

"I've missed that hand on my cock," he says.

"You knew where to find me."

"I was punishing you."

"Sounds like you were only punishing yourself."

He drops me, grabs a fistful of my hair and forces me to my knees.

"I missed fucking that disobedient mouth even more."

He shoves inside of me. He's so fucking hard and when he thrusts forward, the head of his dick hits the back of my throat and I gag.

He tsk-tsks above me. "Be a good girl and take it," he says and thrusts in again causing my belly to burn bright with a deep-rooted, so fucked-up sense of pride.

He fucks me hard and fast, his hand still tangled in my hair, guiding me over his length.

"Fuck," he says. "You will be the end of me."

Precum fills my mouth and he slows his pace, straining to hold back.

"Get up," he orders and strips me of the rest of my clothes as his eyes burn bright red in the dark.

I can feel the wetness coating me, slipping down my thighs. My clit is swollen and needy.

The *norrow* appear beside me.

"What are—"

The dark shadowmen grab me, flip me around and slam me to the floor. I huff out a breath and dirt crusts in my mouth. Wrath kicks my legs apart and sinks between them.

I flail beneath the norrow, but their hold is steady and a seed of panic blooms in my chest as my heart slams in my ears.

Wrath's fingers slip beneath my mound, hitting my clit. I pant against the floor, filled with a too-big feeling, like I might burst open at the seams.

"Wrath," I moan. "Please."

He slips two fingers inside of me, slides a third forward against my swollen bud.

A flare of pleasure burns at my core.

"Fuck." I'm trying so hard to catch my breath. "Fuck me."

His fingers disappear and he cracks me across the ass. The pain is immediate and catches me off guard and I can't help but yelp in the dark.

"Beg for it."

I groan. He cups me between the legs and I squirm, mindless and buzzing trying to burn friction between us, to feel the edge of pleasure.

It's too much. It's too much. It's all too much and not enough.

Blood is crusting on my arm and down my chest. Dirt grits on my open wound.

I can feel the primordial shiver of the norrow on my skin, like a dark daydream.

I am mindless and found all at the same time.

Found by Wrath, the dark Demon King.

"Please." The buzz between my legs is a flame I need stoked. Right fucking now. "Please fuck me."

He grabs me by the hips and yanks my ass up, baring me more.

When the head of his cock comes to my opening, I almost weep with relief.

A breath stutters out of me.

The norrow disappear.

Wrath rocks back and drives into me, seating himself to the hilt.

Pain blooms at my core, he's so deep.

He fucks me hard and the sound of our primal fucking echoes through the cavern.

The pleasure builds.

And builds.

Wrath groans as he pounds into me.

His dark magic writhes around the cavern floor, then pulls in tight, and when I feel the diving caress of it at my clit, I almost lose my mind.

"Come for me, *dieva*," Wrath says. "Call out my name."

"Wrath," I say on a moan.

"No," he scolds, his grip tightening on my hips. "Try again."

The darkness writhes around my pussy, teases at my clit, coaxing the pleasure from my well. It's a divine swirl, a featherlight touch with just the right rhythm to drive me wild.

Fuck. I'm a quivering, wet mess.

"Go on," he says, punishing me by slowing his thrusts. In and out. In and out.

The cuffs on my wrists light up and the metal grows hot as the orgasm reaches out for me.

"Fuck. Oh fuck. Wrath."

He takes another fistful of my hair and wrenches me back. The growl of his anger rumbles in my ear. "Say it, *dieva*."

"My king," I correct.

"Good girl," he says and thrusts deeper.

The darkness circles my clit with a divine rhythm and the wave crests, then spills over, burning through my veins, all of the muscle in my body tensing up.

Wrath drives deep and comes with a deep, guttural groan, the sound echoing around us in the stone cell.

He pulls back, sinks in again, the head of his cock swelling inside of me, hitting deep at the center.

I tremble through the aftershock of the orgasm, racing like an electrical current through my veins.

When we've both ridden the wave out, we collapse on the dirt floor on our backs.

We both pant into the dark.

Where the fuck do we go from here?

He might have controlled that descent into dark pleasure, but we both know he's as mad for me as I am for him.

We are the thorns in each other's side and every time we try to pluck the other out, the thorn sinks deeper.

"Let me out of this fucking hole," I say.

"I like knowing exactly where I can find you."

I lift my arms and the metal cuffs sink down my wrists. "You've literally handcuffed me."

"I know. I like that too."

I groan into the dark.

"At least let me have a shower."

"So you can clean my cum from your pussy?"

"Wrath."

He rolls to his knees, then scoops me up effortlessly.

One second, we're in the dankness of the dungeon and the next we're in the warm hush of his bedroom.

I almost weep.

But I'm not going to let him know how badly I wanted out of that prison. I'm just going to pretend that it was a mild annoyance, a slight inconvenience.

He promised to torture me and any sign of discomfort would be a mark on his side.

I will not let him win.

I keep my arms locked around his neck as he carries me into the bathroom and sets me down on the black stone floor of the walk-in shower.

Only the undercabinet lighting is on, so it's easy on my eyes considering I've spent the last two weeks in almost total darkness.

He reaches around me and flips on the showerhead, dials in the temperature.

I try not to like that he's taking care of me. Of course I fail at that.

I wanted to believe that I was just an innocent bystander yanked into Wrath's darkness, but the truth is, whatever it is we have here makes me euphoric in all of its dark, fucked-up glory.

Turns out living on a knife's edge is exhilarating.

And being cared for by the infamous Demon King is like holding the flame of a god in your hand.

It'll surely burn you, but the thrill of holding it is so fucking worth it.

When steam fills the stall, I walk in beneath the water and a moan escapes me.

"You have ten minutes," he says.

"Yes, warden."

He growls before disappearing in a whirl of black magic.

3

When I'm showered and wrapped in a towel, I come out to Wrath's bedroom. There's a bedside lamp on, but Wrath is nowhere to be found.

I tiptoe around the room and put my ear to the door. I don't hear anything beyond it. I go to the balcony next and pull open the French doors. Wrath's bedroom is on the second floor and the balcony overlooks the back garden.

I'm sure I could scale down the railing and hop down to the ground and run away through the woods.

But running seems futile now.

And besides, I'm naked again with no clothes. Why the hell do I keep finding myself in this predicament?

"Thinking of trying to escape already?"

His voice finds me on the balcony and a shiver runs down my spine. I turn to him and clutch at the towel.

I'm not a liar—most of the time—so I dodge the question entirely like the artful little scamp I am. "It feels like it's been months since I breathed fresh air."

He rolls his eyes. "It's been two weeks and no more. So dramatic. Get inside, *dieva*."

There's a satisfied thrill low in my gut hearing him use my pet name.

It feels like I'm standing on solid ground again.

I come inside. He disappears and pops up beside me a half second later. He wraps his hand around the back of my neck and steers me over to the bed where I notice there's a chain screwed into the headboard.

"I didn't know we were going full BDSM," I say as he tosses me on the bed, grabs one of my arms and clamps the chain to the cuff around my wrist. "Is this really necessary?"

He gives me a sardonic smile. "You've run from me twice, betrayed me multiple times, stabbed me, and summoned my brother only for him to take one third of the triad, putting us both at risk. So yes, it's absolutely necessary. Unless you'd like to return to the hole?"

"No," I say, a bit too quickly, then twist my mouth into a salacious smile. "Chained to your bed is fine by me."

He snorts and turns away.

"Where are you going?"

"I have work to do, *dieva*." He glares at me over his shoulder. "And a mess to clean up."

Then he's gone.

"You could have at least offered me a drink!" I yell.

He doesn't respond, so I just lay in his bed, naked and chained, and a little miffed. I mean, this is definitely a step up from a stone floor. Wrath's bed feels like laying in a cloud. And it's definitely a lot warmer than the dungeon. But the cuffs and the chain are chafing and frankly, really fucking annoying.

I test the chain by giving it a few hard yanks, but of course the Demon King is no slouch. The damn thing is screwed in tight.

I drop against the pillows, forcing air out of the fluff and I'm immediately surrounded by his scent.

Now I'm soaring. Wrath's scent might be a fucking drug and I think I might be an addict.

It's like wintertime beneath the stars, a crackling fire, and something spicy in a hot mug between your hands.

I take a deep inhale, filling my nose and my lungs with it.

I could huff this fume all day. Begrudgingly, of course.

Trying to find a comfortable spot, what with being chained to the bed, I curl onto my side and tuck my arm beneath the pillow. The stuffing is just thick enough to soften some of the sharp edges of the chain and cuff.

I breathe out.

From this moment on, I will never take a comfortable bed for granted.

I'm realizing that the *animus* might have shielded me from physical ailments my entire life. I never gave it a second thought, but looking back, I wasn't ever sick. What few scrapes and bumps and bruises I suffered were gone within a day.

But sleeping on a stone floor for a week? The dark god's power can only do so much.

I decide I'll just lie there in Wrath's bed for a while and rest my aching bones before I start strategizing my next move, but before I know it, I'm fast asleep.

And it isn't until hours later that I feel the bed dip beneath the Demon King's weight, the warmth of his chest at my back and his arms around my body.

I'm barely awake, but I swear, even through the sleepy fog, I hear him sigh into my neck.

Almost like he's relieved to have me by his side.

4

When I wake in the daylight, the Demon King is gone again. But I'm still chained to the bed.

Annoyance flashes through me. I feel the now familiar sensation of my power lighting up, but the force of it is quickly snuffed out by the magical cuffs around my wrist.

"Goddammit," I mutter. Then, "Wrath! Hello!"

Because I'm the world's luckiest girl, it's Lauren that responds to my shouting.

Rolling my eyes, I lie back against the pillows, tugging the blanket around me.

"Naked in the Demon King's bed again," she says. "Why am I not surprised?"

"Yes, yes. I know. Get it out. Go ahead. The slut is bending over for him. Blah blah blah. Can I please have some clothes?"

She yanks the drapes open and sunlight pours into the room, burning my eyes. Groaning, I throw an arm over my face.

"I'm not sure if I have any more clothing to spare. You keep finding yourself without yours. I'm running out."

"I'll owe you."

She blows out a breath. "As if you have anything to give me."

"Can I be unchained?"

"I don't have the key."

"Of course you don't. Where is Wrath?"

"The Demon King is currently in Saint Sabine meeting with Kat."

"Why?"

"If he wanted you to know why, he would have told you, I'm sure."

Being chained to this bed is punishment enough—now I have to be forced to endure Lauren's snark.

I don't think she'll ever warm up to me and her bad attitude has me constantly questioning why Wrath keeps her around.

If I were a vindictive asshole, I'd be scheming to get rid of her.

Do I have that power with the Demon King?

There's a snarly little flare of pride that tells me maybe I do.

"For the love of all things holy," I beg, "can I please have some clothes?"

She rolls her eyes, lets out a long grumbly sigh, and leaves the room.

I test out the chain again and don't get it to budge. It'll be much easier to investigate once I'm dressed.

Lauren returns with a tangled ball of clothing and dumps it on the end of the bed. "There you go, princess," she says and leaves again.

"Hey! I can't reach them!"

But of course, she's not here to make things easier for me.

I spend the next fifteen minutes stretched out on the bed like a man about to be quartered and hung. I manage to grab the clothing with my toes and yank it up the massive length of the bed.

The panties and shorts are easy to put on, though it takes some shimmying around. I get the bra on—thank god it's a hook closure—but have to leave one of the straps off for the chain.

"Now we're in business." I stand on the bed and kick the

pillows aside. Using all of my strength, I wrap both arms around the chain and yank.

My teeth grit together. Sweat beads on my forehead.

I blow out a breath. "Okay, new strategy."

I prop a foot on the headboard and use my leg for leverage. When that doesn't work, I pull the chain taut and brace both feet on the headboard like I'm a climber rappelling down a mountainside.

"Come...on...god...dammit!"

Nothing.

Doesn't even budge.

I fall back to the bed, sweaty and spent.

"A spirited effort," the Demon King says.

I wince and bury a grumble. "It's unbecoming to watch a girl struggle from the shadows."

"Here, let me help you."

The darkness kicks up around me. Inky tendrils trail up my legs, up my thighs, and a shiver courses up my body.

The dark ribbons steal beneath the hem of my shorts and the anticipation of their destination makes my heart thud loudly in my head, and a tingle buzz in my clit.

"Wrath." I pull myself up against the mountain of pillows.

The Demon King drops into one of the wingback chairs in the shadows.

"What did I promise you, *dieva*?"

The darkness slips around the hem of my panties and cups me, pulsing against me.

"Fuck you."

"What did I promise you?"

"That my suffering has only begun."

"Yes."

The darkness pulls in closely, a whisper against my clit.

I sink back against the pillows and close my eyes.

This doesn't feel like suffering and the fear that it could flip at any moment somehow makes the pleasure that much more potent.

The ribbons of darkness rock against me, swirling and teasing at my bud.

I'm wet in an instant and the darkness pools together to a swollen head, sinking to my opening.

I hear the shift of fabric as the Demon King rises from his chair.

"As a king," he says, "I've learned there are different kinds of suffering."

The darkness pushes inside of me, filling me up, and fucks me slow and steady.

The chain rattles as I writhe on the bed and I wrap my arm around it, as if to anchor me there.

"There is the suffering of pain."

A ribbon winds up across my torso, steals inside my bra and caresses my nipple.

"There is the suffering of want."

The pace of the darkness picks up, driving into me over and over. My pleasure builds, my breathing quickening.

The crest is rising, rising.

"Oh fuck, keep going."

I spread my legs further apart letting the darkness take me.

I'm so close.

The pressure builds.

And then—

Gone.

"And there is the suffering of loss."

"Wait. Wrath, please—"

I writhe on the bed and yank at the chain.

"Wrath."

He's at the bedside now, peering down at me, the sunlight limning him in silver, his face hidden in shadow.

The orgasm is haunting me like a ghost, so fucking close, just out of reach.

I'm still buzzing.

It would take just the slightest bit of friction and I'd be spilling over the edge again.

Wrath climbs on the bed and my inner walls clench, anticipating the feel of his cock inside of me.

Kneeling between my legs, he scoops me up and sets me on his lap. I can tell he's hard through his pants and the bulge rocks against my hot center.

The chain grows taut.

"I think I've suffered enough," I say with a ragged breath.

"No, you haven't." His mouth is close to mine. He has the softest lips and the most punishing of kisses.

I lock my legs around him and grind over his cock.

"Fuck me."

He leans forward, presses his lips against mine, lets me taste the sweetness of his tongue.

I moan into his mouth. He's going to give in to me. I know he will. If I just keep him here and—

Suddenly, I'm weightless and falling back. I yelp and collapse against the bed.

Wrath disappeared.

Fucking hell.

I scurry back into a sitting position and find him at the end of the bed, leaning against the bed post. He's watching me with hooded eyes and a satisfied smile on his face.

"Asshole," I say. "As usual, a girl only has herself to count on. I guess I'll just finish myself."

I'm baiting him, but he doesn't bite.

I slip my hand down the flat plane of my stomach and then beneath the waistband of my shorts and into my panties.

I'm so fucking wet, my fingers are immediately slippery and when I slide them over myself, the sensation is exquisite.

I rest my head against the headboard and close my eyes.

I go slowly at first, tempting him.

My clit begs for more as the pressure builds, but I want to drag this out. I want to punish him as much as he's punishing me.

Wanting more lubrication, I dip a finger into my slick channel and then drag my finger back up, drenching the rest of me.

When I open my eyes and look over at Wrath, his irises are glowing molten red.

I love getting beneath his skin.

I slip my hand out, bring my fingers to my mouth and suck each fingertip clean with the roll of my tongue.

He growls.

I sink back to my clit and pick up the tempo, turning quick circles with the pads of my fingers.

Fuck. Fuck I'm close.

I like him watching me.

My breathing quickens, chest rising and falling with the building orgasm as my body tenses up, ready for the pleasure to burst through.

"Oh fuck," I moan.

There is a moment when I'm about to spill over the edge that I think he'll stop me, and the anticipation of the pleasure being stolen from me makes the actual orgasm slam through me like a bright flame.

I cry out. The chain rattles as my body tenses up. My thighs rub together, muscle and bone quivering as the pleasure rides through me.

I jerk and the chain goes taut again, then bangs against the headboard when I fold into myself.

The bed sinks as the Demon King comes up between my legs and forces my knees open.

My hand is still curled over my mound. Just the slightest movement might send me over the edge again.

"Give me your hand," he tells me.

I breathe out quickly, trembling beneath him.

"*Dieva*," he scolds.

I pull my hand from my clit, from my panties. My fingers glisten in the light.

Wrath wraps his hand around my wrist and brings me to his mouth. He sucks one finger in, drags his tongue over my fingertip, cleaning off my juices.

He moves to the next finger and cleans that one too.

The feel of his tongue is a sensation I wasn't prepared for and butterflies ignite in my belly.

This is the hottest fucking thing I've ever seen him do.

I'm quivering again, full of a sensation I can't name.

When he's finished, he holds my hand up. "It's as I suspected," he says.

"What?"

"I can still taste my cum in your pussy. From now on, I want your pussy to always be dripping with it." He bends over me and the hard ridge of his cock presses into me. "I want every vampire, demon, and shifter within a ten-mile radius to know who you belong to."

The darkness pulls in around us, blotting out the sunlight as Wrath wraps his hand around my throat.

"Then why didn't you fill me up again, huh? Why deny me?"

His jaw clenches, teeth gritting.

"Why, Wrath?"

"Because I can't spend every waking minute buried in your pussy."

"It doesn't sound so bad to me."

"You had your chance."

"You mean if I bound myself to you, I'd have you in my bed?"

"I would have given you the world," he admits and then flinches as if he didn't mean to say it out loud.

"The world for my obedience."

He narrows his eyes.

"There are thousands who would give anything to be where you are."

"Full of the Demon King's cum?" I give the chain a hard yank. "Chained to his bed?"

His teeth grind together.

"You know what's hilarious about that?" I counter. "They would have bowed to you, but this power that burns through my veins? They never would have been strong enough to contain it. I don't bow to you because I don't have to. Because I am not your inferior. Start treating me like your equal and maybe we can come to an agreement."

"You are not equal to me."

I snort and roll my eyes. "Tell that to the *animus*. Go on, she's listening."

He growls and climbs off of me as the darkness pulls back and the sunlight fills the room again.

The tension of the moment is gone.

He unlocks me from the chain, but the magical cuffs stay on my wrists.

He lingers, bent over me. The air grows charged, electric.

His hand comes up as if he means to push aside a lock of my hair, but at the last second, he shifts and gives one of my magical cuffs a tug to test its strength.

I'm left aching.

"Come downstairs when you're ready," he says and then pulls away.

"You're going to leave me here alone, unchained? Maybe I'll tie a rope out of your silky sheets and scale down the balcony like a girl trapped in a dark fairytale."

He levels me with an annoyed scowl. "I wonder...if I drown you in a shallow pool, will I survive? No blood will be drawn." His gaze goes distant as he considers it. "I'm certainly willing to experiment."

I grumble. "I'll be down in ten minutes."

"Good girl," he says and disappears.

Truth be told, I wasn't planning on running. I just like to rile him up.

If I pretend I hate his guts, then I don't have to face the inconceivable truth—that I don't.

I take my time in the bathroom and comb out my hair with a spare brush I find in one of the drawers. It's been forever since I felt put together and presentable. Not that it should matter, considering I'm a prisoner here.

Now that I'm unchained, I can finish dressing. I grab the t-shirt Lauren found me and hold it up.

"Fuck me."

It literally says DEMON SLUT across the chest.

I've seen these shirts hanging in the windows of the goth shop in the strip mall outside of Norton Harbor. They're Demon King licensed merch, though I don't know who holds the license. Certainly not the Demon King himself. This kind of tomfoolery is beneath him, as my mom loves to say.

Lauren planned this. I have to give her a gold star for patience and ingenuity.

I put the shirt on and make my way downstairs and to the Bourbon Room. Wrath is there with Arthur and Lauren.

When she sees me in my slutty shirt, a smirk spreads across her lip-glossed lips.

Wrath takes one look at me, his eyes dragging over the big block letters covering my chest and a scowl deepens the sharp lines of his face.

He turns that scathing look on Lauren and she braces.

It's a goddamn delight.

There's something I'm learning about Lauren—she's not very bright.

She's so desperate to make me look bad and to have the Demon King's attention that she never stops to actually strategize about the proper way of making that happen.

I almost feel sorry for her.

Her dumb devotion to him is going to get her head lopped off one of these days.

Though I hope that's just figurative and not literal.

I might dislike her, but I don't dislike her that much.

There's a moment where I think Wrath might punish her now, but apparently her cowering satisfies him, because he moves on without calling her out.

Damn.

"Arthur," he says, "why don't you bring our traitor up to speed and show her the news conference from yesterday."

"Will that be my new nickname?" I ask lightly. "It's much easier to pronounce than *dieva*."

He walks over to the bar. "I do like the ring of it."

Arthur busies himself with the TV remote and tries to pretend we're not all at each other's throats. Poor Arthur.

He clicks on the screen and brings up a news conference at the White House podium. Naomi Wright is there and Chaos is by her side.

I cross my arms over my Demon Slut t-shirt while the footage plays.

"Our country has been subjected to far too much carnage." Naomi looks across the assembled press, but then shifts to the camera, to the viewer. She's dressed in her usual blazer, the pearls in her ears and around her neck. I wanted to hate the president for what happened to me in Riverside Park when her soldiers turned on me, but maybe she was in the exact same position I was just a week ago, feeling like she was stuck between two opposing forces with no easy way out.

She made a decision that she thought would protect her country.

I can be mad about it or I can respect it. And I think I respect it.

If only Wrath would take the same outlook and forgive me already.

But I guess that begs the question: have I forgiven him?

I look over my shoulder at him and his gaze immediately darts to me. There's an unreadable expression on his face, but it makes me shiver, nonetheless.

"I'm pleased to stand up here today," Naomi goes on, "and inform you all that we have a solution to the scourge that is the Demon King." She pulls back and gestures with a hand at Chaos, and the Demon King's brother steps forward with a sheepish grin.

He's wearing a camel-brown blazer that diminishes the cut of his biceps. There's a navy-blue tie around his neck that goes well with the white and blue plaid shirt beneath.

The round tortoiseshell glasses that sit on the bridge of his nose hide the gleam of his steely gray eyes.

"Good morning, everyone. You're all probably wondering who I am." He ducks his head, lets some heat come to his cheeks as if he's embarrassed or shy to be there. "My name is Charles"—I snort—"and not to alarm any of you, but I'm Wrath's brother."

There's a sharp intake of breath from the assembled press.

Chaos holds up his hand. "I know. I know how that sounds. But hear me out."

It's like he's studied us, like he knows just what to say and how to say it. Wrath could never stand at that podium and look sheepish and say things like *hear me out* in that reluctant tone of voice.

Chaos is a villain of a different sort.

The kind you never see coming.

And I brought him here like the stubborn idiot I am.

That seed of guilt takes root in my chest and unfurls its arms.

My mom likes to say guilt is for suckers and priests and that the only purpose guilt serves is to make us weak or powerful, depending on which end you're on.

"You can't change the past," she's said to me more than once. "No sense dwelling on it."

But there's no doubt that one of the biggest reasons we're here in this situation is because of me.

If only Ciri were still alive so I could ask her what the hell she was thinking.

It felt like she knew what she was doing, that she'd already witnessed the future. I had blind faith in her and Sirene.

But how the hell can this be a good thing? This all feels like a horrible mistake.

"I want to assure you," Chaos says, "that I'm here to help. As Wrath's brother, I know him very well. Sometimes he throws a tantrum"—the press lets out nervous laughter—"and I'm usually the one there to clean up the mess."

Even though Wrath has already watched this news coverage, I can still sense his vibrating rage. But when I look over at him, his face is blank.

Is it the connection between us? I don't know how I know it, but this news conference is like nettles beneath his skin. It feels like he's on the brink of smashing things.

"I want to help," Chaos tells the crowd. "I *can* help."

Spoken like a true politician.

"I know trusting me will take a considerable amount of proof on my end and I'm willing to put in the hard work so you'll know exactly who I am, and that I'm here to set right what my brother has wronged."

Goosebumps lift on my arms as Wrath's anger sinks a weight in my gut.

"Now, if you have questions," Chaos says, "I'm here to answer."

He calls on someone in the press assembly, a twenty-something woman wearing a pale pink hijab. "As you may know," she says, "Wrath has killed a great many of our soldiers. Can you speak to why he's done so and furthermore, why we should believe you when you say you won't?"

"That's an excellent question." Chaos speaks to the reporter, but I get the clear impression he's speaking directly to Wrath. "My brother can be reckless and stubborn and sometimes he doesn't think through his actions."

The darkness kicks up around us as Wrath's magic writhes in the air.

"And if I'm being honest," Chaos says, "my brother has always been a little bloodthirsty. And I can assure you, I am not."

"No, it's just power he's after," Wrath says behind me.

"I don't wish to harm anyone," Chaos adds.

"I've seen enough." I turn to Wrath. His irritation and anger are almost a living, breathing thing in the room and it's buzzing along my skin like an electrical current. "Shut it off."

"Is it too much for you to face, *dieva*?" Wrath challenges.

"No, I think it's too much for you."

He inhales through his nose, jaw flexing.

"Arthur," I say.

There's a long pause as Arthur hesitates and Wrath faces off with me.

And then Wrath blinks, pulls away, and stalks from the room.

I race after him.

"Tell me how to beat him." I come up alongside him, but my pace is still at a power walk just to keep up with his long strides. "Tell me what to do and I'll do it."

His brow furrows into a scowl. "Now you want to help?"

"I made a mistake." He says nothing. "And so did you."

He comes to an abrupt stop and I have to backpedal to face him.

The darkness pulls in again and I can't tell if it's just his magic or the norrow coming to slam me on the floor again.

I need to figure out how to get these cuffs off my wrists so I at least have a fighting chance of defending myself.

"Nothing has changed," he says. "I still need you to bind yourself to me so that I have the *animus* within my possession. Since you are the *animus*, that means you."

I knew that ultimately it would come to this.

I've had a lot of time to think it over while stuck in that dank hole.

I don't know enough about magic or power or gods or Alius to know what I might be losing by binding myself to the Demon King.

But I know that I can't outrun him and I can't outrun myself.

Sooner or later I'm going to have to face the fact that I'm not who I thought I was, that everything about my life has changed, and that if I want to move forward, I have to start accepting those things.

"Maybe we can come to an agreement," I say as my heart drums in my chest. My head says this is the right move, but the rest of me wants to vomit.

"I'm listening."

"I have contingencies and questions."

He goes stoic on me again. "Go on."

"In Alius, do women frequent your bed?"

A sliver of surprise comes to his eyes, softening the bite of his scowl. "That's one of your questions?"

"Yes."

"Why does it matter?"

"If I'm to spend the rest of my life bound to you, I want to know the lay of the land."

"By understanding the number of women I invite into my bed?"

"By the number of women you fuck, yes." I want to be real clear on what we're talking about here.

He leans against the stone wall behind him, looking as casual as can be, like we're just two people having a flirty conversation somewhere and not discussing something as profound as a magical marriage.

"Before my betrothal," he says, "the number was many. Afterward, fewer."

"And lately?"

"Lately," he says, "just one."

I scream at every muscle and fiber in my body not to react to the triumph of that statement. Like what I want to be doing is running down the hallway hooting at the ceiling.

But I'm a mature, respectable woman.

But also FUCK YES. The Demon King is mine. Even if he does irritate the hell out of me.

There is no sense fighting it anymore. I've been tethered to him not by choice, but by circumstance, so I might as well make the most of it. And if I'm to make the most of it, I'll stake my claim, goddammit.

"And what about after?" I keep my voice level. "After all of this?"

"I haven't thought that far in advance."

I cross my arms. "Then think about it now."

"Are you asking me to stay faithful to you and only you?"

"Well...would you be okay with other men in my bed?"

Nostrils flaring, he lurches upright, shoulders rocking back. "There will be no other men in your bed."

Don't react. Don't react.

Now I'm parkouring off the walls in my mind palace.

Stay cool.

"Why not?" I ask.

"Because you are mine."

"I'm not your possession."

"I've called *dieva*," he says, a little smug. "In Alius, if anyone dared to touch you, it would be within my right to cut off their hands and shove them down their throat."

"Is that the only reason? Because of some barbaric claiming practice?"

He glances away. His black t-shirt sinks on his shoulders, exposing a whirl of his black demon mark as it winds over his collarbone.

I tighten my arms over my chest trying to keep myself from running my fingers over it just to watch him shiver beneath my touch.

"No man will come to your bed," he says when he turns back. "That answer is final."

"So what, you can sleep with whoever you want, but I can't?"

"Is this one of your contingencies?" he asks.

"Yes," I answer because why the hell not.

"Is there more?"

"I want to stay here, in my world."

"No."

While this answer is not really surprising, I'd hoped otherwise.

I don't know the first thing about living in another world.

It feels too much like starting at a new high school where you don't understand the cliques or the rules and you just have to figure it out as you go.

But after living half my life with my mom, bouncing all over the world, that's a situation I know how to navigate extremely well. Maybe I can manage a new world without too much trouble.

"Can I go back and forth?" I ask.

He considers this for a second and then, "That would require permanently opening the gateway. Is that what you want?"

Fuck. If we were playing chess, he's just cornered me.

"No, I suppose not. But can you at least figure out a way for me to visit from time to time?"

"I can."

"But will you?"

He narrows his eyes again. "For you, *dieva*, yes, I will. Are we finished?"

"The people I love and care about."

"What about them?"

"You will not lay a finger on them. In no way will they be harmed. Ever."

He doesn't need time to consider this contingency, but his words are cold, nonetheless. "Your precious mortals will remain unscathed."

"And the women in your bed?"

As if I'd forget.

He pushes away from the wall and stalks toward me. I take a step back.

"I want an heir someday," he says. "Are you willing to bear my child?"

"Umm..."

Even though he insinuated that he'd pump someone full of his demon seed someday—that impregnating a woman with demon royalty was brutal fucking—it never once crossed my mind that he'd want that woman to be me.

Sure, I'd like to test the brutal fucking part, because I'm always up for a wild ride, but...children? I never gave them much thought. And after doing family photography for so long, I started to think I didn't want them.

But with the Demon King?

The thought makes me glow a little inside.

Before he showed up, I'd been empty. Looking back, I see it for what it was: I thought I just needed to find a path, do some internal growing, but being with Wrath...I've never felt so *awake*.

"All right, yes," I answer. "I'll bear you an heir." My voice catches on 'heir' and he hears it.

"Are you sure that's what you want?"

Now he's giving me an out?

And if I said no?

But I won't. I don't want to.

"Yes. I'm sure."

"Then my answer is this—if you bind yourself to me, bear my heir, then I will only bury my cock in your tight little pussy. Does that suffice?"

Heat flares in my face and then travels down my belly and to my clit. I get a flash of what we did last night, the feel of his hands on my hips and his cock shoved inside of me.

I know he can smell me now and can probably sense where my lusty thoughts have gone.

"Okay," I breathe out.

"Okay?" He lifts a brow.

"I'll bind myself to you."

My heart drums hard in my chest as the panic sets in. Have I made the right decision? Will I regret this for the rest of my life? Do I even understand what I'm doing?

Am I seriously considering going to another world with the Demon King?

I'm tired of running and I'm tired of fighting him and if I'm totally honest, I'm tired of pretending that I hate the thought of being only his.

"No more games, *dieva*," he warns.

"No more games."

He licks his bottom lip, then drags it in with a rake of his teeth as he considers me. I get the distinct impression he's waiting for another shoe to drop.

I hold out my hand. "Let's shake on it."

He regards me with the hint of an amused smile on his ravaging mouth, then slips his hand into mine and shakes.

It's done.

I've agreed to marry the Demon King.

"So how do we do this?"

"We need a witch," he tells me as he backtracks to the Bourbon Room.

"Kat?" I ask, chasing after him.

"Arthur," he calls as he reenters the room. "Rain and I are going to House Roman. You make sure things are in order. Lauren."

She launches herself from the couch. I wouldn't be surprised if she saluted him. "Yes?"

"Take off your shirt."

Lauren regards him with a warring look on her face. She wants to obey, but she clearly knows where this is going.

"Lauren." His voice rumbles and the darkness kicks up, tendrils undulating in the air.

She yanks the plain black tee over her head and tosses it to me. I catch it in a ball.

Wrath turns to me, grabs the hem of my Demon Slut shirt, and unceremoniously relieves me of it. He stalks over to Lauren and hands it to her. "Put it on."

She glowers at him but slips it on anyway.

"When we return," he tells her, "she will be a queen and you will treat her like one." She takes a step back and Wrath follows, running her into the wall. A yelp escapes her throat. "No more games, Lauren."

"Yes, my king."

"Louder."

"Yes, my king!"

He swivels around, satisfied, and comes for me next.

I think he's tripled in size because I swear to god we all shrink around him when he demands we fall in line. "And you," he says to me, "you will act like a queen."

"Okay."

He stops a few inches from me and regards me with cool expectation.

I huff out a breath. "Yes, my king."

"Good girl," he says and for some reason, the praise hits me square in the chest.

Lauren didn't get a good girl. Ha.

He slips his arm around my waist and pulls me into him as his dark magic kicks up in a writhing mist.

"Ready, *dieva*?"

"Yes," I say with as much confidence as I can muster.

5

Wrath deposits us in a garden with a massive estate house in front of us and a harbor behind us. I immediately recognize the harbor as Chantilly Harbor in Saint Sabine.

Gus and I come to the city often and I love Second Quarter the most. It reminds me of a quainter New Orleans.

Somewhere beyond the house, jazz music plays from a street corner and laughter and revelry rises above it, despite the early hour of the day.

Much like in Norton Harbor, there's a paved boardwalk that runs along Chantilly, but there's far more greenery here shielding the garden from the prying eyes of pedestrians and tourists.

I gaze up at the estate house.

Gus and I have gone on the boardwalk many times before and I've always admired this house from afar having no idea it belonged to a vampire. Now that I know it, I can't unsee it. It *looks* like a vampire's house.

Wrath takes my hand and guides me through the garden over cobblestone paths mottled with moss. There are hundreds of flower varieties blooming in the garden in shades of pink and purple and orange and yellow. What a dream.

"This place is stunning," I say as Wrath takes us to French doors.

"If you think this is amazing, you should see the royal garden in Alius. It puts this one to shame."

Now he's piqued my interest. "You never talk about Alius."

"I just did."

"Before, I guess. To me."

He looks down at me. "I never saw a reason to...before."

Before I agreed to marry him.

I blink rapidly and break eye contact, suddenly flustered.

I don't know why. I don't know why him sharing details about his home is somehow more profound than him sticking his cock inside of me.

But it is.

And now I'm hungry for more.

Hand on the door handle, he turns it and pushes in, not waiting for an invitation.

We enter into a cool, hushed darkness.

It's eerily quiet.

"Where is everyone?"

"Vampires sleep during the day," Wrath reminds me.

"Right. Of course."

"Kat," Wrath yells.

"Shhhh! If they're all sleeping—"

"I'm here." Kat appears in an arched doorway, looking smashing as usual. She's wearing a pantsuit today in a deep shade of emerald. The shoulders are sculpted like thorns, the collar plunging, showing off her cleavage.

Her dark hair is done in soft waves, her long bangs framing her face.

As seems to be her signature, her plump lips are a bright shade of red.

"She's agreed," Wrath says and lets me go.

"Has she?" Kat arches a brow at me, regarding me from beneath the fan of her lashes.

"She has," I say.

"Mmmm." Kat curls her hands around her hips. "I will never understand you two. At each other's throats one minute, marrying each other the next."

"It's not marriage," Wrath argues. "It's a binding. Much different."

"Is it?" Kat turns that sharp brow his way.

"Yes," he says on a growl.

I don't see much of a difference. In some ways, this is bigger than a marriage because I can't divorce his ass if I grow tired of his nagging.

"So how do we bind ourselves?" I ask. "Is there a ceremony? Do we need witnesses? Should we wait for the others to wake? And most importantly, will there be cake?"

"It's not a spectacle," Wrath argues. "We do it now. The sooner the better. And no cake."

I pout at him. He scowls.

"Come this way." Kat swivels on her heels.

We follow her out into an arched hallway where soft inset lighting guides us through the shuttered house.

We pass several pieces of art in gilded frames. I know from growing up with an artist that several of these paintings are presumed missing and are worth millions.

I think I heard someone say Rhys Roman is a billionaire. And apparently a serious art collector.

Kat turns into another hall and a large-scale photograph of Háifoss waterfall catches my eye. The image is portrait format with the falls taking center stage surrounded by green moss and craggy outcroppings. Mist hangs heavy in the air, turning much of the photograph hazy, almost like a painting.

"That's one of my mother's photographs from Iceland."

Kat stops to glance at the image contained in an ornate black frame. "Is it? I didn't realize."

I get a little flare of pride seeing my mom's work in the hall of a billionaire's house. A vampire no less. Wait till I tell her. She's going to flip.

Kat keeps walking and Wrath sets his hand at the small of my back, spurring me on.

We finally turn into a smaller room, darkened with black shutters that are turned down so slatted rays of light pour in over the room.

It smells like Kat in here, like expensive perfume mixed with exotic herbs and a fair dash of earned pride. There's a long worktable across from the door and an entire wall of cabinets to the right with glass-fronted doors. The collection of jars inside stokes my curiosity and I immediately go to it, scanning the contents. Except, all of the labels are handwritten in a language I don't understand.

"Do witches really use herbs and toads and eyes of newt to do their magic?"

Wrath picks up a corked jar. He scrutinizes whatever is inside.

"I use magic without all the accoutrements," Kat answers, "but some things can help focus, bind, or amplify certain magics. Most witches don't need all of this, but we like it nonetheless."

"Do you need it for a binding?"

"We'll use it," she says as she comes up beside me. "Just to be sure. Are you sure?" She lifts a brow, scrutinizes my reaction.

"Yes. I don't entirely understand what it means to be the *animus*, and I don't know how to use it so it seems silly to keep it to myself while Chaos causes...well, chaos. And anyway, the *animus* doesn't belong to me. The power belongs to the Demon King."

Kat frowns. "So by that logic you belong to him?"

I sense him watching me.

"Are you trying to talk me out of it?"

"I'm trying to understand."

"You're bound to Rhys Roman, aren't you?"

She crosses her arms over her chest, sharp red fingernails curling around her biceps. "I am."

"Do you regret it?"

"Not a chance. He's my best friend, as much as he can be an asshole."

"I know that plight well."

I practically hear Wrath roll his eyes.

"Rhys and House Roman are my family. But"—she cants her head, waves of her hair cascading over her shoulders—"I'm bound to House Roman by oath and blood. This"—she points a sharp nail at Wrath—"this is different."

"How?"

"I could, theoretically, get myself out of my position. My oath is much like those cuffs on your wrists. They can break. What you're doing, binding yourself to the Demon King in this way? That's like putting an orange in a blender and pressing the button. That orange is not coming out the same way ever again."

Goosebumps lift on my arms.

I never would have thought an analogy about fruit could sound so profoundly eerie and sinister.

"What's different about your binding from mine?"

The look she gives me is almost sympathetic. "Everything."

First, Kat takes off the magical cuffs, then undoes the binding she put on me since the spell won't work with all of it still in place. Undoing the binding is nothing more than a few whispered words and the snap of her fingers and suddenly the power rushes back in like a dam that's been broken.

My eyes slip closed and I breathe out with a sigh.

It's like a hot shower after too many nights in the cold.

I'm no longer numb.

"Better?" she asks when I pry my eyes open again.

"Much."

I rub my sore wrists, the skin chafed and red. God, it feels good to have those things off.

I guess we've taken another step in the direction of holy matrimony, because Wrath trusts me enough not to have my magic bound.

I still plan to zap his ass someday soon. He fucking deserves it.

It takes Kat about fifteen minutes to prepare for the binding and my palms start sweating three minutes into her work.

I pace the room.

Wrath leans against the worktable watching me, completely unfazed.

I'm trying not to look at him, but it's impossible not to feel his presence when he's in a room.

He says nothing and lets me freak out.

What am I doing?

I like being an orange.

But orange juice is really great too.

Fuck, now I'm thinking in riddles.

"*Dieva*," he says.

I stop pacing to catch his gaze. He's unreadable, face blank. Does he feel it too? This trembling on the horizon?

"We can't go back to being oranges after this," I tell him.

"I know."

"Do you?" I swivel on my heel and start pacing again. "Maybe this entire time I've been freaking out about being bound to you and you haven't properly considered what it'll mean to be bound to me. I mean...will I age? You certainly don't. What if I become a saggy old bag someday and you're stuck with me, your rotten, sour orange juice?"

There's a snap of air, a kiss of a breeze on the back of my neck.

When I turn, he's there, just an inch from me, filling my space. "I'm not worried."

It's a simple statement, and ludicrous, if I'm honest—*he should be worried*—but it settles my nerves just the same.

"Just to clarify...which part are you not worried about? Being bound to me? Me turning into a saggy old bag?"

The corner of his mouth lifts. There is something profoundly enjoyable about getting the Demon King to laugh. "Both," he answers. "All of your worries. Set them aside. There is only one way for us to go and that's forward."

"That's deep. You should put that on Demon King merch."

He laughs again. I warm.

"I'm ready when you are," Kat says.

My heart drums in my chest. "All right. I guess I'm ready too."

Wrath nods, acknowledging me and my consent.

Kat takes two giant abalone shells over to the worktable. The inside of the shells shines pearlescent beneath a mixture of herbs. "I need a lock of hair from both of you."

"Here, let me," I say and reach over and pluck several jet-black hairs from Wrath's skull.

He curses, growls, then winds several strands of my hair around his index finger and yanks them out by the root.

"Ouch!" I rub at the sore spot. "I think you were rougher than I was."

"I will always be rougher, *dieva*."

Kat gives us an exasperated look and then takes the hair and sets it in the herbs in each shell. Next, she flattens her hands over them and whispers something foreign.

There's a soft WHUMP and green fire ignites beneath her hands, flames licking around her knuckles. She doesn't flinch and the only scent on the air is that of burning herbs.

When she pulls her hand away, there is a small stone in each shell. One is opaque white, the other shining black like obsidian.

"That's interesting," she says as she takes the stones into each hand.

"Which part?"

She brings the opaque stone into a stream of light. "They're different colors. It's just unexpected."

"Were they supposed to be the same?" Wrath asks.

"I would assume they would be. You and Rain, your power, it's all from the same current, you know? I would expect them to be the same."

I cross my arms over my chest. "Is it bad that they aren't?"

"You want the truth or a guess?"

"The truth," Wrath says.

"I don't know."

"And the guess?" I ask.

Kat looks at the stone again. "I don't know."

"Okay. Awesome."

"We'll move forward regardless," Wrath says.

"Of course." Kat clears a spot on the worktable and sets aside the shells. "This is one of those spells that requires us to be quick. Like cutting a baby from a womb. We need to move once the blood runs."

"Will there be blood?"

"Something of this magnitude? Yes. Absolutely." She grabs a length of black charcoal and starts scribbling fiercely on the worktop. When she's finished, there are two identical circles with rune symbols inside. "This is how this will work." She picks up my opaque stone. "We cut open both of your palms. Stone goes in one hand. The other hand will touch the grounding symbols here." She taps at the charcoal. "Once you've connected with the grounding symbols, you'll bring the stones to one another, right over your hearts. The spell will be kindled at that point. You'll feel the current open between you and you will be bound. Any questions?"

"Do I say anything? 'I do,' maybe?"

Kat laughs. "Nope. The power is in the blood. Not the words."

"Got it."

I never gave my wedding day much thought. I've always liked being alone and I've never been in a relationship that gave me marriage vibes.

But if I had been one of those girls that daydreamed about her special day, this wouldn't have been it. Not even close.

"Take your shirts off," Kat instructs.

I pull my t-shirt off and toss it aside.

Wrath grabs his at the back of the neck and slips it over his head in one swift motion, muscles flexing along his shoulders, abs contracting with the movements. He tosses the shirt and stands half naked in the slatted daylight.

I feel Kat appreciating the view beside me and without thinking, I scowl over at her, damn near bristling.

"Calm down," she says. "As if I would be brave enough to cross you."

That pulls me upright and the territorial bitch immediately relaxes.

Brave enough to cross me? Kat is a vicious, gorgeous, badass witch.

I'm just a photographer from a tourist town.

But I detect no bullshit on her face. She's fucking serious.

Grabbing a blade from inside an ornate box, Kate takes my hand in hers. "Both palms. Got it?"

"Yup."

She slices my first hand and I bite against a hiss. The pain is immediate and sharp but fades quickly as blood wells in the wound. She moves quickly to my other hand, cutting a near identical wound.

When she turns to Wrath, he's already got his hands up, blood dripping down his wrists.

"Right. Connected on a physical level. I forgot," Kat says. "Then let's finish the job and make it official on all levels. Ready?"

Wrath looks at me. There's no question on his face, but there's a flash of doubt in his eyes as if he's waiting for me to back out, run away.

I'm not running this time.

I've made my choice.

"All right," Kat says. "Then let's begin."

6

In unison, Wrath and I bring our bleeding hands to the grounding symbols Kat sketched on the worktable. Mine is my right hand and his is his left.

The second our blood hits the charcoal, the symbols burn bright green just like Kat's magic.

There's a heaviness that crawls up my arm and a tugging pressure beneath the palm of my hand that feels very much like an anchor.

My white stone is clutched in my left hand, now wet with my blood. Wrath has his captured between his thumb and forefinger as we wait.

Kat closes her eyes and whispers a string of words I can't comprehend. I smell the sweetness that I now attribute to her magic and it reminds me of an herb garden my mom had for a summer, like basil and bergamot.

"Now. Now!" Kat says, snapping her fingers at us.

Wrath and I reach across the short distance between us and press our stones to each other's heart.

I feel the coolness of the bloody stone first, then the heat of his touch.

And a second later, a gale force shoots across the room. Loose paper flutters in the wind and the slats of the shutters flap loudly as my hair is tossed in my face.

"Is this normal?" I shout.

"Don't let go!" Kat yells.

There's a liquid rushing down my arm as Wrath's stone burns at my chest, as heat and energy charge toward me. Wrath grits his teeth together as the monster comes to his face, sharp and sharper still. His fingers claw at my skin as if he's holding on to me for dear life.

I can't catch my breath. It's like I've turned my face into a tornado, all the oxygen sucked from my lungs.

The heat spreads through the rest of my body, nerves and muscle crackling. My skin grows taut like I've been out in the sun too long, like it could split open at the slightest touch.

Green light flares beneath my palm as the grounding symbol reenergizes, as if it can feel my grip on it slipping.

Wrath adjusts his stance, planting his boots to the floor and the wood beneath him buckles.

I flinch. The wind kicks up, knocking a stack of books off the table. They thud to the floor, pages flapping.

Kat hurries to the wall of cabinets and starts opening doors, rummaging inside.

"What's happening?" I yell.

"Don't let go," Wrath says.

"I won't."

The veins in Wrath's hand stand out, swelling beneath his skin as his knuckles turn white.

The connection between us vibrates and the air balloons around us with a milky green haze.

The door bangs open. Rhys Roman appears in the glow of light with Dane and Emery behind him.

"What the fuck is happening?" Rhys asks.

"Don't come into the room!" Kat yells.

"Should we be worried?" Dane shouts back.

Kat keeps rummaging.

"Wrath?"

His eyes are locked on me. "Don't let go, *dieva*," he says again, but his voice is missing its usual grit and it doesn't feel like a warning to me so much as a plea. As if I'm the only thing keeping him from being swept away.

"I won't," I tell him again. "I'm not leaving your side."

The wind picks up. Rhys puts his arm over his face, shielding his eyes as a bottle of herbs knocks over and smashes on the ground, sending dozens of dried sprigs flying through the air.

"Kat!" he yells again.

"I found it!" She hurries over to us, a metal rod in hand.

"What is that?" I ask just as she positions it over my forehead and everything goes black.

I wake with a start and it takes me a second to come back to awareness, to feel Wrath's body beneath mine, his arms wrapped around me.

There's a pulsing energy running between us like a heat wave over hot asphalt.

That's different.

I look around and realize we're back in the main room in House Roman. Kate, Rhys, Dane, and Emery are in front of me, watching me.

Wrath is sitting in an overstuffed chair, me nestled in his lap and the feel of him this close, his touch gentle, is enough to send butterflies migrating through my stomach.

"What happened?" I sit forward and Wrath spreads his legs,

letting me sit between his thighs. His hands are still on me almost like he's afraid to let me go.

Kat comes forward. "Do you feel all right?" She bows at the waist to scrutinize my face while her hands hover in the air around me.

"Headachy," I admit. "What happened?" I ask again.

"Well..." She frowns at me, then straightens, hands curling around the hourglass shape of her hips. "You were more powerful than I anticipated."

I press at the spot between my brows. "Huh?"

"When I drew the grounding symbols, I put more weight on Wrath's side. He's more powerful than you. Or he should be. But apparently he isn't."

I'm immediately reminded of Ciri's last words right before Wrath killed her.

You're no longer the most powerful person in the room, she said to him.

Meaning me. Meaning *I* was the most powerful one.

I thought it was just bullshit. One last dig before she lost her life.

But now, with this...was she serious?

"I had the balance wrong," Kat admits. "I apologize for that."

I glance at him over my shoulder. His eyes are narrowed as he meets my gaze. There is nothing overtly menacing about him but I can feel something foreign thrumming around me.

It takes me a second to realize it's Wrath's unease.

It's almost a living, breathing thing. Like I could reach out and run my fingers through it, watch the air bristle and part.

I'm more powerful than he is and he's uneasy about it.

The sands are shifting beneath us.

Suddenly, I don't feel so steady.

This was supposed to be a good thing. It wasn't supposed to reveal more weak spots in our relationship.

"So did it work? The binding?" I ask.

"You tell me." He tips his chin at me. "What do you feel?"

"I do feel different," I admit. "Beyond the headache, that is. Almost like—"

Anticipation.

Eagerness.

I can feel him so acutely it's like he's living in my heart and in my head.

I lurch off the chair, goosebumps rising along my skin.

He stands beside me, clearly on edge.

"Do you feel it?" I ask him quietly.

He grits his teeth, sucks in a breath, then, "Yes."

"What do you feel from me?"

"Fear. Worry."

"Fuck," I say beneath my breath. "You didn't tell me we'd have no secrets."

"I didn't know. I've never done this before, *dieva*."

I pace away from him and he comes after me, aching with the need to be near me and then there's a quick flash of—

I whirl around to face him. He reels back like I smacked him.

Was that...

No. *No*.

It wasn't love. The Demon King has no heart.

But there is an ache in my chest right now that feels like it, but I don't know if it's him or me or maybe both.

Fuck. Binding ourselves together was just supposed to be a minor detail, a slip of paper and nothing more.

We're not supposed to actually care for each other. Right?

Tears burn in my eyes and I rub my hands up and down my arms.

This is too much too fast.

Shit. I'm freaking out.

"Rhys," Wrath says with a clipped tone of voice.

"Yes?" Rhys comes forward.

"Will Rain be safe in your house if I was to leave?"

"Of course. The house is deeded to a human and Kat has the perimeter spelled."

"Good. Keep her here."

"Wait." I hurry forward but before I can reach him, he's gone.

7

I start for the door, the one that opens on the back garden where Wrath and I first came in to House Roman.

But before I can turn the handle, Rhys is in front of me.

I'm used to Wrath popping in and out on a whim, but vampire speed is something that still takes me by surprise.

A little yelp bursts from my throat and I stumble back.

"Apologies, Ms. Low, but I can't let you leave." Rhys Roman is no Wrath, but he's still really fucking scary. There's something in the way he moves—not quite ghost-like, but close. Like he moves so fast my eyesight can't keep up, and so his movements are nothing but a blur of color.

"I'm not going to be a prisoner in your house," I say. "I'm done being held captive."

"Not captive," Rhys says and tilts his chiseled jaw at me, a lock of his blond hair falling forward. "Protected. There is a difference."

When he speaks to me, low and evenly with that perfect British accent, I almost want to give in. Almost.

I cross my arms over my chest as the *animus* flares to life. God, does it feel good to have her back.

It's like I can stretch my legs again after being crammed into a closet.

Rhys grits his teeth and throws back his shoulders.

I catch my reflection in the glass in the door—my eyes are glowing embers.

Could a vampire stop me from leaving?

"Rain." Emery comes up beside Rhys and puts her much smaller body in front of the massive vampire. "Why don't you take a walk with me?"

The *animus* immediately retreats and Rhys eases the tension from his shoulders.

"Where?" I ask Emery.

"There's something you might find interesting that Kat and I have been dying to show you."

"What is it?"

"You're overselling it," Kat tells Emery. "It's just books," she says to me.

"Yes, but books are the gateway to knowledge. And you know what Horace Mann said about knowledge? 'Every addition to true knowledge is an addition to human power.'"

Kat screws up her red lips. "Horace Mann was a goddamn prude."

"Wait." Emery blinks. "You knew Horace Mann?"

"Who is Horace Mann?" I ask.

"Can we please stop talking about Horace Mann?" Dane pipes in. "I much prefer we talk about me instead. Do you know what *I* said about knowledge?"

"Oh god." Kat rolls her eyes.

"Nothing. I said nothing about knowledge because I'm not a fucking pretentious twat."

Emery smiles at me and hooks her arm through mine. "Ignore him. He's obnoxious."

"I think what you meant to say, poppet, is, 'He's devastatingly handsome and charming.'"

I snort as Emery drags me away. "How has he not been staked before?"

"Oh, he has. Many times. He's just really good at hiding his heart."

"It's because he doesn't have one." Kat falls into step beside us. "If you tore open his rib cage, you'd find just a stone of hubris."

"Do not leave the house," Rhys calls after us.

"Yes, dear," Emery says over her shoulder.

"I mean it." His voice rumbles behind us.

"Just to be clear—" I start.

"He really does mean it," Emery finishes. "I love the man, but you do not want to cross him. Come. I have a feeling you're going to love the library."

Emery is right.

"Holy shit," I say as I step inside after Emery and Kat push open the thick double doors.

"I feel like Belle in the Beast's library." I gaze around in wonder, craning my neck as I take it all in.

There are two stories with the second floor open to the main floor by a wrought iron railing. A wide set of stairs directly across from the entrance takes you up to a landing where a giant circular window dominates the wall. From there, the stairs branch off left and right to the second story.

On the main floor, several tables fill the space, each with a matching library lamp on top. Vintage sconces cast a soft golden glow around the room, with three massive iron chandeliers above doing the rest of the work to light the space now that the sun has set.

"Kat," Emery says, "will you grab that book on the gods? And I'll go find the one with the—"

"Already on it." Kat starts across the room, her hips swaying, her stilettos silent on the plush Persian rugs.

"Make yourself comfortable," Emery says as she leaves me for the second floor.

I go to the nearest bookcase and run my fingers over the spines. Most of the books seem ancient, bound in leather, the titles stamped in gold and silver. Each shelf has a bronze placard tacked into the wood with a slip of cardstock inside with a printed label. There's 18th century romance and 19th century horror. And then I spot a copy of *Frankenstein* and pull it out, flipping to the front pages.

There's an inscription inside.

Dearest Rhys,

Meeting you was a pleasure. A bloody pleasure, indeed.

Mary Shelley

"This is signed by Mary Shelley!" I yell and the girls laugh.

"If you like that sort of thing," Kat says over her shoulder, "there are signed copies of *Pride & Prejudice, Dracula, Jane Eyre, The Great Gatsby, Wuthering Heights—*"

"And Shakespeare, if you can believe it," Emery adds from the second floor.

"They're just sitting here on the shelves? Like...just shoved in with the rest of the normal books?"

"When you're a vampire," Emery says, "they're all normal books."

I return Frankenstein to the shelf, but before I can locate the other signed editions, Kat and Emery return with the books they were searching for.

Kat's book is thin and near pocket-sized. Emery's book is much bigger by comparison. She needs both hands to carry it and when she sets it on the table, it thuds loudly. The title has no inlaid coloring. I run my fingers over it, feeling the hard edges of the stamped letters.

Mythology of Alius.

"What's yours called?" I ask Kat.

She slides hers across the table to me.

The Tale of the Original Gods.

"They're both from Alius," Emery says.

"We think," Kat adds.

Emery opens the cover of her book and the spine creaks. "After the Demon King arrived, we all got curious about his origins."

"Mostly it was Emery who got curious."

"I like my history." She flips through the pages, careful with the thin paper. "They've always known about Alius." She tips her head at Kat.

"You did?"

Kat shrugs and pulls out one of the chairs. "We thought it was an urban legend. A fairytale."

"So I knew there had to be something about it in the library," Emery goes on. She turns several more pages and I catch sight of black and white illustrations, some depicting battles, others of gorgeous creatures surrounded by more beauty. "I started doing research, trying to see what I could learn about Alius and the Demon King should we need to—"

"Murder him," Kat cuts in.

Emery sends her a sharp look. "No. Defend ourselves against him."

"AKA murder him."

"But you're allied with him," I point out. "You literally did his bidding and bound me."

Kat lifts another shoulder in this casual, flippant way she has that should be irritating but isn't. "I do as Rhys wishes and Rhys wishes to cooperate with Wrath. I clearly had my own opinions about it. If it was up to me, I would not have bound you. I like you. I like you more than I like Wrath. But the truth of the matter is, I hold no loyalty to you. I don't really know you. I've known Rhys for centuries."

"Wait...you're immortal too?"

She smiles at me with a cheeky flare of pride in her eyes. "Comes with being a Redheart witch. We have dominion over magic of the flesh. Means I get to keep this gorgeous body forever so long as I don't lose my head."

"Is that what kind of witch Sirene is?"

"I couldn't tell you," Kat admits. "But the scars on her face make me doubt she's a Redheart. If she was, she would have healed herself."

"She told me she got those scars from Wrath."

"Oh?" Kat lifts her brows in surprise as she thinks that over. "Actually...that makes sense." She picks up her book and flips through several pages, then taps her finger on the printed text. "'... no man, woman, child, or animal is invincible against the power of the original gods. He who angers the gods will forever bear the mark of their insolence.'"

I frown. "The original gods...so, the triad?"

"That's just scratching the surface." Emery spins her book around to face me. "Read this."

"'In the beginning, there was only Night and Day—the Dark God and the Bright Goddess. One did not exist without the other, and yet they did not exist together, passing each other only briefly at the horizon.'

"'It was at that passing that the Dark God learned of the Goddess's warmth and light and he hungered for it more and more every day until finally the God created the Moon.'

"'The Goddess filled his night with light, but she would fade from him, and worse, she was *cold*.'

"'The God's hunger persisted. His desire for Day consumed him until he was so ravenous for her, he devoured her in the sky, stealing all of her light.'

"'It was through their consummation that the world was

born.'"

I look up. Emery and Kat are staring at me. "That's some heavy mythology."

Emery reaches over and flips a few more pages. "Read this."

There's a symbol at the top of the page that looks like an eclipse, which makes sense with the story. Night consumed Day.

I keep reading. "'As the world grew, Night watched Day give birth to more and more. To the grass in the fields and the flowers in the meadows, the birds in the sky, the trees in the forests. At night, her moon controlled the ocean, swayed the seas. The Dark God grew jealous of her power and her dominion over all that lived and breathed. He wanted that power for himself. He was the King and he would be the only ruler of the world.'"

Dread runs along my spine, raising the hair at the back of my neck.

"'Night tricked Day. He lured her from the sky and trapped her beneath the earth. She raged and raged until she bore a mountain and her rage spewed into the sky, shrouding the world in darkness.'"

I push the book away. "I can admire the symbolism," I say. "The sun and the moon, the eclipses, the volcano. But how does this relate to Wrath?"

"The stones," Kat says. "The stones that contain the Demon King's power, right? The triad? They're said to be from the Dark Father God, but I think the story is wrong. They belong to the Goddess. It was the God who stole them."

I frown at her, trying to digest what she's saying. "It's still only a story."

"But is it?" Emery sits in the chair beside me, but she's sideways so she faces me. "Think about it. The stones are black, like volcanic rock."

I only saw one briefly when Chaos stole the *oculus* from Wrath, but even before then, Wrath described them to me as being black, carved with the old language.

My chest tightens as this weird feeling invades my body, a feeling like there might be weight to what they're saying.

"The Demon King rules with borrowed power," Kat says.

I snort. "That's not true."

Emery and Kat share a look.

"What? What is it?"

Emery rakes her teeth over her bottom lip.

Kat says, "Night and Day have many names in the mythology just like the gods and goddesses that belong to your Greek and Roman mythology."

"Okay?"

Emery grabs Kat's tiny book and flips to the back to a glossary, then hands it to me.

I skim the section.

Day | Bright Goddess

Known also as Sun, Sun Goddess, Divine Mother, Giver of Life, Sola, Borna, Mater Dea, Reginae, Reignyabit, Reign

My heart stops. A cold sweat breaks out along my hairline.

I immediately jump to the memory of Wrath at my mom's cottage, the way he reacted to my name, how he insinuated it was supposed to be Reign and not Rain.

I just thought he was pissed about Sirene helping to name me something that literally meant stealing his throne from him.

But now—

I look up. "This doesn't mean anything. I don't...I *mean*...I'm just some rando girl."

They're both staring at me with pinched eyes, furrowed brows.

"Right?"

When they don't answer, I slam the book shut. "I'm not some reincarnated goddess or whatever. Is that what you're saying? I'm just a photographer from a tourist town with a new age mother who likes tea and patchouli and...and I drink too much. I mean, does a goddess really drink too much wine and fall asleep on her balcony so she burns in the sun? No." I lurch away from the table. "This is just a story."

Kat stands up. She doesn't approach me. I think she knows I'm on the verge of running. "If it was just a story," she says, "then why are you more powerful than the Demon King?"

"You messed up the spell."

She snorts. "I take offense to that. I don't mess up."

"Then it was because he lost the *oculus*."

"You have one stone. He has one stone. It should be equal at the very least."

"It's because I weakened him."

Emery finally cuts in. "Listen, we're not going to jump to any conclusions, okay?"

"Okay." Tears are suddenly burning in my eyes. "Have you told Wrath any of this?"

"No," Emery answers.

"Please don't."

"He must know that—" Kat starts, and Emery cuts her off with a sharp look.

"We're not going to mention it to Wrath," Emery says. "We just thought it might be fun to know more about the legends and Alius."

Distantly, I'm aware that Emery is just telling me what I want to hear, but I can't handle this. Not right now. Now when I just bound myself to the Demon King and I felt the connection between us thrum with...

And then he abandoned me here.

That's because he knows, the voice in the back of my head says. *He has to know the mythology behind his power.*

And now Kat's spell proves it.

Fuck me.

8

We're eventually pulled away from the books by the sound of a child yelling.

"That sounds like Gabe," Emery says.

"Who's Gabe?" I follow the women from the library and back to the main living space. There's a little boy spinning round and round on one of the barstools while a woman behind the bar empties the trash.

"Gabriel Luis Visser," the woman says. "Get off that stool this instant."

"I'm breaking a record, Ma!" he yells.

"Gabe." Kat comes up beside him and flicks her wrist and the stool lurches to a stop. Gabe sways as if he's still spinning and has lost his equilibrium.

"Ahhh come on, witchy woman!"

"Gabriel!" the woman says again.

"It's all right, Lisa," Kat says. "You know we tolerate this little demon because we love you the most."

Gabe snorts and hops down. "Ma ain't your favorite. I am. You tolerate Ma because you love me."

Lisa comes around the bar with a bag of trash clutched in her hand. "I swear to god, young man, you will be the death of me."

Gabe laughs and darts away as his mom reaches out for him.

Except he slams right into Wrath.

Gabe bounces back and Wrath's hand snaps out, taking a fistful of Gabe's shirt, catching him before he falls. It doesn't take the Demon King any effort at all. He barely moves a muscle.

Eyes wide, Gabe looks up. "Holy shit," he says. "The Demon King."

Lisa makes the sign of the cross over her body.

No one moves.

Gabe just hangs there, dangling by his shirt.

Do I step in? Do I try to get the Demon King away from the poor innocent little boy?

Wrath said he wanted his own children, but that tells me little about how he actually is around them.

Using Gabe's shirt, Wrath pulls the boy closer so they're face to face. Gabe holds his breath.

"Respect your mother," Wrath says in his deep, menacing voice.

Gabe exhales in a rush. "Okay. Sure. Whatever you say Mr. King. I mean, sir."

"He's really harmless," Kat says. "Just a bit of a pain in the ass from time to time."

Wrath lets Gabe go and the kid stumbles back before finding his footing and straightening his shirt. "I'm not a pain in the ass."

"Yes, you are." We all turn to Rhys at the sound of his voice as he comes into the room and goes behind the bar. He grabs something from beneath the counter. It isn't until he's drinking it back, lips stained red, that I realize it's a bottle of blood.

Ugh.

I'm glad Wrath doesn't have to do that.

No, he just bathes in the blood of his enemies.

"Hey Mr. Demon King," Gabe says, his bravado back. "You

think I can see those shadow soldiers? They're so cool, man. I wish I had those guys around. I'd be kicking asses left and right." He curls his hands into fists and punches at imagined enemies.

"Gabriel!" Lisa shrieks.

"Sorry, Ma," he says looking sheepish this time. But even that isn't enough to deter him. "You think I can see them?"

Wrath peers down at the kid. I literally have no idea which direction this will go. For all I know, he could turn into the monster and scare the crap out of Gabe.

But then the shadows pull in closer and take shape.

Gabe's mouth drops open, his eyes glinting with excitement.

My belly warms with a feeling I can't name.

"Tell me, Gabriel," Wrath says, "do you like roller coasters?"

"Oh sure. Me and my friends go to the boardwalk all the time to ride the coaster there. I like to fly, man."

Lisa clears her throat loudly.

"I mean, sir. Mr. Demon King."

The norrow bleed together, then flow around Wrath like a wave. They perfume the air with that primordial scent, like chilly air and rich spices.

Then they dart forward, taking hold of Gabe and lifting him off his feet.

"Whoa!" Gabe yells.

The darkness tosses him in the air and he bellows with laughter as he comes back down only for the darkness to catch him again.

Lisa clutches at her chest, muttering what sounds like a prayer beneath her breath.

Wrath's darkness tosses Gabe again, then spins him around, then dangles him by his ankle.

Gabe roars with laughter the entire time.

I steal a glance at Wrath and find him fighting a smile. The connection between us warms and the warmth flows to me, catching me off guard.

Wrath's eyes dart to me.

Gabe falls through the air, screeching. Rhys hurries beneath him, arms spread out to catch Gabe, but the darkness swoops in at the last second, gently setting him to his feet.

"Holy shit," Gabe says again.

"Gabriel Luis!" Lisa scolds.

"Can you do that again? Please? That was awesome!"

"That's enough for tonight." Rhys ferries the kid toward the door. "Before you give your mother a heart attack."

"Awww, come on, old man."

Emery laughs at the perceived insult, even though technically Rhys *is* an old man. I'm in a room surrounded by old people.

"Thank you, Lisa." Rhys gives the woman a squeeze on the shoulder. "That'll be all for tonight."

As they leave, I hear Lisa castigating the kid, but he's not having any of it. "But Ma! Didn't you see that? It was awesome! Wait till I tell the boys the Demon King threw me around the room with his dark magic!"

Their voices fade away.

I look back to Wrath and find his eyes squarely on me.

The connection thrums again. Something is bothering him. Some emotion that he's trying really hard to bury.

I want to go to him, desperate to reassure him, even though I don't know what he needs reassurance from. But before I can, a guy comes hustling into the room, a backwards baseball cap taming dirty blond hair.

"What is it, Cole?" Rhys asks.

"There's been another attack." Cole's eyes land on Wrath. "And they're blaming him for it."

Wrath bristles but says nothing.

Dane comes in around Cole and grabs a remote. Pressing a button, two panels retract in front of us revealing a giant flat screen TV hidden in the wall. When the screen brightens, Dane flicks to the channel and Grand Central Station comes into view.

People are screaming and flooding from the main doors as darkness ribbons around them.

My stomach drops.

A news anchor ducks and then the camera jostles, the image bouncing.

"Go. Go!" the newsman says.

Darkness shoots behind him.

"It's the Demon King!" someone yells.

The giant arched window that stands over the entrance shatters and glass explodes outward. More screams fill the air.

"Is this live?" I ask and look over at Wrath, suspicious of what he was doing while he was gone.

"Yeah, it's live," Dane answers and I expel a breath of relief.

Wrath frowns at me and I can feel his annoyance echo back to me. "You think I'd do something like this?"

"I don't know," I admit. "You are a villain after all."

"Attacking people in a train station is not only callow at best, but it's also beneath me."

"Damn," Dane says. "The Demon King has standards when it comes to his villainy."

Wrath scowls at the vampire but lets it rest.

Rhys snaps his fingers at Cole and says, "Check on Last Vale. Take a few of the sentinels with you."

Before I can ask what any of that means, Wrath says, "This reeks of Chaos. He's baiting me."

"Then we should do something about it," I say.

There's pandemonium on the screen as the ground rocks and the cameraman loses his footing.

"They think it's you. If you show up to stop him, they'll know you're not the bad guy."

"But I am, *dieva*. I am the villain, as you keep reminding me."

"This isn't a time to be petty."

"Wrath," Rhys says. "If you have the power to stop this, I'll ask you kindly to do so."

Fear flashes through our connection, burning and bright. I inhale sharply and Wrath's attention shifts back to me, his brow furrowing.

He's afraid of facing his brother.

He has so little power left to lose.

"I'll go," I say, taking myself by surprise.

The truth is, I'm a little worried about him too. This is my fault. I'm the reason Chaos is here causing all of this. I'm the reason why Wrath lost part of the triad.

I can fix this. Somehow. I have to do something.

"You will not leave this house," Wrath says, squaring against me. "If you faced my brother, you would lose."

"Why?" I wave my hand in his general direction. "Because I'm not seven feet tall and all bristling muscle?"

"Bristling muscle?" Dane says behind me. "And I doubt he's over six-five."

"I have power, you know." The *animus* comes to me easily, answering my call.

Emery sucks in a breath and Rhys shifts in front of her, shielding her with his body.

Bright, fiery light shines around the room.

I'm suddenly flush with warmth.

I am the *animus*. The power is mine. I can do with it as I please and—

Wrath disappears with a snap of air. I sense him behind me before I can turn to meet him, and that fraction of a second costs me.

He grabs me by the neck and kicks my feet out from beneath me. I'm suddenly blinking at the ceiling and falling fast for the floor.

He catches me before I hit.

Just like Gabe.

I'm a defenseless child next to him.

The power flickers out of me like a spent filament and I'm left with nothing to fight with.

"You won't go up against my brother," he says above me, his face all hard lines and fury. "You don't know the first thing about fighting, let alone controlling your power. You would lose and if he hurt you—" He grits his teeth, cutting himself off.

Pain shoots through the connection. Real and visceral and he tries to tamp it down, but he's not quick enough.

There is nothing we can hide from one another now.

Did he know this would happen when he decided to bind me to him?

I don't think he did. This will be a weakness in his eyes and the Demon King would never choose vulnerability.

"You will not engage with him," he says and winds his arm around my waist, pulling me to my feet.

"So teach me."

"Teach you?"

"Yes. How to use this power. You had it for several hundred years. If anyone knows how to use it, it's you."

He regards me with narrowed eyes. I suppose the old him is thinking anyone having control of the *animus* other than him is a very bad idea. But he'll never have it back. It will always be mine.

Be me.

"I should know how to use it," I try again. "I'm bound to you. I'll always be a target. Not teaching me is a liability at this point."

"She has an excellent point," Rhys says.

A growl rumbles in Wrath's chest as he sends a scathing look at the vampire, but Rhys holds his ground.

I cross my arms over my chest. "Say yes."

He mulls it over, then, "Fine."

"Yes!"

He growls at me. "This is no victory, *dieva*."

"Oh, I beg to differ."

"You'll change your mind soon enough." He tightens his hold on me, draws me into him and then says to Rhys over top of my head, “My brother has one weakness: fire. That information is yours to do with as you please, but I’ll not be getting in the middle of it. Not yet anyway.”

The air crackles. I know by now what that means.

“Where are we going?”

Wrath peers down at me. “You’ve requested that I teach you how to fight. Who am I to pass up an opportunity to put you in your place?”

9

WRATH'S DARKNESS RIPS US FROM RHYS'S HOUSE. I FEEL THAT FAMILIAR sensation of being pulled and twisted and popped from one dimension to another and when we reappear, I find us in a training room in what appears to be the castle. There is an entire wall of weapons displayed on a peg rack. Swords and axes, scythes and spears.

My stomach sinks.

What the hell have I gotten myself into?

"Lauren," he yells as he walks over to the weapons.

Since Lauren doesn't have the ability to travel through the sub-dimension, we have to wait for her to make her way to us.

I think it takes her five minutes at least. She looks from Wrath to me and then to the sword in his hand. "Our little *animus* wants to learn how to fight and you're going to fight her."

Lauren's mouth curves into a sinister smile. "About fucking time I get to slit your throat."

Wrath tosses her the sword and she catches it by the hilt easily.

"Where's my weapon?" I ask.

"You don't get one," Wrath says.

"You must be joking."

"Do I joke, *dieva*?"

No. No he doesn't.

"If she cuts me, she cuts you," I point out. "Is that really what you want?"

"No. It is the opposite of what I want." He circles us. "You should do everything in your power to keep your skin intact. Do you understand me?"

I huff out a breath. "I wanted to be taught. Not thrown into hand-to-hand combat with a demon."

Lauren pulls off her t-shirt. She's wearing a black sports bra and black Lululemon pants. Almost like she's been ready for this moment the entire time.

Her demon mark cuts across her chest and arches over her shoulders. Hers isn't as complex as Wrath's is, but it's still impressive.

Can a person vomit from dread? Because I feel like I want to start hurling. Lauren isn't going to go easy on me. Maybe that's why Wrath is pitting me against her.

"Begin," he says.

Lauren gets into a fighting stance.

Fuck.

She circles me for several seconds, sizing me up. I mirror her movements, trying to keep as much distance between us as I can.

I don't know how to approach a fight. What little I learned in self-defense was, well, self-defense. I know nothing about offense.

So I guess the best thing to do is wait for her to—

Lauren charges at me. I yelp and dart away.

"*Dieva*," Wrath warns.

Lauren slices with the blade. I barely get out of the way before losing a chunk of hair from my head.

I dance back and Lauren advances, the blade cocked back. She swings. I duck. But the move costs me precious concentration and

Lauren closes the distance between us, slamming the hilt of the sword up into my jaw.

My teeth crack together and a sharp ache zings through my face, throbbing in my eye sockets. Blood wells in my mouth. Wrath stalks around us and spits blood on the floor.

At least he's suffering with me.

But then his gaze darkens, a warning scowl. The more he suffers, the more I suspect I'll suffer the consequences later.

Lauren steps into me again, swings, the blade catching me across the arm. Searing pain shoots down my body as blood immediately fills the cut, several beads sliding down my bicep.

I have no time to assess how deep it is before Lauren is after me again.

She stabs for my gut. I bow my body, just dodging the hit.

The first flare of anger wakes the *animus* and heat races down my arms.

A flicker of flame burns in my hands, except I don't know what to do with it. Can I shoot fire from my fingers? Send magic arcing through the air?

When I faced off with the soldiers in Riverside Park, I conjured flames from nothing. And with Chaos, the *animus* burned away the norrow like they were nothing more than kindling.

But all of that happened in the heat of the moment. I can't remember the actual mechanism to make it work again.

The only thing I really know how to do is call it.

But once I have it, I don't know what to do with it.

Lauren yells a war cry and comes running at me, the blade poised to impale me.

Come on, *animus*!

Flames roll down my arms and when Lauren gets within a few feet of me, the acrid stench of burning flesh fills the air.

Lauren shrieks and scurries backward as smoke rises from her shoulders and her skin turns blistering red.

She has demon magic at her disposal though and she's healed within seconds.

My own magic slips away.

"Nice try," she says and charges again.

I evade her, try to yank the *animus* back up, but the power is being a stubborn bitch and nothing comes to my call.

"Stop thinking about it as separate from you, *dieva*," Wrath says. "It is you and you are it."

Lauren clenches her teeth, rolls her wrist so the blade swipes in an X in front of her body, then comes at me again using fancy footwork to get in beneath my guard. The blade catches me across the chest, cutting through shirt and skin. It happens so fast that the pain comes seconds later.

I shove Lauren back.

"This is stupid," I tell Wrath. "Teach me how to use the *animus* so we can stop Chaos."

"That's one of your problems," he tells me, crossing his arms over his chest. "You're too impatient."

"I've waited long enough, haven't I?"

Lauren ignores our banter and keeps on fighting. She slices through the air, I dodge, then kick out with my foot. The blow makes her knee buckle and she goes down to the floor.

"Use the power," Wrath orders. "Finish the fight."

But when I reach for it, it isn't there. "I can't."

"Why not?"

"I don't know. It's like trying to catch water."

"What brings it out when you do use it?"

I lick my lips, keep my eyes on Lauren as she climbs to her feet. Sweat is starting to bead on her forehead, so at least she isn't indefatigable.

"*Dieva*," Wrath coaxes.

"Rage, mostly," I answer. "When it comes to me, it's usually out of rage."

"Rage burns quickly," he says. "It's not kindling, it's gasoline. If you want to control it, stop letting it control you."

"I'm not."

"You are." He stalks to the weapon wall. I split my attention between him and Lauren. Big mistake.

Lauren comes at me with the sword, swiping through the air just as Wrath pulls a dagger from the weapons wall and sends it sailing toward me.

The blade glances off my cheek and the pain of the cut burns through my face just as Lauren reaches me and slices through my thigh with her sword.

The *animus* roars to life as white stars blink in my eyes. The pain is overwhelming, nauseating.

"Control it," Wrath says. "Don't let it get away from you." Lauren spins and comes at me with her fist this time just as Wrath grabs another dagger from the wall, cocks his arm back, and throws it.

I am the *animus*.

I shouldn't have to think about using it.

I just can.

I will.

Time slows. I take several settling breaths and anchor myself in my body.

The blade comes sailing right for my throat. The *animus* blooms excitedly at my core.

Without thinking, I snatch the dagger from the air and spin around, sinking the blade into Lauren's shoulder. The fire burns around me, blistering the skin down Lauren's arms, charring it along her collarbone.

She screams, drops to the ground, shaking and crying.

And just when I think I've won—

Wrath slams into me from behind and I go down, pain jolting through my knees. He's on me again in a second, hand wrapped in my hair, yanking my head back. A blade is suddenly at my throat.

"Never let your guard down." His voice is rough at my ear. The blade scrapes painfully against my skin.

"Okay," I say. "I won't."

He lets me go and I lurch to my feet.

"Call it again," he says.

I'm covered in sweat and blood is drying at my wounds, but I put all of it out of my head and focus on the breath in my lungs, the beat of my heart in my ears.

I am not angry. I won't let it control me. For once, I give up the control entirely, letting the power run through me like water instead of me trying to corral it, grip it in my hands.

At first there's nothing and the anxiety at being incapable swims to the surface.

Another deep breath.

Just let go.

The room burns bright orange with a resounding WHUMP.

Wrath circles in front of me and I can see the reflection of the power in his irises.

"Good," he says and tosses another blade up the air and uses his dark magic to shoot it across the room at me.

Sharp awareness takes over me and I can see the blade clearly, can snatch it from the air as if it were a feather caught in a lazy wind.

Once the hilt is in my hand, I spin and throw the dagger back at Wrath. His darkness deflects it, but then he disappears and I turn, focusing on nothing but the here and now, the needling along my back.

I whirl around. He slams into me, but I spin with him and use his own move against him. I kick his feet out from beneath him, slamming him to the floor and quickly climb over top of him, settling over his waist.

Smiling like a maniac, I lord over him. I'm breathing heavily, but new energy wells in my veins.

I'm giddy and a little drunk on power.

"Am I done?" Lauren asks as she slowly climbs to her feet.

Wrath doesn't even look at her. "You're dismissed."

With a grumble, she shuffles to the door and leaves us.

"Well done, *dieva*," Wrath says.

His words are potent, but the pride that thrums through our connection means more.

I can feel him so acutely and my belly soars because of it.

"Thank you," I say.

"You still have a lot of learning to do, but perhaps there's hope for you after all."

I roll my eyes. "You're such an asshole."

Without warning, he grabs me by the waist and rolls me to my back so it's his body covering mine. "Never let your guard down," he warns again, his mouth now inches from mine.

"Yes, daddy."

He grumbles, low and deep in his chest, then gets to his feet and offers me his hand. "You need a shower."

"Speak for yourself."

He wraps his arm around me, sending butterflies charging across my belly, and yanks us to his massive bathroom. Grabbing the hem of my shirt, he peels it none too carefully from my body, the material now glued to the wounds by dried blood. Instinct has me pulling away, anticipating the pain, but there is none.

"Sit," he says and nods at the closed toilet seat. I do as commanded. Using a wet rag, he cleans the wound on my arm, but once the blood is gone, we find the skin intact, not a wound in sight. We find the same on my cheek, on my thigh, and across my chest.

"You're healing quicker." There's a troubled look on his face.

"That's a good thing. The quicker I heal, the less you suffer."

"Mmm," he says and tosses the rag to the sink. "Undress. Get in the shower."

He doesn't have to tell me twice. I may have healed, but my body is still aching and I know the hot water will feel good.

Naked, I step into the stall and turn on the hot water, letting it bead on my skin, soak my hair.

A second later, Wrath is naked and beside me.

"Turn around," he orders.

I turn and face the showerhead.

He takes shampoo in his hands and works it through the tangle of my hair. His fingers on my scalp are almost orgasmic and I have to put my hands on the tiled wall just to keep myself upright.

Suds trail down my back, down my ass. Once he's lathered me up, I turn and rinse out the soap, eyes closed against the hot spray.

When I open them again, Wrath is staring at me, his own gaze crimson red in the murky light of the all-black shower.

His bare chest is rising and falling in a rhythm that spells agitation and the connection beats with curiosity.

"What is it?" I ask.

"Why aren't you afraid of me?"

The question catches me off guard.

"I am afraid of you," I admit.

"No, you're not. I wanted to believe you used your stubbornness to hide your fear, but now with the connection, I know the truth. You're *not* afraid of me. Not like you should be. From the moment I first met you, you refused to bend to me."

"Why does it bother you so much?" I ask, turning it around on him.

"Answer the question, *dieva*."

I lean against the shower wall, giving him the showerhead. He steps beneath it, puts his face into the spray, scrubs away the sweat.

"If you want the truth," I say, "I don't know what the answer is. Maybe it was the *animus*, maybe it recognized you."

"You have to stop talking about it like it's separate from you." He turns sideways and the water glances off his broad shoulder, trails down the cut of his bicep, down the nip of his waist.

I don't want to look down at his cock, because I know what the sight of his nakedness will do to me and it doesn't feel like the right time for that.

"Your turn," I say and reach over, using my thumb to rub off a smudge of blood along his jaw. He lets me do it. Doesn't flinch.

The air nearly vibrates between us, the connection wobbling on its axis if it had one.

"What was the question?" he asks on a rasp.

"Why does it bother you so much that I'm not afraid of you? Is it just the power and the control?"

He comes closer, pinning me into the corner of the shower.

"I thought it was your disobedience."

I smirk.

"But now I realize it's something else."

"Tell me."

The water circles the drain, beading on the tiled wall as steam fills the space that we don't occupy.

"You are an enigma and I've always hated mysteries. But more than that, I don't recognize myself when I'm with you."

He's more terrified of me than I am of him.

I am sure of that because I can feel it rippling through our connection.

"Is that why you left Rhys's house in a hurry earlier? I felt... when we...*you*—"

Love.

That's what I felt.

Love.

He licks his lip, then rakes his teeth over it, avoiding my eyes and I realize I've overstepped. His walls are coming back up.

I quickly change subjects. "Where did you go anyway, when you left?"

"To the place I go to when I need to breathe."

"Which is where?" I'm more curious for this detail than I have been for others before it and I'm glad to keep him talking.

"Finish up and I'll show you."

"Really? Promise?"

"I promise, *dieva*." A smirk comes to his sensual mouth.

I rinse out the rest of my hair and scrub the blood from my body. He finishes before me, towels off and dresses in his dark jeans, a black t-shirt and the black coat I first saw him in, in the alley behind Collie's Tea Shop. The collar stands rigid around his pale face.

I dress in clothes I find hanging in a section in his closet. A section that appears to be just for me.

"Wear a jacket," he instructs me. There's a black bomber jacket in the closet, so I slip into it.

"Ready?" he asks and holds out his hand.

I'm giddy with anticipation. Where does the Demon King go to get away? He can literally go anywhere in the world.

"Ready."

He grabs hold of me and pulls us away.

10

We reappear under a twilight sky. The air is chilled and goosebumps lift on my arms despite the coat. Wind cuts across the foreign landscape and sand skitters over my shoes. It's the only sound save for the rasp of clothing and the rapid beating of my heart.

Wrath lets me go and I stumble back as the ground shifts easily beneath me.

It's sand. All of it is sand.

"Where are we?" I spin a circle, my eyes adjusting to the darkness. There's nothing but rolling sand dunes as far as the eye can see with a row of dark mountains in the distance. It's so quiet, so vast, it feels like another world.

"White Sands National Park in New Mexico," he tells me.

For all of the traveling I've done with my mother, I've only been to a desert once. Mom typically prefers lush landscapes like Scotland or Iceland, full of color and texture and depth.

"Deserts are temperamental," she told me on our way to the Mojave when I was just eight years old. "I'm not full of much hope for this shoot, but I go where they pay me."

It was blisteringly hot. Not hot like Florida where the air sticks to your skin. Hot like you've opened the oven door and stood right in front of it, letting the heat bake your skin from your bones.

I was excited about seeing the desert that day with Mom only because I'd never been and I'd heard that deserts were their own sort of magic.

After that shoot, I hated deserts as much as she did. I was sunburnt despite the layers and layers of sunscreen and the wide-brimmed hat and the sunglasses. "I'm never ever going to another desert," I told her that night while she rubbed cold aloe on my skin.

"Don't worry, baby," she'd said. "I'll die before I go to another."

But standing on a dune of white sand with the Demon King beside me, I have to eat my words.

This desert is much different than the Mojave and I realize I unfairly judged deserts based only on one and only beneath the blistering sun.

This desert at night is otherworldly.

Above me, the Milky Way splits the dark sky nearly in two. There are so many stars in the sky, I get dizzy just looking up.

"This is beautiful."

It's so quiet here, my whispers sound like a shout.

"Your world does have its moments of searing beauty."

I glance over at Wrath, but he's not looking at the sky.

He's looking at me.

My stomach drops, my heart beats a little harder.

The connection between us thrums and this time, he doesn't try to hide it. More and more, he gives and gives and I am desperate to have it.

To have him.

"How often do you come here?" I ask.

"Often enough."

"It's lonely, isn't it?"

He turns away from me, his head bent toward the sky. His footsteps follow the sharp edge of a dune, breaking it beneath each step. “I’m used to being alone.”

I follow him, walking in the imprints of his boots. “I am too.”

He glances at me over a shoulder. A gust of wind rumples his hair and I have to fight the urge to reach across the space between us and run my fingers through it, watch him bend to my touch.

“You are surrounded by people who love you,” he says.

“Yeah, that’s true, but...” I trail off, trying to figure out how to put it into words. “My mother was a good mother, but because I acted like I didn’t need her, she pretended she wasn’t needed.”

“Did you?” His eyes flicker red in the light. “Need her?”

A wave of emotion takes hold in my chest, squeezing the air from my lungs. “Maybe. Yes. Sometimes I did.”

He turns away, keeps walking.

“Have you ever needed someone?” I ask.

“Of course.”

“When?”

“I needed you,” he admits.

“That’s not what I meant.”

“Isn’t it?” He comes to a halt and I lurch to a stop behind him, the ground shifting beneath me. “Do you want to hear something truly fucked up?”

“Oh yes. Please go on. I like fucked up things.”

He’s quiet for a handful of seconds and I think it’s because he’s considering what to say and how to say it, which only builds my eagerness to hear it.

“When I lost the *animus*,” he starts, “I was desperate to get it back. I missed it like a limb and ached with the absence of it. When I met you for the first time, that void disappeared and it terrified me.” He meets my eyes. “I had forgotten what it was to be whole.”

My breathing quickens.

“When you left me again and again...the void yawned open and every second you were gone...” He takes in a breath, the fine lines around his eyes deepening. "Every second you were gone, I missed you."

The breath catches in my throat.

My gaze blurs with tears.

"I thought about you every waking minute. I still do, even when I have you chained to my bed. I can't ever stop thinking about you and I fucking hate it. I hate how the sight of you is burned to memory like hot metal touched to wood, a permanent char mark right here behind my eyes. You are always there." He clenches his teeth, jaw flexing, and turns away from me, speaks to the sky. "I hate that just the scent of you makes me hard. I hate that the sound of your voice makes me want to be gentle.

"But most of all, I hate that when you're quivering beneath me, I feel like I've laid my hands on something that only the gods can touch."

His back is still to me, but I can see him plainly in my mind, the char mark burned to memory. The cut of his jaw, the slope of his nose. The way his Adam's apple sinks when he swallows his frustrations.

He may be a demon, a *king*, but when I love him the most, he is just a man.

I go to him and wind my arms around his waist, hook my hands at his stomach. "I hate you too," I say. He puts his hands on mine, threads his fingers with my fingers.

"I am a man fighting against the wind and you are a gale force, *dieva*. And I don't like being powerless."

My belly is immediately soaring.

I move around him so we're facing each other. His expression is hard-edged, wary.

I feel it too, that inescapable tug at the center of me, even before we were bound. We were always supposed to come together. I am the *animus* and he is the king.

I reach up on tiptoes to kiss him.

He's stiff at first.

We're two lonely creatures unaccustomed to needing someone else, to being needed.

And worse, trusting them.

"No more games," I tell him as his eyes slip closed, as his hands slide to my waist, coaxing a moan to escape me. "I made my decision. I bound myself to you and I plan to embrace it, all of it. I don't ever want you to feel powerless because of me."

"It's too late for that." His mouth comes down on mine, hard. I breathe out through my nose as the kiss deepens, as his hands sink to my ass and he drives me against his hard cock.

I want to sink into him. I want to disappear into him and the pleasure of fucking and nothing more. None of the complications of our relationship and the position we find ourselves in.

Reaching between us, I grope him over his jeans and he growls into my mouth, nipping at my lip. A hiss comes out of me and he swallows it up, his hand possessive on the back of my head.

I fumble with the button on his jeans and when I finally get it open, he's straining against the material of his boxer briefs.

I try to pull him out, but the sand shifts beneath me and I lose my footing.

But his darkness catches me before I topple over. It crests into a wave around me, holding me tightly.

And in an instant, Wrath is on top of me, his darkness suspending us mid-air.

I yelp, unaccustomed to being weightless.

The darkness ebbs and flows, lifting us higher, and I flail against it, fighting it.

"Give in to me, *dieva*," he says. "Surrender to me."

The sand dunes are far below us now and we're so high in the sky, I swear I could reach out and touch the moon.

"Do you trust me?" he asks as his eyes brighten, more crimson than grey.

Do I? I don't know that I've fully given in to anyone in my

entire life. I've always been alone because I've chosen to be alone, because it's always easier to rely only on yourself.

When you only rely on yourself, no one can disappoint you.

Or betray you.

The darkness steals my shirt, then my pants, leaving me in a matching set of black lace underthings. Wrath's deft fingers slip in beneath the band of my bra, teasing at the sensitive underside of my breast. My nipple peaks, aches for him.

I hang my head back and close my eyes. Maybe if I don't look at the sky or the ground beneath us, I can give in to the pleasure of my body and not the terror.

"*Dieva*?" he asks.

"Yes," I say, a little breathless. "I trust you."

He relieves us of the rest of our clothes and they flutter to the sand dunes twenty feet below.

I make the mistake of looking down and choke on a yelp, but Wrath is clever about distracting me. His hands trail down, right under my ass so that his fingers hit on my inner thighs and coax me open for him.

The head of his cock nestles at my opening and I whimper, desperate for him to be inside of me.

His mouth trails down the side of my jaw, down the curve of my neck. He nips at me, I jolt, and he tightens his hold on me as the darkness ribbons around us, holding us aloft.

He continues his slow, tortuous descent of his mouth and I arch into him, begging him to take my nipple in his mouth. And when he finally does, I mewl beneath him. We may be rising to the stars, but I'm descending into the pleasure of his mouth.

Tongue teasing at me, he brings me to a peak and then bites at me, sucks me back into his mouth, then eases the sting with a slide of his tongue.

His cock presses forward and I rock my hips up, trying to sink him deeper.

The darkness pivots, righting us, and Wrath settles me on his hips and coaxes my legs around him. I use his body as leverage and try to drive him into me.

But he holds himself steady.

"I will always control your pleasure, *dieva*."

I moan into him, a little mindless for more.

"Not even the *animus* can take that from me."

I rock against him again, but he hooks his hands beneath my thighs and lifts me off of him, stealing the heat of his cock from my opening.

I moan at the loss.

"Are you always going to torture and tease me and make me beg?"

"Yes," he admits and slides his shaft up my wetness, the head of his cock hitting my clit. He drags back again, then up, back and up.

The sensation steals the breath from my lungs and I gasp to get it back.

"Then please fuck me."

"Try that again."

"Please fuck me, my king."

"Good girl."

I'll beg for it all day long. This part of myself I can give him. I can give up control when he's fucking me because when he's fucking me, I feel whole.

He sinks inside of me, forcing a moan from my lips.

The darkness tightens arounds us, surrounds us on all sides save for above where the Milky Way glitters and glows.

Wrath picks up his rhythm, driving into me. He's harder than he's ever been and I can feel every ridge of him inside of me.

"Fuck, *dieva*," he says, in and out, filling me up.

The pleasure builds.

I hang my head back and the stars blur into bright white lines.

Wrath pinches my nipple between two fingers, sending a jolt of pain through me and then quickly covers it with his mouth, stopping the pain with a caress of his tongue.

"You will always be mine," he says.

"Yes."

"And I will always worship you if you'll let me."

Worship me. Reign. The Bright Goddess.

It's almost like the moon is taunting me from the sky.

Wrath drives into me harder, and I grow wetter as he brings me closer and closer to the brink.

The darkness envelops us and it caresses against my skin like silk.

My nerves are lit up like lightning. Every sensation is like a revolution, like a star being born.

"Come for me, *dieva,*" he says. "I want to feel that tight pussy pulse around my cock."

He shifts us, so that I'm bouncing on his shaft, my arms around his neck.

Warmth spreads through me and when I open my eyes, a bright golden light is filling the dark cloud around us. It sends a soft flow across Wrath's sharp face, driving away his shadows.

"I don't know if I can," I say. I'm close, but it's all so much, too much.

"It wasn't a request." He flips me over and the darkness nestles me into its dark waves. Wrath drives back into me, buries himself to the hilt. His hand comes to the column of my neck, fingers pressing hard into me.

"Come for me, *dieva*. That's an order."

His other hand sinks between my legs, presses against my mound.

I'm suddenly squirming beneath him, desperate for friction as my clit throbs and my body pulses for release.

He swirls two fingers against me, pulling the orgasm closer and closer and—

I cry out. The pleasure rushes in.

I quiver beneath him as he nestles against my ass, cock buried so deep, it almost hurts.

He pulls out, slams back in, cups me as I ride through the wave of the orgasm, then flicks my clit again, causing me to shudder.

"Fuck," I breathe out, the golden glow intensifying in our nest of darkness.

Wrath pounds harder, punishing my pussy until he slams in deep and fills me up.

His fingers press at my throat, stealing some of the air from my lungs. I hold my breath as he throbs inside of me.

As my body blinks through the aftershocks, Wrath slides out several inches, then slides back in, slow and torturous. His grip on my throat loosens and he finally lets me curl into myself, curl into him.

The darkness undulates, then holds us like a black cloud and Wrath wraps his arms around me.

We lay there for the longest time, the bright sky above us, the darkness below. We're suspended in a dark daydream where none of the shit can reach us.

Soon I find myself drifting off to sleep.

"*Dieva*." His voice is hoarse at my ear.

"Hmm?"

His fingers trail through my hair and it sends a shiver down my spine.

"I can't love you the way you deserve to be loved."

I open my eyes. Moonlight skims the dark clouds with pale silver light.

I know he means it as a warning.

We haven't had this conversation yet. We haven't been brave enough to look it in the eye, give it a name.

But that is what we have, isn't it? Some kind of love, as twisted as it may be.

"Just love me how you can," I tell him.

The moonlight disappears. Wrath pulls us through the sub-dimension back to his bed. He lays me gently on the sheets, pulls the blanket around me as I tremble.

I'm so warm and I feel so safe.

We can figure this out.

I know we can.

But nestled in his arms, as I descend into sleep, I hear him whisper, "But will that be enough?"

11

I WAKE TO LAUREN PEERING DOWN AT ME.

I shriek. Wrath holds me still, his face still buried in my neck, in my hair. "This better be important," he says behind me.

Sunlight is pouring in around the partially opened drapes. I have no idea what time it is, but I've become a creature of the night. It could very well be two in the afternoon.

"Kat is here and she's brought you a present."

Though I can't see Wrath, I sense his curiosity through the connection. "Don't leave me in suspense."

"Apparently they caught someone trying to sneak into Last Vale. They think he's one of Chaos's men. Kat brought the trespasser to you."

Wrath disentangles himself from me and collapses on his back. "I'll be there in a minute."

Lauren nods and leaves.

I suppose when you're the one in charge, there is no such thing as a day off.

"What's Last Vale?" I ask. "Rhys said something about it last night too."

"It's a hidden town in Saint Sabine that Rhys founded a long time ago. It's to be a safe haven for the supernatural."

"Why would this guy want to go there?"

"There's a powerful ley line that runs beneath it. The same ley line that Ciri used to pull me to your world."

I sit up. "Do you think Chaos is trying to open a portal?"

"It's certainly possible. I wouldn't put it past him." He throws the sheet and the duvet back and slides from the bed. I take a minute to appreciate the view of him walking away, his bare ass, the way his back dimples, all muscle and bone.

"Stop leering at me."

"I'm not. I'm appreciating what's mine."

He grumbles as he disappears into the closet. "Clever little girl."

I sigh and collapse back against the pillows that smell like him.

"You should dress as well," he calls out to me. "I'd like you by my side."

A thrill buzzes through me. "Really?"

He comes out dressed in his usual—black jeans, black t-shirt, black boots. He is a dark vision. He runs his hand through his equally dark hair, raking it back. Even though we showered last night, his hair is somehow perfectly coiffed in that roguish, careless way only someone like him can manage.

"From now on," he says, "I want you always by my side."

It sounds perfunctory, cold, but the connection doesn't lie—this isn't about appearances. He doesn't want to be without me.

It's been so long since I've had an obsessive crush that I forgot what it felt like to be so wound up in someone that you couldn't imagine walking away from them.

I can't call this a crush, though. This is something else. Something deeper.

But the overwhelming need is still there, echoing back to each other through the vein of energy that runs between us.

I don't even have to say anything. He already knows.

I'll be there. I'll stay by his side.

"Get dressed," he orders and waits for me on the balcony.

I throw on the first thing I see—a white t-shirt, black skinny jeans. I find a row of shoes on a shelf on the bottom of my section in the closet. Tennis shoes, flats, stilettos, and several pairs of booties.

I go with a pair of black booties.

In the bathroom, I rake my hand through my hair, but mine is flat and limp, and doesn't do that roguish wave like Wrath's does. Maybe when this is all over, I'll make a hair appointment. I deserve a treat-yourself day after marrying a demon and battling his demon brother.

Back in the bedroom, Wrath turns away from the balcony. Even though I'm in nothing more than jeans and a t-shirt, he drinks in the sight of me like I've donned a princess dress, hair curled and pinned.

My chest warms.

He comes over, hooks his arm around me and plants a kiss on my mouth, his hand sinking to my ass. A flare of desire wells at my core and Wrath tsk-tsks.

"Sorry," I say, even though I'm not.

"Business first, fucking second."

"Shouldn't that be the other way around?"

"Not when you're king and queen."

I pout up at him and he smiles easily, his gray eyes glittering. "I may not know how to properly love you, *dieva*, but I do know how to fuck you. I'll make it up to you."

"Promise?"

"Always."

He pulls us from the bedroom and deposits us in a distant hallway where voices carry out from an unmarked room.

Inside, we find Kat and Lauren with a man tied to a chair.

There are no windows in the room and only one door. There's no furniture save for the chair.

Blood is crusted along the man's jaw and his left eye is turning a bruised shade of violet.

"I checked him for location charms," Kat says. "And bound him so no one can use him for a location spell."

Wrath nods his approval.

The guy is veering back and forth between sobbing and laughter. Tears stream down his face and his eyes are wide open, giving him a crazed look.

"It doesn't matter," he says.

Wrath stalks over, circles the guy slowly. The guy fights at the ropes binding him, causing the chair to creak, the ropes to groan.

"Did Chaos send you?" Wrath asks.

The guy laughs and the laughter descends into sobs. He's not much older than me. He might have been a college student or an office drone. There's nothing special about him. Maybe working for a demon is the height of his potential.

"You'll never stop him," the guy says.

"Stop him from doing what?" Wrath asks.

The guy spits on the floor just missing Wrath's boot. "Stealing your girl and your throne."

Wrath bristles. The connection vibrates and I want to crawl out of my skin. I'm not made for interrogation, it would seem.

"What were you doing in Last Vale?" Kat asks.

"Looking for the portal."

Wrath and Kat glance at each other. "Did he find it?" Wrath asks her.

"Not as far as we know. He was just outside the city."

"He couldn't have opened it without a traveler," Lauren says. "Right?"

"There are other ways to get through," Kat answers. "None of them easy though."

Something is troubling Wrath.

"What are you thinking?" I ask him.

"Chaos has the *oculus* and your government on his side. A

billion-dollar military at his disposal. I don't know why he'd go to the trouble of opening a gate when it's not soldiers he needs."

The man goes quiet and winces from pain as he shifts in the chair.

"Something else is wrong," Wrath says. "A problem he can't solve." Wrath turns his attention back to the prisoner. "The question is, do you know?"

The man shakes his head, tears dripping from his face. "I don't. I don't know anything."

"If you don't know anything, then what good are you?"

A bead of bloodlust takes hold of Wrath and it wells up inside of me. He's growing impatient and eager for violence. It almost makes my head spin, how quickly he's gone from smiling at me in the bedroom to murder.

"What's your name?" I ask, trying to defuse the tension.

"Zach."

"Zach, if you help us, maybe we can help you."

I get a sharp poke of disapproval through the connection. Wrath scowls at me.

"I don't know anything," he says again. "I swear it. I..." He grimaces. "Sorry. I..." He grits his teeth, tendons standing out in his neck from the strain.

"Zach," I try again, "tell us every little detail you might know. Even if it seems insignificant. Can you do that?"

"I can't." He descends into madness again and hangs his head back and laughs.

"What is wrong with him?" I ask. "This doesn't seem normal."

"It isn't. This is what happens when you either don't have the power or the knowledge to use the *oculus* on someone."

The guy turns to crying again, snot running down his nose. "I can't do it. You can't stop him." He laugh-cries. "Please help me."

"This is a waste of time." Cold impatience reverberates through our connection. Wrath stalks forward.

"Wait!"

He puts his hands on either side of Zach's head and gives him a violent twist.

The sound of bones cracking makes my stomach see-saw. Zach's body goes limp, his head turned at an unnatural angle.

I clamp my hand over my mouth.

Wrath points at Lauren. "Clean this up." Then he stalks from the room.

I hurry after him, still queasy. "Why did you do that?"

"He was useless and his mind was scrambled."

I race ahead, cutting him off.

"He was a human being."

Wrath frowns down at me. "And?"

"And. And! He deserved...something..."

"He was an enemy and he needed to be dealt with. That is how this goes."

"No. I don't want that to be the way we deal with problems. That isn't—"

He looks away from me, his gaze going distant as if he's hearing something I can't.

"What is it?"

Horror washes over his face. He reaches out for me, but an explosion rocks the floor as debris fills the air. I'm tossed backward and slam into the wall. All of the breath is knocked from my lungs and I slink down to the floor gasping.

There's shouting and yelling. Dust plumes around me while flames grow in the background.

I can taste sulphur in the back of my throat.

Another explosion goes off and the heat intensifies.

I still can't breathe. Everything hurts. I think I broke a rib, maybe punctured a lung.

"*Dieva*!" Wrath shouts.

"I'm here," I try to say, but my voice is barely more than a whisper.

At the other end of the hall, a gun lets out a pop-pop and

bullets whiz by.

More shouting fills the halls. Another bomb, then another and the castle rocks on its foundation. Someone screams.

I'm disoriented. My head is ringing. I should run. I should do something, right?

I need to get out of the smoke, get fresh air, clear my lungs so I can think straight.

Arm clutched over my body trying to keep the pain at bay, I drag my hand along the stone wall until I find the next break in the hall and go right, and finally stumble into an exterior door. I burst outside, drag in a breath.

When the dust clears from my eyes, I realize I'm not alone in the back garden.

And worse, it's someone I recognize.

Ryder, the leader of the Men Against Wrath. And standing beside him is Tom, the man from the farmhouse down the road, the very same man I was dumb enough to inform of the castle. The Demon King's castle. The one hidden by magic unless you know where to look.

Fucking hell.

I'm such a fucking idiot!

"Rain!" Tom says and hurries over to me. "Are you okay?"

"What is going on?" I whisper and try to stand upright but my back is killing me and there's a sharp pain in my side that hurts like hell when I take a deep breath.

Ryder stalks over, shoves Tom aside and stabs me in the gut.

A scream claws from my throat. The pain is so intense, I immediately drop where I stand.

The world spins.

"What are you doing?" Tom tries to attend to me, but one of Ryder's men yanks the old man back. "We're supposed to be saving her!"

Taking a length of my hair, Ryder winds it around his knuckles and yanks me to my feet.

My vision goes bright white as the pain overwhelms every nerve in my body.

"Yes, but a little pain can't hurt. Especially when it weakens the Demon King." Ryder smiles at me as he produces another blade.

Somewhere at the other end of our connection, I can feel the Demon King struggling through the mirroring wound while he fights the people swarming the castle's halls.

And with the pain, I can feel his panic.

He can feel me slipping.

There's so much blood. It's just pouring out of me, soaking my shirt, my pants, running down my leg.

"This isn't right," Tom says.

Ryder nods at one of his men. "Percy, escort the old man home. He's done his part."

"I'm sorry, Rain." Tom reaches out for me, but Percy yanks him away. "I didn't know."

A second blade flashes in Ryder's grip and he plunges that one into my shoulder with a swift, downward thrust.

My knees buckle. I let out a pathetic sob as I hit the dirt.

"Chaos said she needed to be alive," one of Ryder's men warns. "We should probably hold back, boss."

Ryder screws up his mouth. "I'm sure she can take it," he says as he twists the blade in my shoulder.

The pain is so intense that my vision blurs on the edges and tears stream down my face. I'm going to vomit. I want to leave my body so I never have to feel this kind of pain ever again.

"Get her up." Ryder stalks away. "Bring her to the car."

Two men hook me through the arms and drag me across the back garden to a waiting SUV in the driveway. I'm tossed into the backseat and fresh pain wends through my body.

Make it stop.

I need to make it stop.

"Burn the place to the ground," Ryder orders before he climbs in behind the wheel and tromps on the gas, tearing us away.

I pass out in the backseat of the SUV.

I have no idea how long we're on the road.

The next thing I know, I'm waking on a couch in a darkened room and Chaos is sitting in a chair in front of me.

"Hello, Rain," he says.

I lurch awake and pull myself into a sitting position as far away from him as I can.

But as I blink the grogginess from my eyes, I get a good look at him.

He looks like shit.

The tortoiseshell glasses are gone and the whites of his eyes are bloodshot, dark circles marring his skin beneath. His lips are dry and cracked and his skin is so thin and pale, it's almost translucent.

Worse, his veins are turning black.

"What's wrong with you?" I ask.

I just saw him on the news and he didn't look like this. Though I bet there was some magic of TV makeup going on.

"It's the *oculus*." Sirene's voice comes from my left. I find the shape of her in the darkened corner, her arms folded over her chest. "He can't hold on to it."

Chaos grimaces, clearly miffed about this turn of events.

"It's eating away at him from the inside and that little show at the train station only made it worse."

Chaos leans back against the chair and sighs. There is the barest flicker of relief in his eyes as if sitting upright caused him a great deal of pain and discomfort.

"I thought you were stronger?" I turn to Sirene. "You and Ciri had a plan and you manipulated me into joining you. I thought this was your goal."

"This *was* her goal." Chaos rolls his head along the back of the chair so he can glare at the witch. "She and Ciri knew it all along, didn't you? You knew exactly where we'd end up. You knew I was the only one who would have the power and the desire to steal the *oculus* from Wrath." He recenters, looks at me. "She knew I'd steal it, but could never hold it, forcing me to give it to you because I'm certainly not giving it back to my brother." He coughs, grimaces, and blood speckles the corner of his mouth. "I was just a pawn in her game and so are you."

I rise to my feet and Chaos flinches.

He's afraid of me.

"So now what? You attack Wrath's castle using MAW to do it? Ryder is a fucking psychopath, by the way. Then you bring me here and...what? What the fuck do you expect me to do now? And where is Wrath?"

I can still feel him through the connection, so I know he's alive, but he's very far away and I can't tell what state he's in.

What I do feel is *terror* at being separated from me.

Sirene pushes away from the wall and comes over. Her long dirty blonde hair is braided into three tight braids that run along the side of her head. She looks better than Chaos does, but there are fine lines of stress crowing at her eyes.

"When I first held you," Sirene says, "this wailing fat little baby, I thought, 'This is a mistake.' I thought the gods were surely laughing at me because you wouldn't shut up." She comes closer. "It's easy to doubt something when you can't see the shape of it yet."

I frown. "I hate riddles."

Chaos puts his hands on the arms of the chair and uses them as leverage to bring himself to his feet. He winces, grunts, and then takes a long breath once he's standing, chest wheezing.

So much for the mighty Chaos.

I don't know why we were ever afraid of him. I could probably punch him in the balls right now and he'd keel over.

With trembling fingers, he undoes the buttons on his shirt and then pulls it off. He may be withering away, but he's still cut like a fighter. His biceps bulge as he moves, his abs contracting as he tosses the shirt aside.

He hasn't lost muscle mass, but something is very, very wrong with his demon mark.

It's jagged and fading away and there's a raw, festering burn mark over his right collarbone.

That must be the *oculus*.

On Wrath's demon mark, there's a gaping hole at the center of it where I think the *animus* used to be. Now I wear the mark between my shoulder blades.

Chaos puts his hand over his infected wound and grits his teeth together.

"What are you doing?"

He groans.

"Sirene, what is he doing?"

His face turns blue while his eyes glow bright red.

The demon mark moves beneath his skin like slippery ink and then his knees buckle and he hits the floor with a loud thud.

"Sirene!"

"Stand back," she says evenly.

I scurry over to the end of the couch.

The demon mark glows red to match Chaos's eyes.

The hair rises along my arms.

Chaos hangs his head back and roars as the *oculus* leaves his body. And when it's over, he bends forward, breathing heavily. There's a stone clutched in his hand.

It looks distinctly like black volcanic rock, just like from the stories.

Sirene wrenches the stone from him. He knows he can't hold it but it takes considerable effort for him to let it go.

This was supposed to be his silver bullet, the beginning of his brother's end.

Sirene comes over to me. I scurry off the couch, slide along the wall. She follows me, the *oculus* sitting innocently in the palm of her hand, innocent like an unlit bomb.

"What do you plan to do with it now?" I ask.

"What I did with the *animus*."

"Ummm...no." I backpedal. She mirrors me. "Sirene. No."

"Why?"

"Because. It belongs to Wrath—"

"No, it doesn't."

"—and if Chaos isn't strong enough to contain it then neither am I."

"Yes, you are."

"No, I'm not."

I hit the corner of the room and Sirene stops in front of me.

"I'm not taking it."

"You don't have to *take* it," she says. "I'm giving it to you."

"Wrath will never trust me if I have two-thirds of the Demon King's power. I barely know how to control the *animus*, let alone the *oculus*. It'll probably burn me up inside and—"

Sirene tosses the stone into the air.

My eyes track it as it arches above my head.

Without thinking, almost as if of their own accord, my hands snap out and catch the stone before it hits the ground.

Heat races up my arm. Light flares in my field of vision.

Sirene staggers back as I mash myself against the wall, as some unseen force roars through the room.

I'm filled with fire. So much fire. It's like I've touched the sun, like my skin is pulling back from meat and bone, incinerating every fiber of my being.

I can't contain it. I'm not meant for this.

It feels like my insides are being rearranged, my cells reborn, my bones hollowed out and filled with molten lava.

I hang my head back and scream.

12

When the pain finally ebbs, I'm on my butt on the floor, but at least I still have eyelids.

Sirene and Chaos peer over top of me. "I told you," Sirene says.

Chaos curses.

"What. The. Fuck." I sit upright and— "Holy shit."

In a blink, I'm on my feet. It's like I've snorted coke and downed a bottle of liquor. Not that I know what it's like to snort drugs. I'm just guessing here.

There is no pain. No aches. I'm full of so much energy, I think I could touch the sky.

I want to run. Fly. Fight. Fuck.

Holy shit.

Holy shit.

Have I finally lost my mind? Maybe Zach wasn't the crazy one. Maybe I've gone mad.

I bring my hands in front of my face. I can see the blood pumping through my veins, the tiny whirls of my fingerprints when I focus on them.

I can hear the birds chirping outside, the worms moving in the earth, and the distant churning of a motor.

"What is this?" Even my voice sounds different, richer, more complex.

"Two-thirds of the Demon King's power," Chaos says begrudgingly.

I pace the room. I can't sit still. "This isn't...how do I...Wrath will... *Why*?" I stop and look at Chaos and Sirene. "Why would you give this to me? I'm not your ally. And I'm bound to the Demon King."

Sirene smirks. "Really? You hold power majority. I think it is *he* who is bound to *you* now."

"No. No no no." I keep pacing. "He's going to kill me. He's never going to believe that I didn't want this. He's going to think it was all part of the plan and—Sirene. Take it back." I hold out my hands. "You need to take it back."

"I can't. I won't."

"Why not?"

Chaos settles himself back into his chair. I can hear the unsteady thrum of his heart. He's not doing well. I don't know how I know it but I do. The mighty demon brother, laid so low by nothing more than his ambition.

"Because," he says, wincing as he looks up at me, "she believes you're the reincarnated goddess Reignyabit and if that's true, the power was always yours. It was always meant to be yours."

13

I LEAVE THE ROOM. WE'RE IN A STERILE OFFICE BUILDING FROM THE LOOKS of it with prison gray walls and cheap tiled floors and fluorescent lights that buzz above me.

The buzz is so loud it makes me wince.

At the end of the hall, I find a stairwell with a placard that says we're on the second floor.

Sirene comes after me. "Rain, wait."

"Fuck off." I burst into the stairwell, the door's push handle clanking loudly.

Wrath is going to be pissed. How will I explain this one? We had just gotten on solid ground again in our relationship.

Sirene's footsteps echo behind me. "Rain."

"I'm just going to give it back to him," I tell her. "So your plan was stupid and fruitless and it cost Ciri her life."

"Ciri knew what she was doing."

"She wanted to die?"

"She knew she had to."

I snort and the sound boomerangs back to me. "I'm giving it back to him."

"You can't."

"Yes, I can."

"No." She vaults herself over the stair railing and cuts me off at the next landing, her braids flipping over her shoulder. "You're not listening to me. You *can't* give it back to him."

"I'm not a reincarnated goddess. Okay! I know the stories. I read about them in a vampire's library. The dark god and the bright goddess. I know how the story goes. But that's not me. I'm just a girl."

"If you were just a girl, then how can you possibly possess so much power and contain it?" She comes up a step. I go up one more. "Chaos is a demon of royal blood and he nearly died holding on to just one part of the triad."

My throat thickens.

"Now you have two. Tell me, Rain, do you feel like you're dying?"

Fuck.

She comes up another step.

My vision blurs as tears well in my eyes. "This isn't supposed to happen this way."

"Answer the question."

"No, all right? I feel like...like..." I tip my head back, close my eyes, purging a tear. I quickly swipe it away. "I feel bigger," I answer. "Not physically though. Something else. Something *other*."

Not even thinking about it, my senses expand beyond the stairwell. Immediately I can tell there are seven men on the ground floor. Two of them are drinking coffee. The third is drinking cheap whiskey. I know it's cheap because I can smell it.

Ryder's voice cuts through the din. "Fucking bitch bleeds like any other," he's saying. "There's nothing special about her."

One of the others laughs. "I don't know. If she's got a special cunt, I'd like to get a taste of it."

Ryder groans. "She's been fucking that demon for weeks. Tainted cunt isn't my thing."

"Bullshit," someone else says. "Given the opportunity, you'd tie that bitch to a tree and fuck her till she bled."

There's a pause, and then Ryder says, "Yeah, you're right."

They all erupt in laughter.

Sirene regards me with suspicion. "What is it? What are you hearing?"

The otherness at the center of me grows claws and sharp teeth.

I lose my train of thought.

The rage kicks up, familiar and comforting.

Bright golden light fills the stairwell.

"Stop." Sirene puts her hand out and there's a loud WHUMP. The air in front of me ripples and glows and my nose fills with the scent of smoky oak.

This is Sirene's magic. "Not yet," she says.

I blink. "What?"

"You've got the murder face on."

"I...I don't have a murder face."

"You do now."

"I wasn't—"

"You can deal with Ryder soon enough."

I huff and cross my arms over my chest. "What is this, some kind of magical force field?" I poke a finger at the rippling blue light and the air crackles like thin ice before disintegrating into a plume of smoke.

Sirene's mouth drops open.

I wrinkle my nose. I don't think that's how that was supposed to happen.

With an arch of her sharp brow, Sirene says, "Not a goddess, huh?"

"I don't know what that was."

"I'm several hundred years old and one of the most powerful witches in your world *and* mine."

"Hello, hubris."

"No one can dismantle my magic with a poke of their finger."

I worry at my bottom lip, trying to come up with a good excuse. "Maybe you're tired."

She scowls at me.

"Hungry? Stressed?"

"Can I show you something?"

Sirene has never asked me anything before. She's commanded. Begrudgingly tolerated.

Never asked.

"As if I would be stupid enough to go anywhere with you."

"You're the one driving. I promise no tricks."

"I don't have a car. You brought me here."

"Not a car."

It dawns on me what she's jiving toward. "I don't know how to travel through the sub-dimension. At least not on purpose."

"I saw you use it once before. It should be a piece of cake now."

Now that I'm a goddess, apparently.

It's all bullshit.

"Okay, fine. But it's not my fault if you pop up on the other side split into a dozen pieces like ice cubes popped out of a tray."

"I'm not worried," Sirene says.

"So where am I going?"

"I doubt you even have to think about it." She places her hand on my shoulder. "Where do you feel drawn?"

I regard her with suspicion. "What do you mean?"

She just stares at me as if urging me to answer my own question.

And then—

Distantly, somewhere far, far beyond this office building, there's a subtle tug. The feeling I get reminds me of playing hide and seek as a kid, like I need to get home free, and put my hand on the bark of the oak designated as home.

There's a pop, a rushing in my ears.

The stairwell is gone and replaced immediately with four stone walls.

When I speak, my voice echoes. "Where are we?"

Weak light shines through a domed glass ceiling. There are more windows along the perimeter, most of them coated in grime and overwhelmed by roots and cobwebs.

It reminds me of the mausoleum where we brought Chaos over.

But this isn't the same place. This one is bigger, more ornate, and at the head of the room above the stone doorway is a new symbol.

The bright sun.

"This is another *porta limina*," Sirene says. "Portal of Worship."

"For who?"

But I already know before she tells me.

"The Bright Goddess."

Divine Mother, Reignyabit, Reign.

I'm going to be sick.

I bend over in the corner and retch, but nothing comes up. I brace myself on the wall, choking on air as my stomach tries to revolt and comes up empty.

Sirene's hand settles between my shoulder blades, then moves my hair aside.

Bile comes up, burning my throat, burning in the back of my nose.

I keep gagging.

This isn't real.

It can't be fucking real.

When the retching stops and I'm able to take a deep breath, Sirene tears a strip of cloth from her shirt and hands it to me to wipe my mouth.

If the power, the names, the portal of worship wasn't proof enough, this wet length of cloth is.

Sirene isn't the type of woman to destroy her clothes for a bit of common spit.

Somehow, it's that that makes me break.

"I can't do this." I love him, is what I don't say.

And he'll never forgive me for this.

He's terrified of losing his power and his throne.

I can't have power majority.

My nose burns again, but this time with unshed tears.

"Yes, you can," Sirene says.

"Then I don't want to."

"You were born for this."

"Because of you." I grit my teeth. "*You* did this."

"Do you want to hear it?"

I ball the strip of fabric in my hand. "Hear what?"

"The story of Reignyabit and why I betrayed a king to give birth to a goddess."

14

I WANT TO GO HOME BUT WHERE IS HOME NOW? WHERE THE HELL DO I belong?

All of me has been carved out and filled with something new that I don't recognize.

I find a stone bench and drop onto it. Sirene goes to the closed portal and admires it, her back to me. "Everything I've told you is still true. Wrath did give me these scars." She runs her fingers gently over the puckered skin as if the scar still hurts. "Chaos did start WWII, but Wrath was just as complicit. He didn't try to stop Chaos and he should have. They had both grown too powerful, too greedy for their own good."

She steps away from the portal wall. "When there's war, Oracle activity intensifies. Are you familiar with them? The Oracles?"

I nod. "I met one with Ciri when she first came to the castle."

"What did it tell you?"

I sit forward, prop my elbows on my knees. "Something about Chaos. Umm... 'through Chaos, there is order. Through order, there is peace. Through you, there is redemption. You are the only way. So you must do as you must and do it quickly.'"

Sirene rolls her eyes. "Ciri liked to speak in riddles, but the Oracles are another level." She comes over to me. "The death and carnage of WWII brought out the Oracles in droves. And when there's increased Oracle activity, inevitably there are whispers of the future.

"I kept hearing about Reignyabit. I only had a vague understanding of her. For being the mother of all, she was pretty much wiped from our books and oral histories. Even in Alius, men take credit for everything, even the birth of the world."

She paces away, her hands on her hips. "Those who would *listen* started to *believe* and places like this were built to worship her in the hopes that she would come to end the suffering. When people suffer, they always prefer the feminine hand, the gentle goddess."

Sirene laughs and the sound bubbles around us in an echo. "Of course, Reignyabit was never gentle and of course she didn't come. Gods and Goddesses don't just pop up out of thin air. That's not how it works. Never has, never will. But—"

"You knew that the Demon King supposedly possessed the power handed down from the Dark God."

She turns to meet my gaze. "Exactly. I had never met a goddess, but I had lived my entire life surrounded by *power*. Power that could do incredible things."

I rise to my feet.

"I knew it would be impossible for me to take any of the triad from the Demon King," she says, "but he and Chaos were at odds."

"Why?"

"Do you remember the story I told you? Of the village Wrath destroyed when he was trying to put down a coup to overthrow him?"

I nod.

"There was a girl there...a vampire. She was a daughter of the family that wanted to overthrow Wrath. Chaos was in love with her. Truth be told, she was using him, but his love was real."

The revelation hits me like a stone to the face.

The pain of the loss, even though it isn't mine, is acute.

I know what it is to love something. But I can't imagine what it is to lose it.

It must feel like your heart is being torn out of your chest.

I don't want to feel sorry for Chaos, but it's impossible not to.

"So when you approached Chaos with the idea of taking the *animus* from Wrath—"

"He was more than willing to do it."

"What did you tell him though?" I trail her as she circles the room. "Obviously, you didn't tell him you planned to birth a goddess."

She snorts. "Obviously. He did try to keep it at first, but he ran into the same issue he had with the *oculus*. There's a reason Wrath was chosen to be king. Chaos was never strong enough. But hubris is always the best way to make a man bend to your will. I told him that I'd hold the *animus* in a safe place until it was his time to rule. That surely it was his destiny. He was happy to believe me."

At the portal, she stops again, crosses her arms over her chest. "I've always believed that whatever I want done, I can do. I don't doubt myself." She looks over at me. "But you"—she gestures at me with a wave of her hand—"what you've become... to be honest with you, Rain, I doubted this was even possible and yet here you are."

Here I am.

The supposed reincarnation of an ancient goddess.

I keep waiting for someone to pull a prank card and laugh at me for even believing a grain of it as truth.

But it never comes.

Sirene doesn't laugh. She levels me with an intense gaze and it's her belief in me, in what I am, that scares me the most.

"What do you want me to do?" I ask. "What do you think I *can* do?"

She looks me right in the eyes and says, “You’ll take the last of the Demon King’s power and you will reign.”

15

I'M NOT SURPRISED BY HER PLAN, BUT I AM GOING TO IGNORE IT.

"I'm not going to overthrow the Demon King and steal a throne to another world. That wasn't one of my life goals."

Sirene stands in front of the stone portal. "The Demon King has reigned long enough. His entire ancestral line, all of them men, ruling with brutality and greed. You have the opportunity to stop him."

I scoff. "I will admit that using the whole feminine power thing is pretty potent on me. You know my mom."

She gives me a genuine smile. "Why do you think I picked your mother as a vessel? Sunny Low is a badass bitch."

I laugh. "Yeah, she is. But...this is more complex than the patriarchy."

She nods. "You're more than a symbolism of feminine power."

"Symbolism." I snort. "I'm no symbol."

"You will be."

"I can't be your Joan of Arc, Sirene."

"I don't want a saint, Rain. I want a fucking god."

"Well, you're not getting that either." I turn to the nearest wall and start running my hands through the tangle of vines, looking for a door. "Now how do I get out of this place?'

"Rain."

I ignore her and keep searching.

"Rain."

"What?"

"Your back—it's glowing."

"What?!" I spin around, but of course I can't see my back.

"Here." Sirene goes to the nearest window and with nothing more than a flick of her wrist, the vines disintegrate, revealing the glass. There's just enough of a reflection that I can see between my shoulder blades where a distinct bright glow is emanating from my skin.

I yank the shirt off to get a better look.

"It's my birthmark." The same one that Wrath freaked out about when I was caught naked and soaking wet. "Why is it doing that?"

"I don't know," Sirene admits.

"How do I stop it?"

Her eyes are wide.

"Sirene."

"I don't know. This is new territory for me."

"Fucking hell. How do I—"

Like a bell tolling, I sense Wrath searching for me, drawing nearer.

My first thought is—thank god he's all right.

My second thought is—oh shit.

"What is it?" Sirene asks. "Is it the mark? Are you okay?"

"No. I mean...yes. It's Wrath. He's coming for me."

Her eyes narrow. "Of course he is."

"You should go."

"What do you plan to do?"

"I don't know. How the fuck do I get out of here?"

"You can literally transport yourself anywhere in the world."

I grumble. "I'm still learning how to drive, all right?"

The connection between Wrath and me intensifies, thrums brighter. He's close.

"You need to go," I tell Sirene.

"Fine. But if you need me—"

"I'm sure I can find you."

She waves her hand in the air, eyes glowing green. The vines pull away to reveal a door to a forest beyond. I follow her out.

Night has fallen wherever we are and the air is cool. It's mostly hardwood trees with a few tall, skinny pines. I marvel all over again at being able to hear things I should not hear. Like the rasp of pine needles, an animal digging beneath my feet, the skittering of claws on tree bark somewhere far away.

I want to deny that any of this is real, but how can I when literally everything has changed?

"Good luck, Rain," Sirene says.

I get the distinct impression she means *Reign* this time and it makes me shiver.

She starts off and disappears through a grove of pines.

My belly warms as Wrath draws nearer. I get a sense of panic followed by relief through our connection. He knows I'm all right—he was worried I wasn't.

My heart drums in my ears.

He's going to be pissed.

What happens after this?

I have two-thirds of the Demon King's power. He's not going to handle that well.

When he appears several yards away still shrouded in darkness, I can see all of the hard lines of his body, the slant of his cheekbones, the sharp cut of his jaw.

"Hi," I say, trying not to be awkward as fuck.

"You're all right," he says. The connection thrums with relief.

"I am. And you?"

"Alive."

"Good."

He comes closer and finds a pocket of moonlight. "Who took you?"

"It's a super long story and—"

"Rain." His expression sharpens, his voice rumbles. "Who took you?"

"It was MAW at first, but they were working for Chaos."

His jaw flexes.

"But I'm okay now."

"But something is different." It's not a question.

I swallow loudly and of course, the Demon King notices. His eyes narrow, gray flecks flaring red in the night as he reads me as easily as an open book.

"You have the *oculus*."

A coyote howls in the distance.

"Not on purpose."

The red in his eyes intensifies.

"Chaos couldn't hold on to it."

The monster swims to the surface.

"I didn't ask for it."

"And yet you have it just the same. Tell me this wasn't your plan all along."

"Of course it wasn't! They tricked me into taking it."

He cants his head, his body going rigid with distrust. "Tricked you into taking one of the most powerful objects in the world?"

"I—yes. I swear it. This was not my plan. I had no plan!"

"Poor, innocent Rain, gifted with power she never wanted."

"Hey." I jab my finger into his chest. "That's not fair. I had a life before all of this, you know."

He stalks away, forcing me to chase after him.

"Wait. Will you please stop?"

He whirls around, his eyes glowing bright crimson now. The monster lurks just below the surface.

"Funny," the Demon King says, "I had a life before you too."

"Okay, asshole, but how was that going for you? The whole reason we're in this mess is because you burned down that village with the *animus* and killed that woman Chaos loved."

He comes to a halt, body rigid.

"So it's true?" I suddenly feel sick.

He turns his head, the sharp line of his jaw standing out in stark relief against the darkness beyond him. "It was a coup. What else was I to do?"

"He loved her."

"A king can't bend for love."

I stagger back as if he's slapped me.

He warned me though, didn't he? He told me he couldn't love me the way I deserved. I thought we could figure out a way to love each other the best ways we knew how. I thought maybe we could be equals, that we could do this together.

But as usual, I'm alone in this. I've always been alone. I've always done everything myself.

"Do you wish to steal my throne, *dieva*?"

I swallow again, take in a deep breath. "Is that all you're worried about?"

Slowly, he turns to me, all of the light gone from his eyes. "Answer me."

Tears blur in my vision. Through the connection, I can almost taste his fear and his undying devotion to doing what he must. Love doesn't factor into it at all. And neither does trust.

"You are terrified of being powerless," I say, "so you do terrible things to prove you aren't. What will you do to me?"

"Answer the fucking question."

In this moment, the only thing I want to do is hurt him.

I don't care how I do it.

I don't care what the consequences are.

I just want him to feel this aching pain, the sharp cut of heartbreak.

Teeth clenched, tears burning in my eyes, I say, "And what if I did?"

The connection between us thrums immediately with rage as the monster comes out and he darts across the clearing, taking me by the throat. He runs me back, slams me into a tree and the old me braces for the impact, waits for the ache of lost oxygen and the overwhelming feeling of being powerless.

But it doesn't come.

There is no pain.

The impact barely registers at all even though the tree shakes and the leaves tremble from the impact.

The only thing I feel is the tug of more power.

The last bit of the triad.

The *dominus*. The only thing the Demon King still possesses.

And it's calling to me.

In this moment, there is one thought running through my mind: *take it.*

If you want it, take it.

I can render him completely powerless and make his worst fears come true.

He doesn't love me. He can't possibly love me.

The only thing he cares about is power.

He's no better than the Dark Father God, destroying what he must to have what he wants.

Wrath's eyes go wide.

His demon mark flares beneath his shirt.

His grip on me tightens. "*Dieva.*" My name is a growl in the base of his throat, filled with pain and surprise.

A knot untangles, a bow comes undone.

Heat flares beneath Wrath's grip, but it's not coming from him, it's coming from me.

The connection vibrates.

"*Rain.*"

He strains against me, fingers pressing hard on my throat as he tries to pull away. But he can't. He can't break the contact because I control it.

"*Dieva*!"

Power flares through me, igniting my insides, beating at my core.

I'm overcome with a sense of rightness that fills my veins, hollows out my bones.

Fire crackles along my skin. Golden light blooms in the clearing.

And as the glow of Wrath's demon mark fades, a new mark appears on my chest, ancient ink sinking beneath layers of skin.

I know the second the *dominus* comes to me. It's one final piece clicking into place.

I don't even have to take the stone from him. I don't need a vessel to claim it.

My belly soars at the victory of it.

Wrath backpedals, skin pale, eyes dull gray. He's breathing heavily, dark brow sunk in a V.

I took the last of his power.

I took it with barely any effort at all.

And worse, the connection between us is gone, leaving that steady thrum between us silent and broken. I immediately feel hollow without it and left out in the cold.

But maybe this was our destiny all along.

Maybe we were never meant to love and be loved.

He warned me and I didn't listen.

The Demon King can't love.

But I wanted him to. I wanted us to be different than we are.

"I didn't want your throne," I tell him. "I wanted you to trust me."

"How could I?" he counters. "When you betrayed me around every turn."

I don't know what to do with myself or where to go but I know I can't stay here.

I turn around to leave, feeling both flush with power and overwhelmed with heartbreak.

"*Dieva.*"

I look at him over my shoulder.

"It takes more than power to rule."

I know what he's left unsaid—do I have what it takes?

Hell no, I don't.

But I'm caught in the hurricane now, battling forces beyond my control.

I'm desperate to anchor myself to something and the first person that pops into my head is Gus.

I need Gus.

I need my best friend.

This time, I don't even have to think about it.

My completed triad of power—the *animus*, the *oculus*, the *dominus*—pulls me away, leaving the Demon King alone with nothing.

16

I don't know where I'm going when I think of Gus. Only that I want to be by his side.

Somehow the power knows where to find him and I pop up in his kitchen in his condo in Norton Harbor.

Adam is there with him.

"Holy shit," Gus says and drops the bottle of ketchup in his hand. The top pops open and red sauce squirts on the white cabinets and splatters on the floor.

Adam has pulled a gun in two seconds flat and has the barrel pointed at me.

I hold up my hands. "I come unarmed."

Sort of.

Does an ancient triad of divine power count?

Fuck if that doesn't sound like the craziest shit ever.

"Rain," Gus says and then he's rushing me, wrapping me in the wide span of his arms. I take in a deep breath, grateful to smell his familiar smell. Tea and baked goods and beneath that, the scent of his soap, his shaving cream, and a hint of Adam.

When Gus lets me go, I turn to his boyfriend. Stoic, all-business

Adam doesn't hesitate to envelop me. And for some reason, it's Adam's comfort and compassion that makes me start bawling.

And as my body shakes and I lose control of the tears, Gus comes up behind me, sandwiching me between them.

"It's okay," Gus says.

Adam hugs me, steady and solid. "We got you, Rain."

I don't know how long I break down in their arms, but they let me, holding me close in their warmth and their love.

I wanted to think that I could handle this alone, always alone, but now I realize how much bullshit that is.

I need them.

I need someone who knew me before all of this happened.

Before I became—

I'm not going to think it. I'm not going to say the word.

Because there is no way in hell I'm a reincarnated goddess.

No. Way. In. Hell.

Adam has a tissue ready for me when we pull apart and I make a mess of it, drying my eyes and blowing my nose.

"Sit," Gus says and pulls out one of the barstools at the L-shaped counter. The same place we spent many nights getting drunk and bullshitting about anything and everything.

God, I miss that.

"Here." Adam pours me a glass of wine. Gus fills me a plate with homemade sweet potato fries and waffles, then drenches the pile of food in local maple syrup. "Eat," Gus says.

"I'm not sure I have much of an appetite," I tell him and then literally three minutes later the plate is empty. "Ummm...ha...okay, maybe I was hungry. What else do you have?"

"Dessert?" Gus lifts a brow. "I have several leftover pastries from Olga's from the tea shop. If you want—"

"Yes. Gimme." I waggle my fingers at him.

Once it's in my hand, I devour two of the treats. Usually by now I'd be stuffed and near comatose. But I feel like I haven't eaten a thing.

"Are you okay?" Gus finally asks.

Adam pours me another glass of wine. The alcohol hasn't even touched me.

"I don't know."

I feel so...different.

"Talk to us." Gus sets his wine glass down. The cross earring that dangles from his ear swings back and forth as he folds his arms on the counter and hunches toward me. "You know you can tell us anything. We're here for you."

I wave him away. "While I appreciate that, what I really need is for us to *not* talk about me. Give me something normal. What about you guys? What's going on with you?"

They share a look and a clever little smile comes to Gus's mouth.

"What?"

"You want to tell her or should I?" Gus asks Adam.

"The honor is yours." Adam leans into the corner of the L-shaped counter and props the heels of his hands on the edge. The sleeves of his t-shirt rise on the dip of his biceps, revealing some of his ink.

"Tell me what?"

The smile on Gus's face widens and his heart starts beating faster. I can hear it as plainly as if I had my ear to his chest. In fact, not only can I hear it beating, I can smell his excitement, this tangy, sharpness on the air.

And then, faintly, almost like a whisper, I hear him think —*married.*

"You're engaged?" I blurt.

Both he and Adam look at me wide-eyed.

Oh, fuck.

Which part of the Demon King's power can read and manipulate minds?

I don't remember, but I have it now and now I can...fuck.

"How did you know?" Gus frowns at me. "Way to steal my thunder."

"This...you...I'm sorry." I stumble away from the barstool.

Worried about her.

She's different.

Now I can hear Adam and Gus. Both of their voices in my head, but none of the words spoken aloud.

No no no.

"Rain?"

Swallowing, raking my teeth over my bottom lip, I focus on getting my shit together.

I can't let on what's happening. Gus will never feel comfortable around me. Maybe there's a way to control it. Maybe I should ask—

I almost thought to ask Wrath for pointers on how to shut it off. I'm sure he'll be all too happy to help.

Yeah, right.

I'm on my own with this one.

I swallow, smile as genuinely as I possibly can and clap my hands together. "This is such great news! Congratulations!" I give them both hugs and feel a little hollow inside as I do.

This should be the happiest news I've heard in a long time. My best friend is getting married!

And I'm fucking breaking inside because the Demon King thinks I betrayed him—again—and I stole his power. All of it.

All of it is mine and I don't know what the fuck I'm supposed to do with it.

I can't rule a world.

I don't want a throne.

My entire life, I've been alone, depending mostly on myself. But the thought of doing this without Wrath leaves me hollow inside.

And hearing my best friend is getting married to someone he loves makes me burn with envy.

I want that.

I didn't know I did until—

Adam's phone chimes. He checks the screen and silences the ring. "I gotta take this." He gives Gus a squeeze on the shoulder and disappears into the other room, shutting the door behind him.

Gus must catch me watching his boyfriend, because he adds, "Lots has been going on in the military lately. As I'm sure you can imagine."

I nod, blink, and turn back to him. "Do you know what their plans are? For Wrath?"

I hate to get nosy and use my best friend for inside info, but this is one instance I'm willing to throw down all my moral codes.

"I know they're planning something with Chaos at the helm and that he's been making them promises they're salivating over."

"What kind of promises?"

Gus tilts his head, his mouth turning down. "What do old white men in power do best?"

They invade. Conquer. Enslave. Steal.

"They can't seriously be thinking of going to Alius, can they?"

Gus straightens, scratches at the back of his head. "You know I only hear the barest of details. It's all highly classified. Blah blah blah." He rolls his eyes. "But—and I didn't hear this from Adam, just to be clear. I'm not breaking his trust. I got it from Harper."

"Harper?"

Gus nods. "She overheard her dad and General Briggs talking about it. Chaos has promised to help the military take out Wrath so that Chaos can assume the throne. But in exchange, he's asked to take several troops with him to his world. Apparently, they don't have guns there, so soldiers with big weapons might help him keep control of the world.

"But you think they seriously mean to just hand him a throne?"

"Hell no. Long term game plan is to kill Chaos too."

I lean in. "Do you know that for a fact?"

"That's what Harper said.

"How long ago was that?"

Gus shrugs. "A few days, I think?"

That was before Chaos lost the *oculus*, before I was the one who took on the triad.

I'm not sure if this is a good or bad thing. They'll still want to handle Wrath. They won't leave that threat unchecked, regardless of how much power he still has.

But when they find out I technically have the Demon King's power...that I'm the way to the throne...

Did Sirene think this one through? Did Chaos, for that matter?

I can hear Gus's thoughts again, like a quiet breeze whistling through a crack in the wall.

Worried. So worried. Different.

I need to get out of here. The room is starting to feel stuffy and suffocating. I need...

"Want to go up to the rooftop?"

Gus looks over his shoulder at the closed bedroom door. "He'll probably be a while. Why not?"

"I'm bringing a new bottle of wine."

"I'll grab the corkscrew and a blanket."

Just a few minutes later, we're making our way down the hallway and to the stairwell and up to the rooftop access.

The wind cuts in across the roof, tossing my hair in my face. I spin into it and somehow smell everything.

Literally everything.

It's like watching a movie for the first time in technicolor.

Sensing my distress as a chill, Gus drapes the blanket over my shoulders and tugs it tightly to my chest.

"Thanks," I say.

Using the corkscrew, he pops out the cork from the wine and drinks straight from the bottle. Leading me to the north side of the building where the harbor glitters with moonlight three blocks away, we climb up on the emergency stairwell and sit on the first landing.

We've spent so many nights here that they all blur together, but it's as familiar as a bed.

"Tell me about the Demon King," he says. "What happened?"

I sigh heavily. "It's...complicated."

"I figured as much."

He takes another swig off the bottle and hands it to me. Down on the quiet street, a car passes playing loud pop music. The people inside sing along laughing.

"I bound myself to him," I tell Gus and he somehow takes this news with barely any reaction. "And then I found out from Sirene—"

"The witch."

"Yup. I found out that she thinks I'm a reincarnated goddess from Alius." I snort, laugh, take another drink. "As if I didn't have enough problems on my plate."

Gus rolls his eyes. "I hear you, babes. To find out you're a reborn goddess? I mean, come on. Who even has time for that?"

I laugh. He smiles.

"I mean it, though. Like...she really thinks I'm a goddess. Or something."

He looks over at me, the moonlight skimming his face, streaking his curls in pale, silver light. "I know. I *hear* you. I always do."

"But aren't you shocked?"

"I'm not sure anything could shock me at this point."

The fact that he's not freaking out, that he's taking the news calmly, rationally, makes me want to sob in his arms. Gus makes me feel sane.

"I miss you every waking minute we're apart," I tell him.

"I miss you too."

Stealing the bottle back, he takes a long pull and then winds his arm around my shoulders, drawing me into his side while he sticks the bottle between his knees.

Gus feels like home too. Familiar and safe.

"You know, I'm not surprised that you're a primordial being."

"Stop! I am not."

He makes a *pffftt* sound. "Should we return to Ben Hightower?"

"Me punching Ben Hightower in his stupid nose has nothing to do with being a reincarnated goddess."

"I beg to differ."

I meet his gaze and then we both burst out laughing.

"You ever wonder what stupid Ben Hightower is doing?" I ask and wiggle my fingers for the bottle.

"Actually, yes. I am a glutton for punishment, remember? I look him up from time to time. You'll never guess what I saw on his feed last time I stalked him."

"Oh, do tell!"

He smiles devilishly. "He's gay. Like legit has a boyfriend. Damn fine too if I'm being honest."

"What?" My voice echoes down the street and a dog barks in an apartment across the intersection.

"Shhh!" Gus puts his finger over his mouth even though we're both laughing uncontrollably now.

"That fucking asshole called you a fairy. That's the whole reason I punched him."

Gus shrugs. "I guess he was projecting."

"I guess so."

The dog keeps barking. Our bottle of wine gets closer to the bottom.

"I'm really happy for you and Adam."

Gus squeezes my shoulder. "Thank you. You'll be my best man, right?"

"Absolutely. It would be my greatest honor. Did you set a date yet?"

"No. We figured we better wait until all of *this* settles down." He gestures vaguely with his free hand and even though he doesn't say it, I know he means me. Me and the Demon King.

I take another drink, leaving one last gulp in the bottom for Gus. His cheeks have turned rosy and he's starting to slur.

I still feel nothing.

In fact, the longer I have this power running through my veins, the better I feel. The more *other* I feel.

"Gus," I say, my gaze trained on the harbor in the distance where a moored sailboat bobs with the waves.

"Yeah?"

"How do you know it's love?"

He drains the last of the bottle and sets it on the roof behind us. "Well..." He rubs his hands together like he's cold, so I open the blanket and yank him into it. We huddle together as the night grows colder.

He thinks on his answer for a minute, his attention fixed on the flagpole on the roof across from us. The flag snaps in the wind and Gus tightens the blanket around us.

"It's like this," he says, gesturing to the blanket. "It's that feeling you get when you've had a shitty day and you come home, you strip out of your clothes and you make a hot drink or a stiff one and you curl up in the blanket watching *Great British Bake Off* and suddenly everything feels fuzzy and warm."

He smiles to himself, running his tongue over his bottom lip. "I have that feeling every time Adam wraps his arms around me. Being with him is like a deep breath. Both the inhale and the exhale."

I immediately flash back to being in Wrath's bed, to him taking me in his arms when he thought I was asleep.

Him breathing deeply, then sighing against my neck.

Like a deep breath.

My chest tightens.

My chin wobbles.

"Rain?"

"I have to go."

"What? Where?"

I throw the blanket back and climb down from the stair landing.

"Rain!"

"I have to go to him."

"Who?"

Gus catches up to me and grabs me by the hand, pulling me to a stop. "You're crying. Why are you crying?"

"Gus."

"Talk to me, babes."

"I think I love him."

"The Demon King?"

I nod. "I know it sounds crazy. It *is* crazy."

"It's not crazy."

I pull to a stop. "It's not?"

"I mean...okay, it's a little out of this world. Maybe literally. But you can't help what the heart wants."

"Spoken like a true greeting card."

"Adam would be proud."

"I've yet to see his romantic side. Can we force him to write his own vows and say them in front of everyone at your wedding?"

"I'll bribe him." Gus winks at me. "I am persuasive."

"I have to go," I say again.

"Okay. But promise me you'll let me know you're all right."

"I promise."

He pulls me into one last hug and kisses my temple. "Go get the demon."

I laugh. "He might try to murder me, but what's love without murder?"

"This doesn't sound healthy."

"I'm a goddess, apparently. I'm sure I can survive."

I step back and think of Wrath. I know in an instant where he is and my newfound power pulls me away without any effort at all.

17

I REAPPEAR AT THE STABLES AT THE CASTLE, WHICH INSTANTLY PUTS ME ON guard.

The castle is no longer a safe location and I can smell the burning wreckage of it across the property.

The stables are mostly dark, but with my new power, I can see every grain in the wood in the walls, every divot in the stone floor. The muskiness of horses and the earthiness of hay fills the air.

But beneath that is fear, panic, dread, and Chaos.

I spot the brothers at the end of the stable aisle.

Out of sight, I sense several men and women hidden in the stalls and beyond.

I know for a fact one of them is Ryder.

Oh, how I yearn to tear that man's spine through his nostrils.

"I told you she'd come," Chaos says.

A lantern flickers on, shooting soft golden light across the aisle.

Wrath is at the end with Sirene beside him, Chaos and his stolen *norrow* lined up in front. Even though he lost the oculus, he apparently still holds some sway over them. But for how long?

And that begs the question—can I control the *norrow*?

There is a deep-seated awareness of them that runs along my skin like a spider in the darkness. I've never felt it quite like that before.

To my left, Ryder and several of his men stand equidistance apart like sentinels at a gate, their massive guns in hand, fingers poised dangerously close to the triggers.

"What is this?" I ask.

"*Dieva*," Wrath says with a labored intake of breath. There's blood on the air, *his* blood. Somehow the mighty Demon King has been cut and I'm left untouched.

I sensed our connection dying when I took the last of the triad, but it still surprises me that I am not connected to this wound, that I can't share in his pain.

I did this to him.

I left him vulnerable.

I never should have run from him.

"You did what none of us have been able to do," Chaos says. "You rendered the Demon King nearly powerless."

I step closer. "I don't want his throne. I've never even been to your world."

Chaos waves my fears away. "It's a lot like yours. Just with more demons and vampires and witches."

"Somehow I doubt that. What do you want from me, Chaos?"

"You hold all of the power now." He steps forward and the *norrow* follow him. "I can't take it from you and I don't want to."

"What you mean to say is, you can't."

He laughs, nods and then pushes his glasses back on the bridge of his nose with a press of his index finger. "I can help you, Rain. You have the power, I have the knowledge and the clout. Half of Alius has wanted Wrath gone for a very long time. They'll be happy to follow someone else, especially someone as pretty as you."

Wrath growls. Sirene waves her hand and magic glitters on the air. She's holding him hostage somehow.

"What you want is a puppet," I guess and though I think he's trying very hard to shield himself from me, I still hear his thoughts.

Tell her what she wants to hear.

"We will be equals."

It's like he's been eavesdropping on me and Wrath this entire time.

That's what I always wanted.

I fold my arms over my chest. "You do know that the president and the general plan to get rid of you too, right?"

He flinches. He didn't know.

"They're plotting a coup behind your back. Once Wrath is gone, you'll be next." I nod at Ryder. "I bet he knows the plan."

Ryder rocks his shoulders back. "She's lying."

But his thoughts say otherwise—*fucking bitch is about to blow this thing. Keep it calm. Can wait to gut her and fuck her and show her how powerless she is.*

Wrath taught me how not to let the rage take hold, but even he must know that sometimes it's the only thing.

If Ryder thinks of me that way, I can only imagine what he's done to other women who don't have a Demon King to save them and an ancient power running through their veins.

Does he really think he can rape me?

Sometimes rage is warranted.

I disappear and slip into the sub-dimension. It's nothing more than a blink, a slight pressure, and I've left one place and reappeared in another. Right in front of Ryder. He has a foot on me and easily a hundred pounds of weight, most of it muscle.

He flinches, recovers, then sneers down at me.

"Did no one teach you how to respect women?"

He runs his tongue along the inside of his bottom lip. "I respect those who've earned it."

"You shouldn't have to earn the right to be treated like a human being."

"Rain," Sirene says and starts toward me.

But it's too late.

I've had enough of Ryder and the desire to tear his limbs from his body is overriding anything else.

How dare he.

How fucking dare he.

When my eyes glow, the golden light is reflected in Ryder's gaze. He clenches his teeth and moves his finger to the trigger.

"Rain, wait!" Sirene darts forward.

Chaos curses and orders the *norrow* to stop me.

Flames ignite in my hand and lick up my arms.

Not afraid of this demon cunt, Ryder thinks as his soldiers grow antsy around us, sensing the impending violence.

I reach out with my hand and Ryder whips his gun forward, pointing the barrel at my gut.

He pulls the trigger and nothing happens.

All of the smug bravado slips from his stupid fucking face.

"Now what, asshole?" I say, but I don't give him the chance to answer.

I place my hand on his forearm and his skin chars and starts flaking away into ash.

His mouth opens in an O but no sound comes out as the flames eat away at his body like dry tinder in a wildfire.

One minute Ryder is standing in front of me and the next he's disintegrating into ash.

His soldiers take formation around me. "Kill the bitch," one of them says, and bullets start flying.

"Rain!" Wrath shouts. There's the telltale sound of cloth snapping in the wind and then Wrath is behind me, wrapping his arms around me, shielding me as bullets pummel him.

His body jerks taking the hits and I slam into a horse stall as his weight comes down on me.

Blood permeates the air.

"Stop!" Sirene yells. "Fucking stop shooting!" There's a sharp crackle, grown men groaning and then slamming against the opposite stall.

"Wrath?" He's dead weight on top of me. "Wrath!" I shimmy out from beneath him and push him over so I can see his face and—

There's so much blood. Too much.

The Demon King isn't supposed to bleed so easily.

Fuck. Fuck. This isn't happening.

I have to do something.

Ryder's men climb to their feet, guns back in hand.

"Wrath!" I shake him but he doesn't respond, his eyes closed, his mouth slack. Is his heart still beating? I don't have time to check him.

The big guy at the front sees the Demon King down and triumph flickers in his eyes.

I'm not letting them take him.

I'm not going to let him die.

Planting my butt on the stone floor, I hook my arms beneath Wrath's and pull him back.

Please, divine power, don't fail me now.

Pressure builds around me as heat ignites in my chest.

In a blink, we're gone.

18

Like most of my primordial travel, I don't think about where to go, but my instincts carry me anyway.

And when we reappear with a crash in my former biological father's studio, I'm shocked and relieved to see my mom there.

"Mom?"

"Rain? What the—is that the Demon King? Rainy baby! Why is he...he's bleeding everywhere."

Jeffrey rushes over. He's still wearing his work apron and flecks of marble cover the front. "What happened?"

I try to explain but I'm sobbing and I can't catch my breath.

He's going to die.

I can't lose him.

I can't do this without him.

"I need help," I manage to choke out.

Jeffrey cleans off the nearest table with a quick swipe of his arm. Tools, chunks of marble, and several bottles of solvent crash to the floor.

Mom and Jeffrey are all business. "Get his feet," Jeffrey says. "I'll get under his arms."

Together, all three of us carry Wrath from the floor and hoist him up on the table.

He's so incredibly pale. Blood is smudged across his face, painting his lips in streaks of crimson.

Jeffrey tears off Wrath's shirt to assess the wounds. "Sunny," he says, "grab my tool bag over there. It's on the bench."

Mom hurries over and grabs what's needed. She pulls out a pair of hemostats and hands them off. "Rain," Jeffrey says, "we'll need some wet rags and a bucket of water. Do you think he needs sterile tools? Isn't he invincible?"

"He was...before I took his power."

"You *what*?" Mom's eyes go round.

"I didn't mean to."

"There's a small kitchenette through that door," Jeffrey says, focusing on the problem at hand. I'm glad someone else can think straight. "Start boiling water. Can you do that?"

I gulp, catch on a sob.

He's not moving. His face is so still. I am gutted. Hollow.

"Rain?"

I blink back to Jeffrey. "Yes," I say. "I can do it."

"Go. Hurry."

I grope around for a light switch in the side room before I realize I can see everything in the dark. I grab a pot from the sink and fill it with water, fidgeting while I wait for the fucking thing to fill up.

Faster, goddammit.

Once the pot is full, I set it on the stove and light the burner and then return to Wrath. Jeffrey is currently digging out bullets from over two dozen bullet holes, Mom assisting him.

"Is he..." I trail off, unable to ask the question out loud.

"His heart is still beating," Jeffrey says as he gingerly removes a bullet and drops it into a bloody Mason jar.

Hope steals my breath.

Jeffrey pulls out two more bullets.

"I have his power. I can probably heal him." I rush over to the table. "Maybe I should just—"

Jeffrey puts his arm out. "No. Not yet. The bullets need to come out first before he can be healed, magic or no magic."

"How's that water, baby?" Mom asks.

I return to the kitchen to find the surface flat. "Fucking hell." This needs to go faster.

I call on my power and then stick my hand into the pot. Immediately the water is boiling hot.

Okay. I can do this. I can be useful.

I dunk several cloths I find in a cupboard into the water and pace the tiny kitchen. How long does it take to sterilize cloth? I don't even know.

When I think enough time has passed, I carry the pot out into the main room. The Mason jar is filling up with bullets and the table is drenched in the Demon King's blood.

I don't feel his pain anymore but I'm gutted just the same.

"We need to get him on his stomach," Jeffrey says. "The rest of the bullets are in his back."

It takes us some effort, but we manage to turn him around. There are nine more wounds dotting his skin from his shoulders down to the small of his back and as Jeffrey pulls out the bullets, I mop up the mess, being gentle with the swipe of the cloth.

By the time Jeffrey is done, the sun is rising in the windows of his studio and Wrath is still unconscious.

"I have a small bed in the back room." Jeffrey nods at a closed door beyond his latest marble sculpture. "We should move him there."

It takes us another ten minutes to shuffle Wrath across the studio, his massive body suspended between all three of us. Mom grunts beside me. Jeffrey does his best with Wrath's legs.

When we set him on the bed, the wooden frame lets out a loud complaint.

"Can you heal him, baby?" Mom asks. She hovers behind me, her arms crossed over her chest. There's blood on her hands.

"Maybe. I think so."

"We'll give you a minute," she says and Jeffrey follows her out.

I go to the bedside. There's a large window above the bed that looks out over the field behind Jeffrey's house. The sunlight paints the tall grass in saturated gold.

And on the bed, the Demon King is so fucking pale, it terrifies me.

Why did he step in front of me? What the fuck was he thinking? I have the triad. I would have been fine—I think.

It doesn't make any sense.

I kneel on the floor and take his hand in mine. Veins bulge beneath the skin, twining around his knuckles. I run my fingertip over one, trace it across his wrist and up his arm.

He doesn't even flinch.

"Don't do this to me," I whisper. "I've always thought I was strong enough to shoulder things alone. I've always just taken care of myself, depended on no one but myself. But now I realize...I was just terrified of loving something so much that losing it would break me."

Tears blur my vision and I sniff them back. "And look, I think that's turning out to be true. If you were awake right now, you'd be rolling your eyes at me and saying something in that cocky, smarmy voice of yours, '*Did you learn your lesson, dieva?*' Well, yes. Okay. I learned my fucking lesson. I can't do this alone." I thread my fingers with his and squeeze. "I need you to wake up."

I stare at his face so hard, my eyes burn.

"Wrath."

Nothing.

"Wrath!"

My power rushes to the surface filling the room with bright light. Maybe if I push it toward him—

The acrid scent of burning flesh permeates the air.

"Fuck!" I drop Wrath's hand as his skin blisters and peels back leaving raw, festering wounds. "Fuck!"

The rage, the despair overwhelms me, engulfs me.

I'm like a bomb about to explode.

I can't think straight. My vision pulses white on the edges.

I did this.

I didn't want this.

My hands tremble and burn with fire. Heat blooms in the room.

"Rain!" Mom comes into the doorway and then throws up her arm as the heat ribbons around her.

I have to get out of here.

I want to destroy something.

I let the power carry me away and disappear, then reappear in the middle of the field beyond Jeffrey's house, the sun cresting the horizon line.

The rage takes over, pounds at my chest.

I can't do this without him.

I don't want to.

How do I fix him?

How the fuck do I have all of this power and can't figure out how to fucking fix him?

Fuck!

Hands balled at my sides, I tip my head toward the sky and scream. I scream and scream and scream.

The ground shakes.

Energy builds in the air, electric on my skin and I can't contain it. I don't want to. I want the world to burn.

Light flashes across the clearing and then—

BOOM.

Power leaves me in a blast, rippling outward.

The pines bow, the trunks snap, and the forest topples like dominos.

Dust and dirt plumes in the air and I collapse to my knees, breathing heavy.

I fold into myself and sob.

What is this? What does it all mean? I'm terrified of who I am and what I am and what I can do and—

"*Dieva.*"

I go still and my heart seizes in my chest.

I can hear his footsteps on the brittle grass. Can hear the steady rush of blood in his veins.

Please don't be an illusion.

Tears stream down my face when I turn and look over my shoulder.

He stands in a patch of field grass, the sunlight burnishing him in gold.

He's alive.

He's alive.

I climb to my feet and race across the field and he opens his arms for me.

When I crash into him, he grunts, and wraps me into him, tightens his hold on me, buries his face in my hair and inhales.

"*Dieva,*" he starts.

"How did...how are you okay?"

"You, I assume," he says. "And whatever power you just unleashed."

"But I don't know how—" Does it matter though? Maybe it doesn't. He's here and he's alive and—

"Why did you do it? Why did you step in front of me?"

He cradles my head against him. "You wish to torture me further?"

"Please."

He sighs with a ragged breath, then puts his hands on either side of my face and pulls me back. "I had already lost everything and the only thing I had left"—he meets my gaze, the flecks of white-gray flashing in the early morning light—"was you."

The tears well in my eyes again and Wrath pulls his thumb over my cheek, wiping them away.

"*Dieva,*" he scolds.

"I love you."

He frowns at me, as if this is the most unfortunate turn of events.

"You don't have to say it. But I know you love me too. I know you love me the only way you can and I'm telling you right now, it's enough. If you're willing to look past the fact that I stole all of your power, I want you in every—"

He kisses me.

He kisses me as the sun bakes us and burns the mist from the ground.

He kisses me, not with gentle hands, but with fierce conviction.

And I hear him in that kiss.

I hear him like a resounding thunderclap.

I love you too.

19

For most of my life, I wanted to be talented like my mother. At her events, I'd watch people stare at her work and get lost in it, marvel at the light and the color and the mood. It was just pixels in a camera, an image later printed on paper, but what my mother created through her camera wasn't just a picture, it was a feeling.

Studying Mom and how she worked, I could mimic what she did. I knew how to find the light, how to turn down the aperture to get that gorgeous bokeh. But I didn't know how to put feeling into an image.

I didn't know how to love a subject the way my mother loved the mist on the Cliffs of Moher or the cloud cover in a mountain range. I never connected with those things. They didn't move me.

It wasn't until I took those pictures of Wrath that I finally *knew*.

I knew what it was to be moved by something and it terrified me.

I'd been chasing a dream and once I was living it, it became too fucking real.

And Wrath...

He had always been terrified of being powerless.

And now, as we stand surrounded by the wreckage of the forest, we have both been laid bare.

I look up at him as the sharpness of the sunlight gives way to the cloud cover. “I can probably give it back to you,” I tell him. “The *dominus* and the *oculus* and—”

He shakes his head and spins me around so we face the blast zone. “Look at this.”

“I am,” I say, a little embarrassed. This takes a tantrum to a whole new level.

“I’ve never done anything like this,” he says.

“What? But—”

“I wanted to prove to you over and over again that I was more powerful than you. But deep down, I knew that wasn’t true. I could feel it. I think I felt it the first moment I crossed paths with you in the alley.”

I look up at him. “Sirene believes I’m a reincarnated goddess. That I’m—"

“Reignyabit.” He tightens his hold on me, draws me in. “I pretended that your name didn’t set off alarm bells in my head, and then when your mother admitted that Sirene had a hand in naming you—” He sighs and turns us, walking us back to the house.

“Do you think it’s true?” My heart hammers in my head waiting for his answer.

“Yes.”

“But—”

“You just destroyed a forest.”

“Yes, but—”

“No more buts. The sooner you embrace it, the quicker we can defeat my brother.”

“Are we still doing that?”

“Do you want him to take your throne?”

I roll my eyes as we crest the hill and the field grass turns into packed gravel around the house. "I'm not taking your throne."

"Someone has to. It better be you."

We come to a stop beside the house's front porch. A hummingbird zigzags around a red feeder at the end of the roofline. When I focus my gaze on it, I can see its wings, the quick beat of them as if time has slowed.

I quickly look away.

I think I might still be terrified of what this all means. Of the power that now runs through my veins.

"I think General Briggs is looking for a way to cross over to Alius."

Wrath's gaze fixes on a point beyond the top of my head. "Of course he is." His eyes narrow and flash red. "Chaos will be looking for a way to leverage that greed. And Briggs will be looking for a way to turn Chaos's ambition into a tool. But both of them lack one thing."

"What's that?"

"You."

"I don't want the throne."

"As you keep reminding me and yet you have the Demon King's power."

But do I? Or do I have what belonged to the goddess? It's ludicrous to believe a myth is now my reality. So maybe I won't look at it too closely.

Not yet anyway.

"Tell me what you loved about being king."

He frowns at me. "We don't have time for this—"

"Tell me."

He sighs again. "I suppose I'll have to get used to you demanding things of me and me being powerless to deny you."

"I could get used to it. Now answer the question."

"Being king was a great honor and I meant to take it seriously in the beginning. But the longer I was king, the more I realized I would always be used for something, and when I wasn't being used, I would be plotted against and betrayed.

"I had to be more powerful. More ruthless. In the end, I held onto my power with a firm grip because it was the only thing that never stabbed me in the back."

"I plotted against you," I say. "I betrayed you."

"Yes, but the difference between you and those who came before you? You never did it for power. You were just a soaking wet puppy pedaling to stay above water."

"Hey!" I give him a playful shove and he catches me by the wrist easily enough, wrangling me into him. I maybe have the triad now, but he is still twice as big as me. "And now what am I?"

He glances at me. "Still a thorn in my side, surely."

"And you're still just as cantankerous."

A hint of a smile lifts the corner of his mouth and then, "Why did you come back?"

"What?"

"You came to the stables. To me."

How do I sum it all up? I left Gus on a mission to declare my love to Wrath, but I had no clue how I was going to declare it.

We've been through so much; we've fought each other around every corner.

We may not be connected any longer, but I can feel him just the same and something has irrevocably changed in him and in me.

"Like you, I've always felt alone," I tell him. "In different ways, for different reasons, but I realized that when I'm with you, I don't feel that way. I don't *want* to be alone."

He looks down at me, eyes squinted against the light, his hand wrapped around my wrist. "I still stand by my earlier warning," he says. "I will not love you gently."

"I know." I let power surge to my arm and it zaps him with heat. He snaps his hand back and shakes out the pain. "And I will not bend easily."

"Perhaps we were made for each other after all, *dieva*."

I think of the story of the dark god and the bright goddess.

"Maybe we were."

"Now," he says, "let's go plot a war, shall we?"

I hold out my hand to him and he takes it without hesitation even though I just burned him. "To the war, daddy."

He grumbles as he pulls me from the clearing.

20

We find Mom and Jeffrey in the cabin's kitchen.

"Feeling better, Wrath?" Mom asks.

"I am." He gives them each a curt nod. "I am grateful for your help."

"Of course." Jeffrey sets his cup down. "You two want a cup of coffee? I'm having mine spiked if you want to join me."

"We have to go, actually."

Before coming back inside, Wrath and I came up with a plan. It starts with visiting Rhys and his house.

"Baby, so soon?" Mom frowns at me, long, dangly earrings swinging from her ears. She's changed clothes, since hers were covered in the Demon King's blood. Which means she has a bag here, which means she was planning to stay. I'm not going to pry, but knowing Mom has reconnected with the man she thought of as my biological father for most of my life makes my chest warm.

"We have some stuff we have to deal with," I tell her.

"Something to do with the Demon King getting shot full of bullets, I'm guessing?" Jeffrey says.

"You would be correct in that assumption," Wrath answers.

"Rainy baby." Mom comes forward, her drapey ruana tucked closed beneath her folded arms. "I'm worried about you and the big guy. He didn't look too good when you just popped up here out of thin air. You never did tell us what happened. What is going on?"

"Ms. Low," Wrath says, "I can assure you, Rain is capable of handling herself."

"I know. She always has been, but—" She frowns at me, then reaches over and squeezes my arm. "I know you've always been able to take care of yourself, but I've been worried about you. I just want you to know that."

"I know, Mom." I wrap my arms around her neck and give her a long hug and as we're locked together, I hear her thoughts.

My baby doesn't need me anymore. Not that she ever did. Never needed me like I thought a child would. Always older than her years.

I'm not going to cry again.

I inhale deeply, memorizing all of the layers of her scent. Patchouli. Lavender. Herbal tea. Tea tree oil. Coffee and weed. I'm immediately settled by the familiarity.

Maybe I haven't given my mother enough credit over the years. She was a hands-off parent, but I never asked her for help. I never asked her to come home. I always kept her at a distance. "I'll be okay. I promise."

She kisses my cheek. "I know."

When we step back, Wrath takes my hand in his.

"You still owe me a cup of tea, Ms. Low," Wrath says. "Perhaps I'll take that promise next time we cross paths."

"I'd like that." She smiles up at him. "Bye, baby. Call me when you can."

"I will." I give Jeffrey a nod before my newfound power pulls us away.

Rhys seems to be expecting us. He and the others are assembled in their main living room with another dozen vampires spread throughout.

And I spot Lauren and Arthur there too.

I'm immediately relieved to see them both alive and well. Even Lauren.

I rush over to her and wrap her in a hug and she goes rigid in my grasp. "What the hell are you doing?"

"I'm glad you're okay."

"Okayyyyy."

When I let her go, I find her frowning at me and fighting a snarl. "We can hate each other all day long, but I don't want you dead," I say.

The snarl softens, but she crosses her arms over her chest. "I suppose I could say the same. Right now, that is. Not a few days ago. A few days ago I wanted you dead. Tomorrow...probably also the same."

Wrath has always been searching for loyalty only for people to disappoint him. Lauren has always been by his side. She's earned her spot and I won't take it away from her.

"Arthur." I'm gentle with my hug for him. He's holding up well, but I can hear his thoughts like a distant buzz in the back of my head. *Hurts. Hurts. Hurts.*

He hugs me back, pats me affectionately. "I'm glad you're okay, Rain."

"How are you?"

"I'm good."

If Wrath was able to help with the pain, could I now that I have the triad? I've been given the launch controls to a rocket ship but I don't know which buttons to push. Wrath might have taught me how to control the *animus*, but I think there's more to it now.

And anyway, I'm different than Wrath.

I have to embrace that if I'm to get anywhere.

And finally accepting that fact, that I am something other than human, but something other than Wrath, is almost like a briar finally pulling loose.

There's instant relief.

I take Arthur's hand and instead of pushing out with the power, I pull in. We're in the far corner of the room, shadowed by heavy drapes and low lighting, so when I start glowing, it's immediately noticeable.

The room goes quiet behind me and Arthur's eyes widen before his face goes slack, all of the tension leaving the fine, aged lines around his mouth.

I hear his thoughts ease out.

Better. So much better. All the pain gone.

When I let him go and step back, he sighs. "Wow. Rain. Thank you. I haven't felt this great in a very long time."

"I'm glad to hear that."

He stretches, rolls his shoulders. "In fact, I think you healed me."

"For now," I say. "Just like Wrath."

"No." He shakes his head. "This is different." His eyes are glassy and his Adam's apple bobs on a hard swallow. "Thank you. Truly."

"I didn't...I mean..."

He wraps me in a hug, squeezing me with renewed strength and I can't help it—I get a little teary-eyed too.

I don't know if I healed him entirely, but any sign of relief is a good thing.

When Arthur lets me go, I turn to the room and everyone immediately looks at my chest. For a hot second, I wonder if I've burned away my t-shirt and bra and am flashing the room.

But when I look down, I find a demon mark, not unlike Wrath's, glowing almost phosphorescent beneath my skin.

And on the next breath, it disappears entirely.

"Whoa. What is that?" I can't hide the panicked edge to my voice. "Does that mean I'm a demon now?"

I don't know that I necessarily want to be a demon.

Wrath comes to my side. "Where you are concerned, *dieva*, everything is a mystery. We'll learn as we go."

I smile over at him, so fucking grateful to have him by my side while I figure this shit out.

"Wrath." Rhys comes forward. "We should discuss our strategy before they get ahead of us."

I frown. "Before who gets ahead of us?"

There's a look shared between Rhys and Wrath. A look that says, *Are we letting the girl sit at the table?*

Steeling my spine, I step in front of Wrath and say to the gorgeous, slightly scary vampire, "I can read your mind if I need to. So I suggest you just tell me instead of going about it the hard way."

He narrows his eyes, lip curling back as if he means to bare his fangs at me.

Truth be told, I'm bullshitting on the mind-reading thing. I might be able to read his mind. I really don't know. I can't hear anything right this second. But like Wrath says, everything about me is a mystery and Rhys Roman doesn't know if I can or can't read his mind. Something tells me he's not the betting type. He wouldn't have a massive estate house like this if he was.

Wrath, for his part, keeps his mouth shut, watching.

I sense his pride in me and it makes me fucking glow.

"Chaos has found a way into Last Vale and he and the United States Government are currently assembling outside my city's perimeter and intend to infiltrate it," Rhys explains.

Well. That's not good.

"The ley line," I say, remembering what Wrath told me before. "You think they're getting ready to open a portal to Alius?"

"I would assume that's precisely what they're planning on doing," Wrath answers.

"How do we stop him?"

Rhys gestures to the rest of the vampires gathered around the room. Most of them are in pockets of conversation, their voices low as they wait for orders. “These are my sentinels,” Rhys says. “They’re ready to move when I give the word. I have another dozen vampires at my call.”

I look at Wrath. “Do you still have the army you were building? The one I saw in the castle?”

“I’ve lost some of the norrow.” His expression is blank, emotionless, but I think it kills him to admit it. “I still have an entire army of demons.”

“What about the witches?”

Overhearing the mention of her kind, Kat pipes in, “Any witch we could have called an ally is deathly afraid of being exposed.”

Dane hangs his head over the back of the sofa to add, “You may or may not know this, but last time witches were exposed, they were burned at the stake. Witch-kabobs around every corner.”

“Hey, asshole!” Kat makes a move to slap him upside the back of the head, but he catches her by the wrist and laughs.

“Okay, so with those numbers, do we have a chance? I mean... vampires and demons up against a mortal military. That shouldn’t be a big deal, right?”

“Normally, no,” Rhys says.

“Why do I get the impression this is not a ‘normally’ situation?”

He cants his head and a lock of his dirty blond hair falls out of place over his forehead. “The other witches, the ones we don’t count as allies? They’re quite all right with being exposed. And I’ve got word they’ve aligned with Chaos and the president.”

“Why would they do that?”

“Because they hate me and they want Last Vale.”

I grimace. I don’t know much about magic, but I guess a town that sits over a powerful ley line must be something to covet.

“How long do you think we have?”

“Not long,” Wrath surmises.

“So what do we—” I cut myself off when I feel a distant tugging and a whisper inside my head.

Wrath angles his body toward me as if he means to jump in front of me, shield me from whatever might be wrong. "What is it?"

"Something is calling on me."

"In what way?"

Rain. Come bargain with me.

"It's Chaos," I answer.

Wrath scowls and drops his arms, hands fisted at his side. "How is he speaking to you?"

"I don't—" I feel the tug again and know right away where he is. "He's at Reignyabit's *porta lima*."

"What is that?" Rhys asks.

Wrath is looking at me when he answers. "A place of worship for the goddess Reignyabit."

"I told you," Kat tells Dane.

"Just because she feels some phantom belly poking doesn't mean she's an actual goddess," Dane argues.

Wrath is still pinning me with his gaze. "I think that's exactly what it means."

"I need to go to him."

Wrath lashes out and grabs me by the arm. "No, you don't."

"Yes, I do."

"*Dieva*."

I get in close to him and lower my voice, even though it won't do much good in a room full of vampires. "Do you trust me?"

He takes in a deep breath, nostrils flaring as his jaw flexes. "Yes."

"Then let me do this."

"It's my brother I don't trust."

"If I'm really a goddess, then it won't matter what he does."

Again with the bullshit, but a girl has to do what a girl has to do. Even ones pretending to be goddesses.

"What do you plan to say to him?" Wrath drops my arm and

hunches closer, bringing his face level with mine. “What could this possibly accomplish, *dieva*?”

“An opportunity to bargain with him before people die.”

He scoffs. “Casualties of war are to be expected.”

I look at Rhys. “Is that what you want for your vampires? Just to be casualties?”

“Obviously not.”

“So let me talk to him first. See if we can find a better way.”

“You’re wasting your time,” Wrath says with a growl.

“I’ll be back soon.”

He grits his teeth, then, “Be careful.”

“I will,” I promise.

21

I find Chaos in the mausoleum that is supposedly dedicated to worshipping me in a former life.

If someone was to worship me now, they would be dealt a healthy dose of disillusionment. I barely have my own life together, let alone the ability to bless someone else's.

Chaos stands at the stone gateway, hands clasped behind his back. When he hears me appear, he turns just slightly, his face coming into profile. He's wearing his glasses again and a navy-blue cardigan over a white and blue plaid button-up.

He certainly looks better than the last time I saw him.

"What do you want, Chaos?"

"I wasn't so sure you'd come. I wasn't so sure you'd hear the call. Looks like I was wrong on both counts."

I know what he's insinuating—he's as surprised as I am to be given further proof that I'm Reignyabit.

"I'm here. So tell me what you want."

He finally turns to me and comes down the three steps from the dais in front of the gate. "We haven't really had a chance to speak alone."

I scan the rest of the mausoleum. It's only one room, but there's an open corridor that circles the sunken center and plenty of stone columns and tangled vines for someone to hide behind.

"I'm listening."

"You're different than the last time I saw you." He starts to circle me. "Did you take the last of the triad?"

I cross my arms over my chest. "Did I take it? No."

Technically true. I didn't intend to take it.

"But you have it just the same."

"Yes."

He nods, continues to pace around me. "Maybe Sirene and Ciri were right after all. And if they were right—" He comes to a halt. "You have no idea how much power runs through your veins or what you could do with that power."

"Tell me. It sounds like you have it all planned out."

"We could rule Alius together."

"Power was never a thing I wanted."

"What *do* you want then?"

"I don't know. What does every girl want? A pumpkin spice latte and a good book to curl up with?"

He snorts. "You're funnier than I would have expected."

"And you're not as tall as I would have expected."

He laughs, keeps circling.

"Join me."

"No."

"Why?"

"Because—"

"Because you think you love him." He sighs. "Lots of women, and men, think they love him. You go to Alius with him, you'll be fighting them off every single day. He will never be yours. Not entirely." The line of his jaw hardens. "My brother has always been adored, even when he's at his worst."

"It sounds like you're jealous of him."

Chaos laughs. "Are you surprised? I did try to take his throne, after all." He keeps walking. "Did you know I was betrothed?"

"Yes."

"Do you know he killed her?"

I swallow, take a breath. "Yes."

"And yet you would still follow him into war? Spend your life in his bed?"

I pivot to keep him in front of me. "I know he's done terrible things. I know who he is, Chaos. He's the villain, and I love him."

He nods, slows his pace. "Nothing will change your mind?"

"No."

There is the distinct sound of stone grinding over stone through the vines. A second later, the vines pull back and the president of the United States walks in. And she's not alone.

She has my mother in tow.

"What the fuck?"

"I'm sorry, baby," Mom says. "When the president called and invited me to tea, what was I supposed to say?"

"*No*, Mom! You were supposed to say no!"

She clasps her hands together. "I'm sorry." She lowers her voice like she's telling me a secret. "It's Naomi Wright! You know how I feel about Naomi Wright!"

The President comes forward. She's wearing her usual blue blazer, tailored chinos, and pearl necklace. She is the picture of perfection while clearly on the verge of threatening my mother for my cooperation.

I know this because I can hear the buzz of her thoughts like an annoying gnat in my ear.

"Now before you get brave," Naomi says, "and use your power to poof out of here—go on, Sunny."

Mom's thoughts start bouncing around in her head.

Unfortunate position I've put us in. I hope my baby will forgive me. I hope she'll get out of this all right.

And beneath that, a strong current of fear as she pulls open the drapey front of her ruana to reveal a vest that appears to be rigged with wires.

"A bomb," Naomi says. "I don't have the detonator, but rest assured, we could trigger it within seconds."

Fear spikes through me and my stomach drops.

When I look back at Mom, she's got her arms spread, shoulders hunched in a shrug like, *What are ya gonna do?*

But in her mind, she's thinking one thing: *I'm sorry, baby.*

"I respected you," I tell Naomi. "I liked you even. I thought you were one of the good ones."

"I am. But sometimes even the good ones have to do unfortunate things in order to accomplish what is, ultimately, the right thing."

"Which is what? Infiltrate another world?"

"We need cooperation, between us and Chaos. He can help us stabilize our country and—"

"Steal a throne."

"No. We don't want the throne."

I snort.

"Think about it Rain. Now that the world knows another world exists? It'll be a race to infiltrate it, control it," Naomi goes on. "It'll be the lunar landing all over again. But I promise you, not all of those who desire to cross over will have honorable plans. There are men like Ryder and MAW who would love to go rogue in a new world."

"What do you want me for?" I ask.

"Chaos informs me you hold the power that would control the throne."

"I guess."

"It only makes sense to have you on our side."

"Except that will never happen."

Naomi puts her arm around Mom's shoulder. "I'd like you to reconsider that, Rain."

Mom presses a hand to her chest, eyebrows drawn together.

What the hell am I to do?

Pick between Wrath and my mother?

"Do you have a way through?" I ask.

Naomi looks me dead in the eyes. "Half of a way."

Her thoughts confirm that.

They have a traveler but they need me and my blood to finish opening it, just like Sirene and Ciri did.

Fucking fuckery.

I turn away from them, hands on my hips as I think. I've never been one for strategic thinking. I'm an action kind of girl. Boots on the ground, get the work done.

I don't have very many options. Would they hurt Mom if I left here now so I could regroup with Wrath and figure out a way to rescue her? Something tells me that Naomi might be more vicious than I gave her credit for and General Briggs would probably torture a schoolteacher if it got him what he wanted.

I can't use the sub-dimension to transport us out of here. Not with a bomb strapped to Mom's chest.

The more I analyze it, the worse my options look.

I pace to the gateway and look up at Reignyabit's symbol—the blazing sun.

Help me, I think to her. *If I'm really you, help me figure this shit out.*

I'm sure an ancient goddess can appreciate twenty-first century cussing, right?

Hello Bright Goddess! Is anyone listening?

Of course there isn't.

I'm almost ready to give up when warmth spreads through my body and the first thread of an idea comes to me.

It has no shape yet. It's just a shadow growing long on the wall.

But it springs hope at the center of me and I need more time to work out the details.

I need to stall them. I'm not usually a liar, but desperate times call for shady tactics.

"Okay," I say and turn back to them.

"Okay?" Naomi lifts a razor-sharp brow.

"I'll help you," I answer. "In exchange for my mother's safety, I'll help you get what you want."

22

NAOMI TAKES MY MOTHER AWAY AND PROMISES SHE'LL BE SAFE—FOR NOW.

Chaos and I go to Saint Sabine to a desolate street that curves uphill and is surrounded on both sides by woods.

I can't recall ever coming to this part of town.

On a deep inhale, I smell the distinct smells of the Second Quarter to the north—gumbo and the fish market and sweet tobacco.

Judging by the aromas and the faint din of the city, I don't think we're more than a mile away from the Second, but it feels like another state.

There's something indistinct about this street, something quietly unnoticeable.

"Here?" I ask.

Chaos nods and starts forward on a dirt path through the woods.

When I step through the hollow between bramble bushes, Sirene appears out of the mist. She's wearing all black. There's thick leather ribbing around her shoulders and her torso. Knives strapped to her forearms. Two more around each thigh.

Her blonde hair is braided along the crown and tied into a tight ponytail at the back of her head.

She is a vision of a warrior queen.

At this point in our relationship, I'm never sure if I should be thanking Sirene or strangling her.

"Take her to the field," Chaos instructs. "When we get through, take her to the gate in Last Vale."

"Where are you going?" I ask him. I need to know where everyone is if I'm going to plot an escape.

"I have to go back for Naomi and your mother."

Don't react to that news.

The closer Mom is to me, the easier it'll be to poof her out of here when the time is right.

Chaos gives Sirene a quick nod and then disappears.

"So that ability, traveling through the sub-dimension, who has it?"

"Just the royal line," Sirene answers. "Wrath, Chaos, the princes, and the lords. The rest of the demons have to use the power of their own two legs."

"And now me," I say.

She looks over at me with a glint of pride in her eyes. "Yes, and now you."

We start walking, following the trodden dirt path as it winds through the misty forest as night descends around us.

"I can't believe you haven't murdered him yet."

"Chaos?" she asks and continues before I've confirmed it. "He's just a means to an end. He wanted to think otherwise, but he's never been able to see the world beyond the end of his own nose."

"Don't you feel bad using him?"

"No. He doesn't feel bad using you."

She has an excellent point.

"So, exactly which side are you on?"

She's behind me on the path, her footsteps quiet.

"I'm on your side."

I snort. “That’s the biggest line of bullshit.”

“Ciri and I had a plan and the plan was always you. Some elements of the plan were not fun and will not be fun, not for you. But we do have an end goal.”

I stop in the path to glance at her over my shoulder. “Which is what?”

She stops too, face blank.

“Am I meant to succeed or fail in your master plan?”

“That’s entirely up to you. Ciri always made it clear to me that we could only set things in motion. We were not to influence them.”

I snort. “So make me a cog in your elegant machine. I see.”

“Or,” she says, “maybe you’re the machine and we’re all the cogs clicking into place.”

“You really think I’m a goddess?”

“I think you’re the better version of Wrath.”

The light to his dark. Just like the stones Kat made for our binding spell. One white. One dark.

I think back to the myth, the Dark Father God, the Bright Goddess.

The shadow of an idea takes on more shape.

A thought prickles along my subconscious.

Dark and light. Light and dark.

Two halves of a whole.

Butterflies fill my stomach.

I keep walking, ignoring the shiver that wracks my shoulders.

When the woods open up to a field, we come to a stop. Not because of the change in scenery, but because of the soldiers.

The military is lined up on the edge of the field dressed in army fatigues, massive guns in hand. I don’t know their numbers but I’d guess there are easily five hundred men and women.

And at the other end of the field is Wrath and Rhys and Kat and an army of demons and vampires.

Wrath spots me and his eyes narrow.

He's devastatingly handsome in the shifting light of torches and spotlights.

He's wearing armor I've never seen before. All black leather and black metal with reticulated plates over his shoulders, and leather straps that run across his torso.

There are blades strapped to his back. Not that the Demon King needs them.

Even without the triad, I suspect he's more than most of us can handle.

It's why he had the triad in the first place.

When we lock eyes, I push one singular thought to him: *Please trust me.*

I have not betrayed him.

I *won't* betray him.

Beyond Wrath and his army sits a sprawling town nestled between the field and the ocean. I immediately smell the salty sea air, can hear the waves crashing against the rocks.

On the edge of a cliff, a massive estate house overlooks both the town and the ocean, but its windows are dark. In fact, most of the buildings seem to be settled in a state of waiting.

I don't know where the gate is here, but I can feel the massive pulse of the ley line.

The energy of it ripples along my skin, lifting the air along my arms.

"This place literally beats with magic," I say.

Sirene nods. "That's why everyone wants it and the world that lies beyond it."

As if on cue, Naomi's soldiers are joined by men and women dressed in street clothes. Not soldiers, but witches.

The air grows charged with the promise of violence.

I might be in over my head.

What the hell am I going to do?

I scan the crowd for Naomi and my mother but don't spot them. How far away will they be?

I look at Wrath again and find his eyes glowing red, his face growing sharper as the demon king comes out to play.

If he doesn't trust me, he'll likely be plotting my death right about now.

If only the connection was still open between us, I could tell him...

"Now what?" I say to Sirene.

She shrugs, clasps her hands behind her back. "I'm not running this show."

The air settles and almost as if the world senses the building promise of war, the waves quiet, the sea grows still.

A breeze crosses the field rattling the grass and lifting the hair from around my face.

"You can turn back now," Wrath calls, his voice booming in the clearing. "Or you can die soon enough."

Several yards to my left, the soldiers part and Chaos walks through.

Where's my mother? Where's Naomi? Fuck.

A cold sweat breaks out along my spine.

"We both know you've grown weak, brother." Chaos stops at the head of the assembled army. He's still in his cardigan and looks painfully out of place among the army fatigues. "I think it's time you retire. You've had the throne long enough and now you no longer possess the power to rule it."

Chaos cuts his gaze to me and Wrath follows it.

Both demon brothers pin me with their heavy stares and my skin crawls.

I backpedal, but Sirene is behind me, and I bump into her.

"I don't like this," I say to her. "This is going to be a bloodbath."

"And I wonder," she says to me, "what will the goddess do?"

The knowing burning through my veins solidifies.

Come on, Rain.

If you're a goddess, you can figure this out.

Light and Dark. Night and Day. God and Goddess.

Yes, that's it.

God and Goddess.

It was never one or the other.

The thought comes into clearer focus, the outline taking shape.

I'm grasping at straws, but that's all I have right now.

"Let us delay this no longer," Chaos says.

And all hell breaks loose.

23

Bullets start flying immediately and the smell of blood fills the air. The witches stay nestled amongst the soldiers and begin chanting in unison.

That can't be good.

That can't be good at all.

"What are they doing?" I ask Sirene.

"What they do best."

"Which is what?"

"Shielding the soldiers and weakening the enemy."

Several vampires go down across the clearing and immediately burst into ash.

Sirene's mouth drops open. "They're using wooden bullets," she says. "They're smarter than I gave them credit for."

Kat is on the other side. And Rhys and Dane. As annoying as he is, I don't want him to die. And Emery...if she lost Rhys...

If I'm going to do this, I have to do it now.

I pull on my power and my hair flutters around my face.

Sirene turns to me. "Where do you think you're going?"

"I'm sorry, Sirene. I already picked my side and it isn't this one."

She frowns at me and for a second, I think she still sees me as that fat, wailing baby making a fuss.

Before she can respond, I disappear and pop back up on the other side of the clearing right in front of Wrath.

"I can't wait to hear your excuse this time," he says.

"They have my mom," I tell him and his face falls.

"They have Sunny?"

More bullets fly through the air. Someone screams and then a gust of wind shoots across the field kicking up dirt, forcing some of the vampires to fall back. Witches, probably.

We're running out of time.

Heart racing, I grab him by the arm and yank us from the field and deposit us hundreds of miles away in the belly of the castle.

Water drips somewhere in the background and the air smells like charred wood.

Wrath looks around. "Why bring us here?"

"We're going to lose."

He frowns at me. "I don't run from war."

"I don't want to run *or* lose. I want my mom back. They have her tethered to a bomb."

There is a noticeable rumble deep in his chest. "I'll make them regret threatening Sunny. You have my word."

It's almost endearing hearing the Demon King promise revenge for my mother.

"I appreciate that, but...we need a better plan than the one we've got."

"If you have one, *dieva*, I'm open to hearing it, but be quick with it."

I move past him and start searching the stone floor.

"I'll admit, this isn't quite what I thought you had in mind," he says.

"Shhh. I'm looking for something."

"On the floor?"

I finally spot it, the rock from my favorite game of Reach for the Rock.

Plucking it from the floor, the rock is cool in my grasp, sharp on its backside.

Turning to Wrath, I find him with his arms crossed eyeing me warily.

"I've been thinking about the myth, the one about the Dark Father God and the Bright Goddess. The Dark God was jealous of the goddess. Do you remember?"

"Yes. I know the story."

"The Dark God didn't want to believe that they were equals so he stole the goddess's power."

His face darkens. He and I both see the similarities between the story and the way he regarded me when he realized I had the *animus.*

He didn't want to believe we were on any equal standing.

But I think we've moved beyond that.

I have to believe we have.

"The Dark God broke the power into three pieces," I go on. "Because it's much harder to be equal when there are three parts."

"What are you getting at?"

Excitement drums in my chest.

Please let this work.

"They were Night and Day, darkness and light," I say. "Two halves. They were always supposed to *share* the power."

Palm flat, I hold out the rock. I don't know what I'm doing. It's like I've walked into an advanced calculus class with nothing more than a strong wish and desire to make the math work.

It has to work.

I have faith it will. I can feel the surety of it rushing through my veins.

"What do you plan to do?" Wrath asks, narrowing his eyes at me.

I close my fingers around the stone and the sharp side slices through my palm, blood immediately welling in my grasp. Heat cascades down my arm and pools in my fingertips. The beat of the power is like a war drum and the harder it beats, the more I believe in it.

The rock heats up and glows in the cage of my fingers.

Wrath unfolds his arms, eyes widening.

Focusing on the stone, I put my heart into what I want for it, knowing that it isn't the stone so much as it is the *desire*.

I never wanted the power in the first place and Wrath wanted it so badly, he lost it.

But I'm not the light without the dark. And he is not the dark without the light.

I don't want to do it alone.

Without *my* dark god by my side.

When the light cuts out a second later, and I open my hand, the slick, black stone has been etched with runes.

"It was always meant to be us," I say. "We've been fighting each other this entire time, terrified of what this was, deep down knowing that it was *something*. I don't want to do this alone. And I don't think I'm meant to." I hold out my hand. "Take it."

He frowns at my palm, then regards me with cool detachment. "You would so easily give up your power?"

"Half of it. But yes. *For you*, yes."

I don't even have to think about it. And neither does he.

Without hesitation, he reaches over and slides his hand into mine, covering the rock.

The second our skin touches, both connected to the rock, the light returns, but this time it shoots across the cavern like the swirling light of a lighthouse.

The castle foundation rocks and the floor cracks and Wrath puts his hand on the wall to hold himself steady as he's remade.

Remade into something new.

A dark god and a bright goddess.

Two halves of a whole.

Night and Day.

The light flickers like flame, then pulls up his arm, winds around his chest, and glows in his eyes before it settles along the edges of his dark demon mark.

When the light dies out a second later, Wrath is breathing heavily. He nods at my chest.

I look down to see my phosphorescent mark glowing beneath my skin, now outlined in black.

It worked. It fucking worked.

And even better, I can feel him again.

The connection thrums strongly between us and through that connection, I let him know exactly how I feel.

I love him and I trust him and I made my decision—I want to always be by his side.

He gives me the smallest of nods, acknowledging what he feels echoing through the connection.

"I don't know how to use the power," I admit to him. "Not like you do."

He holds out his hand to me. "I'll teach you as much as I can."

"You have a deal."

How can you not believe in gods and goddesses when you've met demons and witches and vampires?

How can you not believe in ancient myths when they come true right before your eyes?

We were always meant for this. Ciri knew it. Sirene knew it.

The darkness and the moon. The sun and the shadows.

Night and Day.

One is never meant to exist without the other.

"Now let's go kick some ass," I say.

Wrath gives me a nod. "Let's rescue your mother. She owes me a cup of tea, after all."

The simple mention of the tea brings tears to my eyes and I think I fall in love with this man, the *villain*, all over again.

24

When we reappear, it's pandemonium.

"About fucking time," Rhys says to my left.

Blood is smeared over his mouth, drips down his chin and his eyes are glowing in the dim light.

"We're getting our asses kicked," he shouts as a loud boom goes off and three vampires are thrown back.

They're throwing grenades.

Wrath looks down at me. "Are you ready?"

"With you by my side, abso-fucking-lutely."

"That mouth of yours, *dieva*," he says and lets the thought hang in the air. I know what he means and smile up at him.

"Do you feel any different?" I ask. "Can we win?"

He nods. "Somehow I feel more power than before."

I feel it too. It's this surety at my core. We are somehow greater than our individual parts. I feel unstoppable right now. I don't know if it's true or not, but I'm willing to have faith if it means getting my mother to safety.

"Come," he says, "and let us have our retribution."

My own mark lights up with the thrill.

Wrath and I surge forward into the field.

I've never really fought for anything in my life.

I had opinions, ones I made sure everyone else knew too.

But I never put action behind those beliefs, never risked life and limb.

When Wrath and I cross the field, my heart beats loudly in my ears as the blood pumps fast through my veins.

We don't speak, don't strategize. Somehow we know what to do. It's a feeling that needs no words.

He lifts his arm and the darkness kicks up like a tidal wave, then crashes down through the assembled army. They're scattered like tin soldiers.

The fire builds up inside of me and the darkness burns away as I take several steps.

The witches come forward, mouths moving in their chant, then one throws her arms out and bright light shoots out from her hands.

My power flares into a shield and the hit bounces off.

The witches have no idea what they've gotten themselves into.

I pull the shield down and throw my arms out.

Fire rages across the clearing then ignites in a towering blast when it reaches the assembled troops. Several witches drop, engulfed in flames.

To my right, Wrath disappears and reappears behind the enemy's line. Shouting erupts as they realize he's in their midst, but they aren't fast enough to pivot. His darkness shoots out like an arrow, piercing several of the soldiers. They go down, blood painting the air.

I'm not a vicious person—I'm no villain—but there is a beat of something vicious-like at my sternum, a building crescendo, a whisper of something darker and older and it says:

You will not fuck with what's mine. You will not fuck with those I love.

You will pay for this.

I never considered myself powerful but, in this moment, I am swept up in it, in being invincible.

In this moment, I believe.

I will reign.

I am Reign.

And these motherfuckers are about to learn.

25

The carnage paints the night in shades of fire and blood.

It doesn't take Wrath and me long to make our way through the enemy line and once bodies start dropping, whoever is in charge calls for the rest to fall back. They scatter like dry leaves. Even the witches.

Rhys and Kat and Dane come up behind us. The vampires are covered in blood, their eyes bright with a predatory glow.

Kat is breathing heavily, but the smile on her face is wide. "Those witches bit off more than they could chew," she says.

"We should pay them a visit after all of this," Dane suggests. "Really drive home our point."

"There will be plenty of time for that." Rhys drags the back of his knuckles over his chin, wiping away more blood. "You need anything further from us?"

I have to find my mom, but I don't think we need the vampires for that.

Wrath must sense my thoughts. "I think we'll tackle this one alone. Take care of your people."

Rhys nods. "If you need me, you know how to find me."

They head down the field, the moonlight painting them in an outline of silver.

"Before I gave you half the power," I tell Wrath, "I could sense people. I did it when Ryder and MAW took me. There was this casting, like a net, and anyone within its reach popped up on my awareness like a buoy in the water. Did you ever feel that?"

"Before I lost the triad? No. Now..." He turns his attention beyond us, his eyes narrowing. "Things are different now. This is new territory for both of us, apparently."

"But we'll figure it out together. Right?"

His gaze cuts back to me. "Of course, *dieva*."

"I can still sense people, I'm realizing, but I don't sense my mother near. And I wonder if the net isn't big enough, if we're going to continue on that analogy."

"Perhaps we need both of us." He offers me his hand. My heart kicks up just at the mere thought of touching him and he must catch it, because the corner of his mouth lifts in a smug, knowing smile.

"We're in the middle of war. There's no time for your filth."

He cants his head. "Very well." But he's still got that smirk on his kissable mouth.

I slip my hand into his and immediately, energy ignites between us and the air glitters like oil on water, crackling in our wake.

"Focus on what your mother feels like," Wrath instructs.

I close my eyes and focus on her.

My mom is the realest thing about me, I'm realizing. Even if I do embrace the fact that I might be a reincarnated goddess, my mother still carried me for nine months, she still gave birth to me.

She is as much a part of me as the power is now.

Sunny Low, with her boundless energy, her unflinching belief in the good in all things, her love of Earl Grey and patchouli, her love of chasing adventure.

When I find her, her presence glows for me almost like a beacon.

I smile, giddy, and look over at Wrath. There's a new emotion in his gaze, one that I haven't seen before and I would almost swear to the gods was veneration.

"You've found her," he says. Not a question.

"Yes."

"Slide into the driver's seat, *dieva*, and carry us to her."

With his hand firmly in mine, I pull the power to me and let it transport us.

We reappear in a windowless room surrounded by gray walls with a concrete floor beneath us. It is decidedly governmental in its lack of taste.

Chaos is there with Sirene and Naomi, General Briggs too. I spot Harper's dad in the background with several other men in suits.

There are TV monitors bolted to the wall displaying several aerial feeds of the battlefield and the destruction that was wrought.

Our arrival causes the room to go quiet.

We must pose a striking contrast, Wrath and I covered in blood, them in their spotless designer suits.

These are the people behind the scenes pulling the strings while everyone else dies for their cause.

It makes me wonder about all of the chaos in our world and whether or not it can be attributed entirely to Chaos himself. Humans have their own free will and they've pissed all over this world. And now they want to piss all over Wrath's too.

"You've clearly lost," I tell them. "Now give me my mother."

Chaos comes around a table set up in the center of the room.

He is unassuming in his cardigan and glasses. "Perhaps there is more to discuss, dear brother, just you and me."

Wrath shifts, his leather armor groaning.

I wanted to think Chaos was the better half the first time I met him. I wanted to like him.

Now I want to destroy him.

And I can feel Wrath's desire for the same thrumming through our renewed connection.

We've never talked about how Wrath felt about his brother, but I can sense it now. There is an overwhelming desire to make him pay for what he's done, but beneath that is a deep-seated sorrow.

It's his brother and Wrath doesn't want to murder him.

He is a villain second, a brother first.

My heart immediately aches for him.

So I make my first promise to him, shield him from the pain, the anguish, and shoulder the burden.

I disappear and reappear behind Chaos and wrap my hand around the back of his neck.

Fire licks down my arm and bubbles the skin at the nape of Chaos's neck.

He fights me at first, tries to twist in my grip. Several of the norrow appear, summoned by Chaos I guess, but they take one look at me and immediately vaporize into a swirl of dark mist.

"Wait," Chaos says around gritted teeth as the power eats away at him. "Rain. Can we...Wrath, *brother—*"

He flails, tries to get hold of me behind him, but it's no use.

Veins of embers break open in his skin, burning him from the inside out. He finally sinks to his knees and grows frantic, swinging, lashing out in any way he can.

But it only takes seconds and all that is Chaos is nothing more than ash on the air.

And when I look across the room at Wrath, his gaze is fire and light and I hear him as if he's spoken directly in my head —*thank you.*

Together, we turn to the rest of those assembled in the room.

"I'd like my mother, please," I say.

"She won't ask nicely again," Wrath adds.

No one moves, stunned in silence, frozen in shock.

"Now!" Wrath shouts.

Suddenly everyone is moving. Two military men work on the vest Mom wears while Naomi and General Briggs stand just behind her, watching with rapt attention.

Once the bomb is removed, they stand back and Mom hurries over to me, wrapping me in a hug, blood and carnage be damned.

"Oh, baby. Are you okay?"

"I'm fine, Mom. How are you?"

"Oh, don't worry about me. They gave me tea and cookies and an old copy of Better Homes and Gardens. I was occupied easily enough."

"With a bomb strapped to your chest," I mutter.

"Well...sometimes you have to weather the storm, baby."

Wrath steps forward. The crowd shrinks back.

"Tell me, *dieva*, what will their fates be?"

I give Mom a quick squeeze and then motion for her to stand behind us. Then I take my place at Wrath's side.

"I think the president has learned not to fuck with us," I say.

"Mmmm." He crosses his arms over his chest and his armor groans again.

Naomi clutches at her stupid pearls.

"I think Harper's dad is just plain greedy and if anyone here was on the edge of pissing their pants, it's him."

"I would agree," Wrath says.

"The others...they're just caught in the game. But General Briggs..."

The older man is wearing his military uniform decorated in a rainbow of bars and medals. I think he might be the driving force behind wanting to steal Wrath's throne and infiltrate Alius. He wanted to gut the world, strip it of its jewels and resources.

I've never liked that man and I like him even less now.

"General Briggs is the biggest risk to your throne," I tell Wrath.

"Our throne," he reminds me.

Yes, our throne.

"Now hold on a minute," General Briggs says as Wrath and I close in.

Unfortunately for him, the rest of those in the room shrink away. No one wants to have his back.

The darkness kicks up around Wrath, undulating in the air. The florescent lights still buzz above us, but Wrath's power still robs the room of light.

"Wait!" Briggs yells.

The darkness shoots across the room.

The sharp edge of it sinks into Briggs's chest with a heavy, wet thunk.

The man's eyes go big and blood sputters from his mouth as he tips forward and slams into the table, sending it crashing to the floor.

A coffee cup spills, then wobbles on its side before finally spinning to a stop.

No one moves.

The room is silent.

Wrath steps forward.

I swear, if the people left in the room could melt into a puddle and disappear through a crack in the floor, they would.

"You will always be inferior to me," he tells them. "I don't know how many times you need to force me to prove it to you."

He pauses and then looks at Naomi.

"If you lead this country, you need to make a decision right now—do you want peace or do you want me to destroy everything you love?"

The pearls disappear in the grip of her hand as she sucks in a deep breath. "You can't blame us for defending our country and—"

"And what of invading mine?"

Naomi clamps her mouth shut.

"Make a decision, Ms. Wright. I suggest you make the right one."

She licks her lips, lets the pearls drop against the base of her throat. The president comes back, the authority resounding in her voice as she says, "Let's consider this a truce then."

"Yes, let's. But if you threaten Rain's mother ever again or force my hand, I will strangle you with those fucking pearls and watch the life drain from your eyes."

Goosebumps travel down my arms at the threat. I know Naomi Wright is one of the smartest women around. She must know she doesn't stand a chance at this point. She's just gotta play the game whether she likes it or not.

"I understand," she says.

"Good." Wrath turns back to me. "I believe we're done here?"

"I think so." I take Mom's hand in mine. "Hold on tight."

"Why? What are you—" Before she can finish the question, we're gone.

26

We pop back up at an estate house that feels distinctly European and old. I had let Wrath guide us so I'm not familiar with the place.

Rhys is there in front of us, a glass of something dark in his hand. Emery is wiping blood from his face with a wet rag, fussing over him.

Dane and Kat are leaned against a bar, elbows on the top, drinks in hand.

"Oh good! You found your mom!" Emery comes over. I didn't see her on the battlefield and there's no blood on her, so I'm assuming she wasn't at the fight. Her hair is wound up in a messy bun. "It's a pleasure to meet you, Sunny." Emery holds out her hand before realizing there's blood on it and pulls it back.

"You are adorable," Mom says. "You remind me of a green witch I met in rural Virginia once. Any relations there?"

Emery smiles. "I don't think so, no. I'm a demon."

"Oh? Oh! That's the most interesting thing I've heard today. Do you know I used to keep a journal of the most interesting things I heard? You should try it."

Emery smiles. "Maybe I will. I like that idea."

Wrath bends down so he can speak quietly at my ear. "I need to speak with Rhys a moment. Will you be all right?"

"Of course."

He gives me a nod and then motions for Rhys to follow him out.

"This place is magnificent." Mom crosses the room, but her gaze is on the domed ceiling and the mural that covers it. There are cherubic angels and mighty gods and mythical monsters all done in the soft jewel tones reminiscent of 18th century renaissance art.

"Here." Kat hands me a glass of what smells like bourbon. "Figured you could use it."

"You have no idea," I tell her, but leave out the part about not being able to get much of a buzz anymore. Or can I? Honestly, I don't know what this new power situation is, but I'm certainly willing to give a buzz the old college try.

I follow Mom to the end of the room where she marvels at a painting of a gray-haired god carrying a torch. "If I was an interior photographer," she says, "I'd be itching for my camera."

"It is pretty magnificent."

She spins, taking in as much as she can.

"Mom."

"Hmmm?"

"I have to tell you something."

She looks at me over her shoulder. Her hair is half tied back with an elastic, but several wispy strands flutter around her face.

"I sorta married Wrath."

"Ahhh!" Mom claps her hands. "Congratulations! Does that make you a queen? I guess you did reign after all."

"I don't know the particulars yet. But listen..."

"What is it, baby?"

"I'm leaving to go with him. I think. I mean, I assume he'll want to return to his home to lord over his land and sit in his throne looking ridiculously hot and all and—"

"It'll be your life's greatest adventure," she says and takes my hand in hers, squeezes, then pats at my knuckles. "You'll remember this for the rest of your life."

Of that I have no doubt.

"I was wondering...do you want to come with?"

"To the Demon King's world?" The line of her brow rises in an arch.

"Yeah. Think about it," I say. "New land to photograph, new mountains and cliffs and oceans and waterfalls. An entire world of brand-new sights to document."

"I don't want to cramp your style."

"You won't."

"Well...it does sound like fun." She trails off in a laugh. "Who knows, maybe I'll be the first photographer to document another world for ours."

"See, yes! That could be amazing."

"But...Jeffrey..."

"Oh. What about him?"

She smiles to herself, then presses her hand to her mouth as if to hide it.

"Could he come with too?"

"Oh? I mean...I would think so? I'd have to ask, but I'd love to have him there."

"Okay. Sure. What the hell! I'd love to come with you, baby." Mom reaches over and gives me a half hug, her arm tight around my neck. "I've missed you. It'll be nice to spend some time with you."

"I agree."

I may have pretended I didn't need my mother for most of my life, but the thought of having her by my side when we literally cross over to another world...well, it makes me feel a whole lot better.

I'm realizing that I have always needed my mom—I was just too stubborn to ask for her help.

I won't make that mistake ever again.

Emery shows Mom and me to spare bedrooms in the giant manor house. Wrath's castle is officially out of the question, so Rhys apparently agreed to house us in the meantime, and I learn that it's the giant manor house on the cliff on the edge of Last Vale.

Mom decides to take a shower and lie down. I clean up in my attached bath and then head back downstairs. I find Kat and Dane in the kitchen and the second I step inside, my stomach growls.

Dane looks at my mid-section. "Are you about to give birth to a demon?"

"What? No. That's my stomach. I haven't eaten in a while."

"Goddesses eat?" Dane asks.

"Who told you I'm a goddess?"

"It's like literally everywhere," he says and rolls his eyes, then snaps his fingers. "Keep up, Rain."

Kat whacks him on the arm. I wonder how many times a day that happens? Probably more than one can count.

"I could eat," I say."

"I'll make you waffles, poppet. I make the very best around."

I look at Kat. She shrugs. "Say what you will about the prick, but he is an excellent cook for being a vampire."

Dane already has the ingredients out and a bowl for mixing.

"Can vampires eat human food?" I ask.

"Unfortunately, no. But I can smell it while it cooks and that's close enough for me."

When Emery returns, Dane hands her a plate too and we all sit at the banquet table nestled in an alcove at the back of the kitchen. Large, mullioned windows overlook the ocean though it's still too dark to see it.

By the time Rhys and Wrath come back, Emery and I are deep into our stacks of waffles while Dane recounts a hilarious story of how he once snapped Rhys's neck and then dragged the poor guy into a hospital and told the staff he was dead.

"You should have seen their faces when he came back to life!" Dane says.

"How pissed off was he?" I ask.

"Very," Rhys answers as he enters the room.

Wrath pulls out the chair next to me and sits, his body turned toward mine.

"Is everything all right?" I ask him.

"Yes. I asked Rhys if he wanted to return to Alius with us."

Emery shifts her gaze to her vampire husband. "And what did you say?"

"I said I needed to speak to you about it first."

"That's the right answer."

"Yes, little lamb, I know it was." He leans over and kisses her cheek and Emery beams.

We spend the next hour eating and drinking and I come to realize waffles and bourbon make an excellent pairing. When we're done, I'm pleasantly surprised to feel just the slightest bit of a buzz, though it took me nearly an entire bottle of bourbon to get there.

"I should probably go take a shower," I say. "I'm still grimy with war."

Wrath has been mostly silent while we hung out, but now he stands and holds out his hand for me. "Come."

I can feel the others watching us. What must they think? Not that long ago the Demon King was a ruthless, scary as hell villain.

Now he's...

Mine.

I slip my hand into his. He looks at the others. "We'll prepare this week and leave after. If you'd like to come, I'd like to have you. I need more people I can trust.

"And in my world, you can be exactly who you are. You don't have to hide it."

Dane leans back in his chair. "I have to admit, that does sound awfully enticing."

"The decision is yours to make," Wrath adds. "If you decide to come, be ready by week's end."

He doesn't wait for a response.

When we reappear in the room Rhys has given us, I look up at Wrath. "End of the week? I thought we'd at least have a few days of rest."

"I've left my throne unattended long enough." He strips out of his shirt. It's still covered in blood and gore. I try not to look too closely at it.

Just thinking about going to another world with the Demon King has my heart racing.

"Don't be nervous, *dieva*," he says, hearing the panic in my chest. "I'll be by your side."

"Easy for you to say. It's your school and you're the cool kid." I tear off my shirt and toss it in the wastebasket.

The room is all European elegance with ornate furniture and plush rugs and artwork hung in gilded frames.

I don't hate it.

"You're a reincarnated goddess," he counters. "You are the literal vision of cool kid."

I snort, then laugh. Hearing the Demon King refer to me as the cool kid gives me a sick sort of giddy satisfaction.

"Do you really believe that?" I ask.

He undoes his belt, yanks it out of the belt loops, and the leather snaps. "You took the last of the triad from me without even thinking about it. Yes, I very much do."

I lick my lips as he comes closer. "Isn't it a little insane to believe in some ancient myth from your world?"

"No. I think the definition of insanity is loving you. Yet here I am."

"You're an asshole."

"There she is." He closes the distance between us and takes my hair, winding it around his fist. "But just because you're a goddess doesn't mean I won't make you bow at my feet."

"Just because you're a god doesn't mean I'll do it."

He tightens his hold on my hair and a sting of pain radiates over my scalp. A goddess and yet I can still feel things. That's good because if I couldn't feel pleasure? I would riot in this bitch.

I grab Wrath around the wrist and power surges to my grip. His skin blisters immediately and he pulls back, eyes flaring red.

"You'll pay for that one, *dieva*."

"You have to catch me first." Laughing, I disappear and pop up at White Sands National Park.

I'm in only my pants and bra and goosebumps lift on my skin.

Will he find me here? Will he know how to find me?

The air snaps and I whirl just in time for Wrath to grab me in the wide span of his arms. The darkness spins around us. And threaded throughout are filaments of golden light.

"Bow to me," he says.

I sink to my knees in the sand. This isn't about submission so much as it is about trust.

We'll continue to fight each other. I think he likes it as much as I do. But I want him to know that he can trust me. And that I have faith in who we are.

The light burns brighter and the darkness writhes.

I look up at Wrath, his eyes glowing red and then he sinks to his knees in front of me.

"If you bow to me, *dieva*," he says, "then I will bow to you. My queen. Forever and an eternity." And then he threads his fingers through my hair and kisses me.

27

THERE IS NOTHING LIKE SLEEPING IN THE DEMON KING'S ARMS AFTER HE fucked me senseless, and when I wake up the next day bathed in late morning light, I marvel at how far I've come and *who* I've become.

Wrath has his arm around me, his large body spooning mine. We're both naked after fucking in the desert and showering when we returned to the house.

I am happy beyond words. And full in a way I've never been before.

"Your feet are freezing, *dieva*." His voice rumbles at the back of my neck, sending a shiver down my spine.

"Then warm me up." Neither of us misses the suggestive tone of my voice and I feel a very distinct hardness pressing into my ass.

"You wore me out last night," he says, playing a game with me. "I'm not sure I have anything left to give."

I roll to face him. His eyes are still closed, long lashes fanning over his pale cheeks. He's rumpled in the sexiest way ever. I just want to stay in this bed with him forever, screw the real world, screw his throne.

But I know the man that wears the crown would wither and die without something to rule.

And me? I'm ready for something else and I'm not so sure this world can offer me the same thing Alius can with the Demon King by my side.

I'm so ready for this adventure.

"Should we get up and have some coffee?"

He groans.

"Wait...I just had a horrible thought. Do you have coffee in Alius?"

Still grumpy, he says, "Yes."

"What about ice cream?"

"Yes."

"Wine?"

"Yes, *dieva*."

"What about *Great British Bake Off*?"

His eyes finally open, pupils shrinking in the light. "I don't know what that is so I'm assuming no."

"Wait. You don't know the absolute gold of *The Great British Bake-Off*?"

He groans. "Judging by your excitement, I will assume I don't want to."

"We need to change that."

He groans and rolls to his back. I quickly scramble over top of him, settling myself over his cock. I'm still leaking cum from last night and I slide over his length easily, the head of his shaft throbbing at my clit.

I pretend that doesn't send a thrill to my core and fireworks across my belly.

"As a goddess, I wonder if I can manifest *The Great British Bake-Off* in Alius."

"What is this bake-off anyway?"

"Oh, you'll love it."

"I doubt it."

"It's an adorable, cozy baking show where contestants all gather in a tent in the British countryside and bake pastries and pies and fuss over sponges."

"It sounds insufferable."

I rock against him, punishing him for the *very* audacity.

He groans, fingers pressing harder on my hips, guiding me over him. All of the muscle in his body tenses up as he grows harder.

"Promise me you'll watch it with me."

"No."

I slip my hand between us and take him in my grip. He's already soaked from my pussy so stroking him is easy. "Promise me."

His eyes slip closed. "Fine."

"That's what I thought."

With a growl, he takes hold of me and rolls us over so he's on top. "I should punish you for your insolence."

I boop his nose. "We both know I'll like it."

Without warning, he flips me onto my stomach, kicks my legs apart and covers my body with his. The head of his cock nestles between my legs. His hand wraps around my throat, forcing my head back.

All of the levity is gone. Now I'm the one groaning.

"Never do that again."

"Yes, daddy."

He rams into me and I let out a little yelp.

"I'm not sure if sharing cosmic power with you is a gift or a curse." He's holding himself steady, filling me up, but robbing me of the rhythm of his cock inside of me.

"Clearly, it's a gift," I say, a little breathless.

He pulls out slowly, then slides back in and I whimper.

"That's what I thought, *dieva*."

Grip tight on my throat, he picks up the pace, hitting so deep inside of me, it almost hurts.

"My queen will learn to do as I say."

"Oh, she will, will she?"

He stops again and I wiggle beneath him, pushing my ass back. Slipping his other hand around my hip, he cups me, forcing me still.

"She will."

How the hell do I say no when he's like this? I can't. I won't. He knows it. I'll push his buttons all day, every day—*outside of the bedroom.*

But here, beneath him, I'm just a girl craving the Demon King's brutal love.

"Fuck me," I beg.

"Try that again."

"Fuck me, my king."

"Good girl."

And then he slams back into me and loves me the way only a villain can, roughly and without restraint.

EPILOGUE

A WEEK LATER, I TURN A CIRCLE IN MY CONDO. THE MESS HAS BEEN cleaned up from when Ryder and his men tortured me for information on Wrath. I had to toss my TV and some of my furniture. Just as well, I suppose. Wrath warned me that I can only bring a limited number of belongings through the portal to Alius.

It's not like we're going to carry a couch through the gate.

I have two bags packed. Wrath promised me I would have the pick of whatever clothing I wanted on the other side, that money was no object. It's hard to wrap my head around it all.

In quiet moments, especially now when I'm surrounded by my belongings and the smudges of my old life, I still feel like a girl just trying to get by the best way she knew how.

Gus comes up behind me and drapes his arm over my shoulders. "We'll take care of the rest," he tells me. "We'll get it cleaned out and listed."

"Thanks, Gus. Keep whatever money you make off of it."

"Babes—"

"I insist. Put it toward your wedding. I'll be back for it once you decide on a date."

"Can you get emails in another dimension? Save-the-dates? Wedding invitations?"

"That's an excellent question and I'm guessing no." I wind my arm around his waist. "I'll come back to check in. So decide on a date sooner rather than later."

"We're discussing it over dinner next week. I think we'll be able to narrow it down."

"Fabulous." I turn into him and give him a hug. "This part is going to suck."

"Which part is that?"

"Saying goodbye."

He rubs his hand up and down my back. "We'll still see each other."

"Come with me."

He laughs. "I'm embarking on a new chapter in my life by getting married. I need to do that first in the world I know and understand before I throw in a world of witches and demons and vampires."

Rolling my eyes, I heave out a big sigh. "Fine."

"Maybe someday you can bring us over for a visit."

"I'd like that."

On the other end of the connection, I can feel the Demon King calling for me.

"Time to go," I say.

Gus squeezes me hard and then lifts me off my feet, whirling me around in a circle. "I'll miss you, babes."

"Miss you too." When he puts me back down, I reach up on my tiptoes to plant a kiss on his cheek. "Behave while I'm gone."

"Never."

I pull away and scoop up my two bags. I guess this is it.

I give my condo one more look. I'll miss this place, but I'm going to live in a palace. I really can't complain.

"Love you," I tell Gus.

"Love you too."

I give him a wink and then I'm gone.

When I reappear, focusing on Wrath instead of a specific location, I pop up in a subterranean chamber below Last Vale.

There's another stone gate in front of us, this one newly constructed in the last week by several demons and vampires that work for Rhys.

"I said to pack light," Wrath chides.

"You saw my condo. This is light."

Rhys, Emery, Kat and Dane are there, as are Mom and Jeffrey. When Mom pitched him the idea of sculpting new work for another world, he was all too ready for the adventure. I'm so glad they're together, and that they have each other.

"Are you ready?" Wrath asks Kat.

"I think so."

"You guys really aren't coming with?" I ask.

Emery comes over to give me a hug. "Not yet. But we will."

"I want to reestablish Last Vale first," Rhys explains. "We need the city's border secure and the gate protected so that you, and we, can come and go as we please someday."

That will make it much easier to return to see Gus. I don't hate this plan.

"I'm going to need familiar faces," I tell them. "So I hope that happens sooner rather than later."

"We'll do our best," Rhys promises.

Kat steps up to the gate. "This should be interesting," she says. "Considering I've never opened a portal between worlds."

"Once you've done it, it'll be easy to do again," Wrath tells her.

"I hope that's true. Which one of you wants to bleed for the magic?"

"I will," I offer.

"Give me your hand."

I hold mine out to her and she pulls a dagger from a sheath at her waist, then drags the blade over my palm. And nothing happens.

Kat frowns, tries again.

"That might be my fault," I say and gesture for her to hand over the dagger.

The longer I'm a goddess, the harder it is to wound me, I think.

I turn the blade on myself and drag the sharp edge over the meaty part of my palm. I feel no pain, but the skin opens up and blood wells up. When I want something to happen, it will. It's as easy as that.

Kat takes the dagger back and wipes it off on her dark jeans, then resheaths it. "To the doorway with you."

I step up the three steps to the stone doorway and Wrath comes to stand beside me. Mom and Jeffrey are behind us. Wrath says to them, "Follow us through immediately. Do not hesitate."

"Of course," Jeffrey says and takes Mom's hand in his.

Wrath turns to me. "You ready, *dieva*?"

Through the connection, his hope radiates back to me.

"I'm ready."

I place my bloody palm to the stone and behind us, Kat calls out a string of foreign words.

The stone melts away and light shines through from the other side.

It's impossible to make out what lays beyond.

A little sliver of fear jams into my heart, but Wrath takes my hand in his. His is warm, solid, and real.

"Whatever we do," he tells me, "we do it together. I will be by your side."

I take a deep breath and nod.

"You take the first step, *dieva*," he says, "and I will follow."

I look back and Rhys and Kat and Emery and Dane wave goodbye.

And I take the first step into a new world with the Demon King by my side, now his queen.

And I will Reign.

I can't believe the trilogy is finished! This was such a joy to write. I loved Wrath and Rain and every single time they were on the page, it was a delight.

If you want to spend just a little more time with the characters, how about a bonus scene?

Rain finally talks Wrath into watching *Great British Bake Off* and then they take a break for *other things*.

Sign-up for that bonus!
https://www.subscribepage.com/nikkistcrowebonus

WANT MORE VILLAIN PARANORMAL ROMANCE?

The stories were all wrong — Hook was never the villain.

For two centuries, all of the Darling women have disappeared on their 18th birthday. Sometimes they're gone for only a day, some a week or a month. But they always return broken.

Now, on the afternoon of my 18th birthday, my mother is running around the house making sure all the windows are barred and the doors locked.

But it's pointless.

Because when night falls, he comes for me. And this time, the Never King and the Lost Boys aren't willing to let me go.

START READING THE NEVER KING NOW!

ALSO BY NIKKI ST. CROWE

WRATH & RAIN TRILOGY

Ruthless Demon King

Sinful Demon King

Vengeful Demon King

Wrath & Reign Omnibus

VICIOUS LOST BOYS

The Never King

The Dark One

Their Vicious Darling

The Fae Princes

CURSED VAMPIRES

A Dark Vampire Curse

MIDNIGHT HARBOR

Hot Vampire Next Door (ongoing Vella serial)

Hot Vampire Next Door: Season One (ebook)

Hot Vampire Next Door: Season Two (ebook)

Hot Vampire Next Door: Season Three (ebook)

ABOUT THE AUTHOR

Nikki St. Crowe has been writing for as long as she can remember. Her first book, written in the 4th grade, was about a magical mansion full of treasure. While she still loves writing about magic, she's ditched the treasure for something better: villains, monsters, and anti-heroes, and the women who make them wild.

These days, when Nikki isn't writing or daydreaming about villains, she can either be found on the beach or at home with her husband and daughter.

Nikki's Newsletter:
https://www.subscribepage.com/nikkistcrowe

Follow Nikki on TikTok:
https://www.tiktok.com/@nikkistcrowe

Follow Nikki on Instagram:
http://instagram.com/nikkistcrowe

Gain early access to cover reveals and sneak peeks on Nikki's Patreon: https://www.patreon.com/nikkistcrowe

Visit Nikki on the web at:
www.nikkistcrowe.com

tiktok.com/@nikkistcrowe
instagram.com/nikkistcrowe
facebook.com/authornikkistcrowe
amazon.com/Nikki-St-Crowe/e/B098PJW25Y
bookbub.com/profile/nikki-st-crowe

Printed in Great Britain
by Amazon